TRICKS OF THE TRADE

TRICKS OF THE TRADE

BEN TYLER

KENSINGTON BOOKS
http://www.kensingtonbooks.com

Truth is said to be stranger than fiction, especially in Hollywood. However, aside from a sprinkling of legendary names, the people and events portrayed in this novel are merely facsimiles. They exist only in the author's imagination—and nightmares.

KENSINGTON BOOKS are published by

Kensington Publishing Corp.
850 Third Avenue
New York, NY 10022

All Kensington titles, imprints and distributed lines are available at special quantity discounts for bulk purchases for sales promotion, premiums, fund raising, educational or institutional use.

Special book excerpts or customized printings can also be created to fit specific needs. For details, write or phone the office of the Kensington Special Sales Manager: Kensington Publishing Corp., 850 Third Avenue, New York, NY 10022, Attn. Special Sales Department. Phone: 1-800-221-2647.

Kensington and the K logo Reg. U.S. Pat. & TM Off.

Library of Congress Card Catalogue Number: 00-110392
ISBN 1-57566-813-0

First Printing: July, 2001
10 9 8 7 6 5 4 3 2 1

Printed in the United States of America

For
W.C.B.

ACKNOWLEDGMENTS

Writing a novel is essentially a solitary endeavor. However, at least in this case, it occurred with tangible and intangible contributions from many. Most notably (but in no particular order) they are: Robin Blakely (agent extraordinaire), John Scognamiglio at Kensington, William Relling Jr., Kevin Howell, J. Randy Taraborrelli, Allen Kramer, Julia Oliver, Muriel Pollia, Ph.D., Susan Taylor Chehak, Dana Rosenfeld Gordon, David Hyde Pierce, Karen Carpenter, Eve Arden, Doris Day, Florence Henderson, Sandy Duncan, and George of the Jungle (er, Brendan Fraser).

Hollywood. They take your soul, give you indigestion,
ruin everything you ever create, and what do you get?
Nothing but a lousy fortune.
—Academy Award–winning screenwriter Frances Marion

Question posed to Sylvia Plath: *"Why are you*
writing a novel [The Bell Jar]*?"*

Answer: *"To take care of a few people."*

PART ONE

PROLOGUE

"You're a vicious son of a gun, aren't you?" said psychiatrist Dr. F. Ecle after listening to his patient, Bart Cain, read aloud from what Bart referred to as his "daily dirt diary."

"Well, pardon me if I'm sick and tired of Hollywood and the bullshit it takes to get ahead, survive, and somehow deal with the satanic personalities who have abused me for years. Anyone who's ever worked for a tyrannical idiot of a boss—no matter what their occupation—would cheer my plans for vengeance."

By vengeance, Bart meant bringing to their knees the flotsam and jetsam that covers the putrid cesspool of the entertainment industry. Bart had filled a dozen steno books with handwritten observations chronicling, in particular, the venomous capers of his boss, Shari Draper, executive vice president of motion picture publicity at Sterling Studios. "The Gayest Place in the Universe," as it was known throughout the cosmos—all of which the parent company, Sterling, Inc., practically owned.

Bart worked at Sterling as a staff copywriter. For his journal, he carefully recorded many top-secret publicity-strategy meetings and telephone conversations with his nefarious boss. He transferred obstreperous telephone calls from irate actors or their managers or bombastic producers to Shari and then stayed silently on the line eavesdropping and transcribing their caustic conversations. He soaked up gutter-variety gossip about George Clooney, Jennifer Love Hewitt, Stephen Sondheim, Richard Dreyfuss, Whoopi Goldberg, Woody Harrelson, Kathy Bates, Nicolas Cage, Alec Baldwin, Bill Murray, Kevin Spacey, and Rosie O'Donnell. Some of his best material was drawn from what he overheard while sequestered in one of the men's-room stalls. He imagined himself playing Agent 007. Sean, of course. Not Pierce, who always looked so constipated.

"I'm merely archiving life in modern-day Sodom and Gomorrah," Bart said, defending his creative journalistic actions. "Don't forget, you're the Dr. Frankenstein in this Mel Brooks-meets-Brian De Palma-meets-James Whale movie of my life. Keeping a diary was your brilliant stroke of genius. My genius is just more diabolical. There was a time when I used to just get mad, then forgive and forget. I don't know when the change took place. But now I want to get even."

"But to publish this thing," Dr. Ecle cautioned. "To expose the people who have been your family for so many years. Why? Remember what they say about biting the hand that feeds you."

"Family?" Bart cried, incredulous. "Listen, I sold my soul to work in Hollywood. Now I want it back. I'm a freakin' Faust, for crying out loud! These notes, which I'll turn into a book, are a means to an end. I'm only biting the hand that bit me first."

"Are you prepared for the end?" Dr. Ecle asked.

"I think so," Bart said. "I'll probably be fired, but I'll use the severance money to make a new beginning. I have enough dish to write a dozen sequels. Like Harry Potter. Only in my volumes Harry's queer and having a true-life romp through triple-X-rated Hollywood. I always thought those stories were metaphors for the film industry, anyway. The horrible Dursleys and their abominable son Dudley live in Hollywood, particularly at Sterling.

"By the time I'm ready to write the next installment, I'll be somewhere far away. I imagine myself imitating *Out Of Africa*. 'I had a farm in . . . *Scotland*.'" Bart was paraphrasing the opening line of the Dinesen novel and Redford/Streep movie. "And Meryl Streep can play me in the movie, 'cause she's got all those great accents in her trunk and my voice is kinda high anyway. She can stretch. A little *Victor/Victoria* thing. The rest of my first line will read, 'with a cute boy hired from the village who spent less time plowing the fields and more time plowing me!'"

"Imaginative," said Dr. Ecle.

"A variation on a theme by Merchant Ivory."

"Something like the film *Maurice*."

"With me as the Hugh Grant character."

"The village boy will be a Rupert Graves type, no doubt?"

"Now you've got it!"

Dr. Ecle rolled his eyes. He wrote something in Bart's file, then said, "I don't usually give my clients advice, Bart." This was Dr. Ecle's mantra, repeated for the umpteenth time since they first began seeing each other professionally. "I merely make suggestions and point out possible courses of action, which is why I prescribed the diary. But this? This farce!"

Bart made a face. "*You* suggested I make notes as a catharsis for my 'demons.' I'm purging, all right—and taking a few egomaniacal Hollywood fools with me." Bart assumed a pose of self-satisfaction.

"You make that studio sound like something out of *Richard III*."

"Exactly! Everybody at Sterling is conspiring against everybody else."

"And you're the only one who *doesn't* want to get ahead in the business?"

"I just want to do my job, write this book, and get out of the glitz biz. My so-called colleagues, Hollywood publicists, are as intolerable as those television ads for new drugs. All those creamy voice-overs that seem so pleased to remind potential consumers of a few minor liabilities. 'The drug Zentrimorphinium isn't for everyone.' You can just hear the snide smile in the actress's voice," Bart said. "'Side effects may include dry mouth, nausea, halitosis, excessive bleeding during menstruation, high blood pressure, increased risk of stroke and heart attack, as well as uncontrollable, oily rectal discharge. Extreme cases may include, but are not limited to, death.'"

"But your diary makes most of these people appear subhuman, like vermin," Dr. Ecle said.

"With their little lab rat–like brains, sniffing around film sets and premieres. Their little lab rat tails scurrying through a complicated maze, reaching toward that elusive goal of being a Hollywood titan. That's not an errant dab of Max Factor African makeup #2 on their respective noses."

"But you can't be serious about the raging insanity? Your bosses are famous in this town! Each year they make *Premiere* magazine's 'Hot 100 List' of the most powerful people on the planet! I can't believe such atrocious behavior as you describe occurs in a motion-picture studio's offices. Especially Sterling, which is supposed to be, as the ads say, 'the Gayest Place in the Universe.'"

"Which is bulltwonk! It's 'the Queerest Place in the Universe.' And I don't mean that as an adjective to identify the employees—although . . ."

"That's what I'd say about your notes, Bart. They're queer. They sound like something out of *Sex and the City* or *South Park*."

Dr. Ecle scribbled in Bart's file folder:

> *Patient appears to be suffering from a series of systemized delu-*
> *sions. He projects interpersonal conflicts and ascribes such to the*
> *presumed hostility of colleagues. Threatens aggressive acts in self-*
> *defense and seems on a mission. Clearly a Don Quixote syndrome.*
> *Or Sonny Bono.*

Bart took a deep breath. He wondered how much more he should reveal to Dr. Ecle. Paranoia had become so rampant at Sterling that he
suddenly didn't trust the unspoken, yet taken-for-granted patient-thera-
pist-confidentiality agreement. There was no way to know if his boss
Shari was a patient of Dr. Ecle's. Or perhaps studio chairman Cy
Lupiano had a weekly session. Bart had no way of knowing whom Dr.
Ecle treated.

"It's all true," he said. "I've only written the facts. Shari's sleeping
with Cy. Cy's sleeping with Shari *and* his new protégé, April. He's rewarded whisky-voiced April by elevating her to vice president, a job she
keeps fucking up. Shari thinks she and Cy together will eventually run
the studio. April, with her big tits and hard nipples, thinks Cy will toss
Shari into the meat grinder of working exclusively on Jerry Bruckheimer
films, then give Shari's job to April.

"And all of them have threatened to clean house of all the gay men
and lesbians, starting with Owen Lucas, president of motion-picture
marketing. He's gay. He's out. He's smart. He's the only genuine human
being ever to occupy that office. And he's in their way. But I have the
feeling that if it comes to a showdown, he'll win. He's so much brighter
than those two battery-operated clones from Altman's *The Player.*
They're windup dildos who go around fucking over as many people as
possible. And I've become a pawn in their 'hour of power' sideshow
games."

For the remaining half-hour of his fifty-minute consultation with his
shrink, Bart continued to read aloud, sometimes haltingly, from his
often illegibly scrawled notes. The material he was collecting was so in-
flammatory that he had locked the first ten spiral notebooks in his
bank's safe-deposit box. He carried the others in a Velcro-sealed com-
partment of his zippered shoulder bag.

When he had to be away from the office for a meeting and couldn't
take his bag with him, he hid the notebooks in his desk drawer, under
copies of the *National Enquirer,* in an envelope marked "Income

Taxes." His clandestine activities were required in case studio security
or his assistant gained access to his locked desk. If that happened, with
any luck they might overlook an envelope marked as something as innocuous as "Income Taxes." He locked the drawer and wore the key
around his neck as if it were a talisman or garland of garlic to keep the
bloodsuckers at bay.

The information Bart possessed was a bit embarrassing to recite to
Dr. Ecle, for among the things revealed was his increasing overzealous-
ness for sex (after years of deprivation) as well as the probability that it
was only a matter of time before he was terminated from his job. It was-
n't necessarily the details in the notebooks that would get him sacked. It
was the fact that he was labeled a "fairy" by Shari and Cy. And he was
not a political ally or collaborator in his various superiors' respective
conspiracies against each other.

"Think about your life and career and give serious consideration to
your future here at Sterling," Shari, the executive vice president, had
said to him during a recent private meeting in her office. "You're one of
my favorites, Bart," she practically cooed, the way a sexy wet-underpants dancer suckers a client for a bigger tip. "I'd like you to be with me
and continue to be 'Part of the Enchantment' at Sterling for a long
time."

But Bart knew her words were actually a threat. There would never
be any love lost between Shari and Bart. She'd made it clear enough over
the past two years that she'd like to be rid of "the little shit," as she
called him (and not just behind his back). There was something about
Bart that she clearly mistrusted. For one thing, there was his intelligence
and talent. He was as good an actor as he was a staff writer. He could
convincingly don the mask of the innocent and virtuous Mary
Pickford/Sandra Bullock rah, rah team player. But Shari was wary, and
rightfully so. She hadn't achieved her level of success without using her
sixth sense.

Bart told Dr. Ecle about a startling allegation that Mitch, Shari's assistant, had made to Bart one morning. He confided that Shari had been
in serious talks with the publicist who was Bart's counterpart at
Paramount Pictures to come over to Sterling. Mitch was certain that it
was Shari's intention to make life so unbearable for Bart that he would
quit.

"Better be sure the porno is off your computer," Mitch warned.

"Shari will use whatever ammo she can get her hands on to bag you and blow up your career."

"I'm not leaving Sterling until *I'm* ready to leave," Bart charged. "And I won't go without a lot of noise."

"You're not the type to go postal."

"No. But there'll be bodies in my wake. Believe me."

Mitch had also shown Bart a confidential memo from Shari. It contained a list of names from the department whom Shari wanted to replace. One of them was Bart. Seeing this document, Bart was filled half with anger and half with glee as he began to concoct suitable scenarios for revenge.

"They all think I'm such a nice young man," he said to Mitch.

"You're just too courtly."

"I get my work done on time."

"And everybody likes you," said Mitch.

"Sounds like I'm the profile of the classic serial killer whom neighbors always describe as 'so quiet and unassuming and keeping mostly to himself.'"

"But there's a dark side to you, too," Mitch said. "Which I not only admire but find very sexy."

Indeed, there was an aspect of Bart's personality that few were sensitive enough to recognize. Mitch was obviously one. But so was Shari.

Unfortunately for her, what she was completely unaware of was that Bart had ammo of his own. He had something more powerful than her machete of absolute authority. He had information chronicled in his notebooks. "Knowledge is power," he quoted Auntie Mame, who quoted James Bacon.

Bart concluded his session with Ecle by reading the last line of his entry in notebook number 12. "As I was waiting for Shari to review photo captions, Cy Lupiano walked into the office. He came over to her desk and grabbed her tits and simply said, 'Hey, hot set! Why the fuck don't you get a cute female secretary? I'm tired of men doing women's work!'"

"Perhaps this should conclude our therapy sessions indefinitely," Dr. Ecle said tentatively. "There's really nothing I can do for you except to listen."

"But that's exactly what I need from you, Doctor. I need someone to listen to me! By the time I'm finished, you'll be utterly convinced Sterling is 'the Most Machiavellian Place in the Universe.'

"When I turn these notes into a book," Bart said, "Shari'll be so destroyed she'll be 'voted off the island.' She'll be lucky if she's hired by a dot-com company!"

Chapter One

"She hasn't had her Prozac suppositories properly inserted today," said Mitch Wood, the personal secretary to "Scary Shari" Draper.

Mitch whispered this mercy warning to Bart, who had just been summoned to Shari's office. Bart's sphincter tightened. He gave an appreciative roll of his eyes to Mitch before entering the high-tech, steel-and-glass inner sanctum where Shari held court, like Torquemada at the Spanish Inquisition. Shari's office, which reflected her rusty-scalpel personality, was decorated with as much warmth as this dreary January day. The room was like a cold warehouse: concrete floor, exposed infrastructure and air ducts, a wet bar, and a big-screen television, video players, and workout equipment scattered about the cavernous room.

"Fuck you, Hutton!" Shari was sniggering into the mouthpiece of the telephone headset she wore like a futuristic barrette. She gave a cursory glance to Bart, then ignored him as he took a seat in one of the two Mies van der Rohe chairs facing the glass table that served as her desk.

Bart sat in silence, pretending to be oblivious to the phone conversation. Holding the pages in his hand, he reread the press release he'd just rewritten for the third time. It announced a new romantic comedy the studio would be shooting with the aging, Academy Award–winning Lothario to whom Shari was speaking.

Costarring would be the English tart Mare Dickerson. Mare (known in the industry as "Nightmare" Dickerson) was famous for playing buxom virgins in a series of acclaimed costume dramas set in the eighteenth and nineteenth centuries, for Miramax. Last year she made the fatal publicity boo-boo of letting it slip during an interview that she was having a torrid affair with the very married Australian author of the best-selling novel *The French Sick Room*. The screen adaptation—

which Mare had begged to star in, playing the lead role of the compassionate nurse—was the Motion Picture Academy's forgettable Best Film several years ago. Mare was now trying to make a comeback of sorts— away from the made-for-cable-television films about bulimic prostitutes that she'd recently been forced to accept.

Like all hyperbolic Hollywood press releases that issue from the studio spin cycles, Bart's was filled with bullshit lexicon. He knew his efforts had little journalistic merit and much less integrity. They weren't supposed to. Rabbits could almost do the writing. It was merely a job. It paid for his mortgage, his therapist, and the occasional bag of weed in which he indulged.

Working for Sterling was merely a means to an end. Bart had other plans. He was a closet novelist. Unlike everybody else in town, he did *not* have a screenplay being "shopped around." He was a prose purist. In fact, he had an unspoken disdain for screenwriters. He hoped it was only a matter of time before he had a book deal and could walk away from the unfulfilling and exhausting vice grip of motion-picture-studio drudgery. Until then, he intended to use Sterling as much as Sterling used him.

Waiting for Shari's attention, Bart scanned his latest draft, praying not to find a typo or dangling modifier. Not that Shari would recognize a dangling anything unless she was sucking it.

Draft Number 3

FOR IMMEDIATE RELEASE

Legendary Academy Award–winning director/writer/actor Hutton Brawley and Oscar-nominated Mare Dickerson are set to star in Sterling Studios's new romantic comedy Ticket to Ride, *directed by Gus Girard from an original screenplay by Lowell Pierce and Rachel Drone, it was announced today (insert date), by Shari Draper, executive vice president, Marketing, Sterling Studios. Brawley will also serve as producer. The film, scheduled for summer release, will shoot on locations in Manhattan and London.*

In this modern folk tale, comedy and chaos collide when handsome Jarred Lange (Brawley), a quirky motion-picture writer/director but deadbeat dad, refuses a court order to surrender his beloved Central Park West penthouse apartment to his ex-wife,

Erin (Dickerson), and their six adopted, racially mixed children. Complications arise after Erin decides to take revenge and hires legal eagle Max Skylar (Martin Short) to arbitrate. However, Erin's less-than-virtuous past catches up with her and plays havoc with her battle for control of the multimillion-dollar residence—and the couple's sublimated, yet undeniable, love.
Blah, blah, blah.

Shari Draper was a stereotypical Hollywood bitch. How she got her job was anyone's—and everyone's—guess. There were the typical rumors that she just shtupped the right Hollywood hotshots and parlayed that into her setup as executive vice president of Sterling's publicity department.

She was not one of those strong, smart women who unfairly received the epithet simply because she was successful in the predominantly men's club of motion-picture studio executives. Not by a long shot. In fact, she was more of an idiot savant, a stupid woman whose fearlessness made her appear as though she knew what she was doing. Her greatest talent was that she was quick to make difficult decisions—though her judgments were often scandalously inappropriate.

An appalling example of this was her infamous faux pas that occurred when the ACLU and a vocal contingent from the Gay and Lesbian Center rallied in front of the studio's main gate and wrote bombastic op-ed pieces in the *New York Times* and *The Advocate*. They were decrying a particularly offensive portrayal of Eleanor Roosevelt in Sterling's hit animated musical feature *WACS in the White House* in which a cute, wiseacre rat sidekick character, who nested in the private living quarters of the chief executive's mansion, sang overtly suggestive remarks about the legendary first lady's sexual orientation. Shari was quoted in *Premiere* magazine as saying, "Tell those pansies [in the gay community] to just swallow it, like [sic] they do [everything else], and get a life!"

An unfavorable publicity fallout resulted from the embarrassment Shari caused the studio. Soon there were boycotts of Sterling's films and water-slide parks by the DAR, Hillary Rodham Clinton, and Ru Paul, causing the studio's board of directors to unanimously vote to recall millions of videocassettes of the blockbuster film and change the offending lyric. For the first time in her career, which had begun inauspiciously as a skateboarding mail-delivery girl at Millennium Films, Shari was reeling. Not from the adverse publicity but from the tyrannical tongue-lashing she received from Sterling's CEO Jonathan Rotenberg, a Howdy-Doody look-alike who ludicrously fancied himself heir apparent to the studio's legendary arbiter of quality family entertainment.

Shari's renown for being devious was equally legendary. She once wired herself to a tape recorder before meeting with a furious producer of mindless, explosion-filled action/adventure films. During the marathon screaming match, the short, bearded, beady-eyed producer lambasted Shari and the other Sterling marketing executives, blaming them because his blow-'em-to-smithereens "event" film starring Bruce Willis—they always starred Bruce Willis—opened in fifth position its first weekend of wide release. After the meeting, Shari messengered the tape to Vicki Rydell at the *Hollywood Reporter,* a Cindy Adams wanna-be, who wrote an excoriating diatribe about the director's distended ego and vulgar language directed at a "lady."

Still, Shari's duplicitous character had ingratiated her to at least one person: Cy Lupiano, the bucktoothed Napoleon who ran the film division of the studio, an infamous little dictator whom billionaire CEO Rotenberg called "Rover" behind his back. Cy's implicit backing allowed Shari to revel in the fact that she had the wherewithal to jokingly say, "Fuck you," to Hutton and any other powerful star in the industry. Her distorted sense of self-value seemed solely based on how many people she could lacerate with her tongue. She could turn ordinarily lovely people like Sandra Bullock and Harrison Ford into cross-eyed, hyperventilating lunatics after a marketing-strategy meeting. "If you'd made a better movie, I could have gotten people into the theater," Shari would say without a trace of tact when they would dare impugn her marketing creativity after one of their films flopped.

As Shari continued her phone conversation—which consisted of a lot of nonverbal sounds and low-decibel snorts—she leaned back in her black leather executive desk chair. Her fat, stubby, white-as-cocaine-powder legs were propped up on the table, her short skirt riding up her thigh. She pretended to ignore Bart, which was the exact effect she wanted to achieve: the cornered house cat cowering before a ravenous coyote. Her exhibition continued with cryptic dialogue that suggested it was difficult to talk openly at the moment. Rumor around the office speculated that Shari was sleeping with Hutton. It was the worst-kept secret in the company that she was also working overtime with the much-married, with children, studio chairman in her office at night.

Her secretary, Mitch Wood, usually stood guard at his desk during those private "dinner meetings." One night, however, a menial from the janitorial staff, doing her trash-collecting duties, slipped by the sentinel and opened the unlocked door. The terrified Mexican woman gasped *mea culpa*s in Spanish as Shari, on her knees, took her lips away from the chairman's red lipstick–greased, pathetic five inches of penis, fell back on the floor, wrapping her unbuttoned blouse around her exposed, braless breasts, and screamed like Roseanne Barr/Pentland/Arnold/Roseanne at a story meeting.

Now, looking at her wristwatch and tittering in a confidential tone into the telephone, Shari leaned forward, exposing her cleavage and revealing a curious, single long strand of dark hair that pushed through a mole. Bart found the sight as disturbing as the soft hairs above Shari's upper lip. Couldn't she at least pluck the mole hair, he wondered as Shari snapped her red-lacquered fingernails at Bart with an impatient "Gimmie, gimmie, and make it quick" gesture to hand over the press release for her to review and approve.

For a moment, Shari divided her attention between listening to Hutton and reading the press release. Then she raised her green eyes to Bart with a look of exasperation, picked up a black Sharpie marker, and scrawled *NO!* in bold block letters across the page. She tore the papers in two and flipped them back across her desk. "Hold a sec," she said to Hutton.

She stared at Bart. "'Sublimate?' Who the hell knows what that word means! How much longer are you going to write shit like this? If you can't do this job right, I'll find somebody who can!"

"This is the third rewrite, Shari. I need a little guidance," Bart said. "What exactly do you want me to say?"

"You're the so-called writer. Figure it out! And I want it fast! *Daily Variety* closes in an hour! By the way," she said, her voice dripping with sarcasm, "who ever told you you could write?"

Bart stalled. He hated altercations. Then, innocently, he said, "Ah, my agent. My publisher. The review in *Publishers Weekly* of my book about the making of *Encino Man*. Hmmm. Let me see . . . the Publicists Guild, who gave me that award last year for Most Innovative and Consistent Artistic Achievement."

Outside Shari's office door, Mitch couldn't help eavesdropping. He was chuckling at the eddy of repartee swirling in Shari's den of iniquity. Shari picked up a half-full plastic bottle of Evian water from her desk and threw it out the door, where it crashed and then bounced off the glass-framed poster for *Marie Antoinette*, with Norma Shearer. Shari's favorite movie and star.

Shari was still shouting at Bart. "Don't get smart with me, you skinny-assed sissy!" she sniped.

"No! Not you, Hutton, for Christ sake!

"That's why the stuff you write around here stinks on ice. You're too busy writing for other people," she continued ranting at Bart. "That's gotta change, mister. I'm warning you. You owe me, and the studio, your undivided attention."

"I'll do better, I promise."

"I'll advise you not to tangle with me, dearie.

"No. Not you, Hutton. Outta here, you little shit. I want that press release!"

As Bart exited to the outer office, he shot a look of grief at Mitch, who, in solidarity, blew a kiss from the palm of his hand. Mitch then took the missile of Evian and blindly pitched it around the corner, back into Shari's office. He winked at Bart as the sound of picture frames being toppled from a bookshelf merged with Shari's voice, screaming, "Damn you!

"No! Not *you*, Hutton!"

Sotto voce, Bart said to Mitch, "How can her throat stand the strain of all that screaming?"

"Let's just say her tonsils get lubed regularly." Mitch smiled.

"All I want is enough 'Fuck you' money to buy and jam those damned suppositories up her brass ass myself before I leave this dump. Sorry. That's inappropriate and unattractive language."

Mitch, who, like Bart, did not suffer fools gladly (and was known to scream as loudly at Shari as she screamed at him), said he'd happily help but that the suppositories would be filled with gunpowder. Mitch, in his own way, was a very sweet natured man. His life was devoted to planning his retirement in Palm Springs and luring Federal Express delivery guys into the men's room for coffee-break blow jobs.

He smiled at Bart, batting his thick eyelashes. "At least *I* appreciate you. And don't you dare leave here before we've had a date, you talented stud, you."

Bart smiled back. "You'd be fun," he said. "But I'm a hopeless romantic. I can't do quickies the way you do. I still expect to fall in love and settle down with Dr. Niles Crane."

Affecting a Yiddish accent, Mitch said, "Have I got a guy for you. I know you're his type. He'll cream when he sees your dimple. Now, you're Mrs. Molloy, and I'm Dolly Levi—Barbra's version, of course."

Bart did an impersonation of early Barbra: taloned fingers brushing nonexistent strands of her bouffant hair away from her face. "Just leave everything to me eh?"

"Does the fact that he's rich and used to be famous make any difference?" Mitch encouraged.

"Oh, please! Not an actor!"

"Not anymore. See today's *Variety?* Hint: His initials are Jim Fallon."

"The star of *The Grass Is Always Greener?*"

"Aren't you clever."

"It's been all over the news. I've had his infamous video for weeks!"

"The one where he's caught doing naughties with rough trade? Isn't it fetching? My grandmother *loved* that! She once got me to pinch a copy of *Penthouse* magazine for her, the issue with Vanessa Williams . . . remember she was Miss Something . . . America or USA . . . but was dethroned when Larry Flynt printed graphic pictures of her eating box? You go, girl!"

Bart was too young to remember that cause célèbre. He thought for a moment. "I'm just too vanilla. And Jim's too scary."

"Aw, come on. He certainly needs a sexy diversion about now. You fit all the jeans, er requirements, perfectly."

"Why don't *you* date him?" Bart asked.

Mitch smiled coyly. "Who says I haven't? But you know me. I never do anything twice, is my theme song."

Chapter Two

To be an "old" star in Hollywood, all you have to do is *not* appear in a feature film, sitcom, or made-for-television movie for a couple of seasons. The public quickly forgets.

Jim Fallon was about to be an old star. At age forty-five.

Five years ago, his hit TV show, *The Grass Is Always Greener*, had made an overnight star of the stand-up comic from Alaska. On Jim's program, which had been an instant ratings hit, he played a goofball high school gym teacher with two Neanderthal preteen sons and a perky wife who got all the best deadpan comeback lines of each script's insipid dialogue. The ubiquitous Betty White had been thrown into the cast as the kindly next-door neighbor, to give the show an air of geriatric dignity, elevating it slightly above typical sitcom fare of Set-up. Joke. Set-up. Joke. Set-up. Joke. The canned laugh track didn't seem to irritate the millions who immediately made the show number one.

After only a couple of stints at the Comedy Store on Sunset Boulevard, Jim had been "discovered," and he was suddenly a millionaire, thrust to the top of the Hollywood Hot Heap. The very first season, Jim won a People's Choice Award for Favorite New Male Star and an Emmy as Best Actor in a Comedy or Variety Series. He also received an NAACP Image Award, even though he was white.

He liked being rich and famous. But once the television tabloid *Totally Hollywood* got hold of the skeleton in what Jim thought was a hermetically sealed closet, the Middle America audience, who loved him on prime-time Sunday evenings, loathed him this Monday morning, when bold headlines in the entertainment sections of newspapers across the country all proclaimed variations on: "Ass Is Grass for Green Star!"

Jim's television persona was that of the virile, all-American male, complete with nose hair, on-screen farting, and offscreen promoting of

NRA ideology. In fact, he was a homo hick from Anchorage who happened to have discovered a comedy gimmick that endeared him to all but the most stringent PBS watching demographics.

His now-revealed secret? Jim Fallon, the Father Knows Best of Generation-X, liked young Latin gang-banger types to rough him up, strip him naked, and lash his arms and legs to a St. Andrew's Cross in the wine cellar turned dungeon of his Hollywood Hills mansion. Then, with a cattle prod, the bangers would zap his raw nipples (which were squeezed by wooden clothespins) and testicles (which were snared together with rubber bands). Jim captured all the action for posterity on an elaborate videotape monitoring system. He was like Sheldon Needstein, the cult-favorite Broadway composer whose secluded place in the Hudson Valley was legendary for its store of S/M hardware.

Jim was so naive, he hadn't a clue that the tabloids kept male hustlers and prostitutes (and nurses at Cedars Sinai Hospital) on retainer just to ferret out dish for their scandalous columns. Thus, when "a source close to the star" leaked one of Jim's self-made porn videotapes, the habitually nervous network suits and gynecologic hygiene sponsors of *The Grass Is Always Greener* couldn't keep a straight face. But they also knew they couldn't keep Jim. They used the morals clause in his multimillion dollar-a-year contract to get him off the show. It was only a matter of time before the tape went public, like Pamela Anderson and Tommy Lee's, being passed around the industry like Academy screeners at Oscar time.

The tape that had been stolen from Jim's home-video library vault showcased a particularly innovative scene of sadomasochism. It had been copied and recopied and recopied until it was down so many grainy generations that there was practically nothing left to prove it was actually the beloved television star caught like an idiot on *Stupid Human Tricks*. Only his distinctive voice as he begged for mercy from the excruciating ecstasy of electrical jolts provided by his posse of gangsta Hispanic boys was left undistorted. Although Jim's publicist tried to claim it was a forgery, the tape made the rounds at every party in Hollywood, thus sealing his fate.

After today, Jim Fallon wouldn't even get a guest-starring gig on *Touched by an Angel* or a box on *Hollywood Squares*.

If only Jim had been videotaped begging for electrical prods from a harem of whores, he could possibly have pulled a Rob Lowe, Hugh Grant, or Pee-Wee Herman routine. Leno would have leaped to book him as the opening guest. Jim could have acted sheepish and apologetic and laughed at himself amid all the jokes. Heterosexual America would have adored him more for fessing up and being a *man*. If Eddie Murphy could be caught soliciting a transvestite and then innocently claim he didn't know "*he* wasn't a *she*," things might have worked out for Jim.

But then there was the country's puritanical God Squad of the religious right: the Christian Coalition of homophobe nuts who were the self-appointed arbiters of the world's morals, many of whom had invited Jim into their living rooms and laughed at his silly on-camera muggings. They were no longer laughing. Jim instantly became the new poster boy for the virulent disease known as Hollywood. The public at large couldn't risk subjecting their innocent, gun-toting children to the possibility of subliminal homosexual messages encoded in the program's weekly scenarios.

Jim's routines would have been misconstrued. Baseball bats would have been interpreted as phallic images. Locker-room and shower-room jokes and what weekly guest stars from the world of gymnastics did would all appear to have sexual connotations. If the script called for him to change a fuse while puttering around the house on a weekend, audiences would have squealed uncomfortably as they imagined Jim's delight at being electrocuted.

So now middle-aged Jim Fallon was washed up in show business, without any marketable, real-world work skills. He wasn't even bright enough to earn a realtor's license, which many a failed actor in town got as a backup.

Still, he was determined to make a comeback. Whatever he had to do and whomever he had to use. "As God is my witness," he said, imagining himself as Scarlett in silhouette, a red sunset in the background, with a dirt-encrusted sweet-potato root clutched in her hand, "I'll be a star again!"

But making a comeback in Hollywood is much more difficult than starting out. Ask Eartha Kitt. There are no more *Merv Griffin Show*s or *Mike Douglas Show*s to rekindle the flames of old celebrity. Today the talent bookers at Leno and Dave want only the hottest stars from the latest blockbuster movies or television shows. Jim Fallon feared that his name was soon to be merely a footnote in *The Comprehensive Guide to TV Throughout the Century*. He would be all but forgotten, like Dana Plato from *Diff'rent Strokes,* who'd had to get a job in a Vegas dry-cleaning store before eventually OD'ing herself into complete oblivion.

In the meantime, Lydia, the beard in Jim's life—the woman he'd palmed off as his "live-in companion"—wasn't above filing for palimony, which she had been secretly planning ever since the first season of *Grass* when *TV Guide* profiled the couple in a Valentine's Day issue entitled "Happy Hollywood Honeys."

The grass was getting browner by the minute.

"Holy Christ!" Michael Scott shouted as he grabbed the *National Enquirer* from his assistant, Troy, who brought in the trades and rags bearing the news of Jim's excommunication from his own hit show. Michael was Jim's agent. "Why didn't I know about this before?" he screamed at Troy, who was merely the messenger. "Why do I have to read these things in the trades? Nobody tells me anything!" he ranted, emulating his hero, the character Kevin Spacey played in *Swimming With Sharks*.

Troy said, "I'm telling you now, aren't I?"

"Ah! Scratch the surface of any actor and you'll find an actress." Michael swacked the paper with a backhand. He didn't want to admit he was also kind of amused by all the Jim Fallon stories. Michael looked up at Troy. "That just came to me. It's great. Is it original or a famous line?"

"Got me," Troy said. "Although it sounds like Dorothy Parker. Or Oscar Wilde." Troy knew his boss was basically an idiot who had probably never heard of Dorothy Parker and more than likely thought Oscar Wilde was a hot dog. "I think that you're an Oscar Wilde weenie," Troy sang to himself to the tune of an old Oscar Meyer commercial.

"Find out if that's a real quote," Michael ordered. "I want it to be attributed to me. It's a good line, don't you think? Don't just stand there looking at me, for Christ sake!"

Troy nodded, winked, and walked away. He knew his boss was a wuss. No amount of screaming and bitching could ruffle Troy, who saw through Michael the way that Haley Joel Osment saw dead people.

Michael Scott was not exactly an Actors and Others Agency hotshot power player, although he wanted desperately to be one. He had thought that with Jim in his stable (like common barnyard animals, actors are often referred to as being in a *stable*), he was on his way. He had discovered Jim at the Comedy Store. A couple of blows of coke and a night of pretending to be gay and convincingly offering up his eight inches for Jim to use as a tether, he gave a solemn Hollywood promise for more action if Jim would sign up for personal representation. Was it the blow of coke or the cock that did the trick? Michael wasn't sure. But within days of Jim signing his agency contract, from out of the blue

NBC dropped the no-name comic into a pilot called *The Grass Is Always Greener.* The show went to series, replacing the low-rated Suzanne Somers's comedy *Mrs. C. and the Chimpanzee,* and it became an instant hit.

Now, this dreary Monday morning, faster than a zap from a cattle prod, Michael and Jim were both in *career interruptus.*

Michael's client roster was mostly a disaster: Rose Marie, Jack Carter, Lorna Luft, Delta Burke, Jay North, Ruta Lee, Ali MacGraw, and Darin McGavin, to name a few. McGavin's recent stroke didn't seem to faze Michael, who couldn't get the old fart a job, anyway. Now his only cash cow, Jim Fallon, had dried up—overnight.

Michael, seated behind his huge desk, swiveled his chair around to face the tall smoked-glass windows overlooking the murky, leaden January skies above Beverly Hills. "Am I to be mired in a bog of has-beens my entire career?" he uttered disconsolately. "Jim, you son of a bitch! I'm very disappointed. February sweeps are just around the corner! You've fallen into the same stinking cesspool as my other clients. Is it me? Am I a jinx?"

Michael could barely get his other so-called stars a little work here and there. Mostly they just appeared once a year in guest appearances on episodes of *Law & Order* or *Ally McBeal* or starring in productions of the ubiquitous *Love Letters* on the condo circuit in Florida. Their income was just enough to keep up their SAG health-insurance premiums. But the older they all got, the more demanding they became, insisting on such contractual imperatives as a box around their names in print ads and in *Playbill*s or last-place billing preceded by: . . . AND ALSO STARRING . . . It wasn't hard to see that the less important one's name was in Hollywood, the more important it was to amplify the appearance of status.

For all the lack of viable working talent he now handled, Michael Scott wouldn't have been surprised if the senior agents dumped Sally Struthers or Joyce DeWitt in his lap, too.

Suddenly paranoid about his career, Michael became certain the entire town either didn't know his name or knew who he was but laughed about his client list behind his back. If it weren't for his assistant, Troy, Michael wouldn't even be able to get a table at The Ivy. As a matter of fact, he could only get a table at The Ivy *because* of Troy, who was movie-star handsome and had dated most of the waiters at the Robertson Boulevard eatery. Michael justified the situation matter-of-factly. "With a name like Troy, you just automatically get laid, like a

Tito or a Trampus. Not much he can do about it." Michael hated his too-bright son-of-a-bitch assistant because everything came too easily to Troy. That's what good looks and half a brain will get you in Hollywood—everything.

Troy was an up-and-coming player himself. In fact, unbeknownst to Michael, Troy's ambitions were coming to fruition faster than his well-planned timeline. He was a mere several paces away from taking over Michael's career.

All of Michael's clients adored Troy. More often than not they preferred to deal with him because he was always better able to answer their pathetic paranoid questions about pilot season or a show that they had heard was going into production and how right they thought they'd be for this or that role. Troy could appease them, usually by getting them invited to premieres or at least press screenings of upcoming films. Without exception, each encouraged him to seek an agent's position, if not with Actors and Others, then elsewhere. And they all promised to follow him if he ever decided to jump ship. However, Troy only had his eyes on new talent. Once he left Michael, he planned to leave the Wax Works behind for the coroner's office to eventually collect in plastic zippered body bags.

Tossing the *Enquirer* aside, Michael picked up Marilyn Beck. A cryptic item jumped out of her column:

> As the gophers continue to burrow under the "green grass" of this ex–sitcom star we have it on good authority that his top-secret tell-all autobiog will dig deeper, grave-size holes in the careers of Hollywood's hottest!

Michael's blood was already boiling, but now he was at serious risk for a massive stroke. He gnashed his teeth, guessing at once that the item referred to Jim. Only he, Michael, hadn't agented any goddamned book deal! What the fuck was his client trying to pull on him? Fifteen percent of a big book advance was what? Michael couldn't do the math, but he knew it was a serious chunk of change. After five seasons on a top-rated show, the small fry from Alaska was almost as big a star as Paul Reiser or Jerry Seinfeld, both of whom got ridiculous multimillion-dollar advances for their books. Five million dollars wasn't an impossible sum to consider, especially now, what with the gossip-hungry world craving every bit of dish about Jim's personal life.

Michael barked at Troy to get his now-professionally-destroyed client on the phone. "Oh, how Hollywood loves to see the mighty tumble," he groused as he crumpled the newspaper and once again yelled at Troy to get Jim, even as Jim's phone was ringing.

Michael's voice oozed sanctimony when he put on his telephone headset and greeted Jim. "Poor baby," the agent purred. "What a pity about that damned tape. And the show. And all that money! And the lawsuit filed by the mother of that sixteen-year-old from Pacoima. Oops, you hadn't heard? Check out today's Army Archerd, second to last paragraph. Happy to fax it over. What'ya say I pick up something from Wolfgang and I bring it over to the house. It'll cheer you up. We've got to make some plans, Jimbo. 'Bout an hour? Terrif!"

Before hanging up the phone (without so much as a good-bye), Michael snarled at Troy, "Get Panda Express to deliver a bunch of stuff here, pronto. When it arrives, put the food into something decent. No leaky cardboard containers in my Beemer! Then bring the car up from the garage. Oh, and throw in a couple of rejected scripts, too."

Jim wasn't thrilled to receive Michael's call. They hadn't spoken since Jim threatened to leave the agency a few weeks ago for another agent who he felt would truly care about jump-starting his feature-film career. Michael calmed Jim down, then promised him a special fuck and to work extra hard at getting Spielberg, Coppola, De Palma, the Coens and Mingella, and top producers for his "favorite client."

This appeased Jim for about a week, but they still hadn't exchanged a word since. Now, Jim thought, perhaps Michael was coming to officially drop him from the agency. Or perhaps Michael had deciphered Marilyn Beck's coded item about the clandestine book deal.

"How do these things get out?" he asked himself, trying to remember who he might have mentioned the project to while he was drunk. Then Jim decided to try to view this from a different angle. Perhaps Michael actually had some career-enhancing magic to impart—a deal for a film. He sang, then whistled, an impersonation of Eric Idle being crucified in *Life of Brian*. Without question, there was an agenda to this unusual meeting, because Michael never paid house calls—except to catered parties.

Jim was anxious about all the possibilities. He decided he'd better shower, shave, and put on his cleanest pair of 501s. The younger and more appealing he looked, the better he felt. And he still toyed with the idea of taking his stupid agent to bed again—although he always fantasized more about being banged by Troy, the assistant. Everybody did.

Jim looked around his vast mansion and sighed. Soon he would have to downsize, since the big checks from *The Grass Is Always Greener* would no longer be rolling in. Nor would the large sums from his Ford truck endorsements. Even the lucrative Japanese commercials might be history. Everything seemed in limbo—a state Jim loathed because he had no control over it.

Off Mulholland Drive, between Laurel Canyon and Wrightwood—not the most prestigious location in town but better than most—Jim Fallon's six-bedroom estate was nestled atop a long, steep cobblestone driveway, hidden behind an electric gate and surrounded by tall pines and palms. The pool, which was only steps away from the back door, was clean but needed resurfacing. Because of the profusion of trees, very little sunlight ever got through, so the pool was seldom used, giving lie to the urban myth, perpetuated by porn videos, that all pool boys in Los Angeles are blond calendar models—tanned, muscular, and unable to wait to strip and service their clients. Jim thought he must have been living in a parallel universe, as was evidenced by his own pool boy. Or pool grandfather, as in this case.

The old man came once a week and did meticulous work. However, Jim had only to answer an ad in *Eros* magazine, a freebie gay publication he regularly picked up in West Hollywood, and his Nordic "full service" pool cleaner would be in the cabana and out of his swimming trunks in a flash. Different pool boys came twice a week, but none of them so much as dipped his skimmer into the water. It was doubtful they even owned a net, let alone understood the correct pH level for the water. At five times the expense of the pool grandfather, the *Eros* boys would probably have to be downsized, too—in a manner of speaking.

By the time Michael arrived, much later in the afternoon than he'd promised, Jim had jacked off to one of his infamous homemade videos, showered, dressed, and was stirring his third martini of the day. Michael would later recall that the man who answered the door when the bell chimed the first few bars of *The Grass Is Always Greener* theme song didn't seem to be a man who was a pariah in Hollywood and the hot topic of Dr. Laura's psychobabble call-in radio show. Jim had a bemused smirk on his face when he greeted his agent. Consciously reaching into his tight 501s, Jim adjusted himself.

"Laughing on the outside, crying on the inside, are we, Jimbo?" Michael chirped.

"We?" Jim hated being called Jimbo.

"We're a team. We've both got to be strong. But first a little nosh."

Into the vast kitchen Michael carried a tray of orange chicken, chow mein, fried rice, beef with broccoli, and egg rolls. Jim could see he'd been lied to about where the food was procured. The entrées were obviously not from Wolfgang, but he kept silent. He really wasn't in the mood for eating, anyway. It was too late for lunch and too early for dinner. However, another martini would be filling enough, and so he prepared himself one. He didn't offer a drink to Michael.

As he prepared a plate, Michael asked rhetorically, "What happened to Hugh Grant when he was arrested for getting that blow job from a prostitute off of Sunset?"

"Where are you going with this?" Jim asked.

Michael, plate and eating utensils in hand, continued babbling as he moved toward the library/den. "And what happened to Rob Lowe when he was videotaped screwing a minor? And what happened to Michael Jackson when he was caught having sleepovers at Neverland Ranch with little white boys?" Michael stopped short. "Scratch that one. It's not a good example. Anyway, what I'm getting at," Michael continued, "is Hugh's still very big . . . *in films*. Rob's got *West Wing*. With the right strategy, you'll be back on the tube—or even the big screen—in no time."

Jim whined, "I want to work in films. I want Kevin Spacey to be my costar." His speech was beginning to slur. "I want a fucking Oscar. Just one. Is that too damned much to ask from this fucking town? I've paid my dues. I came from nowhere, and look where I am now."

"Nowhere again," Michael said with a wink.

"Do I have to prove that I'm a *fucking* survivor before I get the *fucking* recognition I deserve? Is that the *fucking* lesson I'm to learn from all this crap?"

Michael looked around the vast mansion, his eyes drawn to Jim's two Emmy Awards, perched on either side of the fireplace mantel under pink spotlights. "My friend, 'fucking' is what got you into this mess. Unless you clean up your act—and your language, for heaven's sake—and do things my way, not only will there never be an Oscar, you'll be hawking those Emmys on eBay!"

Jim began to sob.

Envious of Jim's living in this gorgeous mansion, Michael took a seat in a wing chair opposite the fireplace. "Here's what I want you to do. First of all, read these scripts I brought over. They're all tentative projects that require packaging. But don't read 'em with the idea of playing the lead. I'm going to have to reintroduce you, first in supporting roles."

"But . . ."

"Don't argue with me about this, Jim," Michael insisted. "All the best shows have supporting characters who make the stars look better than they are. Just look at Jack and Karen on *Will & Grace,* and Daphne and Roz on *Frasier.* I think you'll be especially good in this one. It's a feature."

Michael indicated a copy of a script called *Blind as a Bat.* "It's a hoot. It's like Mr. Magoo, only the star character is a near-sighted former Wall Street executive who is now reduced to being the super of a building on a run-down street in New York. The role I have picked out for you is the new gay tenant who is trying to gentrify the neighborhood."

"Gay?" Jim was aghast.

"Let me finish. Everybody knows that *real* men, *straight* actors, play gay better than gays. But the public doesn't know that there aren't really any 'straight'"—he used his fingers to indicate quotation marks—"actors in Hollywood. They think that 'straight'"—again with the fingers—"actors are comfortable enough with their own sexuality that they haven't a problem playing queers. No offense. It's all Scientology . . . or sociology. I get those two confused."

Jim sobbed again. "Scientology my ass. If I joined them, I'd be better taken care of than I am with you. Just look at Tom and Nicole and Travolta and Kirsty."

As Michael finished his plate of orange chicken, he offered some traditional agent-client wisdom: "Trust me." Then he added, "So what's your fortune?"

"It was a high six figures per episode."

"No. Your fortune cookie. But here's a twist. Whatever it says, you have to add 'in bed' to the prognostication."

Jim, in a gin stupor, didn't quite follow as he held a Panda Express fortune cookie in his hand.

"Here," Michael said as he cracked open his cookie into crumbs and demonstrated what he wanted Jim to do. "Oh, mine's a goody. 'Luck will visit you on the next full moon . . . in bed.' Now you try it."

Jim cracked open his cookie and munched on part of it. He took out the small slip of paper with red lettering. Through double vision he read: "'From a past misfortune, good luck will come to you . . .'"

"'In bed.'" Michael completed the sentence.

Jim looked askance at Michael. Even halfway to being drunk, Jim could see he had a butthead for an agent.

Then, as a coda, Michael said, "By the way, how's the tell-all book coming along?"

Jim turned ashen.

Chapter Three

After scurrying back to his office, Bart told his secretary, Chita Contessa Van Nuys—or Cheets, as he called her for short—that he was on deadline and would be behind closed doors until he'd completed yet another rewrite of Shari's press release.

Cheets was a schizophrenic actress with equal parts talent and deep-rooted issues of resentment and hostility toward her boss in particular and mostly everyone in general. Many years ago she had won a Silver Pin Award from some storefront acting academy in East Lansing, Michigan. She subsequently got a job in a Dentyne chewing-gum commercial for television and was on her way—as it turned out, to oblivion. Lately she'd been reduced to playing the Monty Woolley role in a basement production of *The Man Who Came To Dinner* with the Los Angeles Rainbow Theatre Experience.

Cheets divided her time between crying over her bitterness that she had to work as a secretary rather than as a star and attending a dozen different twelve-step programs, including Alcoholics Anonymous, Over-eaters Anonymous, Sexaholics Anonymous, Over Spenders Anonymous, and Alien Abductees Anonymous. Bart wished there were a program called Oversleepers Anonymous, because Cheets couldn't be on time if a curtain call depended on it.

Simply overhearing a Monday-morning chat between her boss and Mitch, standing at the coffeemaker, talking about how great Bette Midler's concert was at the Universal Amphitheater on Saturday night, could ignite a tirade from Cheets about how much better she could have been than Bette. Bette just got all the breaks. "Honey," said Mitch Wood, "to paraphrase Mama Rose, 'If you coulda been . . . you woulda been.' I'll take 'Get Off the Cross for two hundred dollars, Alex,'" he said, pouring a mug of coffee and leaving Cheets in tears.

To Bart, Cheets's most annoying habit involved her personal telephone calls. Trained to enunciate and project, she unwittingly subjected him to every syllable uttered into her phone in her cubicle outside his office. All the whining and crying and personal conversations with her ex-lover, the artistic director of the Los Angeles Rainbow Theatre Experience, grated on Bart.

Her saving grace was that she was good at her job, and she saved Bart much time by fielding unsolicited telephone calls. Bart couldn't risk losing her. Moreover, any other assistant may have ratted to accounting that Bart's expense reports didn't always truthfully reflect whom he dined with at expensive restaurants. Cheets was loyal. Plus, she knew more about Bart's intimate life and the personal writing projects he worked on during company time. As much as Bart tried to keep his private affairs private, she always knew which of his "business" callers were actually dates.

Now, with his office door closed, Bart sat down at his desk and stared at the screen of his computer monitor. Tears of frustration began to blur his vision. The first draft of the press release was as good as any he'd ever written. The second draft was merely a variation on the same theme. The third draft was yet another variation. Bart realized he was simply retyping the same material, barely using different words.

He decided that Shari was toying with him, testing how far she could push before he said or did something that would give her a reason to fire him. To challenge this theory, he went back to the first draft and retitled it "Fourth Draft." He would print it out, waiting until it was nearly past deadline at *Daily Variety* before taking it back to his boss. With the trade publication about to go to bed, Shari would have to approve the release as it was or rewrite it herself.

In the interim, Bart decided to waste time and access America Online and find a chat room to take his mind off his problems. He guided his mouse to the AOL icon.

"You've got mail!" chirped a happy, mechanical voice.

Bart always found the voice rather sexy. It told him something potentially exciting was just a click away.

But this time when he logged on, Bart ignored the mail. Instead, he went to LAM4MNOW. Over the past months he'd discovered this chat room was the best place to troll for cybersex—or at least a lewd interactive interlude. He'd punch in a few member profiles and see what each had to reveal, and he rarely had to wait long before he received an Instant Message from someone who had viewed *his* profile.

This time was no different. Bart had just finished reading the profile of POWERman2 when he heard a trill. In the upper-left-hand corner of his computer screen a box appeared with "Rotoroot4U" in bold letters. The message was simple: "Liked your profile. How's it hanging?"

Bart's fingers dashed across the keyboard to access Rotoroot4U's profile. Within seconds it appeared:

Member name:	Don't ask. Won't tell.
Location:	Send pic, then ask . . .
Birthdate:	All candles still fit on one cake.
Marital status:	No ring.
Hobbies:	Men. Men. Men. Did I mention Men?
Computer:	Yes, I have a BIG one.
Occupation:	It pays my AOL access fee.
Personal quote:	My brain is in my pants . . . Blow my mind. It's a terrible thing to waste.

Bart responded with: "Heavy and horny. U?"
Again the trill. "Where are U?"
"The office. Burbank. U?"
"West Hollywood. When do you get off?"
"Depends."
"Send a pic."

Bart wasn't wild about attaching a photo of himself and sending it to an anonymous E-mailer. Not that he had anything to be ashamed of. In fact, Bart was attractive, intelligent, and talented, had a good-paying job, and never had a complaint about his *accoutrement.* He knew that he was, in the vernacular, a catch.

He responded to Rotoroot4U, saying, "Let's 'trade' pics." No way would he make a date with a guy who could be a pasty-faced geezer with old-age freezer burn on his face or a gut out to there.

Rotoroot4U agreed to send his picture simultaneously.

The downloading time seemed interminable, and Bart was anxious because at any moment Shari could be knocking on his office door, demanding the revised press release. Two minutes was an eternity, but at last the download was completed.

Bart emitted an involuntary gasp at the image on his computer screen. If he were a cartoon, his eyes would have popped out of their sockets on springs. Rotoroot4U was physically unlike the usual guys Bart dated; the accountants and doctors whom Bart imagined he'd eventually marry. No, this was definitely a sex-toy fantasy: a swarthy young Latino.

Rotoroot4U's photo image was cropped just above his pubic hairline. His body was lean and dark and hard-muscled—a combination of Brendan Fraser and Jason Lee's. His stomach was rippled. His shoulders were strong and wide. His chest and pecs glistened either from oil or perspiration. His dark eyes were piercing. His face wore a scowl, almost menacing. He had long sideburns, a goatee, and a tattoo that looked like gang insignia on his left bicep. He was the sexiest man Bart had ever seen—and the most dangerous looking. The combination was exhilarating.

Bart dashed off a quick message. "You're a stud! I don't ever do this, but . . . let's meet. I'll bring the wine."

When there was no immediate response to his message, Bart panicked. Didn't his own picture measure up? It was the one of him in the woods in a hiking outfit: boots, short shorts, a white tank top slung over his shoulder, revealing his own lean, well-defined, hairless torso.

Bart waited anxiously, his eyes glued to the Instant Message box and at the same time to the clock on his screen. At this very moment Elvira Gultch was likely bicycling down the hall to his office. But Bart was frozen in his chair. He couldn't move from his desk for fear he'd miss the hoped-for response from Rotoroot4U.

Bart waited. Nothing.

Anxiously, he typed: "Still there?"

Nothing.

Finally, the announcement trill came. "Forget the wine. Get your faggot ass over here. NOW!"

Just then, Bart's door burst open. Shari, hands on hips, stood in the portal. She was barefoot, with red toenails. "Bart, I've had it with you! I swear I've never had more problems with a fucking writer! Where's that fucking release?"

"Hot out of the printer, Shari," Bart managed. He was red-faced and fearful that she would catch him playing around on the Internet and see the beautiful naked man on his computer screen. He diverted her attention from the monitor by getting up from his desk and handing three pages of text to his boss. She grabbed the press release, turned around, and stormed out without closing the door. "I hate my quote!" she bellowed over her shoulder as she padded back toward her office. "I don't talk like that!"

Desperately hoping Rotoroot4U was still on-line, Bart returned to his desk and quickly typed: "Sorry. Office emergency. Still there? Address?"

The reply came quickly: "427 Heather View Drive. Go around to the back of the house to the sliding-glass doors. My room. By the way, I charge."

"$$$???"

"Fifty dollars. And don't waste my time if you're not legit."

"ASAP. Wait for me."

Logging off, Bart shouted to Cheets, "It's six o'clock. I'm outta here!" He smiled to himself and said under his breath, "And I'm going to get laid."

Chapter Four

Rodrigo Dominguez, a.k.a. Rotoroot4U, wasn't what he appeared to be. If you happened to look over your shoulder and register this buzz-cut, goateed guy in a dingy tank top that revealed tattoos and muscles as he was walking down the street behind you—day or night—you'd quickly look for sanctuary. Rod (as his friends called him) appeared as though he should be mugging old ladies for their Social Security checks or Jehovah's Witnesses—just because. Jessica Rabbit said it best, "I'm not bad . . . I'm just drawn that way," and Rod had sketched his barrio-clone persona to attract a certain kind of guy and to repel every other type of human being.

In the privacy of his own space, however, he was a quiet twenty-one-year-old who worked his ass off, eighteen hours a day, doing whatever was required to support his three passions: the gym, sex, and writing screenplays—not necessarily in that order. At his tender age, he already had six feature-film scripts completed on spec—romantic comedies in the tradition of Ernst Lubitsch—stacked on the desk beside his computer in the small room he rented in a house owned by a former bit player who needed a boarder like Rod to make ends meet.

But hustling was in his genes. Before he was kicked out of his house at age sixteen, he'd learned all he needed to know about self-awareness and street smarts from the people who raised him. He learned that he had to seize opportunities and rely on his instincts, as well as his sex, to get what he wanted from life—and from the people who wanted him. Rod felt it was a fair exchange: money for sex-starved males or females; dancing at wet-underpants parties at the secluded mansions of wealthy old movie stars; modeling naked for horny photographers. His repertoire was vast.

At the moment, Rod was steadily employed three nights a week as a bartender at the Trap, a popular S/M bar on Santa Monica Boulevard in West Hollywood, where he worked shirtless, in jeans that were a size too large at the waist, which guaranteed they'd ease down his hips enough for drooling customers to see where his pubic hair began (and prove he wasn't wearing underwear). He served beers and shots of tequila, handpicking the covetous assholes who packed the place on Friday and Saturday nights looking to blow him, in the stockroom, leaning up against cases of Budweiser. For twenty dollars. "One does what one has to do to survive in this world" was Rod's mantra, handed down by his gang-banger dad, who was still a kid himself when Rod was born. Two other nights a week he bused tables at the Cobalt Cantina on Robertson from 4 P.M. until midnight. On his leftover nights, he solicited in chat rooms and fucked strangers for cash.

He may not have always enjoyed the circumstances in which he found himself, but Rod considered it honest, if not altogether legal, work. More important, it kept his days free to work out at the gym and write. To Rod the gym=sex, and the sex=cash. But his primary focus was on his writing.

Every morning, he woke up believing success was just around the corner. He knew that in Hollywood lives changed with the blink of an eye. He remained confident that he would eventually meet an industry-connected guy who could get one of his scripts made into a film or offer him a job as a staff writer in episodic television. True, it wasn't likely that he'd run into David E. Kelley or Steven Bochco at the Trap, but perhaps the keys to the door of success would appear in the guise of an equally successful but less well known player who would come for a fuck and leave eager to agree to read his work, recognize his talent, and offer to mentor him.

The house in which Rod rented a room by the week was a one-story shingle-and-stucco job, circa World War II, dirty white in color. It had a peculiar, if valuable, feature: The sliding glass door in the back that led to his room was laminated with a reflective Mylar tinting. It enabled Rod to see outside, but nobody could see inside. This gave Rod an opportunity to size up any trick he'd trolled for in a chat room and decide if he was worth the time and fifty bucks or whether he should jack it up to two hundred dollars just to get rid of the creep.

He also liked to watch guys preening at their own mirror images in preparation for meeting him. Most of the guys were too stupid to know it was a two-way mirror. They would check out their hair, their teeth, look up their nostrils, stick out their tongues, and adjust their clothes.

They'd tuft the chest hair out of the top of their shirts or flip open the top button of their 501s, reach inside, and give themselves a quick pump in order to show off how much they were packing. This amused Rod, who was completely confident about what he himself had to sell. Anyone who had experienced his sexual apparatus would agree that the service was cheap at twice the price.

Since it was Monday night, one of the two nights a week Rod had off, he was free to fuck. Although he'd rather spend the time writing, it was the sex work that allowed him to keep his days free—and also provided unlimited character studies. Old Mrs. Carter, who owned the house and was once married to a movie star who, after fifteen years of marriage, traded her in for a human Barbie doll, seldom came all the way to the back of her home, where Rod's room was located. She usually stopped midway down the hall at their shared bathroom.

But although she was generally unobtrusive in Rod's life, Mrs. Carter wasn't an idiot, so she probably knew what was going on under her roof. Especially since her tenant's tricks usually had to use the one bathroom, which was directly in view from where she sat in the living room, reclining in her Lazyboy with her cat, Marcel. It was a blessing to Rod that Mrs. Carter was practically deaf. She kept to herself, watching television day and night, with the volume cranked up so loud it could be heard clear down to Rod's room. Thankfully, the sound of the TV also covered the often-animalistic noises emanating from his bedroom.

For Bart, this night's drive from Burbank to West Hollywood took an inordinately longer time than usual. He began to be afraid that Rotoroot4U might not wait. An accident had taken out the traffic lights at the intersection of Barham and Cahuenga, so the usual ten-minute ride from Sterling to the Cahuenga Pass took a grueling forty minutes.

Once he finally passed over the 101 Freeway, Bart turned left and drove down past the Hollywood Bowl and the American Legion Post, which looked like an Egyptian temple, to Franklin Avenue. There he turned right, passing the big Methodist Church, with its huge red AIDS ribbon illuminated by a bright spotlight, the way the gargoyles on Notre Dame de Paris were blasted by halogens at night.

Bart passed the Magic Castle and then the Highland Gardens motel, where Janis Joplin overdosed on drugs and died thirty years ago. When he hit La Brea Avenue, he turned left. Just a few blocks farther down was the former Charlie Chaplin Film Studios, which were now the former A&M Records Studios, which was where the now-dead Karen

Carpenter recorded her biggest hits. Once when he passed this way Bart found himself listening to a cassette tape by the seventies pop duo the Carpenters and feeling almost overwhelmed by sadness because the velvet-voiced Karen had "bought the farm and moved to Paris," like Janis Joplin just a few blocks back—both of them obviously self-destructive in their own ways.

At Hollywood Boulevard, Bart turned right. The other direction would have taken him to all the famous landmarks: the Chinese Theatre, the renovated and restored El Capitan and Egyptian Theatres, and of course, the Walk of Fame, where hundreds of household names and has-beens were embedded in the sidewalks. Nearly every star from the Golden Era of Hollywood was represented, unconsciously spat upon by inconsiderate tourists or urinated on by shopping-cart transients. Neil Armstrong and his Apollo XI crew, Aldrin and Collins, had their star right at the corner of Hollywood and Vine, and they weren't spared fewer indignities than Lassie. The newer celebrities who received recognition on the Walk of Fame were now mostly inaugurated for publicity purposes—the pomp and circumstance paid for by studios to promote a new film. Therefore, a few mistakes were made in the hallowed pavement, such as adding Charlie Sheen to the mix. Cough up enough money and the Hollywood Chamber of Commerce could vote you a spot in front of the Hollywood Palace Theatre, Amir's Discount Souvenirs and T-shirts shop, or the Allied Parking lot. So far the chamber had managed to evade Courteney Cox-Arquette, probably because the Arquette part would eventually have to be replaced. Whenever an actress hyphenated her name with her new husband's, it was a bad omen. Check out Farrah Fawcett-Majors, Meredith Baxter-Birney, Pamela Anderson-Lee, and so forth.

Cruising down to Fairfax Avenue, Bart pretty much knew where he was going. At least he was familiar with the neighborhood. It was close to the Sports Connection (also known as the Sports Erection), the gym on Santa Monica Boulevard where he lifted weights after work.

Heather View Drive turned out to be a side street just a couple of blocks behind the health club. Finding a parking spot in this part of town was murder. The city of West Hollywood had strict parking policies, and if you were lucky enough to find an empty space, you had to read the confusing and often conflicting street signs two or three times to understand if and how the parking was restricted.

It was after seven when Bart finally found the house where Rotoroot4U said he'd be waiting. Popping a handful of Breath Assure capsules into his mouth and swallowing them without water, he rolled along looking for an open spot into which he could slide his '99 Mustang convertible. But it was impossible. Frustrated and impatient, Bart decided to drive down to Melrose, find a metered space, and jog back.

Twenty minutes later, he was standing, as instructed, outside the back of the house under a bright porch light, opposite the mirrored sliding-glass door: checking his hair, his teeth, his clothes, opening another button on his white dress shirt, perspiring from the jogging and the anticipation of forthcoming sex.

He rapped his knuckles on the glass. No answer. He saw his own look of panic reflected back to him under the bright overhead globe. Tense about what he might be getting himself into with a stranger, Bart found himself looking up at the light fixture. It was grimy from an accumulation of dust. There were shadows from dead and decaying insects inside.

"Dead," Bart said to himself as he flashed on the potential dire consequences of meeting a stranger for sex. "Christ! Am I so desperate that I'm willing to risk God knows what to get off with a guy I just met on-line?"

"Yes!" he said aloud, although he couldn't believe he was actually on the brink of following through with a sex fantasy.

Then, as if there were a devil-angel advocate colliding in his head, Bart thought: *This isn't my MO at all. I play the virginal ingenue. I'm becoming a freaking whore! I'm turning into Mitch!*

Bart winced at that thought. However, his apprehension was quickly overruled by the hard-on he had been sustaining ever since Rotoroot4U's picture flashed on his monitor screen. He decided that for once he wouldn't be a sissy about the propriety of sex. His stupid, puritanical sense of morals was to blame for his being chaste for so long in the first place. Now was the time to take a chance. This could be a once-in-a-lifetime opportunity.

Even if the guy was only half as hot as his cyber image, Bart decided it was worth the remote danger just to feel another man's skin. It had been way too long. He was practically insane with lust. "Gotta be a first time for everything," Bart whispered to himself, now ready for the previously unthinkable act of actually paying for whatever was about to take place behind the mirrored glass door.

Returning to his reflection, he knocked on the glass again. The muted sound of a television came from the front of the house, and he wondered if perhaps Rotoroot4U was up there. However, just as he stepped back and was about to try the front entrance, the outside light went off. A long moment later, like the interminable time between when a theater's house lights are extinguished and a concert diva appears, the glass door slid open.

Backlit by the illumination of a single large candle on the floor, the male figure standing before Bart was practically invisible. The man didn't bother to introduce himself. He simply stepped aside, indicating for Bart to enter.

Although Bart had never paid for sex before, he had read that such transactions were always made up front, though money was never actually handed to the hustler. Apparently the etiquette was to place the cash on a dresser or table. Bart reached into his pants pocket and pulled out two twenties and a ten. "Is this okay?" he mumbled.

"Whatever, man." The voice held a distinct Latin accent.

"I thought your photo was awesome, man." Bart felt himself self-consciously slipping into an unfamiliar character and began using what was to him a foreign vocabulary. He didn't often speak in sentences that required him to use "man" as a noun of address or say things like "awesome" unless he was describing the Grand Canyon. It was as though his entire personality had shifted to match the environment, the reverse of the way it did when he was at the opposite end of the social spectrum, wearing a tuxedo, holding a flute of effervescing champagne, and being overly courtly toward some of the world's most recognizable bitches and bastards at an awards banquet or charity ball.

His eyesight adjusted to the duskiness of the room. The space appeared to have been an addition to the original house. It was a chilly night, and there was no central heating. A small floor heater, plugged into a wall socket, emitted only a slight amount of warmth. The furnishings were utilitarian. The desk, which was just an old door laid across two sawhorses, supported a computer monitor, hard drive, and keyboard. Papers, pens, yellow Post-its, and unopened mail were scattered everywhere. A television and VCR on one side and a four-drawer filing cabinet on the other flanked the "desk." A queen-size mattress lay on the floor. A fitted sheet covered the mattress, but otherwise it was unmade. Two corners of a top sheet were tucked in between the bottom of the mattress and the hardwood floor.

Obviously, Bart decided, there had not been time to make the place presentable to guests. Or, he thought, perhaps this was all part of the mystique of paying for sex. In any case, the mess actually added to

Bart's excitement. Images of other men's bodies having sex on the very same sheets flashed through his mind.

Then he turned around and suddenly got a full view of the real Rotoroot4U: naked, semihard, and holding a bottle of tequila.

"Want some?" Rotoroot4U said, holding out the half-filled bottle. Bart accepted.

He coughed as the fluid burned the lining of his throat. He handed the bottle back to Rotoroot4U, who poured a good amount of the liquid into his own mouth and swallowed. He took another swig, moved closer, and pushed his lips against Bart's, forcing the tequila to surge from his mouth into his visitor's.

Bart's cock filled his Brooks Brothers slacks like a water balloon.

"I don't waste time," Rotoroot4U said. "Am I going to have to force you to strip, man?"

The mild-mannered Clark Kent that served as Bart's secret identity suddenly fell away. What emerged from deep within his soul was like the creature that inhabited Sigourney Weaver in *Alien 3*. Within moments, Bart and the man were bareassed on the sheets, both aggressively pawing each other. At some point during their bestial passion, Rotoroot4U donned a condom and plunged himself deep into Bart, who cried out in agony and ecstasy, competing against the disembodied voice of Regis Philbin in the living room, demanding, "Is that your final answer?"

Later, after both men climaxed, they lay close together, sweating and breathing heavily. The room was still dark except for the candle and dull lights shining in from outdoors through the two-way mirrored window. By now Bart had noticed the setup of the glass door and its obvious purpose, but he didn't say a word.

Although he had had a few sexual partners in the past, he had never been with a man who was so completely out of a wet-dream fantasy. He knew he could go on being the screwee as well as the screwer with this stud for days—nonstop, which was so totally *not Bart,* who could go a month without jacking off and a year without sex.

Until this night, sex had never been a major motivating force in Bart's life. Although Bart knew he could probably sleep with any of a dozen guys he knew, with his demanding career schedule of fourteen-hour workdays at the studio and the intense stress he was under from the demonic Shari, sex was relegated to the back burner. He seldom even noticed an erection, because he was constantly worried about deadlines and making marketing presentations to senior studio executives, producers, and stars. Sure, he checked out attractive men as he dashed from one screening or interview to another, but he seldom had time to exchange even a flash of eye contact.

"Thumbelina and her four sisters" were useless, too, because he was too exhausted to beat off when he got home. And when he woke up in the morning, he was too filled with trepidation about dozens of potential crises that would inevitably crop up at the office.

On the rare occasions when he actually had a date, unless the other guy initiated sex, Bart was too timid to make the first move. He'd been emotionally incinerated by his first lover, who, one night toward the end of their yearlong affair, called him a "grab-ass" and rejected him.

Now, as he felt the warm flesh of this solid man beside him, Bart had to stop and think when was the last time he had made love. All he could remember was that the guy was a self-absorbed actor whom he had to interview for a feature article. The guy wasn't all that attractive, but he made the first move, and Bart went along for the ride—a tedious and tiring one, as it turned out, because the actor merely lay on his back and expected Bart to do all the work. And it was definitely work, because the guy couldn't climax. Bart finally gave up sucking the guy's dick, put on his clothes, and left the man, who had simply fallen asleep on the bed. That monotonous experience alone was enough to put Bart off sex.

After a few moments of silence except for their controlled breathing, Rotoroot4U finally said, "I'm Rod."

Bart panted, "I'm Bart, and Christ, you're the most amazing . . ."

"'Fuck.' Say it. I'm a pretty amazing fuck. You do know the word, you little Ivy League fuck."

"You're . . . amazing."

Immediately, the two men began caressing each other again, both becoming simultaneously aroused. Soon they were launching into another marathon of unconstrained sex that was every bit as powerful and fulfilling as the first time.

After they had both had their second orgasms in less than an hour, Rod told Bart his time was up.

"I don't have another fifty dollars on me," Bart said.

"One price for the whole ride, man," Rod assured him. "Better get dressed. Bathroom's down the hall, if you need it."

"Thanks."

As Bart opened the bedroom door and stepped barefoot out onto the hardwood floor of the hallway, Mrs. Carter was coming out of the bathroom with her cat. She disinterestedly sized up the naked young man whose tumescent member preceded him by eight inches and walked back toward the living room and the cacophony of *Who Wants to Be a Millionaire* coming from the tube.

Returning to Rod's room, the men made small talk as Bart dressed. He put on his clothes as slowly as possible. For some reason he couldn't fathom, he was stalling to remain in Rod's presence.

"What do you do?" Bart finally asked.

"Bartend. Work out. But mostly I write."

"Work out? That's obvious," Bart said. "By the way, I write, too. What do you write?"

"Screenplays."

"Really? I work at Sterling."

Even if Rod had been strapped to a lie-detector machine, there wouldn't have been the slightest response on the polygraph to indicate his sudden piqued interest in Bart. He had become a master of inscrutability. "What do you write?" Rod asked nonchalantly.

"For Sterling? Publicity stuff, for movies. For myself? I've got a novel—unpublished, of course—making the rounds." Then he asked, "Got an agent? Have you sold anything?"

"Can't seem to get in the door."

Bart intuitively felt there was something unique about Rod. There was something of substance here. He took a big leap. "Maybe I know some people who could at least look at your stuff," he said as he slipped into his Kenneth Cole loafers.

"A lot of guys have said that to me before," Rod said. "Nobody in this town keeps a promise. Half the time the dicks I meet on-line don't even show up."

Bart said, "I can at least get a friend in the story department at the studio to do coverage on one of your scripts. If you want."

"That'd be cool," Rod said, still reserved and distant. "It'd at least give us a chance to see each other again, too. Getting the coverage back, I mean."

"Hey," Bart said, still not having completely decompressed from the sex, "can I take you out for a drink? Like now? To talk about your script and stuff?"

"Nah, man. I got this other dude coming at eleven. But thanks."

Registering Bart's obvious disappointment and afraid the opportunity to get one of his scripts read by a legitimate story analyst at the most prestigious studio in Hollywood could hinge on stringing Bart along, Rod added, "I don't have anyone tomorrow night. Why don't we see each other again? Gratis?"

Gratis, Bart repeated to himself, thinking it was not the kind of word an idiot street hustler would use. "Great, man. I'm off at six. I can be back here by sevenish."

Rod picked up a script from the top pile on his desk and handed it to Bart.

"Blind as a Bat," Bart read aloud.

"Yeah. Gave it to a guy who came here once, some cocksucker from Actors and Others. The guy is a freak-o suit who comes into the Trap every Friday night. You know the place, down the street on Santa Monica? It's where I tend bar. He likes me to pee my beer down his throat. See him every week, right on schedule, but he's never mentioned the script. Probably never read it. Like I said, nobody in this town keeps a promise. But I have a feeling you will. Won't you?"

"Absolutely."

Rod smiled. "Hey, man. By the way, if you thought I was great—you were better. No kidding."

Bart felt himself getting hard again. *Down, boy,* he told himself.

Rod was more than just a hustler for sex and a first-class manipulator, but he was telling Bart the truth. It was surprising he hadn't gotten further by now in his writing career by sheer dint of will and aggressiveness. Even a marginally talented hack can be a success in Hollywood. And Rod was better and brighter than most.

"So. Tomorrow. Seven . . . ish." Rod smiled again. Then he came forward and planted his mouth onto Bart's and slipped his tongue between Bart's lips and teeth.

They inhaled deeply, like two *Baywatch* studs rehearsing mouth-to-mouth resuscitation with each other, without a script. Not only was Bart anxious for another tryst with the sexiest man he'd ever met; Rod was possibly getting the career opportunity for which he had been waiting years.

At last they pulled away from each other. Rod unlocked the door and slid it back for Bart.

"Tomorrow, dude," Rod said.

"Tomorrow, dude," Bart parroted back.

Chapter Five

"Tell me how you feel about that," said Dr. Ecle, responding in his best neurotic Dr. Bob Hartley impersonation to Bart's latest career crisis.

Bart was lying on his therapist's black leather couch, detailing the latest scenario of Shari's publicly castigating him during a staff meeting. Bart's supposed transgression this time was that he had insulted superstar Zarita Wetmore by altering her previously approved bio in the press kit for the homoerotic musical comedy *Nuns Are Sisters Too*. The film costarred Nathan Lane as a monk desperately trying to remain celibate, with Kay Ballard in a cameo as the Mother Abbess.

"How do you think I feel?"

"I won't know until you tell me."

Bart rolled his eyes. This Jungian or Freudian or Gestalt passiveness wasn't why he was paying a hundred fifty bucks an hour. "I was humiliated, of course. The entire New York office was on speakerphone, too. Shari embellished the magnitude of the entire situation. She claimed she received an outraged call from Zarita. It's too bad the world outside of Hollywood doesn't know what a twat Zarita is. She makes Lauren Bacall look like a smudgy orphan in *Annie*. But I'm certain that Shari was lying. Zarita would never have made any such call herself. She'd have her lackey manager, Liz, complain on her behalf. That woman is constantly afraid she'll lose her cash cow. She'd make a stink out of Holy water if it kept Zarita from firing her. Trust me, I know. I've worked with Zarita and her type too many times. The Zaritas and Mary Tyler Moores of the world can't fool all of the people all of the time. Mary Richards, indeed! It's amazing how many people can't see through that phony 'Who can turn the world on with her smile' crap."

"And you feel Shari was out of line and exaggerated the details of the call?" Dr. Ecle asked.

"Big-time!"

"What seemed to be the root of the problem?"

"Root? Shari bellowed at me, claiming Zarita had bellowed at her and threatened to pull out from doing all publicity to support *Nuns*. Specifically because I, Bart Cain, made appropriate changes in her self-aggrandizing bio. The changes made her look less like she has the distorted ego of Rebecca De Mornay . . . or Jerry Bruckheimer."

"Rebecca . . . ?"

"Forget it."

"So you see yourself as a scapegoat?"

"Exactly. Everybody in town knows how Zarita likes to hold studios hostage. Early on in negotiations for her to star in a film, she always agrees to do all the print, radio, and television publicity we flacks drum up. Then, at the eleventh hour, after the press junket has been set and the hotels reserved, the party planned and the media invited, she backs out. She says she's too exhausted or the film sucks. Which in this case it does. But then she comes around saying she could possibly be persuaded to work on behalf of the movie if the studio buys her that multimillion-dollar Monet, Chagal, or Mapplethorpe she's had an eye on. After working with her, we'd all like to give her an Andres Serrano original, all right. Like his *Piss Christ*, I'd like to immerse Miss Dreadlocks herself upside down in a vat of urine!"

"So she blackmails you? Could get you an NEA grant." Dr. Ecle tried to interject a bit of levity based on the Mapplethorpe and Serrano comment—and failed.

Bart whined. "Now I'm supposed to buy a magnum of Cristal champagne, no expensing it, and personally go down to LAX tonight and find Zarita before she takes off for New York on the studio's corporate jet. I have to hand her this token gift and, on bended knee, apologize for editing her bio. Which is my *job*, for Christ sake."

"What was wrong with her bio in the first place that made you change it?" Dr. Ecle asked.

"The hyperbole was excruciating. It gave me bleeding hemorrhoids. Honest to God, this is how she wants it to read. I've memorized it verbatim. '*What a moviegoer gets from their two hours in the dark of a cinema house depends entirely on the dazzling, effulgent star, in this case Academy Award–winning, Tony Award-winning, BAFTA, Emmy, Grammy, People's Choice, and NAACP Image Award–winning Zarita Wetmore, the most successful Haitian-American actress in the history of all time.*'

"'In the history of all time?' What kind of cockamamie redundancy is that! It goes on to say, *'She loves telling you, her loyal, devoted audience, a real story and fully developing her characters.'*

"Well, I would hope she'd fully develop her frigging characters! She is, after all, an actress. Excuse me, star. There's a difference.

"*'So we all leave the movies enriched and overwhelmed by her unforgettable roles and excitedly await the next great story she will share with us on-screen.'*"

"And you feel that's all wrong?" asked Dr. Ecle.

"It might be acceptable in a *Saturday Night Live* parody. One in which Zarita accepts a Golden Loom Award from Star Jones, on behalf of the International Ladies Garment Workers Union, for one of her publicity-perfect humanitarian efforts, such as the Save Our Children from Kathie Lee Foundation. But it's not fine in a press kit. At least not in a press kit that has my name as the writer on it."

Dr. Ecle pressed his hands together. "I sense you're filled with anxiety, Bart. Even with the Klonopin I've prescribed."

"It's that obvious?" Bart said sarcastically. "It's my maniacal boss who got me on this drug in the first place. I have too much pressure at work. And now that I should be getting fucked—excuse me—literally by the only man I've ever met who's off the Richter scale of earthshaking sex, I'm forced to work way overtime on arbitrarily created assignments. It's as though Shari knows all about Rod and she won't let me have so much as nine thick inches of a personal life. Anxiety? It takes on a whole new meaning with me!" Bart paused. "Sorry about the 'F' word. I'm using it a lot lately."

"Follow that thought about Rodrigo," Dr. Ecle suggested, his prurient mind making the segue to a more lascivious issue. It was the first time since Bart's session began that the shrink became seriously attentive. "What's going on there?"

Bart finally smiled. Lying on his back with his eyes closed, he flashed on Rod's dark-skinned body hovering above him in all its naked anatomic beauty. Hard as steel in all the right places. "You'll think I'm nuts."

"That's what I'm here for."

Bart sighed. "Well, for most of my adult life, I've equated sex with love. This is the first time I'm seeing sex as play, as extracurricular activity. I've always had to at least think there was a future with a guy before wrinkling the Laura Ashleys with him. With Rod, it's just so damned much *fun*. He's the perfect stud! It's driving me crazy that I can't be with him all the time. I even want to quit my job just so I can stay in his bed all day, even if he's not there. I just want to wrap myself in his dingy sheets and hibernate."

"Bart," said Dr. Ecle, "you're beginning to display rather overt signs of becoming obsessive. You realize that, don't you?"

"Obsessive? Over Rod? You bet your prescription pad, Doctor. I even stole a pair of his underpants. When I put them on, I get so hard I start to come without touching myself. I can actually get off just wearing his goddamned underpants! It's like they have some magic aphrodisiac property! Next I want one of his perspiration-soaked tank-top gym shirts."

Bart paused, then: "I told you, he's a wanna-be screenwriter? Coverage came back on one of his scripts that I sent to a friend in the story department. The guy gave it an *Excellent*. It means Rod has real talent. I'm obsessed with a guy who's a stud *and* talented at the same time. That's a first for me. A breakthrough, wouldn't you say?"

Dr. Ecle shrugged. "That diagnosis is yet to be determined. But tell me more about the sex."

Bart let out a moan of pleasure. "I've only been with him six times, but he's awesome. When I arrive at his house—or, rather, the room he rents—he merely slides open the door. . . . I walk in, and he immediately pins me against the wall. It's as if I'm the only guy he's fucking—I know I'm not—but he can't seem to wait to send his long, hot tongue snaking down my throat. Picture a special-effects shot on *Ally McBeal*."

"He always has a bottle of tequila on hand. We start by taking a couple of swigs. I've gotten very used to the taste. Then I start by slowly disengaging my lips from his and dragging my tongue from his Adam's apple down his chest, over to an armpit, which I thoroughly clean like I'm a cat licking its coat. I go for his brown nipples and gnaw on them. Then I make my way down his arched chest that has a green-and-blue tattoo on the right side. Gang symbols, I suppose. Then on to his stomach. I usually linger for a picnic in his navel, cleaning it out. He's got an 'inny.' Then it's on to the main course, which is feathered in a bed of black alfalfa sprouts and anchored with the pits from two ripe avocados."

Dr. Ecle's mouth was agape. He looked like an asphyxiated fish.

Bart concluded: "We eventually make our way to his bed and . . . and . . . we do it."

Dr. Ecle swallowed and snapped out of his reverie, disconcerted by the abrupt end to the scenario. "Do it?"

"You know. We have sex. Kinda rough sex, I'll admit. I think he intuitively knows he's brought me out of my shell. I'm not so much the mild-mannered little wuss that I appear to be. Years ago, I had a guy say to me he wanted to 'fuck me until my head caved in.' Nothing out of the ordinary happened with that jerk. We had sex, but my head was still intact—just brain-dead from boredom. Rod actually makes me feel my head—and I do mean the one on my shoulders—will explode. He's perfect. Except . . ."

"Except?"

"Every time after . . . you know . . . after the first climax . . ."

"First?"

"Oh, we always go at least two or three full rounds every time. After the first round, he gives me the third degree about his script. He does it furtively. Like he's merely making after-sex, lovey-dovey small talk. First he laughs and says, 'Man, you're really some wild fuck.' Or 'Did you have as bitchin' a time as I did?' Then he always whispers in my ear as we're holding each other, 'Hey, man, any news about our project?'"

"I confess, I've been sort of evasive."

"Haven't you told him? About the coverage?"

Bart shook his head. "Not yet. I keep telling Rod to be patient, that I'm sure my friend will come through soon."

"So basically you've been stringing him along."

"Not stringing . . . per se."

"Why do you think you're withholding this information?"

"I don't know."

"Yes, you do."

"No, I don't," Bart parried.

"I think you do."

"Then *you* tell *me*."

"I can't give you the answers, Bart," Dr. Ecle said.

"But that's why I'm here, isn't it?"

"Are you afraid of something?"

"Like what? That I'm being used? That when he gets the coverage it'll be *adios amigo?*" Bart paused and thought for a long moment. "Maybe," he admitted for the first time aloud.

"Who's using whom?"

"Hey, he's lucky to have me. I'm his entrée to the biz."

"But isn't he your entrée into the world of sex for play? You've bitched about not finding anyone special ever since we started these consultations."

"There's more to it than that," Bart insisted. "I can't explain it in words." He paused. "Do you think maybe I'm falling in love?"

"You tell me. The answer, Bart, is deep in your subconscious."

"Why must it always be the *subconscious?* It's my *consciousness* I'm aware of."

"We're going to have to do a lot of excavating to find the answers to your questions. Very arduous." Dr. Ecle sounded like a Gestapo agent preparing a prisoner for torture.

"I don't usually do this," Dr. Ecle continued, "but let me tell you about another patient of mine."

"Isn't that a tad unethical?" Bart said, lifting his head off the pillow and turning around to look at Dr. Ecle, who was staring into space.

Bart used to get a woody just thinking of his shrink, even though the guy usually took up half their sessions talking about himself and his lack of lovers. Dr. Ecle had explained that the anecdotes he revealed about his own failures as a love machine would be useful to Bart as he progressed along his own journey of self-discovery. Now Bart was getting a little scared of what Dr. Ecle had up his sleeve for therapy. Bart lay back down.

Dr. Ecle wasn't what most gay men would admit to finding sexy. But until Rod came along, Bart's idea of sex appeal in another man wasn't necessarily linked to physical appearance. Bart gave much more weight to how intellectual, talented, or witty the guy was. Dr. Ecle was not a six-foot-five, broad-shouldered, blue-jeaned Marlboro Man. To Bart, however, he seemed pretty smart. He was more a latter-day Professor from *Gilligan's Island,* including the white dress shirts opened at the collar and down a couple of buttons.

Bart used to get hard just thinking of the strands of chest hair revealed through the nearly diaphanous fibers of his shrink's shirts. Although he wasn't anywhere near runway-model handsome, he was what Bart had considered "marriage material." He seemed stable. Had a thriving Beverly Hills practice. Lived above Sunset. Drove a sleek fern green Jaguar. He looked like a guy with whom Bart could comfortably trade sections of the Sunday edition of the *New York Times* in bed in their jammies (bottoms only) each weekend.

Bart's impression of Dr. Ecle changed when Rod came into the picture. Now Dr. Ecle seemed more like a bifocaled Ernest P. Worrel. He made Bart want to shout, "Hey, Vern! KnowwhatImean?"

"I'm not naming names," Dr. Ecle continued. "I just want to suggest that as part of your therapy, you continue to do what this one patient did as a means of catharsis. It may give you a better perspective on how you respond to the people who *appear* to have authority over you."

"Like Shari? And Rod?"

"Or that last major crush you had. Payne, was it?"

"Thane."

"Oh, right. The one with the wife and three kids."

"*Ex*-wife. And three cats."

"Hmmm. Well, the individual to whom I refer is the son or daughter of a big movie star from the old days. Doesn't matter who the star was, but his or her towels would be monogrammed B.D. or J.C. Confidentiality prevents me from telling you the real name—of the star, I mean."

"M-G-M?" Bart asked, ready to play twenty questions.

"It isn't important."

"Warner Brothers?"

"Anyway, I suggested he or she—the nameless son or daughter— write down every sordid detail about the way he or she was mistreated by one of Hollywood's legends, who happened to be his or her mother or father."

"B.D.? J.C.?" Bart pondered aloud. "Old old? Or Bo Derek and Jane Curtin old."

"Too young. And *star,* not just a *celebrity.* But that's enough hinting. The journal he or she—my patient—wrote turned into a best-selling book. Which became a cult-classic movie. Which made beaucoup bucks of—as you've said in the past—'fuck-you money.'"

Bart immediately bolted upright, as if he'd suddenly had a presentiment about who murdered JonBenet Ramsey. "You treated one of the Hudson sisters' daughters?"

Dr. Ecle's face turned beet red, as though Judge Judy had caught him in a big fat lie. "Jane. John. Son. Daughter. Who knows? Who cares?" Dr. Ecle exclaimed.

"You know I'm a slave to Joan! A guy I knew had her dog's ashes in a Chock Full O' Nuts coffee can!"

"Yes, we've had that discussion. I'm not at liberty to say precisely who the star—"

Bart persisted. "Didn't her daughter end up with a stroke? And being disinherited and losing her husband and all kinds of personal disasters after she destroyed her mother's perfect image? All because of that tell-all book? What was the title, *I've Handwritten a Thank You Note to Mummsie, My Precious?* And you told her to write that? Oh, m'god!"

"Hour's up," Dr. Ecle said defensively. "Anyway, it's not like she—or he—owned the Hope diamond, for Christ sake. She—or he—didn't suffer all those calamities because she or he was cursed, for crying out loud."

"If you have Blanche or Jane Hudson for a mother, you're pretty much doomed."

"I never said it was anybody you've heard of," Dr. Ecle cried nervously. "It could have been Elsa Lanchester, for all you know."

"Wrong initials. Married to Laughton. Gay."

Dr. Ecle looked around his office as if half-expecting a parade of members from the California State Board of Psychiatry to burst through the door and confiscate his perma-plaqued medical degrees, like Rose Hovick pilfering Papa's solid-gold retirement award from the train company.

"I'm diligently keeping the diary you suggested," Bart said in a wary tone.

"I know. Keep doing that. Meanwhile, we'll pick this up next week."

Bart got up off the couch and left. To him, Dr. Ecle looked as frazzled as Dr. Frasier Crane after a mix-up with his tickets for orchestra seats on the aisle at a Seattle Repertory Theatre production of *The Lisbon Traviata*. It was amazing how much life really was like TV.

Chapter Six

The gates to all Hollywood studios officially open at nine every day—except Disney, where former studio head Jeffrey Katzenberg once avowed, "If you don't come to work on Sunday, don't bother coming in on Saturday!" Or was it the other way around? The admonishment was so stupid, no one ever quite figured out what he meant. The saying was as cryptic as the lame "Love means never having to say you're sorry" on the poster copy for *Love Story*.

For Bart, "business as usual" at Sterling meant that he arrived each weekday morning at six. Today was no different—despite the fact that he had been up until 2:00 A.M. with Rod. Over the years that Bart had worked at Sterling, he was always the first one in the office. The studio was notorious within the industry for its understaffing, thereby wringing every drop of blood, and sweat, from its employees and creating nervous breakdowns, and suicides. Still, Bart enjoyed getting out of bed before dawn because it meant quietly jump-starting the day in peace, even though his sadistically overwhelming workload actually required the long hours.

There was an unspoken, companywide assumption that since Sterling was the most prestigious entertainment empire in the world, hundreds, if not thousands, of would-be Eve Harringtons were waiting in the wings to replace any lackey who deigned to show any lack of gratitude for the privilege of his or her employment. In an eye blink, anyone who wasn't a team player could be history. But though unequivocal loyalty was expected from each worker, Sterling had no reciprocal allegiance to the cogs that ran the big wheel. Anybody courteous enough to resign with two weeks notice was swiftly escorted off the lot that same day by studio security.

Bart was good at mimicking what was expected of a team player. "Yes, sir." "No, ma'am." "I'll volunteer for that unpaid assignment, even though it's in opposition to the collective-bargaining agreement between Sterling and IATSE and even though my mother's funeral is at the same time . . ."

But he felt all that was beneath him. As much as possible, he tried to leave the brown-nosing to the overenthusiastic interns who didn't complain about the slavelike treatment and less than minimum wage and the just-out-of-college assistants who mistakenly thought if they proved themselves tireless workers, they'd enjoy a meteoric rise in Hollywood and make the leap from being under a thumb to being *the thumb*. Invariably, they were all in for a surprise—especially at Sterling.

Bart's mornings were ritualistic: coffee in an environmentally responsible cardboard cup from the commissary. Download the E-mails that popped up overnight. Listen to whining voice-mail messages from below-the-main-title-credit actors or their agents complaining because they had not been asked to do publicity for the film in which their single thirty-second scene was their big break. Then there were memos to write. Post-its to plaster on Cheets's computer monitor screen with instructions to call Holly Hunter or John Turturro to get approval of their bios for use at some upcoming film festival.

Lately, however, Bart had a new objective for arriving early: his diary.

With his Gregg ruled steno books in which to capture fleeting thoughts and feelings, Bart unleashed a torrent of frustrations and run-on sentences of never-before-revealed venom and resentment toward so many colleagues, family, and friends. He was stunned at his own vitriol and use of fairly vulgar language.

He devised codes for his various colleagues in case his notes fell into the wrong hands. For instance, "JtH" meant "Jabba the Hut," in reference to behemoth Harry Wolfman, the most frighteningly obese person he'd ever met. Harry was someone who blustered that most men—especially the younger ones—found him inordinately sexy. An ill-tempered, Nazi-like gargoyle who rode a Harley and led the Hogs on Hogs contingent at West Hollywood's annual Gay Pride Festival Parade, he fired assistants left and right, usually as soon as they proved to be smarter than he and quite capable of doing his job. JtH was threatened by demonstrations of intelligence among his support staff, especially since he had the IQ of a flat Diet Pepsi—and he knew it.

Bart also knew that JtH could be squashed with one of two comments: "Get off my back, you fat-assed yeti!" Or, "How do you find your dick under all that lard?"

It was almost like automatic writing—the words not coming *from* Bart but through him. The sometimes-unintelligible sentences reminded him of one-sided conversations with his schizophrenic next-door neighbor, whose words poured forth with no continuity of thought.

Nine o'clock came too quickly, usually when Bart was on a roll. He resented having to put away his scrawled notes and begin his workday, preparing questions for interviews for a new press kit. For example, his list of those from whom he needed quotes right away included Richard Dreyfuss, Bill Murray, and Jenifer Lewis. (The funniest woman alive, she managed to make her truck driver's vocabulary endlessly entertaining. "You're gonna have to clean this shit up for print, honey.")

By 9:05 the trade papers and Bart's mail were delivered. He finished the dregs of his coffee and scanned Army Archerd. *Daily Variety*'s famed columnist may not have had the biting sardonicism of the Hollywood Kids or DishtheDirt.com, but his clear and polished prose was a breath of fresh air to the stodgy old guard of Hollywood has-beens. But the young Turks who now ran the community found more dish in the *Ladies' Home Journal*.

Several interesting stories peppered the paper today. Something about Robert Downey Jr.'s jailhouse uniform of basic orange. Some wunderkind studio head in his early twenties losing it at the shoulders when his latest Chevy Chase comedy and a spate of Catherine Zeta-Jones films flopped at the box office.

Bart shook his head. "Poor son of a bitch. Washed up at twenty-three!" He really wasn't worried about the studio head, whose parachute was more likely the color of platinum—or Downey, either, for that matter, who still had movies coming out despite his incarceration.

As for the twenty-three-year-old executive, he would do just fine. There was an unwritten law in Hollywood: You can only fall upward. If you get fired from one studio, you always go on to a bigger and better job at another one, regardless of what offense caused your termination. Lying. Cheating. Embezzling. Masturbating on the centerfold picture in a porn magazine in front of your secretary, then making her clean up the mess. No sin in Hollywood goes unrewarded.

Take David Begelman, still the poster boy for dirty tricks in a town with more scandal than Washington, D.C. Begelman and his partner bankrupted Judy Garland. Begelman personally halted Cliff Robertson's acting career and God only knew what other atrocities. But like countless executives before and after him, Begelman was commensurately rewarded with a better-paying job—running M-G-M. The Devil finally caught up with him, though, taking his soul in a suite at the Century Plaza Hotel; made it appear to be a suicide. "Ah. Karma," Bart said triumphantly at the time. "Film producer Don Simpson paid the Devil big-time, too. Yes!"

Even though he'd already cashed in, Simpson's name was on the Gregg ruled steno pad under "Bart's Top-Ten List of Disposable Assholes." He just hadn't gotten around to crossing him off. Simpson accompanied John Landis, Oliver Stone, Jerry Lewis, Michael Feinstein, Dr. Laura Schlesinger, Rob Schneider, Zarita Wetmore, and of course, Shari Draper and Mare Dickerson.

Each day, the mail boy brought a stack of newspapers as well as resumés from hungry freelance writers hoping for a chance to do some work for Bart and thus add Sterling to their list of credits. There were also the screenings and premiere invitations from his counterparts at rival studios and announcements about awards banquets. Stacks of crank letters from disgruntled filmgoers completed his daily haul from the U.S. Postal Service.

One of Bart's myriad duties was to personally respond to the morons who had nothing better to do with their lives than complain about the tarnished image of Sterling Studios. Nine out of ten letters quoted the Bible and ended with some unimaginative, clichéd prophecy that the studio's famous grandfather-like founder was "spinning in his grave." "He's frozen, you dunderhead!" Bart often screamed mentally at the semiliterate letters. "Ever hear of cryogenics? He ain't spinning unless he's on a spit roasting in hell!" Which was a definite possibility, considering the several unauthorized biographies that brought up evidence of his Nazi affiliations and homophobia.

Bart's written responses to the sometimes-hostile letters were unfailingly polite. He protected his professional integrity while maintaining the appropriate image and preserving the rich culture and history of the studio, which had been built primarily on the success of the country's biggest hit song ever from the sound track of one of Sterling's short films from World War II. The ballad, "Meet Me at the Zoo (When the War is Through)" from *Over Dover*, was still raking in royalties more than fifty years later.

Bart's letters sometimes sounded as if they were written by an automaton with the same affected congeniality as a recorded voice at Disneyland admonishing parents to keep a tight leash on their dysfunctional brats.

Bart had long ago run out of original ideas for his responses to these letters. Now they were all pretty much uniform:

> *Thank you for taking the time to write. We appreciate your patronage and promise to continue to strive to live up to your highest expectations for the finest in family film entertainment . . . you cocksucking, ass-wiping, dildo-fucking, shithead.*

The tag never made it into any of Bart's correspondence, but he often fantasized about insulting the cretins who took up his time with their lame protests and threats to never again buy Sterling's videos at the local K mart or spend their yearly vacations at any of the company-owned theme resorts. Instead, he strove to sound as sincere and sickly sweet as possible when he imagined the ignoramuses who bitterly complained about profanity in the studio's films or asked why the young hero or heroine in so many stories was always fatherless or motherless or orphaned. Nine out of ten times that loathsome phrase "family values" appeared in their idiotic missives.

It was a testament to Bart's tact that he was able to respond with diplomacy one time when a barrage of letters with nearly identical sentences was delivered by the sackful day after day from the Coalition for Traditional Nuclear Family Unity, a faction of the so-called Religious Right who were having a field day with Hollywood and and with Sterling in particular. Their general content was:

Dear Sirs:

My family and me we always take Christ along when we go to your Theme Place in Texas each and every year for over five years in a row now. But now we hear you got yourselves a Homo Day. Our pastor over at the Weeping Mary Praise the Lord Who Is Nailed to the Cross for Our Everlasting Sins Worship Center here in West Crumbutt says you close the place to Christians, the only true religion, and let queers with AIDS have all the rides to themselves for a spell. My question is, if they stay in your hotels, we want to know what you do with the sheets after them queers use them because we know what they do on those sheets and hope that you do too. Also, do you let them go to the toilets?

*Please contact me for an answer because then we can plan our
vacation this year and maybe you won't see us so much which
would be a real shame for the little ones.*

Yours in Christ,

*Mrs. Mylanta M. Pepsid
(Married to my husband who is a man
for twenty-seven years now. Nine born-again
sons. Soldiers for our Savior.)*

"Let me see if I understand that last part," Bart mocked aloud.
"Mylanta here has been married for twenty-seven years to her husband
who is a man . . . or is it for twenty-seven years her husband has been a
man? And she has nine sons, or sons who were born nine times? That's
really clear, Mylanta. Or Mydol. Or Placenta. Or Gynalotramin." (The
names were interchangeable.)

There was always a postscript:

*P.S. Please repent while you have time. I will pray for you and your
employees. Stop your evil. Only God can save you. We have to go
back to family values.*

"Yea, yea, and you don't hate the sinner, only the sin," Bart jeered,
parroting Pat Buchanan–like rhetoric.

Bart bet that if the writers of these letters knew about the bulletin
board outside his office door, where he posted the week's most asinine
complaints for all to read, there'd be fewer letters for him to answer. He
would have loved nothing more than to take his red pen, write "Suck
my queer cock!" across the letters, and send them back without any further explanation.

But Shari insisted on reading every one of his responses, especially
since her *WACs in the White House* debacle. "Too arch!" she scrawled
with her Sharpie across one of his typical replies. "Your condescension
is too obvious!" she wrote in the margin of another "Don't patronize!"
she declared on still another response to which he attached a patron's
frayed sheet ripped from a spiral notebook.

After flipping through the pathetic, typo-filled crap he'd just read and
adding it to the hundreds of its nearly identical sequels into his "To Do"
file box, Bart picked through the rest of his morning's mail. To his sur-

prise, there was an invitation-size envelope with his name and the studio's address handwritten in elegant calligraphy.

"I hate weddings" was Bart's muttered response as he sliced the top edge of the envelope with a serrated opener. However, when he withdrew the ecru-colored engraved card, he was surprised to discover it was an invitation to a black-tie soiree.

> *Your presence is requested at the home of Jim Fallon,*
> *February 9th*
> *To commemorate and screen his final appearance on*
> *The Grass Is Always Greener.*
> *Regrets Only.*

A handwritten message was scrawled at the bottom of the Benneton Graveur stationery card. It read, "Mitch says you've got the cutest dimples. Please cum." It was signed with the initials J.F.

"Please cum?" Bart groaned. "That's so tasteless and just plain high school juvenile!" However, he looked again at the date on the card and then checked his calendar. As a rule he hated Hollywood parties, but this one was taking place on a night when Rod was scheduled to work at the Trap. Rather than sit at home alone wearing Rod's underpants and fantasizing about his Latin lover, Bart decided he should probably accept the invitation and at least make an appearance. But he really didn't want to show up alone, unwilling to give the obviously lecherous Jim Fallon the impression that he was available. Bart wondered if he should talk to Rod and see if perhaps he could switch shifts that night with another bartender. Bart thought aloud, "It would certainly be a novelty having an actual 'date' with Rod."

Thus far, Bart had been content to keep the relationship on a purely sexual basis. The "old-fashioned boy" shackles that Bart had cast aside since meeting Rod made the idea of dinner and a movie not an option if instead they could spend their time on the sheets igniting each other into a sexual conflagration.

Dates are for people who were testing the waters or were tired of making love to each other, Bart thought. This was his time to quench his nearly insatiable thirst and appetite for Rod's naked body, and he didn't want to share Rod with anybody.

Reevaluating the party situation, Bart thought, *In a town that pays absolutely no attention to me, if I make a grand entrance with Rod on my arm at Jim Fallon's, even Hollywood's most jaded movers and shakers would probably do a double take. We'd be King and King of the Prom.*

Bart confessed to himself that, just once, he'd like to know what Eliza Doolittle really felt when she appeared coiffured and couturied to the nines at the top of the palace staircase as royalty and servants alike whispered to each other, trying to deduce her identity. The same thing might actually happen at Jim's. "Who's the stud—and the lucky stiff he's with?" Bart could practically hear the covetous crowd murmuring.

By 9:30 the office was alive with the sound of the Xerox machine spewing out stapled copies of film reviews, the fax machine pouring out memos from the New York office, phones ringing everywhere. Secretaries usually preceded the arrival of their bosses in order to make coffee and flag meetings and luncheon appointments on daily calendars and clip stories from the major daily newspapers and trades about the studio's films and stars. The exception to this rule was Cheets. She sauntered in when she damn well pleased, and more often than not, it was Bart who got Cheets *her* coffee. If he was going to the commissary, he figured he might as well be gracious enough to bring her back a decaf. She always thought she was getting the real thing, but Cheets was generally so wired, Bart didn't want to contribute to a meltdown.

After returning with Cheets's java, Bart called Mitch to acknowledge he'd been invited to Jim Fallon's party.

"That's my handwriting on the envelope, silly," Mitch said, pleased with his penmanship and clout.

"You also told Jim I have dimples? There's just the one."

"How do I know you don't have one on a cheek I've never had the pleasure of kissing?"

"Save your lines for the Arrowhead delivery guy." Bart laughed. "You'd better be there to protect me."

"Trust me, you won't have to wear a snackproof codpiece. Jim'll be too drunk on martinis and completely impotent. He'll just embarrass himself, as usual." Mitch sighed. "But you'll meet some stars. Totally A and B list. It's a who's who of Hollywood leeches. They'll be bloodsucking Jim for the last time. Fortunately, I've spiced the list with an assortment of the cutest bag boys from Gelson's."

Bart couldn't care less about the stars or the bag boys, although on second thought Gelson's human resources director was known for having a sweet tooth when it came to hiring soap opera–beautiful young men. The store was a good place for frustrated housewives to get *themselves* bagged. But Bart loathed Hollywood and its pretentious parties. He often vowed that once he found a way out of Sterling, and Hollywood in general, he'd never accept an invitation for anything but intimate dinners of eight or twelve. And he'd never read another *Daily Variety* or the *Hollywood Reporter* or *Premiere* magazine or *TV Guide*, for that matter.

When did my attitude change? Bart occasionally wondered about his intense dislike of Hollywood. *When did my wondering childlike enthusiasm disappear?*

From his earliest memory, Bart had wanted to work in show business. He didn't want to be a star, but he relished the thought of being surrounded by them and other creative people. The stifling mediocrity of living in a small town and growing up with family and friends who were so dull and passionless gave him no other choice than to pursue an alternative life. He identified more with the kids on the television show *Fame* than with anyone in his school. And there was never a question in his mind that he'd make it.

Bart had left home and gone off to UCLA to study English lit. In his sophomore year, when a chance came up to do temp secretarial work at Paramount Pictures, he left college and accepted the assignment. He thought he'd never look back, and for a few years he felt right on track with his life. He even burst out of the sexual closet and fell in love with a man whom he thought walked on water.

Then he was hired full-time at Sterling Studios, and the intense daily pressure blew the fairy dust right out of his eyes.

It was still fun to have Marlo Thomas or Glenn Close call him personally to discuss their publicity bios. And to be urinating in the marketing department's restroom and find that Richard Dreyfuss had sidled up to the urinal beside him gave Bart a small reminder of the gaiety he once felt about making his dreams come true in Hollywood. Bart's real issue with the biz was the gargantuan egos of talentless senior executives and the flash-in-the-pan actors and their maniacal representatives—as well as having to write bullshit about them day in and day out.

"Maybe it isn't so much Hollywood I hate," Bart mused aloud. "Maybe I'm simply burned out."

His reason for attending Jim Fallon's party was almost like peeing next to Dreyfuss, only it had a more historic significance. Jim had been America's number-one comedy star and was still the country's most talked about celebrity in a week that also boasted such headlines as the

Globe's: "Liz and Queen in Palace Cat Fight"; and the *Star*'s: "Child-Abuse Experts Rage as Kathie Lee Turns Daughter into New JonBenet; and Gwyneth's Dating Muddle: Is It Ben or Brad She Wants?"

"If nothing more, we'll have fun dishing the crowd," Mitch assured Bart. "I'm planning to get Jonathan Taylor Thomas and Brendan Fraser together, then separate them from the crowd to see what happens, as an experiment. Sociology 101."

"I think Jonathan's clarified for the umpteenth time that he's straight," Bart said. "And Brendan's married."

"Next you'll be reminding me that Jason Priestley got married, too—for a minute! Don't you trust my infallible gaydar, sweetie? I'm legendary."

"And what becomes a legend most, darling?" Bart sniggered. "A dead Blackglama mink hanging on your shoulders."

Bart knew that in Mitch's mind every man was considered gay until proven otherwise. He lived by the motto "I never met a man who didn't like to get his dick sucked, sweetums."

The rest of the week seemed endless. Between meetings and writing press releases and press kits and cast and filmmaker bios and photo captions and film synopses and answering complaint letters and talking to agents and personal publicists, Bart had little time to think about Rod or Jim Fallon's party. Besides, the only time he could telephone and leave a message on Rod's machine was when Cheets was away from her desk. Her ears were as acutely tuned as a Doberman's. Bart couldn't risk her overhearing any plans he made with Rod.

It hardly mattered. Rod never answered the phone before three in the afternoon. That was when his writing time ended. When he knocked off, he played back his messages. If Bart had called, Rod would return the call right away. Cheets had begun to suspect something was going on, because whenever Rod phoned and she asked in her rapid-fire cross-examination, "Who's calling?" Rod would say, "It's personal."

She now recognized his voice. "Personal's on line two," she announced with a deadpan smugness. Bart picked up the line and whispered his conversations.

Every time Personal phoned, it was obvious that Cheets was eavesdropping, because things became utterly quiet outside Bart's office. Her telephone, which rang incessantly, went unanswered. Bart could make out the silhouette of her shadow as she leaned closer to his door and took mental notes of the one-sided conversation she was hearing. He had to keep everything he said to Rod enigmatic and ambiguous. A cryptic code evolved. Bart spoke in brief, monosyllabic sentences. Rod understood. Cheets thought she did, too. She was always projecting what she "thought" people were thinking, especially about her. Unfortunately for Cheets, she was usually right.

"Same time?" Bart would inquire.

"Later, dude."

That night, another traffic snarl turned into a harried drive to Rod's room. The moment Bart arrived, he could tell his lover was not in the best of moods. The sex was perfunctory, as if *the* stud of West Hollywood were physically present but his sexy goateed and buzz-cut head was off spinning somewhere in cyberspace. Still, it was mind-blowing sex for Bart, who, after only twenty minutes of his prostate being massaged by Rod's jackhammering, could no longer control his climax.

Rod, however, got himself off soon after, simply to get it over with. He lay on his back, his smooth, dark-skinned body barely touching Bart.

Bart took a handful of Rod's load and mixed it in with his own as it began to drip down his stomach, then cool and congeal. For Bart, this was bliss. But he could feel tension in the air.

Finally, Rod gave out a heavy sigh of dissatisfaction.

"What?" Bart asked.

Another sigh. "How long before your friend reads my script?" Rod whined.

Oh, shit, Bart thought, *no more fooling around.* "As a matter of fact, you sexy, talented stud, I wanted to surprise you."

Rod rolled onto his side and propped his head up into the palm of his right hand. "Yeah?"

"Good news. I talked to him today." Bart smiled, drawing on his best PR bullshitting skills. "He apologized for taking so long. Lots of other scripts to read. But he loved *Blind as a Bat.* In fact, he said in his report he gave it an *Excellent.*"

"Cool, man." Rod was obviously thrilled but didn't want to sound overly enthusiastic. "So what's next? Do you think the studio will buy it?"

"You can't even submit it without an agent," Bart said, quickly bringing down Rod's euphoria.

"But if the guy likes it, can't he recommend it to one of the studio's creative execs?"

"He could get in deep trouble for accepting unsolicited material."

"Then what's the use?"

Bart made a snap decision. "I've got a plan. There's a party on Saturday . . . at Jim Fallon's house."

Rod whistled. "Jim Fallon. Wow. That's one sick motherfucking dumbass."

"So he has a penchant for rough trade, so what? You're not exactly Roma Downey, all lit up with a star-filter aura, saying, 'Gawd looves yeh,' twelve minutes on the dot before that computer-generated white dove freeze-frames. Anyway, there'll be plenty of stars and agents and managers there. If you switch your night at the Trap, maybe you can join me and we can network. Parties are where it all happens."

Rod quickly agreed. "I'll definitely get the night off. So what exactly did he say about the script?"

"He's going to send me his written report tomorrow," Bart lied, having received the coverage over a week ago. "But he said it was one of the best scripts he'd read in a long time."

"I'm totally jazzed, man. And this guy's legit? He's good at his job?"

"He's been at it for a long time. The studio takes his coverage seriously. As soon as I get the written report and your script back, I'll bring it over. We'll celebrate. That okay?"

"More than okay, you little shit. I'm celebrating now."

With those words, Rod rolled over onto Bart's sticky body and the two men began to deep-kiss each other, sucking one another's tongues. The mutual feeling of their hard muscles and velvet flesh made any further thoughts about anything other than physical pleasure disappear. Rod was back to his old self again, giving his undivided attention to sex. This time, their play lasted an hour before either man climaxed. Rod then swallowed a pull of tequila, took another swig, and drooled it into Bart's open, waiting mouth like the Actors and Others suit in the stockroom at the Trap.

Before dressing to leave, Bart met Mrs. Carter and her cat in the hallway. Apparently she was getting used to seeing him—or else she was just horny, because for the first time, she stopped and smiled. Her eyes scanned him from top to bottom. When he returned to Rod's room after sponging himself off, Bart dressed and said, "By the way, you need a tuxedo for this party. I'll pay for it, if you like."

Rod took the offer in stride, as if he expected the invitation would come with all additional expenses paid for. Bart added, "Just go down to Larry's Tux Rental tomorrow. Don't forget the shirt and shoes, too."

"We'll be Prince Charmings at the Fire and Ice Ball," said Rod.

"Ever been to a glittery Hollywood party?" Bart asked, knowing the truth.

"The only glitter at parties I've been to are what you see after a tab of LSD."

"You're in for a shock . . . or treat . . . depending on how you look at it."

"What's the big deal? A lot of phony baloneys all dressed to the hilt. But Jim's place is spectacular."

Bart thought that was an odd statement, but he brushed it off, thinking Rod had probably seen the Barbara Walters Oscar-night special that featured Jim and his "girlfriend" lovingly ensconced in the star's multi-million-dollar estate.

"Do you have business cards?" Bart asked.

"Should I?"

"You need to hand 'em out to everybody you meet. I'll have our graphics department make up a box for you."

"De rigueur?"

Rod surprised Bart with his choice of words. What one minute seemed like a limited monosyllabic vocabulary with a heavy Latin accent, the next minute became a mouthful enunciated with a genuine French inflection. That's the writer in him, Bart surmised. Or the actor.

"If I could just meet an agent and get him to represent the project, I'd be set," Rod said.

Bart cautioned, "These things take time in this town, so don't be too disappointed if, after all the alcohol and drug-induced bonhomie, you don't hear from anyone. We may have to go to a lot of these things before people start remembering you. Just stick with me, Rod."

Although Bart was once again horny for another round of sex, it was time to call it quits. Plus Rod said that another on-line trick was due to arrive soon, which made Bart furious, although he tried not to show it. Bart was, if not *in love* with Rod, at least *conquered* by him. He was envious of the other men Rod was screwing—for fun or profit, it didn't matter. He wanted to be the only man in Rod's life, just as Rod was the only man in his.

"Can I ever expect to be the only hole you're interested in?" Bart asked, surprising himself with his blunt question.

"Hey, man," Rod said, enfolding Bart in his arms, "I'm really keen about you. Grateful, too."

"Because I came through with my friend at the studio?"

"Yeah," Rod said. "But also because you're still a good fuck after a whole two weeks. You definitely came along at the right time in my life."

"All I can do is open the door. It's up to you to walk through it." Bart tried to sound like a benevolent mentor. "You came along at the right time for me, too," he added before a long, passionate kiss good-bye.

Chapter Seven

The next morning arrived too quickly. Before Bart even had his coffee, Shari was on the warpath. She'd left a voice-mail message at his apartment the night before, insisting he call the moment he got in. He didn't respond. By the time he'd gotten home from seeing Rod, however, it was way too late, although calling her at 2:00 A.M. and waking her up would have been a fun prank.

An identical message was on his office machine: "Rumor has it that you're not finished with the press kit for *Gratuitous Explosion*," he heard her husky voice shout through his speaker.

"Fuck you, Shari," Bart said aloud. It was still early, and the office was fairly empty, so no one heard him.

"If I come in there tomorrow and find this to be true . . . well, you can only imagine what I'm going to do to you. You little cocksucker. Think about it."

Is this what they call harassment? Bart wondered as he reached for his bottle of Klonopin and dumped twice the prescribed dosage into the palm of his hand. He chased the pills with a swallow of coffee.

He stared at the wall opposite his desk, on which was framed a poster from *The Day the Earth Stood Still*. "*Klaatu barada nikto!*" he said aloud, a mantra, wishing it would rid Shari from his life. The words from the film were an alien pronouncement to summon the robot policemen of the universe to zap Shari with a deadly ray. He'd love to see a giant robot cornering Shari, making her faint from sheer terror, like Patricia Neal in the movie. Or better yet, it could disintegrate her altogether.

The press kits were indeed late, but no later than others had been. As usual, it wasn't due to Bart's lack of diligence. Shari herself had held up production for a full two weeks by failing to read and approve the material. His work, which needed her endorsement, sat in Shari's "In" box day after day. Call after call from Bart, but no amount of appealing for her attention caused action. Shari seemed determined to undermine his reputation and make him look incompetent. But because she had the ear—as well as the cock—of the chairman of the studio, there was no one Bart could go to for help.

He'd discovered over the years that *everybody* knew somebody with authority in the industry. The gopher you confide in turns out to be Michael Eisner's son's college roommate. Your hairstylist also coiffed the secretary to Sharon Stone. The whole town was so incestuous, no one could ever talk to a stranger about anything to do with the business.

With Shari, there was always an excuse. "I left your press-kit notes on the airplane." Or, "It must have dropped out of the cab in New York." Or, "The sentence structure was so poor, I couldn't go on. If they were done properly in the first place, I wouldn't have had to make any comments."

It was a no-win situation for Bart. Nothing he did would ever please Shari. But at least the Klonopin was kicking in, so he decided he might as well just be himself and stop worrying about his personal Cruella De Vil.

In Bart's imagination he envisioned a time when Sterling would be making a film adaptation of one of his novels. As executive vice president of publicity and marketing, Shari would have to be involved with the project. In Bart's fantasy, he walked into the executive conference room with Steven Spielberg, the producers (of which he is one), "Rover," and Shari. She would be all smiles, taking credit for having been a mentor to Bart during his formative years in the industry.

As the meeting began, Bart, with a glass of sparkling Pelegrino in his hand, suddenly stops the proceedings.

"This is the film with the highest budget for any movie you've ever made here," he announces triumphantly. "I'm so delighted that you out-bid Warner Brothers, Fox, Disney, Paramount, and Sony. It's great that we've got Ben Affleck, Angelina Jolie—is she back from rehab?—Meryl Streep, Leonardo DiCaprio, Gary Sinise—sans his hairpiece, for once—and Angela Bassett. I love them all. And Steven's directing. Wow! I smell Oscars for almost everyone in this room. I always thought this would happen. I just never imagined my alma mater, Sterling, would be the studio to make the picture.

"With that said, please indulge my one artistic idiosyncrasy," Bart continues. At this point he stands up. Shari is shocked to see that he's grown from five-seven to a wide-shouldered six-five just since their arrival in the conference room. His piercing blue eyes look first upon Mr. Spielberg, and he smiles. Then to "Rover." On to the duo of inconsequential producers. Finally, his smile fades. His eyes bore into Shari. Pointing a well-manicured index finger, he roars, "If this cunt's on the project—in any capacity—I walk away from final negotiations this very minute. Paramount, Universal, Miramax, and everybody else in town are just as eager to make this film as you are. *No Shari!* Do I make myself perfectly clear?"

By now Shari has withered away in her chair, a child swallowed up in a grown-up's clothes. Security arrives to escort her off the lot and out of Hollywood altogether. *Premiere* magazine runs a cover story about the incident, and the whole town secretly applauds, just the way they did when Dawn Steel—bless her departed soul—got a brain tumor and found herself edited out of this world. There were few people around who would mourn the passing of Shari. No love lost there. No more than for Dawn's early exit.

Bart's reverie was interrupted by the ringing telephone. His heart raced when he saw whose number appeared on the caller ID: Shari. Ext. 666.

Giving it his most effusive, bullshit-publicist greeting, he answered the phone. "Morning, Shari! I was just about to return your call from last night. Got in too late to disturb you at home. What? Who's spreading that naughty rumor? The press kits will definitely ship this week. Right on schedule. Where'd you get that information? Don't pay any attention to that. Cheets is in rehearsals for an all-female version of *Raging Bull.* She's a bit distracted. Yes. Of course they'll be mailed—by Friday. Great. See you at the staff meeting at ten."

Bart replaced the telephone receiver on the cradle. "Fuck you, bitch!" he whispered.

When Cheets finally wandered into her cubicle at 9:45, Bart could hardly control his impatience. "Afternoon, Cheets," he said, his tone dripping with sarcasm.

"I'm sorry. I flushed my miniature electrolysis machine down the toilet. Had to call the plumber." It was one of her more wild excuses for being tardy.

"Last week you locked your dog in your car—with the engine running—all night and asphyxiated the poor thing. Whether fact or fiction, I wouldn't tell those stories about myself if I were you. They really make you sound like you're a few planks short of a full stage. Anyway, I need you to call the printer right away and find out when the press kits for *Gratuitous Explosion* will be ready. You told Shari they weren't available, but I told her they'd be shipping this week. Don't make me out to be more of a liar than I already am, please."

The day was not starting out auspiciously. Not only were the press kits for *Gratuitous Explosion* not ready; other projects, such as the synopses for the studio's entire slate of films for the remainder of the year, weren't ready to be mailed to the press. The other publicists in the department needed the material to pitch stories to the muffin magazines: *McCall's, Ladies' Home Journal, Redbook;* as well as the glossies, such as *Vogue, GQ, Premiere,* and *Maxim.* It was time for Bart to stop thinking about Rod and start concentrating on the fearsome deadlines he was facing.

But as soon as Rod called to confirm he'd been able to switch with another bartender and could go to Jim Fallon's party, after all, Bart fell back into his lackadaisical "God I don't want to be here working today" mode. Hearing Rod's voice just made him crazy with desire. If it weren't for Rod's unbreakable writing schedule, Bart would surely run over for a nooner. But Rod was extremely disciplined. He had his routine. The gym, writing, hustling, and Bart. In that order. Bart felt doomed to be a puppet to Shari—and to Rod. He hoped things would change after the party.

Once he and Rod were seen together in a social environment, people would automatically jump to conclusions and think of them as a couple. Bart hoped that Rod, too, would start to see them as partners and begin to think of their relationship as more than a business arrangement. Bart wasn't ready to rock the boat by making domestic demands of Rod, but the prospect of being Rod's only man was definitely high on his wish list. If they were a success at the party, perhaps Rod would keep him around.

Saturday afternoon finally arrived. Bart—dressed to the nines—drove over to Rod's. Parking was easier now that Rod had arranged a street-parking pass for him, but it was still hard to find a spot.

After the glass door to his room slid open and revealed Rod in all his splendor, Bart uttered, "Oscar De La Hoya has no competition in the sex-appeal ring." Rod looked sensational—wearing anything—or nothing at all. But he was especially attractive in his black tuxedo.

"You like?" Rod asked.

"Ah, ha."

"The guy who altered the pants paid me twenty bucks to let him suck me off after hemming my cuffs." Rod laughed, pleased with himself.

It was typical narcissistic Rod behavior, and Bart was never in the mood to hear about his sexual exploitations with others. It was one thing to hear Rod was totally turned on by Scott Speedman from *Felicity.* ("Great lips, man.") That was just insipid observation. Bart himself admitted to Rod that he was floored by Alec and Billy Baldwin. ("You think *they're* cute?" Rod had said with incredulity.) But whenever Rod flaunted how much sex he had, it cut to the core of Bart's insecurity and fear of rejection. He knew he could never expect Rod to be monogamous. Hell, he made a good part of his living by letting freaks and geeks suck him off. But it was way too late for Bart not to have become possessive of the only man who had ever given him an erection merely by talking on the telephone.

"I was buck-naked," Rod continued. "I looked great. And there was a plate-glass window, so anybody could have looked in, which just made it more exciting. There I was, on a carpeted platform in front of a three-paneled full-length mirror, while this ravenous pig knelt on pins and buttons and a pair of scissors, completely oblivious to the sharp pricks."

"Except yours," Bart said snidely.

"When I shot my load, he gagged so hard I thought I might have to call 911!"

"How amusing," Bart said sarcastically.

"It was. What a kick watching from three different mirrored angles as this punk almost choked to death. He foamed at the mouth like a rabid wolf by the time I finished with him." Rod laughed again. "I told him he had to lick his chops like a 'Got Milk?' commercial and swallow everything or else I'd kick his ass. His tongue was like a squeegee. He got every precious drop of my hot varnish. Sucked me completely empty. Then, after catching his breath, just to prove to himself how much meat he was able to take, the kid used his measuring tape to get my exact dimensions."

"Did he tell you how much?"

"All the guy could do was stammer, 'F-f-fucking A!' Then he wrote my stats on the back of an order blank. When he caught his breath, he said the tux would be ready the next afternoon. No charge."

"I like that part," Bart said. "I didn't really need to hear all the graphic details."

"Sure you did. Isn't it queer, man?"

"Yes, queer, as in 'I suppose I should be grateful that I no longer have to pay you for the pleasure' kind of queer."

"You've paid me enough with all your help getting the script read and taking me to this party," Rod said, his tone registering genuine appreciation.

"Speaking of which," Bart said, reaching into the breast pocket of his tuxedo jacket, "here's the official coverage on *Blind as a Bat.*"

"No way! Excellent! How cool is this, man!"

Rod grabbed the manila envelope, which was folded lengthwise to fit into Bart's breast pocket. Rod looked at the four typewritten, single-spaced pages. The detail into which the script reader had gone was extremely analytic. Under the heading "Synopsis," Rod's entire story and characters were boiled down for quick reading. Rod skipped two pages of synopsis and flipped to the one that was headed "Comments."

It read:

BLIND AS A BAT appears to be a tightly woven screwball comedy from start to finish. It's filled with memorable characters, enhanced by witty dialogue. There is a payoff at the end that heightens the emotional farewell between main characters Jesus Parez and Maria Esplande. The writer brilliantly puts a perfect spin on the contemporary issues of love and romance in the twenty-first century. In terms of overall appeal, there seem to be many fresh and intriguing elements to this project. Again, the writer (and story) offer much in the way of fresh imagination and inventiveness. The principal characters are nicely drawn, and the dialogue throughout has energy and humor. The writer is obviously good at devising poignant "moments" and character reactions.

At the bottom of the page, next to the heading "Script," was the single word *Excellent*. The next line down, beside the word *writer,* was another single word: *Brilliant*. Next to the word *comments,* the reader had typed: "Don't let this one get away."

"'The characters are *nicely* drawn'?" Rod said with incredulous disdain. "How could he say they were *'nicely drawn.'* They're *perfectly* drawn, for Christ sake."

Bart was baffled. "Rod, that's the best coverage I've ever read! 'Nicely drawn' is a good thing. How can you take those two words out of an entire document that practically hails you as the Second Coming?

You sound like an actor who gets rave reviews from all the respected critics; then a little wuss in some freebie throwaway says his performance was rigid or something equally stupid, and the actor's ego is destroyed. What you've got here is as good as gold! You're validated as a screenwriter! You can probably take it to any agent in town and get a deal!"

Rod, suddenly ashamed for overreacting, admitted he had never expected anything so glowing. He knew it was one of his better scripts, even if that cocksucker suit from Actors and Others hadn't recognized its merit. But he truly hadn't expected quite the effusive reaction from a professional reader.

"So now we get in the car, drive to the party, and start making contacts," Bart said. Then he took out a small rectangular white box tied with a red bow. "Open it," he said, handing the box to Rod.

Rod looked quizzically at Bart, then untied the bow and lifted the cover off the box. Inside he found five hundred white cards. Each was engraved:

RODRIGO DOMINGUEZ
(310) 555-2847

Bart said, "After all our fucking, I've never known if I had the correct spelling of your last name. Does it end with a Z or an S?"

"Yeah, man." That was all Rod could say. He was obviously touched by Bart's gesture. "I've never had business cards before!"

"I guarantee they'll go fast," Bart said. "Everybody at this party is going to want to know who you are. Once the right agent gets a copy of the script and the coverage, everybody will know who Rodrigo Dominguez is. Believe me."

Chapter Eight

"... And all the stars, there never were, are parking cars and pumping ga-a-a-ass! I've got lots of friends in San Jose ..."

Rod was singing that old Bacharach/David song—the Carpenters' arrangement—as they pulled up to the valet sign at the bottom of the private road that led to Jim Fallon's mansion. Rod indicated the two young valets. "Think these guys are 'all the stars that never were?' They're parkin' cars. And probably pumpin' ass." He laughed at his own joke. "But who'd be caught dead living in San Jose, for Christ sake."

He was still on an emotional high from reading the coverage and anticipating his first Hollywood party. The two blond hunks in red vests rushed to either side of Bart's Mustang and opened the doors. "Fallon party?" one asked as Bart stepped out of the vehicle and was handed a pink claim ticket. The valet did not expect a reply to the obvious. He nodded toward a waiting Rolls-Royce at the entrance to the driveway. "The car will drive you up the hill."

"How do I look?" Rod nervously asked Bart. "Is my tie straight? Is my hair okay? Should I have worn underpants?"

"You look great. I guarantee all the gay agents and managers and straight women in this crowd will be choking on their crudities the minute you walk in the house. And the underwear—wouldn't want your panty lines to show."

The two of them got into the backseat of the Rolls for the short but elegant ride up the hill to Jim Fallon's estate. At the top, dominating the center of the circular drive, was a three-tiered water fountain bathed in lights of red, green, and amber. As two more red-vested liveries opened their car doors, Bart and Rod stepped out of opposite sides of the vehicle. The sound of water falling and gurgling in the fountain, combined with a miasma of voices and music emanating from within the house, gave the evening a fairy tale aura. On the outside, the mansion was an ultramodern affair. It reminded Bart of a tacky but trendy Thai restaurant. All that was missing was a neon sign: Jim's Pad Thai Palace.

A card table was set up at the bottom of the steps leading to the front door. A burly black man dressed in a dark gray suit, white shirt, and black necktie was seated on a folding chair, checking off names on a guest list. On the table beside the list was his walkie-talkie, which emitted mostly static, but every now and then, incoherent voices.

"They have a list?" Rod said nervously as he and Bart stood in a short line and approached the table.

Bart smiled at Rod's naïveté. "All the news about Jim's sex play probably makes him a sitting duck for religious freaks. Plus, more than half of Hollywood is here tonight. They love to see the mighty tumble. And it's free food and booze. Blow this place up and the whole town goes with it."

"Then my script would *never* get made," Rod said. That was Rod, thinking of himself first.

"What if we're not on the list?"

"We're on. I've got the invitation. Plus one of the guys I work with is Jim's friend. He set the whole thing up."

When the couple ahead of them had been cleared, Bart announced, "Cain and . . . guest."

The guy at the table didn't have to go far down the alphabetical list to find *Cain, Bart*. "Doesn't say you're bringing a guest," he said, speaking with a West Indies accent in an imperious tone.

"You always bring a guest," Bart said testily. Was the guy an idiot? "Nobody expects you to come alone."

"Apparently Mr. Fallon did." The black man's jaundiced, bloodshot-but-knowing eyes looked up at Bart, judging the young white boy: another yuppie poof.

Other guests were waiting behind Bart and Rod. "What's the holdup?" one complained.

"What's going on up there?" He could hear another's impatience, as if a restaurant maître d' had the impudence to make Mr. Big wait for his usual high-profile table. These were industry people unaccustomed to cooling their heels for a fraction of a moment for so much as a blow job, if not a cup of decaf.

"This is absolutely ridiculous," Bart said. "Call Mitch Wood on your walkie-talkie thing," Bart said dictatorially.

The security man sighed insolently and picked up his black walkie-talkie. He spoke to someone inside the house.

Within moments, the front door flew open, and Mitch danced down the steps to the table. He gave Bart a peck on the cheek, hugged Rod, and went behind the table. He grabbed the pen out of the security guy's hand and, next to *Cain, Bart,* wrote: plus one. "There!" he admonished the guard. "Everything copacetic? Come, boys," he said, and led Bart and Rod into the house.

The mansion's entryway was *Architectural Digest* perfection. In the center of the foyer was a nearly priceless, round Lalique table. Its crystal base of Erté-like vestal virgins, standing side by side in a circle, formed the base platform on which the beveled glass top could rest. A vase containing Casablanca lilies the size of the arrangement found in the lobby of the Four Seasons Hotel was perfectly centered.

"Welcome to 'Fallon's Lair'! Not to be confused with Valentino's *'Falcon*'s Lair,' up on the other hill," Mitch explained. "My, you guys are so-o-o-o handsome," their escort gushed. "It's definitely the man who makes the clothes, not the other way around," he said, giving Rod a long, lascivious look.

The house was stunning in every respect. From the Italian-tile entryway floor and the crown moldings where the walls met the ceiling to the lighted artworks on the trompe l'oeil walls. As they followed Mitch, passing the lilies, to the top step of the sunken living room, both Bart and Rod were suddenly taken aback by the most breathtaking view of the city either had ever seen. Los Angeles was revealed through floor-to-ceiling glass windows, a 180-degree expanse like the view one might see from a news traffic helicopter. A Santa Ana wind was blowing, so the lights of the city below were a sequined cape laid out and shimmering as if it were one of Bob Mackie's bugle-beaded costumes for Cher, magnified a zillion times.

Two steps below, the sunken living room was packed with recognizable faces from television, motion pictures, and music. Bart immediately observed Will Smith, Shania Twain, Melissa Etheridge, Jerry Seinfeld, Jodie Foster, Toby McGuire, Tim Allen, Loretta Devine, Rue McClanahan, Hilary Swank, and Ellen DeGeneres, giving Anne Heche a sneer from across the room.

Rod caught sight of Courteney Love, Ashley Judd, Jewel, Marilyn Manson, Jane Krakowsky, Dylan McDermott, Halle Berry, Milla Jovovic, and shit, Ricky Martin!

Most of the women were wearing New York black, but a few sluts—assistants from agents' offices, no doubt—had slipped in wearing red or teal. They were there to be noticed by any straight man attending—of which there was a definite dearth.

Silver trays with flutes of champagne were passed among the wall-to-wall guests by an array of handsome, smiling blond men and women. Mitch signaled for one of the caterers, a young Brad Pitt type, who appeared and offered Bart and Rod their first drinks of the evening.

"*Cristal,* of course," Mitch preened.

"And where's our infamous host?" Bart asked, sotto voce.

Mitch raised an eyebrow. "This way, boys," he said.

He took Bart by the hand, and Bart took Rod by the hand. They wended their way through the crowd in the living room toward the backyard, Mitch acting as cattle catcher. Jennifer Holiday, the first cow, looked startled, then perturbed, as they shimmied past her big butt, which she still carried despite losing enough weight for two extra divas. Kate Jackson splashed her drink when Mitch accidentally stepped on the toe of one of her black velvet high-heel shoes. Helen Hunt was knocked against Kevin Spacey as Hank Azaria glowered from across the room, splashing her drink, too. Sheryl Crow, Sean "Puffy" Combs, and Jennifer Lopez didn't fare any better.

Soon they were poolside. It was a perfect, balmy Southern California night. Adding to the magical atmosphere, a full moon was hanging over the city. Even Bart was impressed. Rod was bowled over and could hardly maintain his well-trained façade of indifference especially when he inadvertently pushed against Julia Roberts as she started to nibble on a stuffed mushroom. She began to complain, but when she looked at Rod, it was as if she'd just been baptized and seen the light. She absorbed the full spectacle of Rod and smiled the way she did when she couldn't believe the size of Richard Gere's dick just before she put her face in his lap and gave him a blow job in *Pretty Woman.*

Opposite them, across the pool, seated on a chaise longue, was the man himself—Jim Fallon. Holding the stem of a martini glass, the base of which was resting on the arm of the chaise, Jim was surrounded by a group of attractive and successful-looking men and women all dressed in formal wear but looking as comfortable as if they were in jogging togs. Bart could tell that Rod envied their composure. For the first time, Rod understood what was meant by "to the manner born."

Mitch led his charges forward, but he stopped the train a few paces before reaching the depot. He paused to point out the particular people who were fawning over Jim. "The tall one is Brent from over at Fox. Who's he kidding with his so-called fiancée in tow, the so-called woman to his right?" Mitch clucked. "I had him years ago. I'll wager she's a transsexual who hasn't had the whole job done. See the bone structure? Am I right, or am I right?

"That one's Pucky," Mitch continued. "Cute, but he knows it—if you get my drift. Untouchable now. He belongs to his boss, or vice versa. I'm surprised he's not wearing his leash; master-slave, that sort of scene. He's with Writers and Actors."

Bart gave Rod the elbow and a nod, indicating he should keep Pucky in mind for a pitch of the screenplay.

"Standing next to Pucky is what's her name, the new bitch in charge of prime-time programming for NBC. I hear she's a cocksucker by day and a commander in the God Squad by night. There's no way she didn't have something to do with dropping Jim's show so quickly."

Then, practically jumping up and down, Mitch said, "Goody! There's Sue Ann Nivens, the man-hungry Happy Homemaker!"

"Isn't that another Golden Girl behind the chaise?" Rod said, astonished to see Betty White in person.

"How old is Miss Thing here?" Mitch quipped to Bart. "Sue Ann can't be before anyone's time! She's smiling as though she doesn't know the bastard in front of her is in fact responsible for her being out of work. She's a doll, really. One of the goodies.

"Oh, and speaking of man hungry, but doesn't want Mommy and Daddy and the industry to know, is that scummy Michael Scott from Actors and Others. Ick." Mitch improvised a shudder.

"Shit," Rod whispered to Bart. "That's the asshole who comes into the Trap each week. The one I told you about—the one who promised to read my script and then never mentioned it again."

"The guy who likes to have you piss in his mouth?" Bart asked.

A woman who looked like Esther Williams—oh, my God, Bart realized, it was Esther Williams—heard the remark and gave Bart a look of haughty disdain.

"Oh-oh. I shouldn't have said that," Bart whispered to Mitch, wincing with embarrassment. "That's *the* Esther Williams."

"Let the bitch drown in her feigned nausea," Mitch declared, undeterred. "She's the last one who should throw stones. Not after what she wrote in her 'as told to' tell-all about her dates with a cross-dressing Jeff Chandler and him having a fetish for slipping into silk panties, for Christ's sake."

Intentionally turning to Esther Williams, as only Mitch could do and get away with it, he said in a confidential tone, "Always figured Michael to be a perv." He gave Esther a nudge with his elbow, then pointed toward the Actors and Others agent. "He's the Devil incarnate," he whispered conspiratorially.

"Unfortunately, he's my bête noire," Esther said as she waddled away from the area.

"She's packed on more than a few sardines since her swimsuit days at M-G-M," Bart observed.

"She's still a million-dollar mermaid as the old stars die off," Mitch declared, returning his attention to Bart and Rod. "Michael thinks he's a hotshot just because his uncle, who's the chief counsel for Actors and Others, got him a job at the agency. The other agents all hate him. Even his clients hate him. You heard Esther. Unfortunately, Jim's too stupid to hate him. Oh, I can't wait to see Michael's reaction when he sees you here, Rod. Let's go make a splash, shall we?"

Rod was up for it. He hated Michael from the first moment they met at Rod's mirrored door. The feeling was mutual. Michael thought he was degrading Rod by paying him to do what they did in the storeroom at the Trap. But it was Rod who held all the cards, and the deck was stacked. Friday evenings, he controlled his bladder as long as possible until Michael showed up. When he shoved Michael into the back room and forced him to his knees and impaled his cock into Michael's mouth, holding his victim's head in the vice of his two strong hands, he made certain Michael swallowed every drop, topping him off like a car's gas tank—using high octane, of course.

Invariably, Michael choked on Rod's mouthful and then vomited his guts out. "Something go down the wrong way?" Rod chided as he kicked Michael with his steel-toed work boots, sending him rolling across the floor to an aluminum bucket, where he retched and called Rod a fucking freak faggot. Same routine. Week in. Week out.

"I'm the fuckin' freak, eh? Who has his head in a bucket of vomit of piss and chunks of his own lunch?"

Finally, Mitch made his way around the pool to where Jim was holding court. Betty White had wandered off with a cute caterer and his tray of miniquiches. "Jimbo," Mitch cried as the trio neared the master of the manse. "Here's the number I wanted you to meet. Bart Cain, meet Jim Fallon."

"Bart?" a female voice cried with indignation as she turned away from her conversation with Jim.

"Shari!" Bart stammered, startled to see his boss out of context from the studio. He turned to Mitch and whispered harshly, "Why didn't you tell me she'd be here!"

"You'd never have come. Oh, Shari, back off!" Mitch rolled his eyes. "It's a party, for Christ's sake."

"What the fuck are you doing here?" Shari demanded of Bart, her nostrils flaring and her eyes moving up and down him as though he were a toxic odor.

For the moment, Bart ignored her as he extended his hand to Jim. "I'm an ardent admirer," he lied. "Do you know Rodrigo Dominguez, the screenwriter?" he said, trying to introduce Rod to the famous Jim Fallon.

Rod burst into a wide smile when he heard Bart's generous introduction.

"Screenwriter?" Jim's watery eyes met Rod's. "Do you have anything I could look at?" His words were a double entendre and not lost on Rod or the small coterie pretending to pay homage to Jim. In fact, even though the infamous video had been reduced so many generations that nothing was clear on the tape, the overwhelming collective thought was that Rod was one of the gang bangers on the tape.

"Thanks for inviting us," Rod said, holding out his hand.

"You're welcome. Anytime. I'm sure." Jim showed a wry smile. He was obviously drunk. He slurred his words and couldn't make an effort to stand and greet his guests. He kept staring at Rod as if not knowing exactly whether they had ever met before. So many gangstas had been at the house.

Mitch piped in. "Jimmy, Bart's the one I mentioned. The publicist at Sterling? Dimples?"

"Right," Jim pretended to recall. "Guess I could use a good publicist right about now, couldn't I, Brad? Heh. Heh. Heh."

"It's Bart. And I think you'll do just fine, Jim."

"Brad . . . Bart, what's the difference," Jim bellowed. "Just so long as you're cute."

Mortified by Jim's inappropriate behavior, he was suddenly on shifting ground. Grasping for something to hold on to, he caught Shari's eye. "And this," Bart said, looking at Jim and presenting Shari, "is 'the boss lady.' The lovely woman personally responsible for all the hits we have at Sterling Studios."

"We know each other, Bart," Shari said. "We go back, don't we, Jim?"

"If she's responsible for the hits, she must also be responsible for the bombs." Mitch laughed.

"Shari, I just *love* your dress," Bart said, trying to deflect her hostility and dissociate himself from Mitch and his bitchiness. There was something about being with his boss outside the studio environment that emboldened him.

"Hmmm," she said coldly. "You still haven't answered my question."

"Oh, I get out from behind my desk now and again. 'On festive occasions,' as Auntie Mame would say."

"But his heart belongs to daddy," Mitch sang. "Meaning his job, of course. Bart gives Sterling his 100 percent undivided attention, don't you, Bart? Just like Auntie Shari asked, or shall I say, threatened, you to do."

Shari groaned. Looking over at Rod, she immediately summed him up and determined he would be a hot fuck, even though if he was with Bart, he was probably gay. Still, she thought she recognized him. Could she have actually fucked him herself, in a galaxy far, far away, she wondered.

Noticing her flute was nearly empty, Bart asked in an overly courtly tone, "May I refill your glass, Shari?"

"I'll get my own, thank you," she said dismissively, and wandered off into the crowd.

Finding an opening in the awkward small talk, Mitch turned to Michael and said, "You big important agent, you. I had no idea that you and Rod here were friends—almost family—from eons back."

Turning to Rod, Mitch said, "Where again did you say you two studs got aquatinted? Oh, yes, that B&D place on S/M. I always used to think that B&D stood for Black and Decker. Ya know, the power tools?" Mitch laughed at his own joke. "I know B&B is bed and breakfast. But what's S/M?" he asked for the crowd's benefit. "Oh, that's right, sado-masochism. I always wondered what went on in those dark holes."

Michael was demonstrably upset. In a sociopathic talent agent, that can be lethal. The few guests who were still standing beside him—all people he knew from the industry—were looking from Rod to him and clearly wondering how well the two knew each other.

Except for the tuxedo, Rod was the antithesis of everybody else at the party. Although he was more polished than anyone in his own family, there was no getting away from the fact that he was a newcomer to this circle of Hollywood players. And it showed. You could pick him out even in this dense crowd. His discomfort among those who had been there, done that—or at least could pretend to have been around—was obvious. Whereas Bart was effortless in his comportment and knew how to plant an air kiss on anyone he hardly knew, Rod stayed behind Bart and tried to remain anonymous. If spoken to, he merely nodded his head to acknowledge the person.

Nobody other than Mitch or Bart made any effort to make Rod feel comfortable or accepted. The emotional high Rod had felt only a short time ago, after reading the coverage on his script and anticipating meeting the rich and famous in Hollywood, had vanished. In its place was the unsettling feeling that he was a party crasher. He wasn't a Hollywood player, and his discomfort and self-consciousness were compounded by the fact that he knew he was a diamond in the rough at best, with the emphasis on "rough." After all, at some level, he would always be the personification of a dangerous Latin homeboy.

Not only had he little in the way of social graces; Rod knew he would never have been admitted into this rarefied circle on his own. He couldn't help feeling as though Bart were displaying him as a trophy. Rod grabbed the next flute of champagne that passed his way.

Somewhere between meeting Jim Fallon and downing his second glass of Cristal, he lost Bart and Mitch in the crowd. Now Rod stood by the edge of the estate and looked out upon the view below. He wanted desperately to get away from this superficial hellhole. He knew he didn't belong with these cultured, successful, talented people. Even if they were as synthetic as Styrofoam.

"The others are starting to go into the screening," a woman's voice behind Rod spoke in a little girl's whispery tone. Rod turned around. The woman was an attractive sixty-something Barbie doll dressed in a gold lamé outfit that stretched over her tight butt and revealed lovely long legs. She made Rod think of Connie Stevens, whom he'd seen on infomercials. She brushed a hand over Rod's round ass. "Or would you rather stay outside in the dark?" she purred, pouring half her glass of champagne into Rod's empty flute.

"Caught the perp, did you?" another female voice coming out of the shadows asked.

"If it's not the police woman herself," the woman beside Rod stated, brushing her glistening lips against Angie Dickinson's cheek. "Sergeant Pepper, wasn't it?"

"Mmmm. Like the Beatles album. I was wondering for the past hour which of the old leather tits at this cheesy affair would bag Antonio first," she said, as if Rod were invisible.

Ordinarily, Rod would have flirted with these aging beauties. He was a master tease, not just of cocks but of pussy, too. However, this was not a good night for taking advantage of old but definitely attractive ladies. He was too upset about the way the evening had disintegrated. All his previous *joie de vivre* had gone the way of an amyl nitrite high. The rush was over in a flash.

At that moment, one of the catering crew interrupted and announced that *The Grass Is Always Greener* was about to begin. The guests should all find a seat in the screening room.

Rod left the two coiffed and well-dressed women without a word, not knowing both were celebrities dating back to prehistoric sixties and seventies television shows. He went in search of Bart.

"Where've you been, man," Bart said when the two finally met up in the living room.

"Get me outta here," Rod demanded.

"What's the matter?"

"Now, man! I wanna go—now!"

"Yeah, sure. I should just say good-bye to a few people."

"Now, goddamn it!" Rod cried defiantly.

Rod was so agitated that Bart had no choice but to lead him to the foyer and out the front door. If anybody noticed them leaving the house, not a word was said. They slipped into the waiting Rolls and road down the hill. They waited in silence for the valet attendant to find Bart's Mustang and drive it around. Bart tipped the guy five dollars and drove down to Mulholland without hearing another word from Rod.

Chapter Nine

"They're just assholes. They don't mean to be. It's their DNA."

Bart finally broke the silence as they reached the intersection of Santa Monica Boulevard and La Cienega, nearing Rod's place in West Hollywood. Rod was still sullen, despondent from what he viewed as a fiasco of an evening.

"We didn't meet any big agents," Rod said. "Like an idiot, I passed out business cards to all the wrong people, including the lady washing dishes in the kitchen. She looked at me, then looked at the card, and looked at me again as if I was a retard. She shrugged her shoulders and put the card into her apron pocket. Then she said something under her breath in what sounded like Chinese and put her hands back in a sink full of soapy water. It was an evening of free champagne and grazing food, and that's it. And I'm still hungry."

"That's not all of 'it,'" Bart retorted. "You should hear yourself. You've just been to a party that the whole town will be talking about for ages. You may even get into *People* magazine because you bumped into so many stars being photographed."

"Crashed into 'em, is more like it."

"It was crowded. You can't be held responsible for colliding with Nell Carter. She takes up more than her share of the planet. There were journalists from *Rolling Stone* and *Premiere* and *Out* and the *Advocate*."

"I felt completely alone and out of place."

"You were far from alone. What makes you think most everybody at that party wasn't as self-conscious as you? Most of the confident-looking ones have just found a way not to show their fear, or their egos are as big as Jeff Stryker's dick."

"He's not as big as me, so what's your point?"

"My point, 'Mr. Big,' is you're unfairly comparing yourself with experts; people who have had more than their share of practice in the limelight and making entrances and idle chatter at parties. The most outgoing personalities are usually the most insecure. Look at that Carol Channing lady. Ya know why she's so noisy?"

"The tabloids said she hadn't been fucked in forty years. I suppose that'd do it."

"That alone would make her desperate to be noticed."

Rod pouted. "I felt like everybody was staring at me. I didn't fit in. I'm nothing but a stud who hasn't got the social graces of a jackass."

"At least you give yourself credit for the stud part. Some pretty famous people were staring at you—in a good way. Even if you didn't notice."

"Those two broads who looked like Barbie dolls?"

"They happen to be *famous* Barbie dolls. And Julia Roberts dropped her stuffed mushroom when she got a load of you, stupid. And don't tell me Bea Arthur holding you around the waist and resting her head on your shoulder wasn't a neat thing."

"She just needed me to hold her up." Rod managed a small smile. "God, her voice is deep. Three out of four Golden Girls at one party was kinda cool. Almost historical, I guess. Like a reunion."

"And what about Charles Nelson Reilly? He paid more than enough attention to you. I was watching from inside the house. You seemed stuck on each other."

"I didn't even know who he was."

"He did some *X-Files,* and he used to be on game shows in the old days."

"Around the time that Lincoln was shot, I'd guess. I'm so stupid, I didn't know how to get him to take his freakin' hand off my ass without making a scene and having him accidentally on purpose fall in the pool. So I just stood there, frozen."

Bart patted Rod's thigh. "What I'm trying to say is, this was just an initiation. I'll bet growing up you never thought you'd find yourself at such a fancy affair."

"Sure I did. I always planned it. It just didn't turn out exactly as I always imagined."

"Things seldom do. 'Be careful what you wish for . . . you'll get it,' I always say."

Bart empathized with Rod's situation. "When I first came to Hollywood and willed myself into the showbiz clique, I was as much of a hayseed as you seem to think yourself to be. Talk about lack of social graces. I once nodded off to sleep in front of Kathryn Grayson while I was sitting in a chair in her living room after a dinner party—as she was singing an aria from a pretend opera from one of her old movies."

Bart continued. "I know you don't know who Kathryn Grayson is. I didn't, either, until this schmuck I was dating brought me to this fat woman's house in Brentwood. But trust me, she was once a *huge* star at M-G-M. Now she's just huge. I was forced to watch one of her old musicals. She was rail thin when she was famous. I heard she found Shirley Temple boning her husband one time and it made her start bingeing on Ding Dongs."

"Tyne Daly must'a used her recipe."

Bart grinned. "Here's how I knew I didn't fit in. During dinner I had to surreptitiously look out of the corner of my eyes to watch the other guests to see which fork to use for each course of the meal. I had no idea how to properly tear a roll and butter one piece at a time. I didn't even know the correct position to place my utensils on my plate to indicate I was finished eating. I also didn't know a wineglass from a water goblet. I was embarrassed as all hell. What you went through tonight was nothing. Think of it as your coming-out party. You got your feet wet. From here on, every time we go someplace ritzy, it'll get easier. Trust me."

"You fell asleep while some famous singer was entertaining in her home?" Rod backtracked.

"Yeah. She walked over and sang full blast into my ear to wake me up. Startled the hell out of me. The other guests laughed. I went home and cried."

"I probably missed a lot of big tips by not working tonight," Rod complained.

"Tips you can get every night for the rest of your life. How many people do you know had Kevin Spacey offering to get them another glass of champagne and asking where you work out and what supplements you'd recommend he take for a better-developed body? That doesn't happen to many people. Unless, I suppose, they look like you. If it'll make you feel any better, when I come in, I'll put two twenties and a ten on the desk, just like the first time we did it."

Rod smiled, finally warming to Bart's attempt to humor him.

With his own seductive suggestion, Bart got an immediate hard-on. He reached over and picked up Rod's hand from the seat beside him and placed it on his own crotch.

Rod smiled. "That's just what that old guy who once played a tough lawyer on that hit show from when I was a kid, did tonight."

"I think you'll like mine a lot more than his old one."

"Yours is much bigger, too. Get around as much as me and you learn to size a guy up *before* he even pulls it out."

Bart made a left turn off Santa Monica Boulevard down to Rugby. Parking was still a bitch in Rod's neighborhood, especially at this time of night on a Saturday. By the time they had found a spot and walked a block to the rear of the house where Rod lived, they were already smothering each other in deep kisses and unbuttoning each other's tuxedo shirts. Studs dropped in the yard. "Never mind. I'll find 'em in the morning," Bart panted, anxious to shed his clothes and feel Rod's hard, naked body against his own.

Bart was vibrating with anticipation. Every nerve ending in his body pulsated. He was desperate to feel Rod's chest, stomach, ass, and cock with his hands and tongue. His own cock and ass were aching. The moment they entered the house, Bart wrestled Rod to the mattress and stripped him of his remaining clothes. The two voracious animals were immediately engaged in heavy, hard-driving, man-to-man sex.

By now Rod intuitively knew when Bart could hardly wait a moment longer or he might climax. Rod pulled out the last condom from a box beside the mattress. He tore it out of its cellophane packaging, added some lube to the inside, and squeezed out a copiousness amount of cold gel into Bart's asshole.

As Rod donned his condom, Bart rubbed the greasy lubricant in, coating the lining of his anus with the slick goo. Lying on his back, breathlessly looking up to the sight of what Michelangelo would have sculpted if he'd seen Rod before David, Bart was literally out of his mind inspecting every inch of Rod's muscular chest, thick arms, tight abs, and his nine-inch steel shaft that was about to become a fixture in his own body. Bart was aching with desire to have Rod enter him. As Rod began to ease into Bart, Bart reached for Rod's butt cheeks and pulled him forward. The pain at first was excruciating.

"Deeper!" Bart sighed, gritting his teeth. Then a flood of rapture washed over him. "Harder! Yes! Oh, *fuck!*"

Sometime during the night Rod got up to pee. In the pitch-black darkness of the room, he noticed the blinking red light on his answering machine, which he'd failed to notice when they returned in the heat of passion. Rod stopped to count. One, two, three, four. One, two, three, four.

As zealous as Rod was about his weight lifting, writing, and sex, he was equally devoted to his answering machine. He couldn't stand not to know who had called. It was like an unopened Christmas present. If he was not allowed to untie the bow and rip apart the paper, it would drive him nuts.

But it was the middle of the night. He didn't want to disturb Bart with the sound of playing back what might be calls from customers begging to drop by for some action.

Returning from the bathroom, he quietly lay down next to Bart. However, falling back to sleep was impossible. He had to know whom the four messages were from.

Cautiously, with as much surreptitious movement as possible, Rod got out of bed and made his way over to the makeshift desk where his machine was blinking. He turned the volume down as low as he could, then pushed PLAY. He increased the volume ever so slightly, just loud enough to hear the voice coming through the speaker.

However, in the utter quiet of the night, no amount of muting was enough to keep the sound low enough. "What'ya doin'?" Bart whispered, still half-asleep.

"Nothing. Go back to sleep."

The machine's first beep was followed by a man's voice. "Rodrigo?" the voice inquired. "This is Jim. Jim Fallon. I'm glad you gave me your card. Very wise. I'd never have known how to reach you. Listen. I'm genuinely sorry. I'm extremely upset about being inebriated when you and your friend arrived. I'm not a drinker, as a rule, but I was so sad about the reason for the party—you know, my last show and all. Things got out of hand very early. However, I wasn't so drunk that I didn't catch the fact that you're a screenwriter. When I asked if you had anything I could look at, I hope you didn't think I was being too forward. I say things sometimes that come out sounding differently than I planned. I mean, people sometimes think I'm mischievous or something. Anyway, I'm rambling here. Sorry for that, too. But I'm serious about looking for new material. Now that I don't have a series, I've got to line up other projects. I'd really like it if you would let me read something that you think I might be right for. So, here's my private number: three, one, zero, five, five, five, six, two, eight, zero. Again, I'm sorry if I came across as rude or anything this evening. I noticed you left before the screening, and I wanted to apologize. Okay. There you have it. My apology. And my interest in your work. And my phone number. Guess that's it. Hope we have an opportunity to work together."

Beep.

"Rodrigo? This is Jim Fallon again. Sorry to bother you. I called a little while ago, and I don't remember if I left my phone number. I'm at three, one, zero, five, five, five, six, two, eight, zero. Just wanted to make sure I didn't forget to give you my number so we can discuss any scripts you might have with roles that I might be right for. Do I sound desperate yet? Thanks again."

Beep.

"Rodrigo? Jim again. Don't feel like you have to call back just because I'm a big, important television star. If you just want to have your agent send me something, that'll be fine, too. Okay. That's it. No more calls tonight. I promise. Three, one, zero, five, five, five, six, two, eight, zero. Okay. 'Bye."

Beep.

"Rodrigo. It's Jim again. This is so weird. You wouldn't happen to be the Rodrigo Dominguez who wrote *Blind as a Bat?* I have that script here. It says, 'Written by Rodrigo Dominguez.' I don't know of any other screenwriters named Rodrigo, so I'm hoping this is you. I hope so. My agent gave the script to me, so I guess we have the same agent. I hope it's written by you, because it's great. Michael says I should think about playing the role of Doug, the gay super of the New York apartment house in the story. I like it a lot. What do you think? I'll have my people talk to your people. Oh, wait. Your people are my people. Small world. Weird. Anyway, great work. Glad we had a chance to meet."

Click. Buzz.

Rod pushed the SAVE button in order to replay the messages in the morning.

He climbed back onto the mattress, laid on his back, and stared into the darkness. "Fuck," he said aloud in a low, incredulous whisper as conflicting thoughts crowded through his head. *I've been cursing that Actors and Others suit for not doing anything with the script . . . I hated the party because nothing appeared to happen . . . Jim Fallon's interested in my work . . . I don't belong to the WGA . . . Is he serious about liking the material . . . Why hasn't that lying, piss-lapping Michael ever said a single word to me?*

Bart rolled onto his side and snuggled up to Rod, placing his right arm across Rod's hard chest. "Told you so," Bart said in a sleepy voice.

"What?"

"Jim Fallon wants you."

"He wants to read my stuff. Then he discovered he already had."

"He wants you to fuck him. Probably on video. For his collection," Bart teased.

"Fuck you. He does not." Rod felt himself getting angry for no good reason. "I thought you were the one who told me my stuff was good. Well, Jim's just saying the same thing."

"Don't get hostile," Bart said, still groggy.

"I'm not hostile. But you're accusing Jim Fallon of having an ulterior motive for calling me. Don't you think maybe he was telling the truth? That he needs a role and really wanted to see what I have? It sounds plausible to me."

"I believe he wants to see what you have, all right," Bart said, still teasing.

"And you know what? I'd gladly show him. If it meant a screenplay sale," Rod said with a voice that spoke volumes to Bart about his lover's ambition and what he'd do to get ahead in Hollywood. "You do what you gotta do in this town, man."

"I was just joking," Bart said in a tone that registered his hurt feelings. He turned and rolled over, his back to Rod. Now, more or less conscious, he said, "Come to think of it, I've been a pretty good stepping-stone, haven't I?"

There was no answer from Rod, but Bart knew he wasn't asleep. In fact, Rod was wide-awake, looking at the blinking red light on his machine.

As his mind raced with thoughts about his career and Jim and Bart, Rod had to acknowledge the truth to himself—that, yes, Bart was indeed a stepping-stone. But who wasn't? Everybody was upwardly mobile in his or her own way. Bart may have started out as a means to an end, but there was no doubt about Rod's physical attraction to him. And there was also no doubt that Bart could do, and had already done, a lot for Rod's career and ego.

Rod would have been content to keep fucking Bart as long as Bart served his purpose; someone who could help him get ahead. But as of this moment, it seemed Bart's time was almost over. Rod and Bart had both thought it would take a while before the right people noticed Rod's work. It was happening faster than either planned.

*   *   *

The silence in the room created a vacuum. Bart was completely awake now and practically reading Rod's mind. It made him feel weak and sick to his stomach. Bart realized he had been falling in love with Rod; there was no mistake about that. But there was more. Although Bart had always been involved with serious, successful, intellectual, and accomplished men, they were practically interchangeable. Although the sex with each of them, to varying degrees, was almost always gratifying, there had never been any man whose sexual energy radiated as intensely as Rod's.

Bart got hard just thinking about being in bed with him. Everything from Rod's macho attitude to his well-constructed body was in Bart's personal theme song: "Mister Sandman."

Rod may not have been the type of man that Bart previously would have thought he would marry for life.

But things had definitely changed.

Rod was definitely the type of man that would always occupy Bart's thoughts during sex with anyone else forever after.

Bart was saddened to think that he might have to give up his sex toy-boy.

"I love you, Rod," he said in a whisper. It was the first time he had ever uttered those words to him.

And although Rod heard the confession, he didn't know what to say. So he said nothing.

Chapter Ten

The light of Sunday morning began to spread through Rod's room. It was that early time just after dawn when, in the past, regardless of how many times Bart and Rod had gotten it on during the night, they both awoke with raging hard-ons. This morning was different only because they did not automatically roll toward each other and begin making love.

Bart sat up, rubbed his crusty eyelids, and looked over at Rod, who was lying on his back, still staring at the ceiling. The bedsheet, pulled to his waist, showed the distinct outline of his erect penis.

Bart got out of bed and began to dress. Parts of his and Rod's identical tuxedos were scattered about the room, and he tried to match which were his.

Things had literally changed overnight. The air in the room was thick with unspoken decisions. Bart didn't bother to dress carefully. He zipped his pants fly, didn't button his shirt, slipped on his black nylon socks (or were they Rod's?), and pushed his feet into his patent leather shoes, not bothering to tie them.

Rod raised himself up on his elbows and looked over as Bart was about to unlock the door and leave. "Talk to you later, man," Rod said. It wasn't a question.

"Yeah. Later, dude," Bart replied in a somber tone. He was thinking it was probably the last time he'd ever use the word dude in a sentence that didn't include the word ranch.

Both men knew that "later" didn't mean later that day. Or maybe even later that year. The incredible joy that Bart had experienced over the past several weeks was suddenly sucked out of him. Part of his being was simply gone. Empty. There was a huge gaping hole where he had allowed someone to occupy space. Now that someone had been ripped away from him.

Bart slid the door open and stepped outside. The cool morning air hit him hard, like a sucker punch. Sliding the door closed, he stood for a moment, staring at his reflection in the mirrored glass.

Bart looked like hell to himself. His hair was tousled. He needed a shave. His eyes were puffy. His open shirt revealed lines on his body from where the sheets had etched crease marks. He realized he was missing his bow tie, but he didn't want to go back inside to retrieve it.

Most of all, he was feeling how much he would miss coming to this strange room. He'd miss meeting Mrs. Carter in the hallway. He'd miss the sounds of her television programs drifting down to Rod's room. Most of all, he'd miss being intimate with Rod.

Rod stared back at him anonymously.

Bart admitted to himself that it wasn't just the sex he enjoyed. There had been *real* intimacy. Or so he thought. But apparently he had been duped into thinking that something deeper than superficial orgasms were shared between them. He didn't want to think that Rod had used him, although it seemed pretty obvious now. He rationalized that he'd kind of used Rod, too; used him for spectacular sex.

Bart turned and walked away.

As he moved down the walkway by the side of the house, he noticed a gold-plated cuff link on the ground, glinting in the weak sun. He picked it up, then gave a cursory look around for its mate. He didn't find it right away, so he gave up and walked off the property. At the edge of the driveway, where the cracked sidewalk began, Bart stopped for a moment.

Bart was trying to remember exactly where he'd parked his car. To Rod, who had left his room and walked down the hall to the living room and was peering out the front picture window, it appeared Bart was thinking about turning back.

The Mustang was a block away and covered with morning dew. Bart opened the driver's side door—which he discovered he had neglected to lock the night before—and sat inside the car, warming up the engine as well as himself before driving away to his own apartment in Silverlake.

Pulling out of his parking space, he drove over to La Cienega Boulevard and took that all the way up to Sunset. The usual bumper-to-bumper street traffic was nonexistent this time of morning on a Sunday, which made the stretch of road an easy drive. He passed Fairfax, then Highland, heading east to Western Avenue. After an inordinately long red traffic light at the intersection, he hung a left, crossing Hollywood Boulevard, and headed up to Los Feliz. Bart passed Griffith Park, ignoring the early-twentieth-century mansions built for silent-film stars and studio moguls that lined both sides of the street. Somewhere along here Lily Tomlin and Jane Wagner had a place. So did Madonna.

Bart had actually been in one of the old gated estates on DeMille one time, which was owned by a cast member of the old television show *The Waltons*. The actress was exactly like the shrew she played on the series. If Rod had been to one of her parties, he would have gotten the full impact of what it was like to be treated as if you didn't belong. It had happened to Bart when he accompanied a friend to an elegant dinner party there. As he remembered, the old woman's complexion was as pale as Max Factor's pancake, as cadaverous as if a vampire had sucked out all her blood. Her hair was dyed Mars rust red, and she wore brown lipstick and a red satin brocade ball gown that was appropriate for the refined ambience of her home but not for the dinner party. She never once acknowledged Bart, even when they were introduced. He could have been invisible.

She was the most inhospitable hostess Bart had ever encountered. Well, almost. She rivaled another glacial personality: Audrey Christie. He remembered being taken by the same asshole who showed him off at Katie Grayson's to a party at the tract home where Ms. Christie lived. She had played Mrs. Upson in Lucille Ball's film fiasco of the musical *Mame*, and she was also the crusty rich lady who snubbed nouveau riche Debbie Reynolds in *The Unsinkable Molly Brown* until Molly became a heroine when she removed her fur coat and placed it around the shoulders of a freezing lifeboat survivor from the *Titanic*. Audrey Christie *defined* rude. When Bart's asshole escort mentioned to the bartender that Bart's cola was flat, she overheard the remark and made a big deal out of this young man, whom she didn't even know, calling *her* cola flat. It wasn't even Bart who'd made the comment. He would have been satisfied to drink whatever he was served. "What a bitch," he now said aloud. "Dead. Too bad. No love lost to the world!"

Once home in his Silverlake apartment, Bart shed his wrinkled clothes, leaving them on the floor beside his bed, and climbed in naked under the cold sheets. Being nude in bed always made his cock stiffen for some unexplainable and uncontrollable reason, as if at any moment some phantom lover would join him.

However, to Bart, his fantasy had come and gone. He couldn't imagine ever having another to replace what had been perfection. Although he was rock-hard, he had no desire to do anything about it. He decided he'd stay in bed the whole day, just to recuperate—from last night and the past few weeks of not getting much rest. He had no other obligations. So that's just what he did. He slept.

Rod didn't waste any time getting in touch with Jim Fallon.

Shortly after Bart left, Rod jacked off, just to alleviate the pressure. He brushed his teeth, got a cup of coffee, went to the gym, came home, shaved around his goatee, and showered. Then, at ten, he picked up the phone and pushed Jim's number on the keypad. After three rings, Jim's answering machine picked up. "You know the routine," Jim's distinct voice advised. Beep.

"Ah, Jim. Ah, this is Rodrigo Dominguez. We met last night at your party. Then you called me. Sorry I'm just now getting back to you . . ."

"Oh. Hey. Ah, hold a sec." It was Jim, picking up the phone. Ear-splitting feedback filled the receiver until Jim turned off the recording device. "There. Morning. Sorry. I was still asleep. The ringer was turned off, but I heard your voice."

"Hey, sorry. Want me to call back? Sorry I woke you up. I thought by ten it would be okay."

"No, this is fine. I should have gotten up by now, anyway."

"So, you called me," Rod said. "You really liked the script? Oh, by the way, your party was great."

"Thanks," Jim said. "Sorry you had to leave so early."

"I hope you didn't think we were rude."

"I didn't think you were rude at all. And you can catch the show when it airs next week. That is, if you have any interest in my swan song. And yes, I really liked the script."

"I'm sure it's a great script. Final episodes of hit shows are usually a letdown, but I'm sure yours—"

"No. I mean *your* script."

"Oh. Far out."

"Is there anyone attached? To the script, I mean. Attached. You know, starring?"

"Of course. I mean, I knew *you* meant attached to the script. No one's attached that I know of."

"I could easily see Kathy Bates in the role of the slumlord owner of the building," Jim said. "And how about Greg Kinnear for the part of Gene, the new yuppie tenant?"

"Is he still doing movies?" Rod said. "I sort of wrote it with Jude Law or Rupert Everett in mind. But yeah, whatever. But it's not a sold script, if that's what you're asking. Michael, your agent, who gave it to you, isn't exactly my agent. He's just someone I kinda know. He never even told me you were reading it. You'd have to ask him what's going on with the project. Michael and I don't exactly talk."

Jim was lying in his bed naked, holding the cordless phone with one hand and stroking his penis with the other. As he spoke to Rod, he was fantasizing about getting his ass fucked by the Latin stud. Jim was beating off even as Rod was explaining the status of the screenplay and mentioning others he'd written that might be equally suitable for Jim.

"My day's rather free," Rod said. "If you'd like me to drop by with some other stuff, I could do that."

At the very thought of Rod's coming by the house, Jim climaxed and shot the biggest load he'd unleashed in a long time, squirting all the way up to his face.

"Jim? Are you there?" Rod sounded concerned.

Jim clenched his teeth in ecstasy, trying not to make any orgasmic noise. "Sorry," he finally said, breathing heavily.

"Is this a bad time?"

"No. I was just trying to find my glasses so I could check my calendar for today." He was lying. Jim had no plans. Sunday was usually the day a draft of the next week's script was messengered to the house. But now that *The Grass Is Always Greener* was history, he had the day completely free. "Ah, would it be convenient for you to stop by around four? Teatime?"

"Sure, that works for me," Rod said. "I'll be at your place at four."

"Great. See you then."

"Ah, thanks again for the cool party."

Jim hung up, a satisfied smile on his face. Then Jim cleaned himself off with a couple of tissues from a box by his bed.

Chapter Eleven

By three that afternoon, Rod still wasn't sure what to wear to his rendezvous with Jim. For the first time in his life he wasn't certain what he was selling—his body or his "intellectual property," as Bart had called his work. He vacillated between his most provocative outfit—jeans and a tank top—or a more conservative look—jeans and a Ricky Martin–style pullover crew neck.

Thoughts of what Bart had said about Jim's motives kept resurfacing. What if Jim really was only interested in Rod for his body and not for his talent? Or maybe he was interested in both? Or maybe interest in his body could lead to interest in his work? People were willing to go out of their way to help sexy people. Bart himself had been proof of that.

In the end, Rod decided on the jeans (sans belt and underwear), his work boots, a tight-fitting, white muscle-revealing tank top that was specially tailored to reveal the contours of his body, and a Shell service-station mechanic's shirt, unbuttoned. The gas-station shirt was left over from a customer whose fantasy was to be lubed with black axle grease and fucked by a grimy, sweaty service-station attendant.

After years of putting out for hundreds of different men, Rod thought he knew Jim's type pretty well. If Rod's intuition was correct, Jim would want to inhale the musky scent of perspiration mixed with semen. Therefore, before leaving, Rod did two hundred push-ups and one thousand stomach crunches. Then he beat off and slathered his discharge all over his body and into the hairs in his armpits. It was a man's smell, one that turned a lot of guys on. Rod knew this. He was just playing it safe in case Bart had been right about an ulterior motive for getting Rod up to Jim's house. However, Rod was confident that if this was the case, he could still wrap ol' Jim Fallon around his cock and get him to do something about making a movie from his script.

At three-thirty, behind the wheel of his dull, green Dodge Dart, Rod was trying to remember the exact location of Jim's place. He knew the general vicinity, and he set out driving up Crescent Heights, which became Laurel Canyon. He followed the serpentine road all the way up to its crest. At Mulholland Drive he made a sharp right onto Woodrow Wilson. This was the tricky part. Most of the houses along here were gated and set far back from the street, secluded from the main road. Rod didn't recall the address, but he remembered that the tall gates to Jim's place were adorned with his monogram—JF—set inside a wrought-iron star.

After driving along slowly and having to pull over several times on the narrow street to let other cars pass by, there it was: the vaguely familiar, long, steep driveway. The gates were closed when he arrived. A buzzer and intercom box stood at car-window height. Rod rolled his window down and pushed the white button on the box. He noticed brown-and-white plastic owls perched on the stone walls on which the gates were attached. He'd seen these things before. They were really disguised security cameras. The owls' eyes were telephoto lenses.

"Come on up," a voice crackled through the intercom. The tall gates opened to allow his car to move up the hill.

Once again, impressed with the lighted water fountain on a patch of green grass in the middle of the circular drive, Rod was happy to see that there was no security man waiting with a walkie-talkie and a clipboard list of invited guests on which his name might not appear. Rod parked by the front entrance, picked up his five scripts, which he'd brought along in case Jim was interested in reading them, checked himself in the rearview mirror, and climbed out of his practically worthless car.

Before Rod could reach the steps and ring the bell, Jim opened the double doors, like a dowager welcoming guests. "So nice to see you again," Jim said, extending his hand and shaking Rod's. The handshake lasted a fraction of a moment too long as Jim's heart raced at the sight of Rod in clothes that advertised his physical endowments and planted the unmistakable suggestion of sex.

"Please come in," said Jim, who was wearing 501s and an expensive black silk shirt unbuttoned far enough to reveal a smattering of graying hair on his chest.

As Rod entered the inner sanctum of Jim Fallon's lair, he noticed that the Casablanca lilies were just as abundant as they were the night before. The house had been so thoroughly cleaned by the maids and catering staff, it was impossible to notice any remnants from a lavish party that had been held on the premises just a few hours ago. But there again was the staggering view of the city. This time it wasn't quite dusk, and the view was a pale gray rather than brilliant Christmas-like sparkling lights that had been so impressive the night before. Still, Rod nearly gasped again at the panorama of Los Angeles over the precipice of the hillside.

"Let's go into the library," Jim suggested, leading the way.

Rod had not been in this room last night. They entered through twelve-foot-tall French doors molded with appliqués of fleurs-de-lis in the center of each door panel. Inside, the room was two stories high, with floor-to-ceiling bookshelves. A narrow stairway leading to a gallery ran the length of one wall. Hanging over the mantel of a huge fireplace on the opposite wall was an oil painting of Jim dressed in a tweed jacket and seated in a wing chair, one leg draped over the other, a golden retriever resting at his feet.

Jim noticed Rod's close examination of the portrait. "The affectation of a wanna-be baronial master," he said as if apologizing for the pretense.

The chair on the canvas was identical to the one in which Jim suggested Rod take a seat. Looking around at the grandeur of the room, Rod noticed shelf after shelf of hardcover books, some bound in leather, others with their colorful paper dust jackets. There was also an array of awards. On opposite ends of the fireplace mantel, bookending numerous other shiny trophies, were two Emmy statuettes. "What's the Grammy for?" Rod asked, impressed that he was seeing an actual Grammy in somebody's own home, not in a museum or just clutched in Carlos Santana's hands on television.

"*Blow Me.*"

"Can't I get a drink first?"

"No. *Blow Me.* That was my first comedy CD."

Rod turned red. "God. I'm so embarrassed."

"Don't be. *Blow Me* went platinum. It's a line I made famous on the show. Like 'Bite me,' only more outrageous, because the network was trying to keep up with the cutting edge of Fox and HBO series. I was supposed to record a sequel."

"*Blow Me, Harder?*" Rod suggested sarcastically.

"You're joking, but that was to be the actual title." Jim smiled. "You're a clever guy. Now, with all that's happened in my personal and professional life, the record company has canceled the contract. We're suing, of course. We had a deal. I don't remember the Rolling Stones getting dumped by their label when they came out with *Sticky Fingers* way back in the seventies. You're probably too young to remember, but the album cover was a pair of jeans—with a real zipper, for Christ sake! Tell me that's not spelling everything out completely."

Jim uncorked a bottle of merlot and removed two Bordeaux glasses from a glass shelf behind the bar. "What do you make of all the fuss? Do you believe all the tabloids? Do you think I'm a total perv?"

Jim set the bottle down to breathe for a moment as he opened a panel in the wall that revealed switches and dimmers. He pushed a button, and flames came to life in the fireplace. He pushed another button, and the recessed lighting in the ceiling illuminated the room. A pink spot directly hit Jim's portrait. Another knob filled the room with soft classical music.

Jim poured the wine and handed Rod a glass. He sat down beside him in an identical leather-upholstered wing chair.

Rod said, "First of all, not only do I *not* believe what I read—except in the *Star,* which is always right—I don't believe what people tell me. Everybody has a hidden agenda. I only believe what I see with my own eyes. And I trust my intuition. Also, whatever you do in the privacy of your own home is your business. You may be a sick, kinky son-of-a-bitch dog—oh, not *you* personally, Jim; I didn't mean that—but I don't believe anyone has the right to judge anybody else who's a sick, kinky son-of-a-bitch dog."

Jim smiled again. "I don't think I'm kinky . . . well maybe by Dr. Laura Schlesinger's standards, but who wouldn't be. I'm no more a dog than any other sexual being—gay or straight. We all have our needs. It's not fair that audiences think I'm just the character I play on the series. People are so ignorant. There's so much more to who Jim Fallon is!"

"I know exactly what you're saying," Rod agreed. "People look at me and immediately think I'm hot and dangerous. Which I am. But that's not all there is to me. I'll bet that not a soul who meets me for the first time doesn't think my brain is in my pants. I think most people would be shocked to discover that I'm a writer. As a matter of fact, the script you read was over at Sterling for coverage. The story guy gave it an *Excellent* and said, 'Don't let this one get away.'"

"My thoughts exactly," Jim said. He was trying hard to look directly into Rod's eyes and not give himself away by absorbing the fullness of his guest's sumptuous body.

Jim took a long pull on his glass of wine. "I had no idea a studio had been approached. Michael didn't tell me that."

"Michael's an asshole. He didn't submit it; another friend of mine did, although Michael will probably try to take credit. (A friend, Rod thought for a fraction of an instant. That's what Bart had been to him.) In fact, he didn't even tell me that he was giving you the script to read. I gave it to him six months ago. He's never mentioned it to me." Rod sipped his wine. "He's a slick one. I don't know why you stay with him. You could do so much better."

"Michael discovered me. I believe in being loyal."

Rod finished his glass of wine and handed it back to Jim in a manner that said, Fill 'er up again. Jim nodded, taking the glass and thinking the afternoon (which was now evening) was going very well indeed. He had planned to come across as sympathetic, get Rod drunk, reveal just enough about his sexual fantasies, and then see what happened. So far, so good.

He returned presently with a refill of the merlot. "Let's move over to the couch. It's more comfortable than these damned chairs that my decorator insisted I buy." Jim indicated the twin sofas facing each other beside the fireplace. A glass-topped coffee table separated the sofas.

Rod moved as directed and placed the five scripts he had been holding on top of the table. "Oh, good, more material for me to read," Jim said, looking at the stack of screenplays, each with a different-color cover and three brass brads holding the pages together. "Tell me a bit about yourself, Rod. How long have you been writing? What have you sold? Do you have to wait tables like so many other actors and writers in this town? God I'm glad I never had to do that!"

Rod gave Jim the most superficial details. "Always been a writer. No sales yet, but there's a lot of interest. (He lied.) As for steady work, I tend bar." He added, "Michael's a frequent customer. You should ask him for the lowdown. I'm not very much at ease talking about myself."

"Oh, you writers. You're so introspective. You have the perfect career. You can be creative, yet maintain your anonymity. Being a star like me is very, very difficult." Jim assumed a wistful, affected tone of world-weariness. "I can't leave the house without paparazzi stalking me. And forget traveling regularly scheduled commercial airlines. Oprah has the right idea. Wish I could afford a jet like hers." Jim paused. "By the way, did anybody see you come to the gate?" He was suddenly panicked. "I should have warned you."

"No one that I was aware of."

"They're sneaky bastards, those photographers. They could be a mile away and with a telephoto get you down to the last detail of your tattoo. I imagine you *do* have a tattoo somewhere, don't you?"

Rod smirked. Then he stood up and took of his grease-monkey shirt. Not only was his muscular body revealed through the diaphanous material of his athletic shirt, but a tattoo crucifix decorated one shoulder, while an ornate gang insignia adorned his huge right biceps muscle.

"You're one hot stud, Mr. Dominguez," Jim said, his pants filling up with an uncontrollable erection. "You must have a girlfriend. Or a boyfriend?"

"Neither one."

"Who was the guy you brought to the party?"

"Just some dude. We broke up last night." A twinge of regret flashed past Rod's mind as he referred to Bart as "Just some dude."

"Oh? I'm sorry to hear that." Jim didn't bother sounding sincere. "You guys looked great together."

"He was jealous. I don't like that."

"I don't blame him."

"Of you."

Jim snorted. "That's absurd. I'm flattered, but I'm hardly someone that anyone on the planet should be jealous of. I'm *persona non grata,* not just in this town but in every American household. My Q-rating's a disaster. If I ever get a chance to make another television series, it will be a miracle. I'll probably be relegated to a Saturday-morning sitcom like *Saved by the Bell* or some such network refuse in roles that they used to call 'the funny uncle.' And that's if I'm lucky."

Jim paused, then asked, intrigued, "Why was he jealous?"

Rod pondered the question for a moment, wondering how much he should reveal and how much he should embellish. He decided to go for a combination of the two. "Bart—that was the guy's name—didn't think my writing was any good, and he said you couldn't possibly want to discuss anything with me other than sex." For another split second Rod felt ashamed for lying about Bart, who had been nothing but completely supportive of his work.

Jim looked appalled at the very idea that he was thought to have had a hidden agenda for getting Rod up to his house. "You were right to dump him. You need someone who understands your creative nature. You're a brilliant writer. Someone has to appreciate your assets. Although, if you don't mind my saying so, I'll bet everybody *is* after your assets."

"Including you, Jim?"

"Listen," Jim said in a tone that read like a confession, "I need a job, and I thought you might have something that Michael could pitch to the studios. Then, when I found out you had written a terrific screenplay, one that I loved and thought was brilliant for me, I simply wanted to meet you and discuss possibilities. Sex was the furthest thing from my mind, I assure you. Until . . ."

Ah, Rod thought, *here it comes. The old man is making his play. What do I do? I don't want to jeopardize his enthusiasm for the project or have him blackball me to Michael or the studios if I rebuff him. Let's just see where he's going.*

Jim went on. "When you walked in here looking . . . well, you can't help it, but looking like something out of a casting call for leading men in a hot daytime drama, only better . . . Naturally I couldn't help but have only a quick fleeting fantasy. Just for a teensy instant. It's elemental. You know what you look like, so you have to agree. But I've regained my composure. I don't want anything to interfere with the possibility of our working together."

Rod was still standing. With a sleight of hand that would have made David Copperfield envious, he had unbuttoned the fly on his jeans and pulled out his cock. "Would this be an interference?"

Jim swallowed hard, mesmerized. He dragged his covetous eyes off Rod's long, thick member only for a moment to glance up at Rod's bulging tank top, tattoos, and goateed face. Then back to Rod's appendage.

"Seen one, you obviously haven't seen 'em all," Jim sputtered. "Would you mind if I—touch it?"

"I'd prefer you suck it. Think of it as a People's Choice Award. This is the choice of a lot of people."

Jim swallowed his glass of wine with one long pull. He slipped off the couch to the floor, onto his knees, and licked his lips.

Sinuously, he slithered his tongue from the helmet-shaped dome of Rod's penis, down the long red-and-blue veined shaft. Then he finally stood up and took Rod by the hand, leading the way to the stairway and up to the second-floor bedrooms.

By the time they entered Jim's lavishly appointed bedroom they were both stripped naked.

Fuck, Rod thought when they entered the well-lit room and he saw Jim completely nude. Jim's body was falling apart. He was already showing major signs of a pot gut. He obviously didn't work out. His butt was falling—if he ever actually had one in the first place—and it had a rash of pimples on both cheeks.

Shit, Rod said to himself, *this is going to be work. I'd better as hell get something in return for plugging this old fart.*

Rod had had to work himself up countless times with some of the trolls who answered his instant E-mail messages, but the stakes were higher this time. It wasn't rent money or saving toward a new computer printer for which he was fucking. It was to obtain Jim's help with getting the script sold and made into a movie. Therefore, Rod knew he had to give the performance of his life and act as though Jim were the biggest turn-on in the world. The actor's ego demanded it. Rod's future rested on how much confidence he could instill in Jim, who, from the language he was now using, was exactly the sick, perverted dog he claimed he wasn't.

Having seen Jim's infamous tape, Rod pretty much knew what it was that this guy liked. He immediately took control, dominating the scene as the gang bangers on the video had done. Rod was tough but not rough. He grabbed a necktie that was neatly folded on the back of a chair and lashed Jim's wrists to the iron slats of his bedpost.

Rod gave him a slap across the face that was just a tad more than playful. "You're a cocksucking asswipe, aren't you, Jim?" Rod said, mimicking the dialogue he remembered from the videotape. He laid himself on top of Jim's body and dry-humped his slave, biting the nipples on his flabby chest and licking the perspiration from his sternum. Jim was in ecstasy.

Rod wanted to vomit.

"You want to suck my big, fat piece of meat, don't you, asshole?" Rod demanded.

"Yes! Oh, please, yes!"

Rod brought his heavy cock up to Jim's face. Jim's tongue darted out just as Rod withdrew the treat. Jim grunted. His animal-like sounds were the nonverbal equivalent of begging for Rod to let him have a taste of his beautifully shaped penis. Rod brought his cock back to Jim's face and slapped him with his tool.

Jim was overcome with anxious anxiety as he smelled Rod's precum and tried in vain to lift his head up far enough and stick his tongue out quickly enough to catch the prize. Finally, Rod gave in and plowed himself into Jim's hot, wet mouth. But Jim was hardly prepared to take the whole large package. He gagged and choked and drooled and parted his lips as far as possible to accommodate the whole thing. Jim groaned in ecstasy.

"You're a good little cocksucker," Rod said, sounding like a school-teacher doling out praise for a child who had learned his multiplication tables correctly. "Let's see how your asshole fares!"

Rod turned Jim over onto his stomach without untying his hands, which meant his arms were crossed over each other. Rod had come pre-pared with a condom in his pocket that he picked up that morning at the 7-Eleven on Santa Monica Boulevard. He noticed there was a tube of sex gel on Jim's nightstand. "Jack off this morning with this stuff, Jim?" Rod asked sarcastically. "While you were talking to me? Well, let's see if how I feel inside of you is anything like what you expected."

Rod lubed up his condom and carefully rolled it over the head of his cock and down his shaft. With Jim still making nonverbal sounds of pleasure, Rod held the tube of Slime over Jim's pockmarked ass and let the cold liquid drool onto his hairy crack. Jim squealed with anticipa-tion as Rod began to massage the lube first on the rim of Jim's hole and then inserted two fingers and coated the inside of his rectum.

"Ready, Jimbo?" Rod asked. He lifted Jim onto his knees and began rubbing the head of his condom-covered cock against Jim's sensitive hole.

"Please. Take it easy," Jim groaned.

Rod laughed. "How easy is easy, Jimbo? This easy?" He slowly eased himself into the hot, dark place that, according to Mel Gibson, was not a portal for entry but rather an exit.

"Or *this* easy?" he said as he forced himself inside.

"No!" Jim cried. "Take it out!"

"Oh, you're too hot, Jim. You are one hot, fucking sexy dude, man!"

Rod suddenly realized he was playacting, something he never had to do with Bart. In fact, to get through this ritual, he started to fantasize about Bart and how much pleasure they had both given each other.

Rod's man muscle rammed itself against Jim's prostate. In only a few minutes, Jim cried out as he automatically shot his load without so much as touching himself. Not that he could with his hands bound. Jim roared with pleasure and pain as Rod continued to hammer away and force Jim to give up his entire load.

Finally, when Jim was spent, Rod withdrew his dick and untied Jim. He rolled him over onto his back and onto the sticky wet sheets, where he'd shot a massive load of jizz. Jim was utterly exhausted, depleted of energy.

But Rod wasn't through. He ripped off his condom and straddled Jim's waist while he stroked his own cock. He groaned until he suddenly drew in his breath and unloaded the kind of heavy cream that only a healthy twenty-one-year-old could spill.

Rod said, "Satisfied, asshole?"

"Yeah" was all that Jim could get out as he continued to breathe heavily. Rod untied him, and Jim rubbed Rod's cum all over his flabby stomach and a chest that was showing signs of becoming breasts.

Rod cast a magical spell over anyone whom he deigned to seduce. From the moment he invited anyone to touch and caress his hard young body they were under his control. Once a man had the privilege of sucking on Rod's cock or getting fucked by him, there was no escaping the bewitchment.

Tough-as-nails Jim Fallon was no exception. In fact, while he was having his brains screwed out by Rod, his mind was thinking ahead to the next time and the time after that and what he had to go through to keep this Latin stud around. He had already decided he'd go to Michael and plead for him to get a studio to package *Blind as a Bat*.

If not Michael, then he'd call in a few favors. There was the Warner Bros. executive's new young wife who, to further her acting career, married a portly upper-management guy who was known for his halitosis. She had made a cameo appearance on *The Grass Is Always Greener*, which Jim had allowed as a courtesy to the old man.

Then there was the closeted Sterling creative executive who had propositioned Jim in the men's room at Merv Griffin's Beverly Hilton Hotel during a break in a salute-to-Angela Lanebury ceremony. Jim wasn't interested in a blow job in a restroom stall, and the guy pleaded with Jim not to tell anybody, especially his wife.

These were just a few of the chits that Jim had planned to eventually collect when the time was right. If Michael couldn't come through, Jim decided he'd start making a few calls. Anything to keep Rod around.

When Jim had regained his strength, the men put most of their clothes back on and returned to the library. The fire still roared, and the sound of Puccini filled the room. Their first bottle of wine was empty, so Rod took it upon himself to go to the bar and uncork another. He was starting to feel right at home.

Jim took a seat on the sofa and began staring into the flames in the fireplace.

"So what do you think?" Rod said to Jim as he handed him a glass of wine and interrupted his reverie.

"About what?"

"The swallows at Capistrano being picked off with shotguns by eight-year-olds out on a class field trip this afternoon. What do you think I'm asking you about? The sex, of course. You're a guy who probably gets laid a lot, and I just want to know if I lived up to your expectations," Rod said, playing coy.

Jim shuddered. "You were certainly born on the wild side," he said. Jim was just as masterful at acting out a character and getting what he wanted from people, too. Only his method was different from Rod's. He wasn't going to let on to this sexy, talented punk that he had practically died from rapture upstairs. "You're a very fine boy."

"A fine boy," Rod mocked, getting only slightly pissed off. "Thanks for the compliment. Would that be your recommendation to anyone who asked you if I was worth the trouble?"

"Trouble?" Jim sipped his wine. He looked at Rod, who had only dressed in his jeans and boots. Starting to get an erection once again, Jim reached out a hand and dragged his fingertips down Rod's chest and sternum. He grazed Rod's nipples and caressed the tattoo on his left arm. Jim's eyes spoke his thoughts loudly, that Rod was the most perfectly endowed man in a city that boasted the most gorgeous men on the planet.

Rod stared into Jim's eyes, and even though it was a total lie, he conveyed the thought that Jim was the sexiest man alive—which was the equivalent of telling Jackie Mason he was as hot as Tom Cruise. And clearly Jim bought into it. Rod's other gift was convincing the people who solicited him that they were an equal in the looks department. That they fucked as well as he did. That they were the perfect size for him—regardless of how incompetent or unsatisfying they may have been. Rod knew exactly how to make people trust him.

Chapter Twelve

The next morning, Bart slept past his usual weekday waking hour of five o'clock. For the first time ever, he arrived at the office after nine. Of course, Cheets was nowhere to be found. The mail had been delivered and was still stacked by his office door. Inside his office, on his desk, the red light on his telephone indicated his messages hadn't been retrieved. Settling in, he turned on his computer and found twenty-eight E-mails had accumulated since Friday.

"One thing at a time," he said aloud, thinking of the mail, the phone calls, the E-mail, and the conversation he was going to have to have with Cheets again about what time she was expected in the office. Mostly, he was irritated with himself for being unable to ease into what was certain to be another frantic day.

He punched in the password number on his telephone to retrieve his messages. "You have four new messages," announced the pleasant, perfectly enunciated voice of the woman who lived inside the phone. "Start of messages," she said amiably. "Message one. From phone-number 666."

Shari.

"Cunt," Bart said to the answering-machine voice, with no more warmth or modulation than "The white zone is for loading and unloading of passengers only."

"Second message. From phone-number 666."

"Bitch," he added in a tone that might as well have been the repeating of an order by a counter girl at Starbucks to make certain she got the request correct: "double latté decaf, venti, to go."

"Third message. From phone-number 666."

"Cooze." By now he was merely reading a roll call.

"Message four. From an unknown number. 'I never said all the things you wrote.'" The voice was Mare Dickerson's, with an accusing tone, referring to the quotes attributed to her in the press notes for her new comedy, *Woodchuck Chuck?* also starring television's Courteney Howard-Giroux and HBO comic John DeSalles.

"Would Chuck, Chuck? Would Chuck-Chuck? Would Chuck, Chuck Chuck?" Bart had played with the title for months, turning it into a title for a porn or snuff film.

"End of mailbox." The woman returned to her natural, nonregional voice.

"Oh, fuck both of you." Bart spoke to the machine, meaning Shari and Mare. He pushed the RELEASE button on the phone to disconnect the voice-mail system.

"By the way, you cocksucking actress, I recorded our interview. Want me to play back the tape and prove my changes were for your own good?"

Of course, Bart couldn't say that to Dickerson. He'd simply telephone the aging star—and nobody but Margot from *Lost Horizon* had aged faster—and politely ask what the thrice Oscar-nominated bitch preferred to be quoted as saying about her experiences working on *Chuck,* as the film title was simplified and reduced for convenience at the office.

Bart had to be diplomatic, which is what he had tried to be when he changed one of Mare's quotes to read, "I'm an actor who enjoys her craft. I'm constantly striving for perfection. I accepted the role of Claudia because, although the character at first seems one-dimensional, I intuitively realized there was great depth to be found in the script. Her arc is such that audiences will relate to the struggles she must face in order to survive the devastating situations she ultimately finds herself trying to overcome as a prostitute in the Pacific Northwest. Thanks to our fine director and the support from the incredibly talented Ms. Howard-Giroux, and Mr. DeSalles and the superb supporting cast, I'm very pleased with this film."

It wouldn't look good in the press kit if the star were quoted verbatim off her tape-recorded interview: "What kind of stupid idiot do you think I am, you little putz. I took the role for one reason, because they offered me a shitload of money. My motivation? It had only to do with the number of zeros they piled behind a number on my check. I don't give a fuck about the audience. I don't care whether or not they like this character. They can stick it up their ass!

"Any American asshole who pays nine bucks to see a movie doesn't deserve quality—he's being ripped off by the studios. Wait a few months for the video—suckers. Most audiences don't have the intellectual capacity to appreciate art, anyway. That's why Jerry Bruckheimer's films make a shit ton of cash. They're mindless diversions for the mindless lemmings who line up in the blazing summer heat to see a lot of special effects.

"Speaking of mindless, where on earth did they find this Courteney hyphenate and the director? Neither stands a chance for another feature once the critics get a load of this piece of celluloid crap. I don't think either of their careers will survive when this mess is released. And they were damned difficult for me to work with. Trying to act with 'no talents' generally is impossible for geniuses such as I."

Yeah, Bart thought. *That would go over real well with Shari. The press would have a field day.*

For him, there was no alternative. It was a simple task of taking the high road and playing the obsequious nobody. He was used to that. It was Bart's life as a publicist, the life of most Hollywood publicists. They took orders and made assholes look like they're the Second Coming of Audrey Hepburn at a famine-relief center in Botswana. However, Bart had a feeling Audrey had been a dream client and perfectly sincere in all her humanitarian efforts.

If Bart loathed Hollywood, this latest fracas with the star of *Woodchuck Chuck?* was just one more reason to think of gaining his freedom. There was the tempestuous Shari, always accusing him of one contrived infraction or another. Then there were the asshole stars who thought they were so far above the rest of the peons who served their every whim that they could be as rude as they wanted to be. Well, Bart decided he'd had enough of the Sharis and the Mare Dickersons and the Michael Manns and the Don Johnsons and the Julia Bobs and Jerry Lewises of the world. And he'd also had it with the fantasy of being with someone as unearthly sexy as Rod Dominguez.

"I don't even have time for a nervous breakdown," Bart lamented. "This is a call for this little wuss to kick some Hollywood ass." He paused, thinking. "But how?"

The easiest target would be Cheets, who, by 9:45, still hadn't made an entrance. But not only was confrontation not in Bart's nature; he didn't want to emulate the jackasses he had to serve by being a bastard to those who served him.

On the other hand, he thought, perhaps a lack of confrontation might be his problem. Look at what happened at Rod's yesterday morning. There was no scene, no flying plates or words of anger that could eventually be mollified by an apology and subsequent make-up sex. Perhaps if Bart had fought for what he wanted, he wouldn't feel as though his life were a case of the tail wagging the dog.

After scrolling through his E-mails for anything that seemed important, Bart came to a conclusion about the course on which he would set his life. From this moment forward, he would buckle down and work extra hard to get out of Sterling. Like Rod, he would concentrate on his personal writing—in particular the diary, which would become a tell-all book. Like Cindy Adams, he'd simply continue to dish whatever dirt he could dig up. And there was plenty of dirt just lying around at publicity staff meetings, stinking up the place like Drew Carey's underwear after an all-night binge on burritos and refried beans.

But if his proposed book was to become a reality, he realized he'd have to conceal himself behind a nom de plume. He remembered that when the identity of Joe Klein, "Anonymous" author of *Primary Colors,* eventually leaked out, he was vilified because of his apparent lack of ethics. Bart used to have ethics. But they were slowly eroded by his working in Hollywood.

"Ha!" Bart uttered as he came to an unexpected realization about himself and his profession. "I'm Laura Petry, for crying out loud! I've unexpectedly walked in on Alan Brady, and he doesn't have any hair!"

But when exactly did that MTM moment occur to Bart, he asked himself. *When did I first realize that Hollywood was actually Alan Brady—a vain star, self-absorbed to the core, a baldheaded egomaniacal beast? When did the façade of Hollywood flip off like a tacky toupee in a wind chamber?*

Unlike the threshold that delineates the moment a puppy becomes a dog, there was no single moment that Bart could remember when he experienced the transformation from wondering child to amoral weasel. He had been an enthusiastic young man when he started in the business. No task at the studio was too small for him to accept with a smile. Simply walking between soundstages during his lunch hour or seeing a parking space that said "Don Knotts" was almost compensation enough for the privilege of working in Hollywood. Even as a lowly assistant, he had felt he was contributing an important ingredient to what filmgoers would eventually view on-screen.

Now, sitting in his corner office, with his own sofa and minirefrigerator as well as an assistant and an expense account and car allowance and weekly invitations to attend private screenings with the stars and directors of new films, Bart realized he was paying a colossal price for the so-called privilege of being privileged.

But in order to continue his existence and status, he had to lie a hundred different ways a thousand times a day. For example, he'd had to tell Piper Perabo after a screening that she was "Brilliant. Simply brilliant!" If that wasn't difficult enough to do with a straight face, he had to push the envelope and say, with his own Oscar-caliber performance of sincerity, that her appearance in *The Adventures of Rocky and Bullwinkle* was destined to make the film that summer's biggest box-office hit.

It was a walking-the-razor's-edge balancing act Bart performed daily. For too long now he had been forced to write obsequious letters to the Hollywood Foreign Press Association, hoping to surreptitiously maneuver the members into nominating Farrah Fawcett for a Golden Globe Award for a "small but memorable" cameo role in the harrowing but true story of a woman's courage when she finds her wealthy new husband has four testicles. And when James Belushi miraculously got a rave in *L.A. Weekly* for his hard-hitting role as a closeted gay aromatherapist in a Beverly Hills salon who discovers that the scent of client Pauly Shore is the aphrodisiac that changes his life forever, Bart had to find a way to make the HFPA and Motion Picture Academy members believe what the lunatics at *L.A. Weekly* had to say and disregard every other major film critic across the country.

Bart got into the movie business because he loved Meryl Streep, Angela Bassett, Jenifer Lewis, and Emma Thompson. Without exception, each of these "stars" was as professional and pleasant as they were gifted. Unfortunately, the Streep/Bassett/Lewis/Thompson wanna-bes were poor imitations. It made Bart morose to recognize that his lifelong passion for showbiz was merely the symptom of a disease rather than the disease itself.

He also decided to put himself on the dating market again. But this time he would go back to his original intent: to find a guy who was educated, emotionally well adjusted, stable in whatever profession he'd chosen, and ready to settle down.

"All my men have had dysfunctional personalities." Bart rolled his eyes as if he couldn't believe his lack of being lucky in love.

Prior to Rod, he'd only had one other lover: "the Asshole" a.k.a. Ed. They had shared a condo on Miller Drive, in the hills above Sunset, in West Hollywood. The Asshole was an aberration, albeit a cutie—or at least Bart thought he was cute, in a Bernie Kopell as the doctor on *The Love Boat* kind of way. But as long as Bart lived, he'd have the horrible memory of the first time he found his so-called lover doing what he did best—destroying Bart's self-value.

It still gave Bart a jolt to recall Ed's numerous acts of betrayal. Bart always went semicatatonic when he remembered the first time Ed cheated on him. Or, more precisely, the first time Ed was caught.

It was an after-midnight hour, a year into their cohabitation. The night had progressed like many others: Bart had stayed awake as long as possible and finally retired to bed—alone. Ed stayed up to watch a porn movie in the living room. Soon, though, Bart was awakened by the dull report of their front screen door being closed and locked from the outside. Then the sound of the ignition turning over in Ed's Jaguar.

Bart recalled waking a couple of hours later to find Ed's side of the bed still cold and empty, the covers never turned down. Bart's first response was one of concern. In the distance were sounds, like hearing the ocean in a shell; muffled, unintelligible words heard through an air vent. Phantom noises came from beyond the closed second-bedroom door like smoke—a demonic apparition seeping through the narrow space between the carpet and door. Sounds that warranted investigation.

Calling out Ed's name in a low tone, Bart moved from the bed, through the room, and out into the hall.

The door to their second bedroom was closed. It was a room whose door had a peculiar attribute: A window had been installed at eye level to enable the previous tenant to keep an eye on her baby without disturbing its naps. Bart and Ed had never bothered to replace it with a proper solid door. Instead, they hung cheap, sheer drapes—the color and density of white nylon stockings—over the glass.

Approaching the door with the trepidation of a survivor come to identify the remains of a loved one, Bart peered through the window past the translucent curtains. His eyes witnessed the first heart-stopping disappointment of his life:

Ed.

Naked.

Embracing someone blond and naked.

Doing what he had taught Bart to do with him in the privacy of their bed.

Then the jaw clenching, wounded animal-like sound of an exhausting climax. The variety that is said to peel wallpaper in its steamy intensity.

To this day, the lingering impression in Bart's memory was that of arms–and legs—flailing like tangled octopuses.

Bart's agony was too large to swallow. Hot misery restricted his breath. He was unable to cry out in grief or express the volcanic rage that churned and melted his self-value. He couldn't even confront Ed or the intruder.

Instead, Bart retreated to bed and buried his face in his Laura Ashley pillow, sobbing for the loss of something intangible—fairy-tale dreams that could never come true. He wept for his own stupidity.

Morning arrived as slowly as payday. Horizontal bars of light, diffused through the slats of the bedroom's shuttered windows, revealed Ed in his accustomed place, sleeping soundly on his back. Naked. The sheet pulled nearly to his waist. An arrogant, conceited son of a bitch, Ed was oblivious to Bart's suffering. Ed was a stranger now. Unknown. Unknowable. An easy target for revenge—if Bart had the balls.

Crimes of passion occur all the time, Bart had almost convinced himself, thinking of the crazy movie actress who reportedly bonded her costar-lover's penis to his leg with Krazy glue while he slept. The story was memorable for its novelty.

Bart was still choking back tears later in the day when Ed telephoned him at the office. Ed had thought he'd gotten away with the infidelity. From Bart came a cold, monosyllabic response to Ed's cheerful greeting. When Bart finally explained his desolation, Ed was, at first, silent. Then he was sincere in his remorse and apologies. Then angry at being made to feel guilty.

By conversation's end, the circumstances of the night before were Bart's fault. "I can't be responsible for what happens when you're not around," Ed said. "It wouldn't have happened if you had stayed up with me last night."

Ever since then, Bart had purposely avoided falling in love. His occasional dates were for sex alone. Now, for a second time, just as he had started to trust a man again, Rod had betrayed him.

"Time to grow up!" Bart announced aloud. "Forget Rod. Forget Ed! Go out and find the ultimate marrying man!"

Bart figured if he couldn't have Dr. Niles Crane, he'd take Miles Silverberg, from the old *Murphy Brown* sitcom. He'd actually seen Miles at the gym one afternoon. The guy had a nice little bod.

But, on second thought, Miles, or the actor who played the wimpy television news-magazine-program producer, must have been an idiot to have left that hit show just before the curtain came down after seven or eight seasons. He wasn't even mentioned in the final farewell episode. It was as though the wrath of Candice Bergen or someone equally strong had closed the iron door on him. He appeared to be *persona non grata* in television.

It wasn't meant to work out with Rod, anyway, Bart decided. In retrospect, he could see that they were on different life paths. Rod was determined to do whatever he had to do in order to become a successful screenwriter. He'd popped so many different guys just waiting for a patsy like Bart to come along, someone he could manipulate into helping him get ahead in the biz. The only thing Bart really wanted was to settle down with a life partner. The guy didn't have to be rich and famous. In fact, the man of Bart's dreams was successful but not in showbiz. Ideally, they'd both want the same ranch-style house, a farm in the country. Their evenings would be spent giving intimate dinner parties and making love at night, before going to sleep, and again in the morning before going off to their respective jobs. They'd hold hands in public. They might even have a commitment ceremony.

Bart had been starting to think these were pipe dreams, but he was not one to give up hope for too long. He was innocent enough to actually believe that the fulfillment of all his dreams was just around the corner.

"CGA!" Mitch called, running into the coffee-break room in a panic, as agitated as if *Will & Grace* had been canceled. He came to a screeching halt beside Bart, who was pouring the dregs of a pot of java that had been left sitting on the burner half the day. "CGA! CGA!" This was Mitch's code. It meant "Cute Guy Alert."

"FedEx just send a new delivery boy?" Bart asked, taking a sip of what looked and smelled like burned molasses.

"No package—and I do mean that as a double entendre, if you get my drift." Mitch smiled facetiously, as if Bart might not get the joke. "This one doesn't transcend your old beau in the looks department, not by a long shot. But that's showbiz. You're in no position to be fussy, young man."

Mitch took a certain amount of pride in being the bearer of bad news just so he could be there to comfort the grieving party.

"What on the grave of Freddie Mercury are you yammering about?" Bart asked. "What's a glorified messenger have to do with me and my sex life in the first place. You know I'm not that kind of guy. That's *your boudoir*, remember?"

"He's not a menial. And he's not my cup of CGA, anyway. But I know you and your off-the-wall, bizarre sort of 'I'll-take-anything-on-the-thirty-one-flavors menu, please, and thank you.' You couldn't care less if it was Ryan Idol, Mitchell Anderson, Dan Butler, or Tom Brokaw as long as they were 'nice.' Whatever that means!"

"What's wrong with Tom Brokaw?" Bart feigned wounded pride.

"Nothing, except he's got a big ol' butt."

"Give Tom a break. That ass spread is from sitting in that damn anchor chair all these years. Notice he stands up now when he reads the TelePrompTer and talks all about what's going down in Bosnia or Chechnya? Don't forget you have a desk job, too. As the good book says, 'He that is with ass, let him cast the first bump and grind.'"

Bart sipped his coffee and made a face. "Is this alleged CGA person Mitchell Anderson cute or Dan Butler sexy?"

"More like that actor-who-used-to-be-on-*M**A*S*H cute."

"I guess Alan Alda's sexy, in a Michael Douglas sort of way," Bart teased, knowing how his offbeat taste in men infuriated Mitch.

"Not A.A. But I always thought Hawkeye was probably well hung. Loretta Swit wasn't named Hot Lips for nothing. No. I'm talking about the one who married Donna Reed's TV brat Mary, what's her face? She used to be on *Coach* when she got old. Hmmm . . ."

"Shelley Fabares?"

"Captain B. J.—blow job—Hunnicutt, that's the one, all right!"

"Mike Farrell?"

"But younger. Much, much, *much* younger. I'm so glad Mike's career has bounced back and he's on *Providence*. He has that *totally* cute son on the show."

Bart's interest was piqued. "UPS? FedEx? Sparklettes? I'm sure you'll let me know before the hour's up all about the 'package' Mike Farrell's Hollywood Wax Museum double delivers." Bart imagined the guy, in a uniform, being escorted to Shari's private powder room and Mitch locking the door behind them.

Mitch said, "Hell, I have absolutely no interest in this one, I assure you. Also, FYI, he doesn't deliver water or do overnighters, either. Well, the latter's just a guess. He looks as square as Alex Trebek. Is that still a word used for his type? Anyway, I leave this one to you, honey. I still feel guilty about the whole Jim/Rod situation. It breaks my heart to see you suffer. After all, it was *moi* who inadvertently got Butch and Slamdance together."

"It's no one's fault," Bart lied. Although he had immersed himself in his Sterling. work day after day since the breakup and wrote copious, mean-spirited, but truthful notes about his coworkers' behavior in his diary at night, he still could just barely summon the wherewithal to think about the concept of going out with another man. It had been only a month since he left Rod's room for the last time. "Broken-Hearted Me" was his new theme song. Damn that Anne Murray! He was on his *way* to being just fine, but if not having jacked off even once since the breakup was any indication, Bart had a way to go to full recovery.

"Rod and Jim as a couple? Pul-eese!" Bart said, mocking the spring-fall "romance." "Rod's not too young for Jim, but Jim's way too old for Rod."

Bart was trying to convince Mitch as well as himself that the match had no valid foundation and therefore was doomed. "Even though Rod's used to tricking with flabby gut relics who have to pay for sex, I give this 'relationship' six months, no more. Jim's a disgusting pig. It only hurts when I realize how much I was merely a means to an end for Rod. Just as Jim is now. If I thought Jim was anything more than a hustle from Rod, I'd actually be happy for both of them. I'd step aside and throw a party or something."

"You do that little thing, dear. If Ephram could let Dolly get on with her life, you can come out of mourning Rod. And here's your chance. Your Walter Matthau is in Shari's office having a meeting right this very *momento*."

"What's he meeting with Shari about? Don't tell me he's an actor or a writer," Bart pleaded. "And I don't do producers. I made the grave mistake of going off track and falling for the last guy on my list of before-I-die possibilities. When I start dating again, it'll be with someone from the top of my sensible list: a brilliant but boring seismologist from Caltech who will charm me with endless pillow talk about tectonic plates, the Richter scale, and volcanic eruptions."

Mitch preened. "I could be a seismologist. I know a lot about the earthshaking volcanic eruptions. As for eruptions with a seismologist from Caltech, forget it. You'll be lucky to get lukewarm oozing. But nothing volcanic, honey," Mitch deadpanned, doing a poor hands-on-hip impersonation of Pearl Bailey.

"Or else he'll be an architect who designs strip malls in Tucson, and his idea of domesticity is to have me for a lover, build a Victorian dollhouse for us to live in happily ever after, and make annual pilgrimages to Falling Waters and all the other Frank Lloyd Wright houses in

America. We'll spend Friday nights playing Monopoly, or entertaining successful, monogamous gay couples."

Mitch rolled his eyes. "Success as in 'filthy rich' or as in the other doesn't know what his lover's doing on the side. 'Cause trust me, sweetheart, you show me a couple who claim to be monogamous and I'll show you a couple who hide their porn and insist on getting the American Express bill sent to his office. Yawn."

What was the point of being gay, Mitch thought, if you didn't set your sights on *the* most beautiful men, not the average, everyday sort of Plain Joe that any *woman* could easily get. God, in His infinite wisdom, created gorgeous men, for one purpose: for other men to walk into lampposts over, to stay awake at night crying over, and to do things together that one's mother would have a heart attack over if she caught you. In other words, gorgeous men having sex with other gorgeous men. "You wouldn't think of sitting anywhere behind row twelve in the orchestra section for the ballet, darling, so why would you for an instant think of settling for a guy who wasn't at least the general population's idea of a sexual Adonis? Or Rupert Everett?"

"The general population seems to think Mick Jaggar is hot," Bart said. "I don't see it."

"Nah. Me, neither. But Garth Brooks . . . chub stud that he may be . . ."

"That's my point!" Bart declared. "I've done that with Rod. I never again want to date someone who'll be courted by every other beautiful man in town. I don't want the hassle." Bart paused. "But just out of curiosity, who is this CGA person with Shari, anyway?"

Mitch gave a cursory is-anybody-else-around-within-listening-range turn of his head and twitched a finger for Bart to come closer and be taken into his confidence. "Shari's interviewing personal dog trainers."

"Finally she's doing something about her barking and chasing after studio executives, er, mailmen," Bart teased.

"That's redundant."

"M-A-I-L. Not M-A-L-E."

Mitch grinned. "Anyway, he certainly must be *someone's* type. I'm placing a bet he's yours. So go dig up a press release, or better yet, a photo of Angelina Jolie—all her head shots need serious retouching, anyway, especially around those puffy, spaced-out eyes—and bring it down to Shari for approval. Come on, now. This is one chance I won't let you fuck up."

Mitch pushed Bart out the door of the break room and gave him a swack on the ass to get him started. Reluctantly, Bart went back to his office, where he picked up a file folder with a draft of a press release announcing new casting of the studio's soon-to-be-produced remake of *Mr. Peabody and the Mermaid.* Hilary Swank just bailed out.

He walked down to Shari's office. "Just go in," Mitch prodded.

Bart took a deep breath and walked with purpose into the room. "Shari?" he called. "Oh. Sorry, I didn't realize you were in a meeting." He paused halfway into the room. Shari clicked her tongue in irritation. "What do you want? Can't you see I'm busy?"

"Sorry. It's the Hilary Swank press release you wanted written in a hurry. I'll just put it in your box. Would you please approve it as soon as possible?"

Mitch was right about the guy sitting opposite Shari. He was very definitely Bart's idea of attractive. In a hazy, sort of out-of-focus way, he looked like a younger Mike Farrell. And there was a resemblance to Tom Wopat, too. Bart made a point of looking straight into the guy's green eyes as he was addressing Shari. The guy smiled and nodded his head, a nonverbal introduction.

"Just go away," Shari snarled. Then she reeled herself in, trying to control her tone of voice. To Bart it suggested she was doing her best not to fly off the handle in front of a guest.

"Again, sorry," Bart said, still looking at the Mike Farrell/Tom Wopat fresh-from-grad-school-spit-polished CGA. "As I said, I'll just put it in your box." Bart placed the manila file folder on top of her overflowing stack of papers. He retreated toward the outer office, turned once, and saw the guy looking at Bart's reflection in the glass of a framed poster of *Marked Woman,* starring Bogart and Bette Davis, behind Shari's desk. Bart had once looked that film up in *Leonard Maltin's Movie & Video Guide:* 1937, "Bristling gangster drama of D.A., Bogart convincing Bette and four girlfriends to testify against their boss, underworld king Ciannelli." Bart always thought that poster apropos hanging where it did.

Back in the anti-office, Bart said to Mitch, "Mmmm. I like. What are his stats?"

"Shall I put it in your 'box?'" Mitch said, castigating Bart's announcement of where he was placing the file folder. "You wish!"

"Sounded stupid, but I was extra nervous!"

"Here. I made a copy of the CGA's dog-training brochure. It speaks volumes, especially if you read between the lines. Grrrr. Now go back to your office and study this, because you'll be quizzed when I send him down to you."

"Oh, don't," Bart protested. "He smiled at me, but who knows? Maybe he's just trying to get a job. He could have been smiling out of sheer nervousness."

"He doesn't need a job. He's doing this as a favor to Warren Beatty. Anyway, from what I can tell, *he's* interviewing Shari—not the other way around."

"Why do I feel like Agnes Gooch and you're Auntie Mame, sending me to a party with Brian O'Bannion?"

"Because 'Life is a banquet, darling!' Are you never going to let me make amends for Fallongate? I consider myself completely responsible for your asshole. And I don't necessarily mean the one who dumped you."

"I'm going back to my office," Bart confirmed. "But do not, I repeat, *do not* send him down to me unless you've thoroughly cross-examined him. If he's found guilty of interest in at least the second degree, okay? No less. Promise?"

"On Shari's grave!"

"That's my real fantasy."

Chapter Thirteen

"I'm closing my door for a while," Bart said to Cheets. "If a dog trainer comes looking for me, let him in."

"Since when did you get a doggie?" she asked in her usual have-to-know-it-all prying manner.

"I'm thinking about buying one."

"Poor little beast. I mean the dog. You're never home. You'll have a latchkey puppy. It'll grow up to be as dysfunctional as—"

Bart closed his door on her and crossed to his desk chair. *As dysfunctional as me?* he supposed was Cheets's unheard assessment.

He sat down, turned on the CD player on the credenza behind him, and filled the room with the sound track from *Somewhere in Time*. He looked at the glossy, three-color brochure, which featured the CGA wearing jeans and a khaki safari shirt rolled up above his elbows. He was kneeling beside four dogs of various breeds and offering a blinding smile for the camera. The photo caption read: *Dr. Rusty Stone (center) and family.*

Bart began reading the text of the brochure:

RUSSELL STONE, Ph.D.
Domestic Animal Behaviorist

A graduate of Exeter Agricultural Institute, with a master's in animal husbandry, and a doctorate in veterinary medicine from UC Davis, Russell "Rusty" Stone is one of the leading animal trainers–both wildlife and domestic pets–in the United States. His devotion to . . .

There was a knock on the door. "It's unlocked," Bart called as he pushed the brochure aside and picked up a sheaf of papers and a red pen, pretending to be editing the text of the press kit for Diane Keaton's new comedy.

The door opened, and the CGA person—or young Mike Farrell/Tom Wopat clone—beamed as he poked his head in. "Bart?"

"Guilty." Bart smiled back, pretending not to recognize whom he was speaking to, let alone that they had just exchanged vibrations in Shari's office.

"I'm Rusty Stone. Mitch said you were having problems with your schnoodle?"

Cheets howled. "Is that what they're calling it now?" She laughed a booming, hear-me-in-the-last-row-of-the-balcony voice.

Bart shook his head in a "Don't pay any attention to her" gesture.

Rusty went on. "Mitch asked me to come down to see if I could help you out."

"Oh, you're the animal trainer from Shari's office. Sorry, I didn't recognize you. You were sitting down. I didn't know you were so tall. Come in. Close the door."

"Is this a good time? I don't want to interrupt your work."

"Yes. It's perfect. Almost time to wrap it up and get the heck out of Dodge, anyway, so to speak. Have a seat. So, you train animals? Shari's certainly an interesting breed, isn't she? She really needs discipline—or, rather, her Jack Russell needs discipline. Shari just needs a muzzle and some doggie downers."

"*Saturday Night Live,* the mock commercial," Rusty said, relating to the doggie downers reference.

"You remember that one?"

"Jane Curtin, wasn't it? How about Quarry, the breakfast cereal?"

"One of my all-time favorites." Bart laughed. "I thought it was a real commercial. 'Bass-O-Matic' and all that John Belushi stuff was too over the top. A lot of great stuff over the years. Wish Lorne Michaels had been able to keep up that originality."

"Love your choice in music, by the way." Rusty indicated the CD player. "That's my favorite score. Actually, anything by John Barry is my favorite, and much of Richard Rodney Bennett."

"The love theme from *Nicholas and Alexandra!*"

"My God. I thought I was the only one who knew about his genius."

Bart said, "Dare I expose my ardent admiration for Karen Carpenter and jeopardize bursting this bubble?"

"My heart is still broken," Rusty said solemnly. "I went to her funeral."

"So did I!"

They stared at one another for a long moment, in that way people do when they visit the Louvre for the first time and suddenly turn around and unexpectedly find Aphrodite. The real, original Aphrodite. There is awe and wonder that transcends words.

Finally coming up out of his reverie, Rusty began telling Bart how difficult it would be to train Shari's dog, since Shari herself could not be bothered with finding the time to be present for any of the sessions. He explained how important it was for the master or the mistress to be there for each lesson and to work with the pet throughout the week. "It's not like sending an inconvenient child away to a convent or boarding school. A dog doesn't just come home for Thanksgiving and Christmas vacations."

As Rusty spoke, Bart surreptitiously broke eye contact for a split second to glance at Rusty's ring finger. No wedding band. The furtive glance was not lost on Rusty, who took a moment of his own to look at Bart's hands. A signet ring adorned his right-hand ring finger. Nothing on the left. They both smiled at each other. If they'd been the stars of that old television series *My Favorite Martian,* this is where their antenna would have protruded from their respective skulls: Their gaydar was transmitting signals back and forth like NASA to the Hubble telescope.

"So, about your schnoodle?" Rusty broke the spell but kept his perennial smile.

Bart decided to level with him. He didn't want to play games or lie and then have to try to remember what he'd said that wasn't true, only half-true, only completely false. "Listen. I'm really sorry. I don't have a schnoodle."

"That's too bad," Rusty said with a mischievous grin.

"Mitch sent you down here because—"

"You were anxious to find a new schnoodle to replace your old schnoodle?" Rusty interrupted. "He said you were in a quandary, that you didn't want to make the same mistake and tackle a big schnoodle when perhaps a standard-size schnoodle would do."

"In a manner of speaking." Bart laughed. "Oh, that Mitch. He always knows how to make a guy uncomfortable."

"No need to feel anything but what you're feeling. I've known Mitch forever. He's definitely a bitch. In dog terms, I mean. But he also said some other things. Since you're about to leave, what do you say we have dinner and talk about . . . schnoodles? Or just teaching old dogs new tricks?"

"Now that's the kind of training I could use," Bart said. "I need a little discipline—about leaving the office at a reasonable time, anyway. Let's go."

Bart quickly cleared his desk, turned off his computer, put his telephone on CALL FORWARD and opened the door, allowing Rusty to lead the way. "I'm outta here, Cheets," Bart called. "See you in the morning."

Exiting Sterling's publicity building, Bart and Rusty walked past soundstages 14, 15, and 16, eventually arriving at the employee parking structure. Along the way, Bart gave Rusty a brief history lesson about the classic films that had been made on the lot.

"Anyplace in particular you'd like to eat?" Rusty asked.

"Anywhere we can talk over a bottle of wine."

"Italian all right? How about La Strega, over on Ventura? Great food and not too noisy."

"I love that place. Meet you there in about twenty. Depending on traffic."

"Don't try the freeway this time of night," Rusty suggested. "Take Riverside to Coldwater, then up to Ventura. I'll call from the car and get a table on the patio. It's such a nice evening, we shouldn't be stuck indoors."

During the ride to the restaurant Bart conjured up thoughts about Rusty: Here was a guy, obviously intelligent (if the academic credentials mentioned in his brochure were any indication), attractive, sensitive enough to work with animals, seemingly unattached, and making the first move to suggest they have dinner. Bart had, just that morning, decided to consider the idea that he might begin to see other men. But he didn't think he'd actually meet anyone, at least not so quickly. He had been busy and, frankly, just not interested. Until now.

"Don't get ahead of yourself, Bart," he said to himself as he drove along the route, staying as close behind Rusty's carnival red Jaguar as traffic allowed. "It's only dinner, for crying out loud. You might not even have anything to really talk about."

He knew that he had a habit of looking on the negative side of potential relationships. God knows, after being burned by Rod, he wasn't getting his hopes up too high.

By the time Bart found a parking space along a side street and walked into the restaurant, it was five minutes after Rusty had been seated at a table exactly as he'd said, on the patio, under an outdoor gas heater. Springtime evenings in Los Angeles were usually chilly. The desert cooled down at night except when the Santa Ana winds were blowing. This was not one of those nights. The hostess escorted Bart to the table, and Rusty stood up like a gentleman and shook Bart's hand, as if they hadn't seen each other in a long time and were keeping a long-standing dinner engagement.

Within moments of Bart's unfolding his white linen napkin and placing it on his lap, the waiter came over with a bottle of Cabernet Sauvignon. "I hope you don't mind," Rusty explained, "I took the liberty of ordering a bottle. You do like red, don't you?"

"Absolutely," Bart said as the waiter displayed the bottle for Rusty's approval. As soon as the cork was removed, Rusty advised the waiter that there was no need for the pretentious gesture of taste-testing the wine before both glasses were filled. "I trust you implicitly," he said, smiling, thus ingratiating himself to the waiter.

It was soon evident that Rusty was the type of individual who charmed everybody he met. The lowliest bread boy and the restaurant's owner were equals in his eyes. They were all treated with the same respect and consideration. *Thank-yous* (but not the obsequious, overly courtly type of gestures) were distributed equally to the shy young man who poured olive oil from a cruet into a ceramic dish for dipping sponges of bread, to the waiter's recitation of the evening's menu specials, to the refilling of their wineglasses before they were empty, to the brushing of crumbs off the tablecloth, to the return of his American Express card after the check had been signed.

By the end of the evening, after exchanging respective, abbreviated life stories, including mention of recent disastrous relationships, both men could hardly believe where the time had gone. Both had enjoyed the same meal: chicken risotto, no dessert, and a cup each of peppermint tea. To their mutual amazement, they found that although their careers were completely different, their appreciation of specific music and literature (classic and popular) and film and theater (they had both seen the same shows during their initial Broadway runs) was practically identical. There had not been a single instance during the night when either had pretended to agree with the other when it came to the merits of particular writers, artists, and political and religious figures, past and present.

"My God. We're like Richard Bach and Leslie Parrish," Rusty said. Bart caught the reference to the author of *Jonathan Livingston Seagull* and *Illusions* and his wife.

"They're absolute soul mates," Bart agreed.

The latter title, they both vehemently agreed in unison, was really the Bible and *not* a work of fiction.

"Well," suggested Bart, "we can't let this be the last of our conversations, can we? What's on your agenda for this Friday night?"

"You are," Rusty said, leaning forward across the table to speak. "I'm clearing my calendar. This time, I'll cook."

"He cooks, too!" Bart exclaimed to no one in particular and yet to the entire restaurant. "What can I bring?"

"Sounds cliché, but just bring yourself. And your schnoodle." Rusty was wearing the roguish grin again. "Oh, that's right." He snapped his fingers in mock disappointment. "You don't have one. Pooh. Guess we'll have to make due with my schnauzer."

Both men were laughing as they got up from the table and exited the restaurant. Once outside, as Rusty was waiting for the valet attendant to bring his Jaguar around, he said, "One last confession before you go. When I left Shari's office, I was the one who asked Mitch who the guy was who had interrupted the meeting. You looked . . . adorable, although I must say a bit intimidated by Shari. I thought to myself, *Hmmm, this guy's interesting.*"

Bart confessed, "You're the only good thing that's ever come out of 'Scary Shari's' office! Usually it's just four-letter words that she hurls at me."

"You deserve more respect," Rusty said seriously. "We all do. After I observed her treatment of you, I told her I couldn't train her dog. I don't work for, or associate with, the kind of people who give off Shari's low-level vibrations. There's too much odious energy emanating from her chi. I could feel it as strongly as I feel the opposite from you."

Bart was speechless, aware that he was definitely smitten with Rusty. Especially with the man's positive outlook on life. Ever since beginning his job at Sterling, Bart had struggled with being surrounded by negative energy. The attitudes of the upper-level managers to whom he reported as well as the egos of the stars and the downtrodden secretaries and assistants combined to make the atmosphere of the publicity department redolent with cynicism, fear, and malevolence. These were among the reasons Bart hated working in Hollywood. It wasn't his job he disliked. The writing was, for the most part, pleasant enough. It was the difficult, unhappy personalities with whom he had to interact twelve to fourteen hours a day that caused his anxiety. It was starting to dawn on him that these caustic attitudes and negative vibrations were insinuating themselves into his own temperament. As if through osmosis he was absorbing the cynical characteristics of those with whom he worked. It was not a pretty sight.

When Rusty's car arrived, he hugged Bart good night. Then he thanked the valet and handed him a five-dollar tip. Rusty raised his hand to acknowledge good-bye as he pulled into traffic on Ventura.

Bart floated the two blocks to his car, realizing that aside from the brief disclosure of his most recent relationship, he hadn't thought of Rod at all during the evening. For the first time since meeting Rod in January, he drove home with renewed interest in his own life.

Chapter Fourteen

Rod closed the sliding-glass door to his room as he sang the theme song from the old television comedy *The Jeffersons.*

He was moving up, all right, to Jim Fallon's dee-luxe mansion in the Hollywood Hills. Rod was leaving West Hollywood for good and not about to look back. After weeks of skillful maneuvering and convincing Jim that their sex life was mutually extraordinary, Rod got the invitation he'd been wrangling for—and a charge account at the Gap.

Rod had quit his job at the Trap and deleted his Rotoroot4U screen name from AOL. He tried to maintain one important vestige of his past—his gym membership—but Jim wouldn't hear of it and surprised him by turning an unused wardrobe closet (the size of Rod's old room) into a weight-lifting area. Jim even promised to hire a personal trainer.

"For yourself, maybe," Rod said with indignation, then quickly realized he'd blundered. "I mean, we're never too young to do cardio," he amended, feigning consideration for Jim's health. He couldn't have Jim thinking that he had any complaints about his ugly body. That could spoil Rod's plans.

The office for Rod that Jim had set up and decorated came complete with a brand-new computer, a huge oak desk, matching file cabinets, and a personal account at Staples for all the supplies he would need to continue his writing. Unfortunately, however, Rod's writing time was becoming less and less productive. Day after day he got to the computer later and later. He'd no sooner sit in the plush leather chair and begin a new scene for his new screenplay than Jim would show up with a martini in one hand and his cock in the other.

As far as Jim was concerned, he was keeping Rod and was therefore entitled to sex whenever he damn well felt horny, which was at least twice during the day, again at bedtime, during the night if he woke up, and of course, first thing in the morning, when he was at his most randy—and least attractive. Halitosis was not a pleasant wake-up call.

Rod, having no place else to go, no job, and no extra cash from the tricks he used to troll for over the Internet, was basically a prisoner, albeit on an extraordinary estate. "The Island of Dr. Morose," he called it. If he didn't submit to Jim's sexual demands, they had arguments, which ultimately led to Jim's feelings being hurt and Rod giving in, anyway, just to appease Jim and maintain the status quo. It wasn't that Rod was afraid of being thrown out of Jim's hilltop manse. He'd find other digs soon enough. He was more concerned that *Blind as a Bat* wouldn't get produced if Jim lost interest in him. Nothing else but the screenplay mattered to Rod.

Michael, too, was coming around more often, doing what he could with what clout he had to resurrect Jim's crash-and-burn career. At Jim's behest, Michael was supposedly representing Rod's work as well.

As far as Rod was concerned, Michael dropped by "Fallon's Lair" too often—especially when he'd arranged an audition for Jim. He made it known to Rod right away that he, too, expected sex in exchange for prestigious Actors and Others representation. "When the cat's away . . ." He grinned when he came to collect his reward for not telling Jim about Rod's past life. And he came to collect often.

Amazingly, sex with Michael wasn't altogether unpleasant for Rod, especially not after all the pawing from the inner-tube-waisted, pimple-butted Jim. A simple blow job wasn't enough for Michael; it never had been. He expected Rod to load up on beer and clean out his kidneys the way he used to do in the back room of the Trap.

So, not only was Rod not getting any work done; he wasn't using the gym equipment, mainly because Jim liked to watch, which inevitably led to his getting horny for Rod's perspiration-soaked body. Now Rod was starting to show slight signs of a gut from lack of exercise and all the beers he consumed to please Michael's predilections. No one but Rod noticed the change in his physique, but the subtle difference was there. Soon, he thought, he'd start to look old, which was a crime in Hollywood. Rod, who had thought he was in control of his life situation, realized now that his career was in the hands of two men he despised.

"March that tight ass into the steam room," Michael demanded one afternoon when Jim was out reading for a bit part on *The Practice*. Rather than have his clothes wet and stinking from Rod's water sports, both men stripped nude before stepping into the custom built steam facility. There, with the humidity turned up to New Orleans in July, both men perspired copiously as they engaged in a variation on their long-standing practice.

Over the past weeks, there had been a couple of close calls when Jim returned home sooner than expected. The first time, Michael and Rod were finished with their business and were zipping up their pants and buttoning their shirts when they heard the bell sound indicating that the electric gate was opening. They had approximately two minutes to clean away any evidence of their games and rush to the office, where they pretended to be discussing a scene from *Blind as a Bat*.

On another occasion, they had not closed the gate when Michael arrived. Therefore, no warning bell sounded when Jim drove up to the house. Fortunately, Rod had already dressed and was back in his office. Michael, however, was still upstairs when Jim suddenly opened the front door and walked in. He stopped in Rod's office and asked, "Where's Michael? His car's outside."

Rod, though startled, pretended to be typing away at a furious pace. He quickly came up with the truth, "Upstairs. Bathroom. Didn't feel well." Rod faked being absorbed in his work but was typing nonsensical words onto his computer. He added, "Maybe the flu. Heard him throwing up."

"He's not using *my* bathroom, I hope!"

"Don't know. He just raced upstairs."

"Don't you have a bathroom right here in the office?" Jim said, scrutinizing Rod.

"For Christ sake," Rod exploded, "you think I want to hear that freak hurling while I'm trying to work?"

"Sorry," Jim said in a conciliatory tone. "Don't fly off the handle. I was just curious."

Just then, unaware that Jim had come home, Michael came down the stairs and swaggered into the office, where he saw Jim standing by a bookshelf. Michael's shirt was untucked and unbuttoned, and his hair was wet. He had looked as white as a sheet after retching his guts out upstairs, but when he suddenly saw Jim, he turned beet red, as if he really had a fever.

Rod immediately took control of the situation. "Feeling any better, Michael?" he asked in a tone that read: Play along with where I'm going. "Hope it's not the flu."

"Er, yeah, I'll be fine. I think my stomach didn't agree with something." Michael quickly buttoned his shirt and tucked the tails into his pants. He combed his hair back with his fingers.

"Probably that all-natural drink you were so enthusiastic about guzzling down," Rod razzed.

"There's some Pepto in the medicine cabinet," Jim offered. "Maybe you should lie down for a while."

"No, I'll just go back to the office. I'll be fine once everything's out of my system." He glared at Rod.

Jim walked his agent to the front door. Before reaching the foyer, he asked, "Are you and Rod getting along? I know there was some hostility in the beginning."

"He can be an asshole sometimes, but I'm keeping him busy. Doing rewrites on the script. It's none of my business why he's here, but it's probably for the best, at least for now—until the studio buys the screenplay and the film is a go. It's gonna happen eventually. Until then, as long as he's happy, we should all be okay."

"With all the changes we're making, I'd say we'll be in a decent position to eventually arbitrate with the WGA to get the screenplay credit." Jim grinned.

"Don't think that's not why I'm having him make so many changes."

"I like Rod being around here just 'cause he's so fucking sexy. The screenplay's a bonus. I may even keep him after the screenplay's sold. He thinks I'm hot stuff."

Jim didn't notice Michael's look of incredulity.

"By the way, the audition you sent me on sucked," Jim complained. "Why do I still have to audition, anyway? Doesn't anybody know I'm a friggin' star, for Christ sake?"

"*Past-tense* friggin' star."

"It's so humiliating. I just know those casting assholes were mocking me as I left the reading today." Jim was almost in tears. "They were thinking of that fucking tape, which they've probably all seen. How come Wayne Knight is working as a regular on three prime-time shows simultaneously, plus he has about five thousand national commercials all airing at the same time?"

"Because everybody likes Wayne Knight. And he doesn't do porn. At least not that I know of."

"Everybody used to like Jim Fallon!"

"Listen. Someday, when you get that Oscar, they'll be licking your boots. Even Wayne Knight. Trust me."

Jim and Michael walked outside and down the steps toward

Michael's Mercedes. Suddenly, Michael put his hand to his mouth, ran to brace himself against the trunk of a tree, and vomited again, this time drenching some newly planted peonies.

"Christ, Michael," Jim said, "the gardener's costing me a fortune. Couldn't you do that someplace else?"

As Michael weaved his way to his car, Jim went on: "Anything else coming up—a part, I mean—that I might be right for? It's driving me nuts to stay in the house all day."

"Hell, at least you've got Rod." Michael wiped his mouth with a tissue and blotted perspiration from his forehead. Getting into the car, he buckled his seat belt and pushed a CD into the stereo. "A stud like that has got to provide hours of diversion. Better than just sitting in your screening room watching DVDs of porn and whacking off."

When Jim returned to the house, he sang out, "Teatime," in a voice loud enough to reach the office where Rod sat staring at his computer monitor.

"Christ," Rod said softly. He cringed.

What Jim meant by "teatime" was that it was time for the first of his six or more martinis of the night. What it meant for Rod was that Jim would become disgustingly amorous. Rod would try to keep up with Jim's drinking just to anesthetize his loathing of the sex Jim would ultimately insist on.

It was during times like these that Rod missed the diverse guys who had responded to his E-mails in the past. At least then it wasn't the same old fart four or five times a day. Rod also conceded that there were many times when he actually missed Bart, who was both sexy and sweet. Bart never made demands. In fact, he was always the one trying to please. Jim, on the other hand, was simply a mean, selfish drunk.

However, Jim and Michael were still stringing him along. Paramount, Fox, Sterling, Disney, and Miramax were seriously considering the screenplay. This kept Rod from going out of his head and literally killing Jim during sex.

Killing Jim wouldn't have been difficult, and Rod had come up with several plot twists in the scenario of their life together. Considering some of the sex toys Jim enjoyed playing with and the drugs he consumed along with the vast amounts of alcohol, a death would be easily accomplished. Jim could drown in the pool, for one. The games he liked could get slightly out of hand and end up wringing the air out of him.

But Rod was a writer, not a killer. Although, he thought, sometimes a person could be both, couldn't he? Books by mass murderers had been best-sellers. But Rod could not see himself in prison, serving a life sentence and becoming some con's bitch. He wanted to be famous, not *infamous*. Therefore, whatever Jim wanted, Rod was resigned to giving him—at least for the time being.

Equally difficult for Rod as sex with Jim was going out to parties with him. On this issue Bart had been mistaken. Dinners and premieres did not get easier to attend. It wasn't comfortable to be the young stud living the high life off the spoils of an older man. Straight men could leech off their famous wives, and women had been doing it for centuries. But two men—one young and devastatingly handsome, the other older, fatter, and rich—still raised eyebrows.

However, a few people he'd met actually tried to be nice to Rod, especially old queens. Whether it was because of his extraordinary good looks or because they were being condescending in their own way, Rod could only guess. But he could sense that people were, if not talking, at least thinking thoughts about him and his relationship with Jim.

Bart's scenario about scrutinizing other dinner-party guests for common procedures of etiquette was nothing like what Rod had to endure. Rod's table manners had become impeccable. He used the correct utensils, learned not to have too many glasses of wine with dinner, and kept himself respectfully distant from the serving help. Inevitably, however, a rude guest would pose a question of the table regarding current political events or moral issues during coffee and dessert, then, in a patronizing tone, ask what Rod's thoughts were on the issue.

"Rod, dear," a face-lifted Nancy Reagan–type shoe store heiress would say, "you're from an ethnic culture that many of us have not had the privilege of experiencing except vicariously through our respective household staffs, bless their hearts. Perhaps you could tell us the views of your people on California's new strict crime codes for juvenile delinquents?"

Guests at the table would invariably become silent. Coffee cups would clink back onto their Dresden-china saucers. All eyes would turn to Rod, from whom they expected nothing more than *"No hablo inglés."* Instead, after a theatrical pause for the curious to come to a prejudged conclusion, Rod would begin to speak. His enunciation was clear and considered.

"First of all, I am an American citizen, as are my, as you put it, 'people' *'Mi familia,'* as you might expect me to say. But I will be more than delighted to offer my personal point of view on the subject to which you're obviously referring: the state legislation in which transgressors—

as young as fourteen—will be subjected to adult-style incarceration to fit certain crimes."

A simple declarative sentence, spoken with authority, as if from a professor of cultural anthropology, never failed to achieve Rod's desired impact: undivided attention and genuine interest.

"I imagine you quite understand that as a result of this law, youths—who in many cases may still be merely suspects in a case—will have their names in the press prior to actually being charged with any specific crime. They may ultimately be sentenced to jail time in adult facilities, thus ensuring negative hope for rehabilitation. This, of course, translates to a virtual guarantee that troubled juveniles will have little choice but to turn to a life of crime as adults.

"In the long run, society doesn't become better off by subjecting youths to adult punishment for their crimes. Countless studies have found that in other jurisdictions in which teens were placed in adult facilities, the youths were more likely to commit new crimes following their release than comparable youngsters from juvenile facilities.

"I would say that to reduce crime, our government might want to consider more rehabilitation for youngsters rather than sending them to adult prisons, where they eventually return to society as adult criminals."

By the time Rod completed his discourse, the other guests, predictably, were dumbfounded. The old bitch who'd tried to steer Rod into the embarrassing corner, hoping he would fumble and reveal himself to be a vapid intruder into their superior society, was the one who was revealed to be the fool. Rod's rapier responses to similar questions posed to him wherever he and Jim went out were the only aspect of these evenings satisfying to Rod. But he nevertheless knew he was on display as the stud Jim Fallon was keeping. He was a sideshow freak: a sexy stud with a mind and the verbal capacity to speak that mind. An idiot savant.

"Now," he would say, addressing his opponent, "perhaps you would care to share your views on the plight of Tibetans struggling against Chinese occupation of their homeland for the past forty years?

"No? How about Chrissie Hynde's arrest for protesting in the window of a Gap store against what she claimed was the use of leather from illegally slaughtered cows in India.

"Not too keen on that one, either, eh? Perhaps you have a view on the new Elizabeth Taylor doll from Mattel? She's costumed as Cleopatra."

That particular dinner ended quickly after this altercation. During the drive home Jim complained, "Don't *ever* embarrass me in front of my friends like that again, you little shit."

"Who's the shit?" Rod retorted. "The bitch who tried to make us both look like fools? Or you? These people aren't your friends. Tomorrow morning they'll all be on the phone with each other, gabbing about who was at the party. That sicko Jim Fallon and his new trick. However, if just one says, 'You know, we misjudged Jim, he's found himself a kid with a brain,' living with you would be worth the god-damned effort."

"If I'm such an effort, you can just move out!"

"Don't think I wouldn't!"

"They're probably saying, 'That's the last time we ever invite those two faggots again,'" Jim yelled, drunk on martinis. "Tell me, how many times have we been to the same home for dinner since we met? Only once!"

"But they're all getting a turn to play host to one of the most famous ex-stars of our time!"

"Don't say that!" Jim cried. "Don't ever say I'm an *ex*-star!"

By now, he was blubbering, seated on the passenger side of his Rolls-Royce. Rod maneuvered the car along Mulholland, finally arriving at their home on Woodrow Wilson. The gates parted, and they proceeded up the long drive. Jim had to be helped from the car and practically carried into the house and laid out on the bed. On nights like these, Rod gave Jim one last stiff drink to get him to pass out, then left him alone.

By morning, Jim had usually forgotten the incident at whatever dinner party they had attended. "Did we enjoy ourselves last night?" he asked Rod, holding an ice pack to his throbbing temple. It wasn't the royal "We"; it was an honest-to-God-I-don't-remember-a-thing question.

"Just fine," Rod said. "As usual, you were the life of the party. Don't forget to call Karen Valentine and thank her for her extraordinary filet mignon."

"Don't they know I don't eat red meat?" Jim protested. "Did I rave about how good it was? How many drinks did I have?"

"Just a couple. But you had a couple before we left, too."

"Who else was there?" Jim asked, making a mental note to let Karen Valentine know he really did have a wonderful evening.

"Let's see, Stockard Channing, who lives down the street; Lorna Patterson and Michael Lembeck, who came all the way in from Malibu; Sally Kellerman, who I think also lives on the street; Lainie Kazan, and

Alan Seus. Oh, and that bitch we keep running into, the department-store heiress. The one who always tries to make me look like a fucking fool? But be nice when you call Karen. I like her. She treats me like I'm part of the family."

"I suppose we have to reciprocate one of these days," Jim said. "We can't keep accepting invitations and not return the courtesy."

"Hell, you just had that big party when your show was canceled. That should keep us in good stead for years! Any idea what that shindig cost you?"

"What do you care?"

"It must have been bloody expensive. You don't know the value of a buck."

Jim rolled his eyes. Now that he didn't have a steady income, Rod kept reminding him that every purchase was a major issue. If anybody knew the value of a dollar, it was Rod. He counted the years he'd hustled for rent and gas money and enough change to buy a cheeseburger at McDonald's. If the fleeting thought of one day suing Jim for palimony, as his so-called girlfriend had (and failed), was ever to be worth his trouble, he didn't want Jim spending everything ahead of time.

"Did we do it when we came home last night?" Jim asked with a grin.

"Oh, yeah, you were an animal," Rod lied, hoping it would keep Jim at arm's length for a few more hours. If Jim had thought he simply went straight to bed, he would have felt cheated. "I'm still worn out," Rod said.

Karen Valentine wasn't too thrilled to hear from Jim when he called to express his sincere thanks for a lovely evening. She was polite but distant.

"So glad someone enjoyed themselves," she said with a cold tone in her voice. She had already heard from nearly every other guest, all of whom, without exception, vowed never to return if that drunken old Jim Fallon and his insolent faggot toy-boy were present. "How can you be friends with those two creeps?" the Nancy Reagan–like shoe-store heiress asked. Karen had tried to smooth things over. "They're really nice once you get to know them," she said.

"I never want to know them," the heiress scoffed, and hung up.

"Yes," Karen said to Jim, "I'd love to have dinner with you and Rod one of these days. I'll call you when I get back from New York." She wasn't planning on going to New York, but it sounded like a good excuse at the time. She just hoped she didn't run into either of them at Gelson's.

* * *

As the weeks passed and the script began to take on a completely different story line than Rod originally wrote, he became angrier with Jim and Michael. The studio most interested, it seemed, was Sterling, the one whose story analyst had liked the script in the first place just the way it was. But still there was no firm deal.

"You read the original coverage, Michael. Why mess with what was considered brilliant in the first place?" Rod demanded.

"Hey, it's not me," Michael countered. "The creative exec wants to package this thing for Ashley Judd and Nic Cage. They need specific changes before they can even approach them."

"Why not just send them the script the way I wrote it, for Christ sake?"

"You don't know the business, you little bastard. This is how it's done, okay? It has to be properly packaged. You wouldn't put Sharon Stone with Julie Andrews, would you?"

"Wouldn't you? They might hit it off."

"Don't be an idiot," Michael scoffed. "Do you want to make a sale or don't you? There are steps and procedures to follow. Got it?"

Rod was bursting with anger and resentment. On the one hand, he had come this far and couldn't let something like "creative differences" interfere with success. On the other hand, all his years of hard work—especially on *Blind as a Bat*—seemed to have been wasted.

There was hardly anything left of the original story. Instead of a Mr. Magoo-like building superintendent in New York who causes all manner of trouble for the tenants and building owner, the main character was now a recovering-alcoholic plumber whose life is turned upside down when a distant relative dies and leaves the building to him in her will. However, an evil Donald Trump–like gazzilionaire plans to raze it, and several blocks of brownstones, to make room for building the tallest skyscraper in the world and tries to pull a fast one on the alcoholic plumber. To Rod, the new plot sucked as badly as Jim Fallon's fellatio technique.

Almost nightly, as Rod lay naked under the sheets beside a snoring Jim, he thought of two things: the screenplay and Bart. With every rasping snore coming from Jim's nose and throat, Rod was nauseated by the idea of having to deep-kiss the oinker in the morning. The only thing that saved his sanity was thinking about the imminent sale of his screenplay and maybe fucking Bart again. Playing this game would eventually be worth the payoff.

God, what a kick it would be if Sterling Studios actually bought the project, Rod thought each night after Jim had passed out from booze or sex or both. *It would mean being on my own again and* working *with Bart, who'd be doing the publicity. Bart would interview me for the press kit, maybe even write a feature article. The title could be: "Novice Scribe at 'Bat.'"* Rod smiled to himself as he considered his clever play on the title of his script, thinking about the publicity fanfare surrounding him when he finally became a famous screenwriter.

How would Bart handle the situation of our working together? he wondered, frowning. *How could I make things up to him and let him know not to take it personally that I dumped him, that it was just a career move.* "I didn't mean to hurt you, Bart," Rod whispered almost inaudibly. "But business is business."

The big guilt trip Rod suffered was knowing that Bart probably would not have done anything similar if given the chance, even for a big raise and promotion or a book deal with a major New York publisher. Bart wasn't the type to screw someone over for personal benefit. Rod knew this, but he tried to rationalize that anyone who didn't take advantage of an opportunity delivered on a silver platter was a loser, Bart included.

But that thought never stuck. Rod didn't think of Bart as a loser. He just wasn't a big winner the way Rod was determined to be.

Nightly, as Rod lay awake thinking of Bart, he invariably got a raging hard-on. He tried to will it away lest Jim should awaken and find him with a boner. If Jim reached over, even in his sleep, and found Rod's meat steaming, he'd be wide awake in a flash, gnawing away at a midnight snack. Same thing in the morning. After his dreaming of Bart, or any of the guys he used to trick with, Rod's pipe would be inevitably dripping. Trying desperately to will himself flaccid so he could pretend to be asleep if Jim began cuddling and investigating between his legs, Rod resorted to jacking off as quietly and with as little movement as possible. The sheets were always a mess when the maid came in, but Rod didn't care what Juanita thought. Thinking of Bart could actually be effective when Jim started in. "Hell, I do what I have to do!" was Rod's mantra. "So screw Bart. And screw Jim!"

Rod rolled over and went to sleep.

Chapter Fifteen

It was late—nearly 8:00 P.M.—when the telephone in Bart's office rang. He considered letting it go to voice mail but decided to pick up on the second ring, thinking any call at this hour might be important.

"I'm all alone in this big old house," the voice said without preamble. "My agent's finally gone. Asshole's at a screening of that new Woody Harrelson film. I'm a loser who thought he'd get ahead faster if he slept with the right guy. I feel like Rita Hayworth in that movie you made me watch, *Cover Girl,* or *Miss Clairol* or *Avon Calling.* Remember how she thought she could get ahead as a dancer by getting her picture on the cover of a *Vanity Fair* or *Modern Maturity* or some other funky magazine. I think that story was a euphemism for sleeping her way to the top."

"Rod?" Bart hesitantly asked, interrupting the stream-of-conscious monologue.

"What other loser do you know? It's me. A voice—make that a fuck—from your past."

Bart was in a drop-jaw state of shock. Hearing Rod's sexy voice conjured up the most erotic memories of his life. In spite of himself, he got immediately and uncontrollably turned on. "What's the problem?" was all he could come up with on such sort notice.

"Nothing. Okay, everything." Rod sighed. "Actually, I guess life's great. I'm living it to the hilt. I just wanted to hear a friendly voice. I don't know why I'm calling. Guess I just had to take a break. Working on the screenplay night and day, you know. No time to make any friends of my own."

"I thought you and Jim had tons of famous friends. Didn't the *Star* just report Jim's name on the guest list of Barbra Streisand's birthday party last week? That must have been fun."

"Sure. Fun. We went. But we never met her. Too many other people. Why would a hostess have a party, then not come meet her guests? She's not very warm. Of course, you didn't read *my* name. I'm an A-list nobody."

"Every *somebody* was once a *nobody*," Bart said, trying to placate his ex-lover. "What about the screenplay? I read in *Daily Variety* that Jim's close to making a deal for a film. I keep thinking it's *Blind as a Bat.*"

"It is. But it isn't. I mean, it's what *used* to be my screenplay. But so many people have made so many changes, you wouldn't recognize it."

Bart said, "Tom Clancy complains about the same damn stuff, but he cashes his checks with no problem. That's the business. You'll have a bundle of money when this thing gets made." He paused. "Listen, I'm just about to leave. I have to meet someone."

"Bart? I don't know what to do," Rod said. "I'm living in a fool's paradise. Everything should be so great. But it's not. I'm just another trick of the trade."

"What can I do?"

"I was hoping you'd say that. You could come up here for a drink, for starters. Jim won't be home for hours. There's a party after the screening, and he's always the last to leave those things. Comes home stinking."

"I mean, there's nothing I *can* do about how you live your life. Rod, I'm running late," Bart said. "I'm seeing someone, and I have to be across town in half an hour."

"Seeing someone? As in dating?"

Silence. Then: "He can't be as great as me," Rod said, sounding doubtful that Bart's romance was anything more than a rebound infatuation.

"There's no comparison," Bart said. "Believe me."

Of course, Rod smugly took that to mean Bart thought he was beyond comparison, that anyone Bart was seeing couldn't hold a candle to him.

"Couldn't we at least have lunch or something? At the studio, maybe? I've got to work something out with this screenplay, and I need your help."

"Is that the reason you called? To get my help with your screenplay?"

"No. Yes. I really do want to see you again and make up for being such a shit. Also, I'm at a point where I need a talented writer to help me out."

"Rod, I'm sorry, but I'm all wrapped up in my own projects. There's my career at Sterling and a new book I'm starting, and . . . everything."

"'Everything'? Meaning the new guy you're fucking?"

"It would only hurt me to see you again."

"So you still have feelings for me, eh?" Rod chuckled. "I'm unforgettable."

"Unforgettable? Hell, do you realize the pain you inflicted on me? No, you probably don't. That's so typical of you. Remember how you just let me walk away? How could you have done that if you loved me, Rod? I don't understand. I'll never understand."

"I don't understand, either," Rod admitted.

At this point, Bart could hear Rod sniffling, as though he were crying. "Rod? Are you okay?"

"I hate Jim Fucking Fallon! He's a total son of a bitch! I hate living up here! I used to call all the shots in my life, and now other people do. What do I have to show for it? *Nothing!* They promised me they'd get my screenplay produced, and I believed them. So far I just write and rewrite and rewrite the rewrites. Nobody's happy with what I produce, day after day. I know it's supposed to be a collaborative art form. But everybody wants to take credit for the good stuff I do and blame me for the bad."

"Who's 'everybody'?" Bart asked.

"Jim and that asshole Michael. He's my agent now."

"The one who . . . ?"

"Yeah. And to answer your unspoken question, we still do it. But it's no fun for me anymore. I'm burned out, man."

"I'm sorry," Bart said.

"Listen," Rod continued, "let me at least give you my cell-phone number, all right? It's the only private form of communication I have. Depending on the circumstances, I might not be able to get right back to you, but I promise I will ASAP if you'll just call."

Bart wrote the number down as he cradled the phone receiver on his shoulder and simultaneously slipped his arms into his sports coat, preparing to leave the office to meet Rusty for a glass of champagne at the Four Seasons.

Rod was pleading: "Promise me. Please, Bart. Promise me that you'll at least think about calling me. I need a friend, and you're the only one. If it makes any sense, I'm really sorry for the way I put my friggin' career ahead of you."

"How early or how late can I call?" Bart asked.

"Doesn't matter. I keep it on vibrate. There's also voice mail. Just leave a message. I check it all the time, but that fucking woman just keeps saying, 'You have no new messages.' 'You have no new messages.' Hell, I don't ever have any *old* messages, either!"

"I'm really late," Bart said again. "You know me, punctual to a fault. If I'm five minutes late for anything, you may as well call 911, because something's happened. I can't keep Rusty—that's his name—waiting."

"Call me, man. Please?"

"I'll try."

"Don't try. Please don't *try*. Just do it."

Still in a daze, Bart gave a cursory wave to the guard at the main gate as he drove off the studio lot. The stereo in his car was playing a CD of Handel's *Water Music,* but Bart hardly registered the usually soothing sounds.

As he drove along Olive to Barham toward Beverly Hills, he didn't even notice traffic signals or the striking union workers picketing outside the Warner Bros. gates or Chris O'Donnell in the Mustang convertible next to him, even though the actor kept looking over at Bart and smiling, probably because he was amused to see someone carrying on such an animated conversation with himself. Bart's thoughts were divided between Rod and Rusty and his conflicting feelings for both.

"Is it possible to be in love with two men simultaneously but for different reasons?" Bart thought aloud. "Sure. But this is stupid because one of them is an asshole. He's incredibly sexy but a total shit. Rusty, on the other hand, is exactly the type of man I always knew I'd marry. Rusty and I don't just have sex; we make love! Rod was just fantasy sex. For crying out loud, you can have fantasy sex with any of hundreds of guys who advertise in *Eros*. But damn it, Rod says *he* loves me, too! And damn it, I loved him fucking me! But that's not the same as love! Or is it? Christ, I'm so confused!"

Bart challenged himself to get a grip. "There's *no* dilemma here!" he insisted. "The only question is, simply: Are you going to pine away for some sexy stud who fucked you over or embrace a sexy stud who fucks you like you're some valuable treasure? A guy with whom you can sit in a room and quietly read . . . and laugh together . . . and share interesting stories and friends. How can there be any question, you dunderhead? How can there be the slightest quandary or hesitation?"

As he drove on automatic pilot, chaotic thoughts blasted through his head. "Fuck you, Rod!" Bart screamed. He pounded the steering wheel.

"Why'd you have to come back now, just when I was getting my life back on course! Rusty and I do things together. You and I only screwed. Rusty and I are equally at home together at the beach as we are at the Getty Museum. We bought a season subscription to the symphony. We wear our tuxedos. But we have just as much of a blast going to dance clubs, working up a sweat and boogying with our shirts off in a sea of other men doing the same thing. We call each other a dozen times a day. I know Rusty likes Indian food, and I go along with it. He knows I'm kinky about Burt Bacharach/Hal David songs, and he surprised me last Friday by renting *Lost Horizon* and going above and beyond the call by sitting through the whole video holding my hand. We do these things because we care for each other.

"Rusty helped me to put you and me into perspective. He enabled me to move on with my life. I didn't think I ever wanted to get into another relationship. I may be stupidly walking the high wire again, but at least Rusty feels like a safety net."

Still speaking aloud, as if to an invisible Rod, Bart continued his diatribe. "You and I didn't have any sort of world outside the sack. That was cool for what it was, but everything was on your terms! You had your inflexible writing schedule, your slutty bartending job, and your freakin' hustling. There was never really any hope for us to have a long-term relationship. Maybe a friendship. Someday."

But Bart couldn't help thinking of the hottest sex he'd ever had—and the heartless way it all ended. He pounded the steering wheel again, this time accidentally pushing the horn and getting the finger from the driver of the car in front of him. "Fuck you, too," Bart said to the pair of eyes reflected in the rearview mirror of the vehicle he was following.

"Okay . . ." Bart continued his solitary debate. "You've known Rod for what, six months? You've known Rusty only a month. You know exactly how Rod plays his games. You were just one of his suckers—literally and figuratively. Rusty doesn't appear to have any ulterior motives. He's got the heart of the Good Witch of the East and the sensitive soul of John Boy Walton and John Denver rolled into one man. While Rod was far better looking than the half-naked guy smiling in the Gillette shaving commercials, Rusty is just as beautiful—because he's Rusty. And his soul is much more beautiful. He's perfect, in every conceivable way!

"There's only one logical choice," Bart declared. "Don't fuck it up!"

He made his way along Fountain Avenue and turned left onto Crescent Heights. He drove down to Melrose, where he turned right, heading for the Four Seasons Hotel. He had made peace with himself. For the moment.

The champagne was Veyve Clicquot, of course. Dominic, the host at the Four Seasons' lounge, didn't even bother to ask for their drink orders anymore. As soon as Bart and Rusty arrived in the cocktail area, two flutes of ice-cold, fizzing champagne were placed before them on a thick beveled-glass coffee table, in front of the sofa, before either had a chance to take his seat.

Rusty, who had turned Bart on to the Four Seasons, enjoyed coming here for aperitifs because of the impeccable service as well as the elegant setting. There were few public places in Los Angeles or Beverly Hills where he felt more at home. That he was considered sort of a VIP among the members of the hotel's staff didn't hurt. But Rusty would have patronized this bar even if he weren't treated like royalty. That he was unfailingly polite and respectful endeared him even more to the waitpersons. Also, he was generous with his allocation of tips.

"To another day of being together." Rusty smiled and raised his glass, touching it so lightly to the one Bart was holding out. "Such delicate, thin glass," Rusty observed. "And yet two equally fragile flutes are able to buffet one another and not result in the slightest crack."

"Like two sensitive souls," Bart added. "If we're careful, we can collide at just the right velocity and not find ourselves broken."

Rusty looked deep into Bart's eyes. There he saw a man who was as attractive on the inside as he was on the outside—a gifted, intelligent, intuitive, and tender human being. He had met too few of those during the journey of his life of thirty-five years. Bart had made a strong, positive impression on Rusty from the moment they met in Shari Draper's office. That impression had never diminished; it had only enlarged as they grew to know one another better.

Although they had been dating for a month, they were a perfect complement to the other. To anyone observing the pair, they appeared to be an ideal couple.

Rusty and Bart. Two successful, confident, and attractive young men living in Hollywood. If *The Talented Mr. Ripley* were recast, Rusty and Bart could play Tom and Dickie—only nice.

Their obvious compatibility was becoming the envy of all the gay and straight couples they met. Observing them in the lounge of the Four Seasons or dining together at Morton's, anyone could see that these two men were what the song *People* was all about. It was obvious that these two "whole" men were first and foremost friends. They clearly adored each other.

If Mitch Wood, for example, could have been a fly on the wall, watching Bart and Rusty fuss over each other during dinner, he would have lost his grip and fallen to a welcome death in a hot bowl of cream of cauliflower soup. Mitch would have declared the relationship disgusting. The two were like Chip and Dale. Or Alphonse and Gaston.

"Would you care for another roll, Bart?"

"Thank you, Rusty. May I refill your wineglass?"

"Thank you, dear. You have perfect timing."

"Doesn't the Chilean sea bass sound interesting this evening?"

"That's exactly what I was going to order."

"Shall we share a Caesar?"

"Good suggestion. Yes, let's do."

"And our waiter's an absolute doll. He's so attentive."

"That's because he has the privilege of serving you, Mr. Sexy."

"That's sweet. But he's so enamored of you, dear. That tie you're wearing really picks up the green in your eyes. No doubt he's the same color because he's so envious of me being with you."

"Stop the insanity!" Mitch would have screamed—like Susan Powter on a major hypoglycemic flip-out. "This is not NBC! You two are not Frasier and Niles Crane!" Then Mitch would collapse into a seizure or stroke, unable to withstand the torture of listening to one more cloying word of sweet talk. Jonathan and Jennifer Hart couldn't come close to these love lunatics. Nor could John Travolta and Olivia Newton-John in *Grease* or Tracy and Hepburn at the beginning of *Adam's Rib*. But Bart and Rusty were having the time of their respective lives.

The salad and Chilean bass, which was exquisitely prepared and beautifully presented, was followed by Rusty and Bart sharing a tiramisù. They concluded the meal with peppermint tea. Then Bart decided to tell Rusty about the call he'd received from Rod just before their meeting.

"I told you all about this guy," Bart explained. "He was the only man I ever really thought I loved—until I met you. But he had other plans. Now he's calling asking for my help. I'm not sure what to do."

"First of all, if it helps, I know he doesn't mean the same thing to you anymore," Rusty said. "The fact that you were once important to each other should still count for something."

"Even after he broke my heart?"

"It's no longer broken, is it?"

"Not a crack. Not a chip."

"Sometimes what appears to be the worst thing that can happen to a person turns out to be the best," Rusty said, referring to the fact that if Rod hadn't left Bart, the two of them would probably never have gotten together.

"I like to believe I still would have found you someway, somehow," Bart said.

Rusty patted Bart's hand. "Hon. Always be honest with yourself. I think you want to help Rod but you're afraid of how it might affect our relationship. Am I right?"

Bart thought for a moment. "I'd never do anything to jeopardize our relationship. Believe me."

"I know that. And I feel exactly the same way about you. Nothing you could ever do would make me change my opinion of you."

Bart frowned. "I should at least call Rod back and find out how I might be able to help him. Is that what you're advising? He did sound awfully sad and desperate."

"I've never understood contentious breakups," Rusty said. "When my only other lover came to me and asked what would be my response to him sleeping with a new guy he'd met, I told him, 'If two people can't be happy together, why continue a charade?' My wish was just that we both be happy people. And we were, only not with each other."

Rusty paused, becoming more thoughtful. "What Rod put you through was devastating. But it's in the past. It's not healthy to keep feelings of anger. Release them. Throw them away. Call Rod and ask if he needs help, from either of us. We're a couple. It goes without saying, but if I can be of any service, I trust you'll let me know."

There was not a doubt in Bart's mind that Rusty's true nature was simply goodness.

By the end of their passionate lovemaking at Bart's apartment, it became a *fait accompli* that Bart would call Rod and meet with him again. Whatever Bart could do to help his old lover, Rusty would provide support.

Rusty was not in the least troubled by, or suspicious of, any amount of attention Bart might pay to Rod. Nor was he concerned about how he measured up sexually next to Rod, who, Bart had confessed, was the hottest lover he'd ever previously known. The only thing that mattered to Rusty was the feel and scent of Bart's smooth skin against his own hard, muscled body, the seal of their lips locked together, and the taste of Bart's delicious tongue, the way his penis filled Rusty's hungry mouth. Rusty knew there was no competition for Bart's affection. They both recognized their mutual devotion with the same clarity as they knew the specific spots on each other's bodies that caused the other to tense up in erotic pleasure and moan aloud, "Oh, yeah! Oh, God! Yes! I love you!"

The first time they made love, Bart was terrified he might accidentally call out Rod's name during a vulnerable moment of passion. He needn't have worried. From the moment he and Rusty kissed, Rusty proved to be such a virile distraction that Bart was completely absorbed in every moment of their time together. He frequently thought of that first night. Their lust was so intense, he could easily recall the precise details: arriving at Rusty's home, entering the house to the lilting sounds of Ella Fitzgerald wafting from the stereo, dogs circling his legs, wanting to be petted, votive candles burning in a dozen different locations of the living room, the intense, loving look in Rusty's green eyes.

After formal introductions to the "family" and receiving a glass of merlot, from which Bart took two small sips, the men stood facing each other for a long moment, staring at each other and uncontrollably smiling. Their eyes spoke volumes about their lust. Their hearts beat as rapidly as their pants expanded. Zealousness overwhelmed them. Bart placed his wineglass down on the coffee table without looking just as Rusty reached out and gently brought Bart's face slowly to meet his own. Their heads were slightly tilted as their lips made contact. Their mouths opened wide to receive each other's tongues. Bart took the lead, unbuttoning Rusty's shirt. Placing his hands on Rusty's warm, bare chest for the first time made him forget ever having been with Rod.

Rusty eased Bart down the hallway to the master bedroom suite. They separated only long enough for each to undress and turn down the bedcovers. Then they caressed each other on the cold sheets, wrestling until one thing led to another and Rusty was deep inside of Bart. They repeated their loving before finally, hours later, falling asleep—Bart with his back pressed tightly against Rusty's strong chest, wrapped in his well-muscled arms.

Now, a month later, the more Bart thought about Rusty, day in and day out, the more he realized he was in love with a for-real angel. As jaded as Bart had become over the years, he was still sometimes afraid. He feared having to repeat the pain caused by his first lover. He was afraid that so-called love might become a cycle of initial ecstasy followed by inevitable suffering. Bart didn't want to endure the nearly un-endurable, soul-consuming grief that accompanied that devastating first breakup or the more recent one with Rod.

Others with whom he had had sex did not have "love" attached to the proposition the way it did with his first full-out love and with Rod. When those other affairs ended, there was nothing lost. Just mild empti-ness, like a twenty-four-hour flu, that lasted only a short time.

Still, awakening in the morning after a perfectly peaceful night's sleep in the arms of his beautiful Rusty, Bart would hear in his head the lyric to an old Rodgers and Hart song, "He Was Too Good to Me." The words echoed in Bart's head. A more casual listener would hear the trite phrase that if something or someone seemed too good to be true, they probably were. But on a less obvious level—using the very same words but with a different inflection—the lyric took on a new meaning. Rusty may have appeared at first too good to be true. But he *was* true. He proved himself over and over. Offering to help Bart's ex, if he needed help, was just another way of Rusty's demonstrating that his devotion went above and beyond any ordinary man's.

Chapter Sixteen

The security guard at the studio gate checked his computer list for drive-on passes and located "Dominguez, Rod." He peeled off a temporary parking sticker, reached in through Rod's unrolled car window, and attached it to the inside of the windshield. "Know where you're going, Mr. Dominguez?" the guard asked, looking straight into Rod's dark eyes and illogically getting a hard-on.

Some of the most beautiful men on television and in feature films passed through this gate day in and day out. There was no justifiable reason for the guard to respond to Rod the way he did. Not only was he inured to the magnificence of the Hollywood's hottest; he wasn't even interested in the cast of the only gay-themed daytime drama, *Shirts and Skins,* all of whom winked at him as they drove to work each day, he wasn't even interested in them. They rarely failed to register more than a smile from the guard. So why was this guy who was going to see senior publicist Bart Cain so utterly distracting?

Rod, completely aware of his impact on the guard, feigned innocence and asked if the guard would mind personally showing him to the publicity building. "I can't leave my post," the guard said, quickly trying to figure out a plan to get away with Rod for a short time. "Tell you what. Park your car. Come back to the kiosk. I'll see if I can get someone to take over for me."

"That'd be cool, dude," Rod said with a smile that made the guard's stomach ache. A line of cars was impatiently waiting for Rod to move forward.

After exchanging a last lustful look into each other's eyes, Rod moved on. It took him a few minutes to find a vacant parking space in the jammed lot. By the time he walked back to the main gate, the guard, in his studio uniform of white shirt, gray slacks, black shoes and necktie with the classic SS logo, was waiting to escort Rod to the publicity building.

"What time's your appointment with Mr. Cain?" the guard asked, his heart racing a mile a minute. With a hand in his pocket, he tried to surreptitiously adjust his erect cock so the head would rest up near his waist rather than bulge out so obviously at his fly. None of this was lost on Rod, who was a keen observer, especially when he was the center of attention.

"Lunch at one o'clock."

"It's only twelve-thirty. How about a little sightseeing tour first? I've got the keys to all the soundstages. By the way, my name's Rich."

"Rich. Isn't this where they film that sitcom *Totally Kewl* with Jared Sumner?"

"Hot, isn't he," Rich said about the blond star of the hit show. "Yeah, that's stage 21. They're on hiatus. Wanna take a look around there."

"I'm all yours, Rich."

Rich was so turned on, he found himself leaking into his white briefs. The stage wasn't very far away. A huge beige-colored structure, it looked large enough to be an aircraft hangar. They entered through a side door with a large placard that stated in bold red letters: CLOSED SET!

Rod was overwhelmed by the enormity of the space. It was cold inside, completely silent except for the sound of their footsteps as they walked through the various sets of the living room and kitchen of the famous New York apartment that was immediately familiar to Rod from having watched the show a few times.

Rich led Rod into the bedroom set. "This is where, each week, Jared's character tries in vain to get his latest girlfriend to take off her clothes."

It was a running gag in the show. It was especially stupid because no one in their right mind on the planet—girl or boy, for that matter—would *not* go to bed with Jared, whose adolescent sexiness made him one of the hottest young men on prime time.

Rod looked around for any sign that they might not be alone. "It's a pretty big stage. Wanna see something else that's pretty big?"

Rich's breathing became harder. Rod reached out and took Rich's hand and pulled it to his crotch. Rich was caught off guard by the massive contents of Rod's basket.

"Shit" was all that Rich was able to manage. Then, as he rubbed his hand up and down Rod's package, which only made the contents grow larger, he finally said, "It's a real bed," meaning the furniture in the room wasn't just Hollywood make-believe.

"I'm ready for the rest of the tour," Rod said as he reached out for Rich's necktie and began to loosen it. Rich finished the job as Rod unbuttoned the security guy's white shirt. He then pulled his own black T-shirt over his head.

Rich was speechless at the sight of Rod's dark skin and muscled body.

Knowing he didn't have any time to waste, he ripped open the buttons of Rod's 501s and fell to his knees to worship the serpent that was released from inside the cave of denim. As Rich's lips closed around Rod's shaft, he raised his arms and placed his hands on Rod's chest and stomach. He blindly felt for Rod's nipples and squeezed them between his thumbs and index fingers as he simultaneously devoured the meat sliding in and out of his mouth and halfway down his throat.

"I'm gonna dry-fuck your sexy ass," Rod commanded.

"Mmmm" was all the anxious agreement that Rich could emit with his mouth full. He then pulled himself free from the feast and untied his regulation security man's shoes. He clumsily kicked them off and stepped out of his pants. Crawling onto the bed and lying on his back, he watched as Rod removed his jeans—no underpants—and joined him on the bed. Rich was looking up at God when he saw Rod. In the heat of the moment, he didn't give a damn about condoms or AIDS or anything other than having Rod inside of him. Rod was happy to oblige and simply spat onto Rich's asshole to give it a bit of lubricant. He moistened his own dick before tearing into Rich, who cried out from pleasure and pain. There was an echo in the huge shell of a building. But the hollow structure was so well insulated, no one on the outside would have heard if a bomb detonated.

Rich took his own cock in his hands and before a half a minute was up, he unloaded his reservoir.

"Sorry I was so fast, man. Hey, I've changed my mind," Rich said. "Don't come inside of me." The moment his own pleasure had been fulfilled, the fear of AIDS slammed into his head. "Do it on top of me instead. I wanna see it," he said, trying to justify his change of attitude.

Rod obliged. He took his weapon out of the sheath of Rich's ass and quickly came on the thick hair that covered Rich's muscular chest.

Resting for a moment to catch their breaths, Rich finally looked at his wristwatch. "Christ. Break time's over." He stood up, used the bedsheet to clean himself off, and began dressing.

"And I've got to get to my meeting with Bart. Just point me in the right direction."

As Rod and Rich tucked in their clothes and left the soundstage, they returned to the glaring light of the early afternoon. Rod said he planned to be back on the lot frequently for meetings with Bart. "Now that we know each other so well, can you dispense with the formality of Mr. Cain having to call in for a pass every time I come through the gate?"

"As long as I'm on duty, which is every weekday from nine until six, I'll just wave you through," Rich said. "Get here before your meetings. We can do repeat episodes on the set of *Totally Kewl*. Might even get Jared to join us when he's back for the season. He's into it. Trust me. He's nothing like his TV character. The things I could tell would have every teenage girl in America committing suicide. He bags men by the six-pack. Even the studio's CEO Rotenberg."

"So the stories are true. About Rotenberg, I mean. I kinda had him figured out. And I'm not too surprised about Jared, either. So, I'll be seeing you around." He left the next meeting indefinite. He really had no intention or interest in fucking the security guard again. This had just been another of Rod's ploys. Now he could get on the studio lot whenever he wanted. Without a visitor's pass.

Rod found his way to the publicity building and checked in with the receptionist on the first floor. Audrey, as her name badge announced, become cross-eyed when she saw Rod. He had the same effect on women as he did on men.

"Hi. I'm Rod Dominguez. I have an appointment with Bart Cain." He smiled at Audrey as she went through the automatic motions of calling Bart's office to announce the visitor.

"I just get his voice mail, Mr. Dominguez," Audrey finally said with a shrug to indicate she didn't know what else to do.

"Just Rod, please."

"Rod," she repeated as uncomfortably as one whom Miss Ross had granted dispensation to address her as Diana the Diva. "Mr. Cain must be away for a moment. We're not supposed to do this, but since you have an appointment, why don't you just go on up and wait. He's in room 1027. Get off the elevator, turn to your left, and go straight down the hall. There's a big poster of *Devil Girl from Mars* just outside his office. Can't miss it."

"You're so lovely, Audrey. Thanks for being so sweet and helpful."

Rod moved away from the reception desk toward the elevator. When the car door opened, Rod stepped inside and turned to face the lobby.

He waved to Audrey, who was leaking between her legs as much as Rich had.

She, too, was used to handsome actors and wanna-be stars, but Rod was in a class by himself. Her heart was still pounding when Bart entered the building's lobby.

"Oh, Mr. Cain," Audrey called out as he passed by the reception station. "There's a Mr. Dominguez waiting in your office."

Bart thanked her and pushed the button for the elevator. He arrived on the tenth floor just in time to see Rod peering into his office. Cheets had disappeared. She took every opportunity when Bart was in a meeting or away for any length of time to run off to God only knew where.

"Rod?" Bart said, coming up behind him. For just a moment Bart stood looking at the man he used to think of as the personification of God's greatest creation. "You look as good as ever," he finally said.

"Thanks, man. But I haven't worked out in two months. I'm getting soft."

"You were never soft," Bart said with a knowing grin. "You're still extremely sexy."

Rod smiled, the narcissist in him coming through. "I'm really glad you called, Bart. I was afraid you wouldn't. I've missed the hell out of you."

"I've missed you, too."

"But you moved on fast. That Rusty guy?"

"How about you and Jim Fallon? That's quite a leap from when we first met. Let's go to the commissary and play catch-up over lunch."

As they left the office and walked out of the building toward the studio commissary, Bart was thinking that Rod was still the sexiest man alive. He couldn't help being aroused by a flood of memories of all the times they'd been flesh to flesh together in bed, screwing each other's brains out.

Bart had thought he'd have his emotions under control. He was involved with the nicest guy on the planet who was also the most tender and loving sex partner. So, he asked himself, why was he still almost uncontrollably attracted to Rod? He decided he couldn't help his animal instincts. But he could definitely help how he responded to them. There was no way he was going to let Rod manipulate him into having sex, no matter what.

After ordering vegiburgers from the commissary grill, getting bottles of Evian, and filing through the cashier's line (Bart paid), they decided to sit outside in the sun on the so-called Garden Veranda. The place was teaming with diners—secretaries, middle-management executives, and a sprinkling of actors—and the noise level would allow them to talk openly without others eavesdropping.

As they made their way to a table by an ivy-covered brick wall, people who were used to keeping an eye on the door at restaurants, to watch the comings and goings of celebrities, couldn't help but look up as Rod passed by. The gay men as well as the straight ones and all the women clearly thought Rod had to be an actor. Nobody as good-looking as he could get away from at least a momentary flash of stardom in Hollywood.

Those who knew Bart all wondered what the hell he was doing with someone who was so painfully handsome and therefore important. In Hollywood, where perception *is* reality, beauty counts for 99.9 percent of any individual's value.

Rod and Bart removed their plates and utensils from their trays and set them on the round table that had an umbrella impaled in the center for shade. Their preliminary small talk included the usual: "Have you seen this or that movie or so-and-so's concert? Any vacation plans? Did you hear that Erykah Badu would be promoting her new CD with a live performance at Tower Records on Sunset?"

Finally, halfway through his meal, Bart asked the big question. "You mentioned problems with your screenplay. What's going on?"

Rod stopped in mid-bite and set his burger down on his plate. "It sucks," he said, his mouth full of whatever goes into a vegiburger." He swallowed. "Just like my life with Jim."

"Literally and figuratively, I presume?" Bart refused to chide himself for being excruciatingly direct. He had often been told he would have made a fine therapist because he was good at poking around and asking the right questions, even if he wasn't always tactful. He always made others feel as though he were interested in them and their problems. "Rod," he went on, "tons of wanna-be screenwriters would kill to be in your shoes. People who can help you get ahead surround you. So what's the problem?"

Rod thought for a moment before he finally spoke. "Things just aren't working out. What used to be my screenplay is now Jim's and Michael's."

"Isn't your name still on it?"

"I don't think there's one original line of dialogue of mine left. Now, instead of being a comedy that would have been super for Hugh Grant and Meg Ryan or even John Lithgow and Chloë Sevigny, it has turned into an edgy drama. Something for Malkovich or Cusack or Penn. Of course, there's a role for the great Jim Fallon," he added facetiously. "It's a big one. He and Michael have written it themselves."

"All screenwriters have horror stories about the way their work is defiled," Bart reminded. "How many books have been written on the subject by some of the biggest names in the business? William Goldman? John Gregory Dunne? You know what the game is. You're not the exception. Your problem is very run-of-the-mill."

"But neither of those guys had to fuck Jim Fallon's pimple butt on an on-call basis," Rod said, and continued eating his vegiburger.

The image made Bart set his lunch aside. "I really hate to say this, Rod, but it's called paying your dues."

"You mean paying off my karma. The remuneration is sick. Talk about the wages of sin."

"The truth is, your own ego is so large that you'll do anything, and I mean *anything,* to be successful. Why are you sitting here griping because you have to suck Jim Fallon's pathetic cock or fuck his fat rash-red ass to get ahead? This kind of behavior has been going on since time immemorial. Sex has been used the way you're using it by probably millions of people through the ages to achieve their goals."

Rod stopped eating and placed the remainder of his burger on his plate. "God, I thought I could count on you for help. Why are you giving me so much grief?"

"I'm not. I'm telling you about the truth. You're no more than a kept boy. Some stars keep their hustlers in red Ferraris. Others buy their boys Rolex watches and fly them all over the world. You see their names during the end crawl credits on movie screens. The credit that reads: so-and-so's 'assistant,' or thus-and-so's 'trainer.' What *you're* getting in the end—hopefully—is a produced screenplay."

"I've come to hate this town," Rod complained.

"It's also been pretty good to you, wouldn't you say?"

"I've sucked and fucked enough in my time. I'm getting tired of putting out, thinking it's going to get me anywhere."

"It has already, hasn't it? Look where you're living? When we first met, you only dreamed about being part of that world. Now your fantasy has come true."

Rod scowled. "I've hustled enough to know when I'm being hustled. I know I'm being used. I just thought it was a reciprocal deal. Day after day, I see how wrong I am. Those two bastards think they've got some idiot for a boy-toy. The thing of it is, I'm willing to put out as long as there are long-term benefits. Right now I don't see any."

"You've never been one to let anybody take advantage of you. Oh, you've taken advantage of plenty of people, myself included, but I thought you were pretty good about not being a victim yourself."

"You weren't at any disadvantage," Rod sniped. "The date on the screenplay coverage was a couple of weeks earlier than when you gave it to me. You were stringing me along. Don't think I don't know."

Bart said nothing.

Rod became conciliatory. "I didn't mean to use you, Bart, honestly. And if I did, it was—just my nature."

Bart nodded. "I don't blame you. And you're right, I got a lot out of our time together, too."

"At least with us it *was* reciprocal. And you always kept your word."

"Is it my imagination, or did we have the greatest time together? At least for me, the sex was primo," Bart said, flashing back in his mind to a conflation of every night they spent locked together in each other's arms.

"Bitchin', man."

"From start to finish."

Rod looked deep into Bart's eyes. "From start to—I don't think we're finished, Bart. I think I just got sidetracked and made an ass of myself. But I'm determined for us to get myself together."

Bart was flabbergasted. "Stop! Hold on! What are you talking about? We've both moved on. We're seeing other people. You can't just call me up and say, 'Hey, man, how's it hangin'? I'm ready to let you back in my life.'"

"Why not? What if I say, 'I love you,' the way you did that last morning when we were lying in bed? I couldn't say anything then. I was afraid. The only guys who ever said they loved me meant they loved my fucking them. Weren't you just saying you were in love with me? Am I stupid enough to think you were so *in love* with me that you'd be available after I got my shit together with the screenwriting thing?"

"I think you're just tired of living with a creep and life isn't going the way you expected," Bart countered.

"And I suppose *your* life is going exactly as you expected?" Rod lashed out. "You're still stuck at this goddamned studio in a job you hate. Do you still have that crazy, nympho, bitch boss Scary Shari? She still have it in for you? How much longer do you think you can take it?"

Bart was silent for a moment. Then, with all the poise he could muster, he said, "As a matter of fact, I'll probably be fired within the month."

"Dude, that can't happen. You're a super writer."

For the first time, Rod seemed to be genuinely interested in someone else's problems. The look on his face registered authentic concern for Bart's happiness and for his future.

Bart explained. "It's all speculation, but it looks like there's a plot to get rid of the president of marketing, a really nice guy who happens to be openly gay. I was actually propositioned."

"By the fag?"

"Please, don't call him that. His name is Owen Lucas. He's a brilliant marketing man and a good executive. It was Shari and Cy who propositioned me. I look like a patsy. They wanted me involved in their scheme to oust Owen. And if I don't play along . . ."

Bart trailed off, then continued. "They hate Owen because he's way smarter than they are. Plus, he's out of the closet. This is the only studio in town where that's such a big taboo—family values and traditions and all. It's such a double standard, because over fifty percent of the guys working here are gay. Many are buttoned-down Armani suit guys by day and full-out cowboy leather drag queens by night."

"What'd you tell me once, 'At Sterling you're considered gay until proven otherwise!'"

Bart laughed. He remembered telling that to Rod one morning while they were both lying together after a long night of nonstop sex. The subject of working for a glamorous company like Sterling had come up, and Bart explained what it was really like around the lot, especially in his back-stabbing, high-tension, dog-eat-dog marketing department.

Bart had once said to Rod, that often, during boring marketing meetings, he'd mentally go around the oval conference table of twenty or so colleagues and say, "Gay, gay, straight, gay, straight, gay, gay, gay, straight, who cares, straight, can't tell, gay, gay, gay . . ."

For the time being, Rod seemed to have left his own problems behind and wanted to know more about this so-called proposition Bart had received. Bart explained how Shari had made the suggestion that he could be in line for a big promotion if he'd help establish the foundation for a sexual-harassment lawsuit they were dreaming up to scare Owen away. They wanted Bart to claim that Owen had made an unsolicited sexual advance toward him.

"The thing of it is," Bart said, "I'd have gone to bed with Owen in an instant. He's sexy and fun and has a great sense of humor and an extremely quick mind. But nothing ever happened. As often as I blatantly made eye contact with him and laughed too loudly at the jokes he made during meetings, he never saw me as anything but the staff writer. And I don't believe it ever happened to any of the guys here. But there's one S.O.B.—a supposedly straight guy name Josh, over in promotions—who I hear is willing to make an accusation of sexual harassment just to *get* a promotion."

"Any chance you misunderstood Shari when she made the suggestion to you?" Rod asked.

"No. In fact, you can be the judge. I taped the conversation."

"No way, man! That's too rad. You could end up owning this whole friggin' studio!"

"Or dead." Bart laughed. "They say Cy Lupiano has East Coast crime family connections. I'll be lucky if I ever get to work at another studio after they blackball me."

"You don't get it, man," Rod said, looking as serious as he did the first night Bart showed up with fifty bucks and made him take shots of tequila from Rod's own mouth. "We both have very valuable assets. You've got a tape that spells out a false sexual-harassment suit . . . and I have something of great potential value, too."

Bart looked quizzical as Rod scanned the Garden Veranda for eavesdroppers. "A copy of a manuscript that ol' Jimbo Fallon's been writing. It's a wild exposé. It tells where all the bodies in Hollywood are buried. Or what closet they're hiding in."

"What are you talking about?" Bart said, looking like Roz Russell in *The Women,* just as the chatterbox, rumormonger manicurist is about to dish the dirt about her best friend Norma Shearer's husband, Steven, stepping out behind her back with Joan Crawford.

"Jim's writing a book. A tell-all." Rod winked. "And I, unknown to him or anyone else, have a copy."

"You stole it?"

"I am not an animal . . . I'm a human being," Rod said, doing John Hurt's line from *The Elephant Man.* "Substitute animal for thief if it makes you feel any better. The idiot left his computer on one afternoon when he went out for an audition."

"I'd call taking Jim's manuscript theft."

"Pilfering, maybe." Rod shrugged.

"Semantics."

"I walked into his office looking for stamps for a letter and happened to see *my* name on his computer screen. Of course, I had a right to know what he'd written about me. I just printed out a copy to read. He has the original, for Christ sake. How's that stealing?"

"So what about this manuscript? What'd he say about you?" Bart was intrigued, as Rod had been when he first came across the book.

"It's not so much *what* he said about me, although there's enough. It's more about all the cocksuckers who run this town, including your nemesis Shari Draper. The people he's met on the way up—and on the way down. It comes full circle in the life of a nobody turned somebody turned nobody again. It could be a primer for every wanna-be and has-been in the industry."

"Is it a novel? *Roman à clef?*"

"If it is, he's using real names. Like Shari's, Barry Diller, Michael Eisner, David Geffen, and Lew Wasserman."

"Wasserman? Why would he lump Wasserman in with those other creeps? He doesn't fit."

"It's incongruous." (There was Rod using his out-of-the-blue ten-dollar words.)

"He actually says nice things about Lew and Edie. I met 'em. They were both real nice to me. But wait'll you read this thing, if you want to. I mean, I can't let it out of my hiding place, but if you want to meet me in private, I can bring parts of it with me. As for your tape, you better make a copy and stash it. You might be sitting on a gold mine."

"More like a ticking bomb," said Bart.

The Garden Veranda was clearing out now, and it was getting too dangerous to talk openly. If Bart had learned one rule while in Hollywood, it was to never talk about anyone in a restaurant. There was some axiom or universal law that made it for certain someone who knew the person you were talking about was within listening range. It had happened to Bart on numerous occasions. He'd be at a restaurant and overhear conversations about people he knew personally. Everybody knew someone who knew the best friend of the hairstylist who kept William Shatner looking so strange with his gin blossoms and his inordinately phony toupees.

Bart looked at his wristwatch. "I've got a screening in ten minutes. We'll have to pick this up later."

"I've got to go, too," Rod said. "Jim'll give me the third degree about where I've been." He rolled his eyes. "Every time I leave the house he thinks I'm running off to fuck some dude." Rod paused for a moment. Then, as if taking Bart into his confidence, he whispered, "Frankly, he's right."

"I thought you gave up hustling," Bart said.

"I have. I just fuck for the release. Gotta keep the tubes clear. I don't want my dick to petrify."

"Mmm," Bart said with obvious longing.

"You're hard for me right now, aren't you?" Rod said, prodding. "I know you are."

Bart blushed. It was true. From the moment he laid eyes on Rod again, he had an erection. "Some things are 'uncontrollable.'" He shrugged, desperate to reach out and just touch Rod's face.

"If you ever want to . . ." Rod's sentence trailed off.

"Wanting is one thing," Bart said. "I think I'll probably always *want* you, Rod. But there's a saying 'If you want everybody, you'll end up with nobody.' Right now I have someone really special. I wouldn't jeopardize my relationship with Rusty for anything." He checked his watch again. "Sorry, man, I've got to rush."

"Wasn't *I* special?" Rod asked as they simultaneously stood up from the table.

Bart looked at Rod for a long moment but said nothing.

"Never mind. Will you call me again?" Rod asked plaintively. "Please?"

Bart smiled. "Of course. You can call me, too. You can practically always reach me here at the studio. Sorry we can't talk longer, but I can't keep Ben Affleck waiting."

Bart winked at Rod to let him know Ben Affleck wasn't really going to be at the screening. Then he made the first move to shake Rod's hand good-bye rather than wait for Rod to advance for a hug or—more inappropriately, given this environment—a kiss.

As the two departed the dining area, they separated and slowly walked away in opposite directions—Rod toward the parking lot, Bart toward the Ella Raines Memorial Theatre. After so many paces, they turned around at the same time and waved to each other.

For Bart, the memory of holding Rod's hard body was a painful distraction. *Damn it! I've made the right decision! I know I have!* he insisted to himself, pushing away all thoughts that life with Rod could be remotely better than with Rusty.

* * *

Rod, on the other hand, smiled, knowing that Bart was still physically attracted to him. In his mind there was always the possibility that they could get back together. Rod, too, was distracted by thoughts of his ex, and just as he reached the guard kiosk, he absently said, "Of *course* he wants me."

Rich, the security guard, overheard. "You flatter yourself, guy," he said derisively. Rod hadn't heard Rich. He simply continued toward his car with a smirk on his face.

PART TWO

Chapter Seventeen

"Let's go over this again," Shari drawled in one of her slow-burn moods. She sat at her desk facing Bart. "You're telling me that Owen Lucas came into your office one night and something happened? What? Tell me exactly."

Bart hesitated for a moment, trying to visualize in his mind the entire scenario. "Okay. It was like this. So I'm working late on the press kit for *The Last Chance,* starring Chevy Chase. The office is empty. Even the cleaning people have done their jobs and left for the night. I'm extremely tired. Suddenly I'm startled when I see a shadow outside my office. At first I think it's probably a security guard making his rounds. Or the ghost of Uncle Ralph, whose supposed to be frozen, but you never know about ghosts. Then I look up again, and there's Owen standing in the doorway."

"Doing what?"

"Just looking at me."

"There isn't any law against . . ."

"Well, he's standing there with his shirt unbuttoned . . . down three or four buttons . . . and his jeans are unbuttoned at the top. The president of marketing wearing jeans to the office always surprised me. Not to mention his sexy hairy chest."

"Forget about the fashion statement or the physiology. Just tell me what happened next?"

"For a moment he just leaned against the doorframe."

Shari prompted, "He said . . . ?"

"Yeah. He said, 'Why don't you blow it off for the night, Bart.'"

"He actually said, 'Blow it off, Bart'?"

"Yeah. I didn't think he even knew my name."

Shari snapped, "I mean, he said 'blow it,' like it was a come-on, right?"

"I didn't think so at the time. I'm kinda naive about these things."

Shari rolled her eyes. "Then he came up and stood in front of you with his, his, his, crotch in your face or something?"

"Actually, his mossy stomach. And he asked if I'd eaten anything."

"Dinner?"

"I suppose. At least that's what I thought at the time. I said I was too busy, that I'd probably grab something at Wienerschnitzel. Then he put his hands in his pockets and started moving them around, like maybe he was feeling for his change or something. He asked me if I liked working at Sterling. I told him I'd been doing it for a couple of years and it was great. I told him I liked my colleagues and . . . and . . . I told him I especially liked that he had taken over as president of the department because he was a creative guy."

"Why would you tell him that?"

"Because I thought he was sexy and—"

"*No! No! No!*" Shari convulsed. She stood up and paced the room like an angry prosecuting attorney, gesticulating with her hands to hammer home a point. "You're supposed to be a victim here, Bart, not some fucking faggot cocksucker looking to score points with his homo boss, you stupid idiot!"

Bart blanched at the scolding. "Sorry. What am I supposed to say again at this point?"

Shari plopped herself back down in her leather chair and exhaled with enough force for the air to scatter some papers on her desk, expressing enormous frustration because they had been at this practice performance for more than an hour and still Bart wasn't getting the lines absolutely perfect.

"Once again! Final time!" she admonished Bart as if speaking to an idiot child. "This is where Owen tells you he's had his eyes on your performance and he's really impressed with how much work you do and how well you accomplish your tasks without complaining and how you should have a promotion and that he'll personally see to it that human resources has a glowing recommendation from him in your files so you can find another department to work in."

"Oh. Right," Bart said, picking up the thread of the drill Shari and Cy had discussed with him earlier that afternoon.

"Continue."

"Okay. So I asked him what he meant by a different department. And he said he was really sorry, but he always made it a practice at all the studios where he'd worked before to never have a special employee that he found too attractive because it was a distraction. And since I was very cute . . ."

"Oh, brother," Shari editorialized.

". . . And I was all he could think about since coming aboard as president. He said it wasn't fair to either of us, because he felt like a lecherous old man—since I'm twenty-seven and he's forty-two—and was certain I'd be uncomfortable with him having these feelings, especially since he'd just made me fully aware of them. He said he didn't want to hurt me or create an unpleasant working environment. He had to think of not only himself and me but the entire department."

"Right. Good. And then you pleaded with him because you love your job and you didn't know what else you'd be qualified to do. And that's when he asked how much you love your job and what you think of him as a man. And what you'd be willing to do to stay on as head writer. In other words, are you attracted to him?"

"And I told him I just wanted to please him. And that if he wanted a blow job every now and again, I'd be happy to—"

"For Christ sake, *no!* No! No! No!" Shari bellowed so hard that the poster of *Marked Woman* rattled on the wall behind her desk. "Jesus, Joseph, and Mary! The guy is forcing himself on you, you imbecile! Remember? You can't stand his guts. You think he's an ugly old troll."

It's your ugly old guts I can't stand, Bart thought. Instead, he said, "He's all of what, forty-two? I shouldn't say he's old, should I? Who'd believe it?"

"You've had nightmares ever since then, right?"

"Well, wet dreams, to be more accurate."

"That's more than I need to know, you little perv. Christ, you're as thick as a brick. Listen, are you with us on this project or what? I'll vouch for the fact that your job performance has slipped way down. You became worthless to the department because you were so traumatized and disgusted by Owen's affection and alienation."

"Isn't that taking it too far, Shari," Bart asked. "I mean, first of all, I'm openly gay. Won't a jury find it unrealistic that I've rebuffed another gay man? An attractive one, I might add. You know how breeders—excuse me—think gay guys are all such horny bastards willing to take on anything in pants."

"Not true, of course," Shari said sarcastically.

"Will a jury believe this story? Secondly, the work I've done speaks for itself. There's no lack of quality in our press kits."

Shari shook her head. "This will never go to any trial; I've told you that a dozen times. We're simply building a case against Owen because we know he wants to get rid of me and bring in his old team from Warner Brothers." Shari was trying to sob. "I can't lose my job. I have a sick mother to take care of and a huge mortgage hanging over my head. Owen doesn't like me. This is just for insurance. Besides, your press kits pretty much suck."

"But you've been approving them, haven't you? What if the court makes me provide all your approval sheets?"

"No court! I've told you! All out of court!" She paused. "On second thought, get rid of 'em right away. And I'll write up some complaints for your personnel file."

"That's not necessary, is it?" Bart said in a wounded tone. As far as he knew, his employee file was impeccable. Never a day late. Seldom a day out sick. There were commendations from Francis Ford Coppola, Nancy Meyers and Charles Shyer, and Maggie Smith offering praise for the work that Bart had accomplished promoting their films either through his writing or when he was on the steering committee for a fund-raising event with them.

Shari said, "Everything bad will come out as soon as this is all over."

How true, Bart thought, but said, "So now you're going to lie about me, too? I'm not the one on trial here, Shari. Perhaps I'm not the guy to go through with this."

"Too late, dipshit. And stop being such a sissy," Shari yelled. "This information will never go beyond my office. Trust me. We're just trying to turn up the heat and scare Owen to let him know we're not stupid."

"That's enough for tonight," Shari finally said, giving up. "We'll try again tomorrow. But get the fucking facts that we discussed straight!"

She thought aloud for a moment. "Maybe we do need a straight guy to do this right . . . Are there any straight guys in the office? I mean, ones who are halfway decent looking? What's with you gay guys, anyway? You're always the best-looking men. It's such a waste."

Bart felt depleted of energy. He walked back to his office and closed the door, then called Rusty on his cell phone. He didn't dare use the company lines because rumor had it they were tapped. The computers, too. It was suspected that all E-mails were downloaded at night. When the names of the CEO or board members or certain four-letter words in the text of a message showed up, the message was selected for review by corporate communications. Nothing was secret—or sacred—at Sterling.

As usual, the extraordinary Rusty was completely supportive of Bart. Although Rusty was already settled in for the night, he suggested they both meet for a late dinner and a bottle of wine. "Better still," Rusty said, "if you don't mind leftovers, my doggie bag from lunch at the Bistro Gardens with Minnie Driver this afternoon is probably more than enough for you. That's it. And I'll open a bottle right now. By the time you get here, it will have breathed sufficiently."

Bart didn't hesitate to accept the invitation. Although they hadn't planned to be together that night, Bart wanted to be comforted by Rusty and reassured by him. Rusty, too, wanted to be near Bart and also to hear all about his horrific day. He also was hot to listen to the tape Bart had made of his latest tutorial with Shari.

As soon as they concluded their conversation, Rusty put aside the book he was reading. He turned on the CD player, loading the disk tray with romantic selections from Doris Day, Carly Simon, Johnny Mathis, Linda Ronstadt, and his favorite, Carole King's *Tapestry*. He then withdrew a special bottle of merlot from his wine closet. He brought out two Bordeaux glasses, then removed the lead seal covering the bottle's cork and neck. When he extracted the purple-tipped cork, he placed it on a silver tray next to the bottle and glasses and set the shining, round serving disk on the coffee table in the living room. He lit some candles as well as the gas fireplace. Then he unwrapped a wedge of Brie and set it on a plate in the microwave, ready to melt the moment Bart arrived.

It was a little after nine when Bart rang the bell at Rusty's home. "Sanctuary!" Bart exclaimed, imitating Tom Hulce from Disney's *The Hunchback of Notre Dame*.

After a long and strong embrace, which included a deep, breathless kiss, Rusty led Bart into the living room. Once they were seated, an exhausted Bart was absolutely thrilled to be in Rusty's gorgeous home in the Fryman Canyon section of Studio City.

It may be the so-called Valley, which got its share of snubbing from those in Beverly Hills and the West Side of town, but Studio City was home to the Radford Studios, which was once MTM Studios, owned by Mary Tyler Moore and her husband, Grant Tinker, and then the studio where *Roseanne* was filmed each contentious week. The area was a haven for a lot of actors. Not always the supersuccessful ones, although there were some of those, too, but certainly many recognizable faces. The ones you'd see at Gelson's, which was just down the street on Laurel Canyon, or at that hole-in-the-wall seven-table restaurant called Vivian's, on Ventura, which was a second home to actors and dancers because it was next door to a well-used rehearsal and audition space.

The clientele didn't necessarily patronize Vivian's for the food. It was the atmosphere (every inch of wall space was filled with autographed eight-by-ten glossy head shots of the famous and not so famous who had been customers) and the camaraderie of owners/brothers Brian and Mario that kept the place jammed.

Rusty's house was on a secluded tree-lined street that could have been a backdrop for a small East Coast town. It gave the feeling of being in an old-fashioned neighborhood. His neighbors included Nancy Dussault, from the old *Ted Knight Show,* as well as Roddy McDowall— until he checked into Forest Lawn after a bout with cancer. In fact, the area was often used as the location for television shows.

"Yikes, what a day," Bart said as he and Rusty settled on the sofa and looked lovingly at each other. "I still don't know if what I'm doing is the right thing, but I've taped another session with Shari. The third so far. She's giving me all these instructions on what to say in the deposition against Owen Lucas."

Ever since Rod first convinced him of the potential value of the tapes he'd made of Shari's duplicitous activities, Bart decided to throw himself into the part of double agent. He'd act out his undivided loyalty to Shari and Cy and Sterling but in the meantime furnish the information to Owen Lucas.

After consulting with Rusty and Owen, Bart had gone to Shari with his tail between his legs. He apologized to her for being a wuss. He had told her that to show how much he respected her and how honored he was to have such an important job at the studio. He would do whatever she felt was best for everybody involved. Shari took the bait without a second thought.

"Let Shari and Cy think I'm going along with their conspiracy in exchange for a promotion," Bart had said to Rusty once his decision had been made. "I have this angelic face. I have a smile that makes people trust me. No one ever imagines I have the capacity for being disingenuous. See, these are the valuable life lessons one gets by working in Hollywood!" Bart laughed.

"She still has no idea that Owen is completely aware of all this clandestine business of hers and Cy's?"

"She's definitely not the sharpest tack in the box. She thinks I'm an idiot because I keep goofing my lines. I just want her to keep reiterating her plans on tape."

"It's going to shock the hell out of her when she finds out that you and Owen are old friends. I think it's such a great 'six degrees of separation' thing."

"I never lose my real friends. We may not stay in touch as often as we'd like, but we always know we're there for each other. I'm in contact with all the guys I knew in college. Owen's like a brother."

"But tell me again. How did Owen know that you and I . . ."

"I have a great relationship with my clients, too. They obviously talk about me. In this case, it was Warren and Annette. She told Gwyneth, whose parents are old friends of Owen's, about me and my new relationship with you. When Gwyneth described you to Owen—cute young guy, a publicist at his new studio, etc.—he put two and two together. When he caught on to all the palace intrigue, he knew he could count on me for help. I'm just sorry for getting you so involved."

"Not a problem. Owen's one of my favorites of all your great friends. I'm thrilled to be doing something that will blow up in Shari's face. If we can just get enough recorded evidence, she and Cy will be history."

"We probably have enough now," Rusty said. "But don't forget, in Hollywood, the type of behavior which Shari and Cy are involved with is completely condoned. There's that old Hollywood maxim When you get fired from one studio, you go on to a better job at another studio."

"That's usually after they get out of jail," Bart said. "You know I don't care about my own career at Sterling. I have enough in stock options to quit anytime."

"And you know I'm not wild about interfering with the course of events in anybody's life," Rusty said, sipping his wine. "But I also can't stand around and watch the people I love, Owen . . . and especially you . . . being abused."

Bart smiled gratefully. "I hate to admit it, but although I can take care of myself when it comes to weathering the storm of Shari, I'm getting a lot of satisfaction from thinking about being part of the team to kick her ass."

Sidling over to Rusty and nuzzling his lover's neck, he said, "When this is all over, I may accelerate my plan to kidnap you and run away to Scotland. To that little farm we've talked about? The place where I can write and you can take care of the village animals. We won't ever have to worry about Sterling or Hollywood again."

Rusty had been hearing about Bart's desire to relocate to Ireland or Scotland ever since their first date. Bart had it all planned for himself before they met and wondered what Rusty had thought of the idea.

As with all things that were Rusty/Bart or Bart/Rusty, there was only harmony. They both agreed they would eventually settle abroad. England, Ireland, Scotland, perhaps a farm on the Hebrides. They weren't sure, but they planned to spend a month traveling as soon as the situation at the studio was resolved or Bart's first book was published and successfully launched.

Bart stared into Rusty's eyes and whispered, "I want our naked bodies pressed hard against each other."

Without further words, Rusty placed Bart's head in his hands and locked his lips over his lover's. Their tongues began tasting the elixir of each other's mouths. Both men were vibrating with electrical energy as they began their slow, passionate foreplay. Their respective moans of ecstasy were uncontrollable. They began to contort their bodies together on the sofa.

"The bed," Bart sighed.

The two rose from the coach, their lips still pressed hard against the other's, their tongues dueling. As they moved out of the living room, candles still burning, Shirley Bassey on the stereo, they found their way to Rusty's king-size bed. Both men were removing the other's clothes, their lips never parting.

Finally, with the sheets pulled down, Bart lay on his back, pinned under Rusty. Bart was panting, his chest heaving, his wrists in a grip that made him unable to move. Rusty lowered himself onto Bart's body. It was as though a lifetime of passion had been pent up inside. Unleashed were the beasts that lie within all men. Their kisses were gentle, then hard, then gentle again.

This was the way they made love every time they were together—love mixed with lust, pouring from their souls as they both whimpered from the ecstasy.

Chapter Eighteen

Jim and Michael were both high on martinis when Rod returned home after another lunch at the studio with Bart a week after they'd reestablished contact.

"Rod," Jim cried. "Great news! *Perfect Love,* er, *Blind as a Bat,* is sold! Sterling bought the script. We just heard from Cy Lupiano. Isn't this terrific? Have a drink."

Rod was stunned. His questions all flooded out in an avalanche of exhilaration and confusion rolled into a stammer of chaotic cross-examination. "Are you serious? What's the deal? Who's starring? The script's not even finished! When do they go into production? How much money? What's *Perfect Love?*"

Rod hated martinis, but he accepted the one offered by Michael. "Shouldn't we have a toast or something," Rod said, hardly able to control his enthusiasm.

"Look at this kid, here!" Jim said to Michael. "It's the greatest thing that's ever happened in his life, and we're responsible. Absolutely we should raise our glasses!"

"To *Perfect Love,*" Michael sang. "May it bring us all a shitload of money and Oscars all around!"

"*Blind as a Bat* or *Perfect Love* or whatever," Rod said incredulously. "I can't believe it sold!" He made a dramatic sweeping gesture with his right hand, an arc high above his head: "*Perfect Love.* Original screenplay by Rodrigo Dominguez. From a story by Rodrigo Dominguez. Executive producer, Rodrigo Dominguez. Brought to you by the new Ford Explorer—and Rodrigo Dominguez." He laughed.

"The details! Details," Rod squealed after a sip of his gin. "And I didn't think the script was ready. I guess you pros know what you're doing, after all. Tell me everything. How much money am I gonna get up front?"

Jim looked at Michael. Michael looked at Jim. They both looked at Rod. "There are still a million details to work out," Michael finally said. "This is just the first step."

"Don't count your chickens and all that sort of thing. It's bad luck in Hollywood. Like actors whistling backstage," Jim added.

Rod said, "But the script is sold, isn't it? Which must mean there's money. You *had* to talk money. How much am I getting? Just ballpark it."

Jim turned around and went back to the bar to pour himself another drink.

"Well, the thing of it is," Michael began, "since you're a first-time writer . . . you don't even belong to the WGA. For Christ's sake . . . things get complicated."

"Loan me the twenty-five hundred dollars it costs to join the freakin' Writers Guild," Rod said, starting to feel a little wary. "Or better yet, I'll just take it out of the check I get from Sterling. I only want to know how much. High six figures? Mid? What? It's worth every penny they're pay-ing—and more."

"Well," Michael continued, "since the screenplay isn't really yours . . ."

"Isn't mine?" Rod said, taken aback.

"Michael and I thought that . . ." Jim interrupted.

Rod waved a hand. *"Perfect Love* isn't my title, but the script is *mine.* I've worked for months on all the rewrites of a perfectly good—no, ex-cellent—original screenplay. Of course it's mine. What are you talking about? I'm the author. You guys acted as consultants. I took creative di-rection from you, but I wrote the freakin' script."

"Let's talk about the specifics after we celebrate," Jim said. "This is a victory for all of us, Rod. You should be thrilled that something which began as a kernel of an idea—granted you contributed to the start of this—is about to become a motion picture, with a juicy role for me."

"No. I want to talk about it now," Rod insisted. "What do you mean, 'It began as a kernel?' And 'I contributed to the start?' That freakin' screenplay is *all mine!"*

Rod was dumbfounded. Surely, he thought, this must be April Fools' Day. At any moment, Jim and Michael would say, "Can't you take a joke, you little hustler? You're a genius, man. We could never have done this without you!"

Instead, Michael said, "I don't think you quite know how things work in Hollywood. No first-time writer . . ."

"God, what a stupid line. 'First-time writer!'" Rod shot back. "No writer is a 'first-time writer.' First time published, perhaps. Or first time produced. But every writer works years for that so-called first-time bullshit."

"What I'm trying to tell you," Michael continued, "is that there's a hierarchy. You have to have a track record—"

"Fuck you. You're not making a bit of sense. Are you telling me that a screenplay that I've written can't be sold with my name on it because I don't have a track record? How else do you get a track record other than selling a screenplay, goddamn it?"

Michael answered in a patronizing tone. "A lot of writers start out doing rewrites or doctoring other people's scripts, but the WGA doesn't officially recognize their contributions. It's just how the Guild works."

"This is a very complicated business," Jim intervened.

"There's nothing complicated about getting credit where credit is due," Rod snapped.

"There's no use talking to you when you're in this kind of mood," Michael countered.

"Mood? What kind of 'mood' am I in? Shouldn't I be in a 'fuck me over' mood? It seems you guys have already done that—with my clothes on, for once. I read the trades. Every day there's a story about a so-called first-time writer getting big bucks for a mere story treatment. I've written the whole damn screenplay. Five others, too! You guys have screwed me, literally and figuratively. You're both going to be so sorry you ever fucked with me. You think I'm some little plaything that just gives great head on command? You think I'll take a slap in the face as well as I take a slap on the ass? You guys invited the wrong stud into your den of iniquity."

Jim and Michael abandoned Rod and congregated at the bar. They poured more martinis and talked among themselves about the film.

Rod stood motionless, glued to the floor, looking as bewildered as Leona Helmsley hearing her sentence of jail time for income-tax evasion, her cushy life literally ripped out from under her.

Finally, still dazed, Rod threw the now-empty martini glass against the framed portrait of Jim. Shards of glass exploded onto the fireplace mantel and hearth. Rod drifted out of the room. As he departed, Jim and Michael looked up at him, then at each other. Nobody said a word.

Rod picked up his car keys from the Lalique table in the foyer, where they were always automatically placed.

Rod left the house and got into his Dodge Dart. He turned on the ignition, put the car in gear, and drove down the hill. The gates parted when he passed Jim's infrared sensor. Turning on to Woodrow Wilson, he drove away angry, confused and bewildered, the way a loyal employee leaves his office after unexpectedly being fired. He didn't know what to do or where to go. His first urge was to call Bart. But he was too numb to take out his cell phone.

Somehow he drove on automatic pilot along Mulholland, down to Cahuenga. He turned left at the light and right onto Barham, on down to Sterling Studios.

Rich was at the gate. When Rod pulled up at the guard kiosk, Rich acted smug and self-satisfied. "Hey, man," he said, smiling. "What took you so long? We haven't done it in a week. Guess you're ready for more action, eh? Meet me over at Stage 21. I can get away in about five."

Rod had already forgotten about their first (and hopefully last) tryst. He tried to turn on his infinite charm but was so drained from his altercation with Jim and Michael that he failed. "Rain check, okay, man? I've got a meeting across town and just need to get Bart Cain to sign some papers."

Rich was obviously disappointed. "The cast of *Totally Kewl* returns in two weeks," he said. "Better make some time before then." It wasn't a polite request. It sounded more like a threat, as if his access to the lot were dependent on another performance on Stage 21. "Don't be a stranger," he finally said as he waved Rod through.

"Yeah. Can't wait to fuck your tight hairy ass again," Rod said without a trace of excitement. "Asshole," he added inaudibly with what little breath he had in his lungs and weakened body as he pulled away to find an open space in the parking area.

Rod's trip from the parking lot to the publicity building seemed to take forever. He felt as though he were walking with lead-filled boots. When he finally reached the reception area of the publicity building, he came up to Audrey, who immediately recognized him and addressed him by name. "Nice to see you again, Mr. Dominguez. I didn't have a chance to say a proper good-bye to you last time. May I tell Mr. Cain that you're here?"

"Mind if I just go up and surprise him?"

"Rules are made to be broken, right?" Audrey giggled.

"Thanks, Audrey," he said. "By the way, great earrings."

She blushed as Rod stepped into the elevator. He gave her a wave.

"Fuck!" said perfect and perky Audrey under her breath. On the outside she looked as if she could play hostess to visiting VIPs and dignitaries at Disneyland. Inside, she was a woman whose libido twitched for almost every man under thirty that she laid her blue eyes on. The few heterosexual mail-delivery boys didn't stand a chance with her. Even Vic Bowen, the executive vice president of film distribution, had had Audrey.

"Why do all the fucking faggots around this fuckhole get all the fucking good-looking guys!" she lamented bitterly, thinking Bart and Rod were probably *doing it.* Then she blinked back to reality and displayed her disingenuous smile for the next man who came up to the receptionist's desk. It was Rupert Everett, asking to be announced for an appointment with Shari Draper. In an instant, Audrey forgot all about Rod. However, since she didn't know who the hell this Rupert Everett was—even later when she told her aghast girlfriend, Bertha, who berated her for not knowing Rupert Everett, for Christ's sake!—there wasn't a snowball's chance in hell of getting this man, either.

Rod stepped off the elevator on the tenth floor and wandered down to Bart's office. As usual, Cheets wasn't at her desk, so Rod simply stood in Bart's doorway until he looked up from his computer monitor.

Bart was momentarily startled. Then he smiled. "Hey, man. What's going on? Time flies. Seems I just saw you four hours ago. But it feels like ages."

"Hope you don't mind me coming back. I just needed someone to talk to," Rod said, staring almost lifelessly at Bart, who sat behind his desk in a plush leather chair, surrounded by movie posters of his favorite films hanging on the walls.

Suddenly, tears began to well up in Rod's eyes and roll down his beautiful, silky cheeks.

"What the hell!" Bart exclaimed. He jumped up from behind his desk and ushered Rod into a chair. He then closed the door, reached for a box of Kleenex, and handed it to Rod. "What's the matter? What's going on?"

"Oh, nothing," Rod said evasively. "Nothing that either suicide or murder or both won't cure."

"What in the world . . . ?"

"Jim. The screenplay. Michael. Sterling. Stealing my material. The end of my career before it's even begun."

Bart opened his small office-size refrigerator and took out a plastic bottle of cold Arrowhead spring water. He handed it to Rod and said, "Sorry, I'm not following. Start at the beginning."

Rod took a long moment to regain his composure as best he could. Then he described the situation he'd just encountered at home—*Jim Fallon's home*—he was quick to remind Bart. "They stole my screenplay. Simple as that. Jim's going to star. They've fucked up my life."

Bart tried to console Rod. "There's nothing to be concerned about. They can't get away with this. There's a long paper trail dating all the way back to the studio's story analyst to prove the script is indeed yours."

"You don't understand," Rod countered. "There's nothing left of the original script or even the original story. Well, maybe a little bit, but not enough to prove I did a damned thing on what's now called *Perfect Love.*"

"What was Dorothy Parker's famous line? 'The only "ism" Hollywood believes in is plagiar*ism*,'" Bart said, trying to lighten the mood.

"She was dead right. And how many years ago did she say that? It's still standard practice. Jim and Michael have it all worked out. I thought this kind of stuff was over after Paramount settled with Buchwald for *Coming to America*. I've been a complete idiot."

Bart shook his head. "This is too insane. There's got to be a logical explanation and something we can do. Let me call a friend in the legal department to find out if they're even telling you the truth. Maybe we haven't even acquired the script."

Rod sat quietly while Bart spoke to his friend Jeffrey in legal clearances. Bart made up a story saying he'd been asked to start a press release announcing a new film called *Perfect Love* and what could Jeffrey tell him about it.

"God, word travels fast," Jeffrey said, astonished at how short the grapevine was—even by Hollywood's standards. "There isn't even a contract yet. But, yeah, supposedly it's been acquired. I've got the file right here."

Bart pressed on. "Just so I can get a head start, can you give me the billing credits?"

"No director yet and no stars attached. But there's a deal memo here that's been prepared for Rupert Everett."

"I've heard Jim Fallon's signed," Bart interrupted.

"That old closet case. Doubt it. There's a Michael Scott as producer."

"Screenplay credit?" Bart asked.

"Same as the producer, Michael Scott. And somebody named Troy Bentley. Oh, this is interesting. It does say, 'Additional dialogue by Jim Fallon.' Hmmm. I don't see that kind of credit very often. Jim Fallon. I thought that dude was through after the s/m video. As long as I've worked in this biz, I'm still surprised at what goes on. Bet there was a lot of gang-bangin' to get him on this film." Jeffrey laughed, thinking of Jim's reputation.

Bart thanked Jeffrey and asked to be kept advised of new developments—casting and start of production and anything else pertinent to a press release. He hung up the phone and looked across the desk at Rod. "Seems to be true. You're not listed as a screenwriter. But hold on, these things often go into arbitration."

"How can I arbitrate if I don't even belong to the fucking WGA?" Rod said.

"You said Jim was going to be one of the stars? There's no one listed yet—except the possibility of Rupert Everett."

"That was one of my ideas, too! I wrote it with him in mind!"

"Jim does however get some strange 'additional dialogue by' credit. What if Michael is screwing Jim over, too? Think that's possible?"

"After what I've seen of this town, anything's possible—and probable," Rod said. "I want 'em both screwed—for life. They're gonna pay."

"Trust me, we'll work this out," Bart said, trying to reassure Rod. "Come on. I'll leave now. Let's go have a drink and talk."

Bart wrote a note for Cheets, whom he could never find when he needed her. He posted the message on her computer monitor.

"Are you okay to drive?" Bart asked Rod. "We can take my car, if you want."

"No. Let's just go over to Ricky's on Santa Monica. I'll meet you there."

"I'll call Rusty to let him know where I'll be. Maybe he can join us. Actually, he'd be a great one for you to talk to about this. He's extremely analytical. Much more than me. Maybe he can come up with some ideas."

"Whatever, man. I just want a drink. And I never want to see Jim Fallon as long as I live. Can I camp out with you for a while?"

With Rod feeling so low, Bart couldn't say no. "Sure, we can turn the office into a bedroom for a couple of nights."

Rod had been thinking of a longer-term arrangement, but he was too physically and emotionally wasted to discuss it any further. He didn't even acknowledge Bart's support. "See you at Ricky's."

* * *

Bart telephoned Rusty from the car and asked if he was available to meet with him and Rod. Rusty was nearly finished with a client, and he suggested that Bart pick him up on the way over the hill.

Rusty actually liked the idea that Bart wanted him to be part of helping out Rod. Not that Rusty felt the least bit of jealousy about Rod, but it would be nice to finally meet the only other man who, at another time, would have been his competition for Bart's love and affection.

When Bart and Rusty walked into the dimly lit Ricky's, which even at 5:30 was alive with loud music and a collection of some of West Hollywood's most drop-dead-gorgeous men, they found Rod at a table, turning away a guy in blue jeans ripped at the left butt cheek. The guy was wearing a black leather vest with nothing underneath but his hairy, muscled torso and nipple rings connected by a silver chain. He was holding a bottle of beer, and he slinked away when Bart and Rusty showed up.

"I may not command respect for my writing," Rod said, "but as long as I have my youth and my looks, the world's certainly interested in hiring me for a roll in the sack. Lucky you two came along when you did. He was the fifth guy in five minutes. Maybe I should stick where my true talents lie."

Bart made the introductions. "Rod, I'd like you to meet my lover, Rusty."

Rusty held out his hand to shake Rod's. Rod, however, didn't bother to look up, brushing Rusty off as he brushed off the five suitors who had approached him before. "I hear you're *nice,*" Rod said sarcastically. "Bart says you're nice. Isn't that nice?"

"Happy to meet you, too," Rusty said, ignoring Rod's lack of manners and ill disposition. "Bart has told me about you, too."

"No way he said I was nice."

"As a matter of fact, the word *asshole* came up the most," Rusty said, smiling.

Rod laughed, involuntarily caught off guard by the quick comeback.

Although such language was foreign to Rusty's everyday vocabulary, he was adept at holding his own with almost any type of individual. He was accomplished at dishing out to others what they doled out to him.

Rod finally looked up at Rusty and smiled, realizing the man was no pushover and was smart enough to know how to level the playing field when it came to interacting with difficult people. "Sorry," Rod said.

"It's nice to meet you. And I actually mean that. It's just been one of those days."

Bart and Rusty sat down and signaled for the bar boy to take their order. When he arrived, wearing short shorts and a tank top, showing off his assets, both men asked for red wine.

"Are you sure you wouldn't prefer beers," the young man said, bending down to their level. In an exaggerated stage whisper he said, "Confidentially, the wine here comes with an aluminum twist-off cap. And there's an expiration date and a skull and crossbones with a warning from the surgeon general—and Bea Arthur."

Rusty and Bart laughed. "Thanks for the words of caution," Rusty said. He looked at Bart for approval, then amended the order to two beers. "Do you have Heineken?"

"*Ya. Das ist gut!*" The bar boy spoke with an affected German pronunciation, pretending to be Colonel Klink, and pranced away.

"So," Rusty said to Rod, "one of those days, eh? What's the scoop? I mean, I don't have more than a slight clue about the reason for our being here, exactly. Something about you getting screwed over a screenplay you wrote?"

Rod reiterated the story for Rusty's benefit. "It sucks" was his concluding remark.

Rusty was reaching into his pocket to hand the returning bar boy a ten-dollar bill to pay for their drinks. "Perhaps you'd better run a tab," he said, giving the cute kid an ample tip.

"Okeydoke."

"I just don't know what to do now," Rod said, nearly in tears again. "This is the worst thing that's ever happened to me. Worse than the time I had to blow Burt Lancaster."

By the time Bart and Rusty were together in Rusty's king-size bed, after they'd enjoyed feeling each other's velvet-skinned bodies and having excruciatingly intense sex, they were still talking about the day's events. They agreed that given the mix of Rod and Shari and Jim and Michael and Cy, no one—not even Rod—was a truly reliable character. Each had an agenda, and each seemed to be more than competent at seducing their way into getting whatever they wanted.

"You gotta be careful of them all," Rusty warned. "I've been around these types of people long enough to know that where money and power are involved, nothing is ever as it seems. It's like families of friends I've had who died of AIDS, or whatever. Everybody seems so compassionate until there's an estate to divide. Then it can turn into a bloodbath.

"The lover of one of the greatest guys I ever knew had to race back to their second home in Manhattan to try and beat his dead lover's mother to the apartment to get his own things and a few mementos out. She got there first and had all the locks changed. The mother would not allow her son's partner of fifteen years to even take his own possessions from the place. The lease was in her son's name, and therefore Kurt, the widow, had no recourse. It happens all the time in the gay community because there are no civil or domestic rights for us."

"But out of that whole bunch, don't you think that perhaps Rod's at least the most vulnerable?"

"Aren't you?" Rusty queried.

"I don't follow."

"Rod hurt you. Shari hurt you. She and Cy are close to destroying your career. It could be argued that even *I'm* using you—in a sense—to help my old pal Owen."

Bart lay cradled in his lover's arms. He looked up at the mural-covered ceiling—a reproduction of Michelangelo's *Last Judgment* frescoes in the Sistine Chapel—which Rusty had painted himself. " 'Using' is when you're practicing something untoward. I don't believe for an instant that you could ever do that to me, or to anyone. It's just not in your nature. We could turn it all around and say I'm 'using' you to help ruin Shari and Cy and maybe to get back at Rod for the way he treated me."

Rusty rolled over on top of Bart and began passionately kissing Bart's lips, his neck, his chest, and his nipples. "Oh, yeah, use me, baby." Rusty laughed as his hands gamboled all over Bart's body, tickling and fondling his partner.

Bart giggled and screamed out, "No! No! Stop!" in mock torment as Rusty put aside their conversation for the time being in favor of ravaging his Bart all over again.

Bart breathed in the scent from Rusty's warm body with as much urgency as oxygen. For a moment, they stopped—merely to gaze upon each other. Bart looked up at Rusty, who stared down at his lover. Time, and the outside world, did not exist. All that mattered was the high-voltage intensity of their feelings for one another.

Rusty rose up and straddled Bart's hips. Rusty began rubbing his hard cock against Bart's own steel-hard penis, which was already oozing fluid. Bart involuntarily moaned in exhilarated anticipation as Rusty's hands began exploring his face, then his chest and stomach and arms.

Bart reciprocated, touching the cleft in Rusty's chin, then letting his hands wander all over Rusty's beautiful torso. In perfect synch, each man anticipated the other's every action and reaction. There was no need for Bart to say when he wanted Rusty to be inside him. It was a natural progression, from deep, harsh kissing to Rusty's gently applying lube to Bart's ass, then slathering his own cock and slowly sliding himself into his lover.

With Rusty cautiously but rhythmically moving deep inside Bart, the nonverbal language that issued from their respective bodies made the world fade to black. The only thing that mattered was this moment, this ultimate in physical pleasure. Both men whimpered and gasped as they engorged one another and tried to keep the loving going on for eternity.

As the sheets became saturated with perspiration from Bart's body, he whispered, "I can't hold it much longer! Oh, God," Bart cried, half in apology and gratitude.

"Let it go, baby! Come for me!"

"I'm ready when you are! Oh, I'm *so ready!*"

Bart abruptly released a loud cry as he climaxed. His explosive discharge reached as far as Bart's nose and beyond, to the headboard of the bed. He continued to come as Rusty's penis hammered at his prostate. Within seconds of Bart's own climax, Rusty clenched his teeth. His throat constricted, and his face contorted, as if he were experiencing excruciating torture. Then he, too, cried out in waves of rapturous groans.

Presently, Rusty eased himself from within Bart's body and lay down on top of his lover, the moist, sticky fluid on Bart's chest and stomach bonding them. Slowly, both men's respiration began to return to normal. Rusty rolled onto his back, his skin still in contact with Bart's.

Suddenly, the bedroom door burst open. Three large dogs raced to the bed, barking. Rusty and Bart both exploded with laughter as their "kids" leaped onto the bed to snuggle with their masters.

"I've never felt more at peace," Bart said as he petted the coats of each of the dogs.

"You're reading my thoughts," Rusty replied. He rolled back to his lover for a good-night kiss that lasted until one of the dogs joined in and began licking Bart's face.

Chapter Nineteen

"Rod can be such a shit," Bart complained to Rusty a few weeks later on a Saturday evening as they lounged together on Rusty's living-room sofa, enjoying their merlot, petting the dogs, and listening to a Betty Buckley CD. "Here I am, playing Lady Bountiful, letting him camp out in my home-slash-office for nearly a month, and he repays me by being a cockteaser, for crying out loud."

"You're seldom home," Rusty reminded him, dismissing the notion that Rod was sexually harassing Bart. "You're with me five nights a week. The rest of the time you're at the office until all hours. It's not like he doesn't know we're a couple. I'm sure he respects the boundaries."

"I don't think he respects anything or anybody but Rodrigo Dominguez and his libido. When I *am* home, all he does is play Jim's porno tapes over and over, saying he's going to someday force Jim into those same scenarios, but for real, no special instructions to take things only so far. Rod's actually got quite a stash of tapes. He stole 'em from Jim's vault. Says he's keeping 'em in case Jim actually gets a shot at being in the movie. He doesn't return Jim's calls. He won't go back to work because he knows Michael, who's deigned to become his agent, would know where to find him."

"Usually it's the agent who stops talking to his client," Rusty said with mock sympathy. "My poor baby. Does it hurt to see the most beautifully constructed man on the planet walking around your apartment without a stitch?"

Rusty set down his glass and began tickling Bart as if Bart were a pouting child, trying to coax a smile and change of attitude. "Is the sight of Rod's silky brown, sinewy, muscled body too much of a turn-on for my little darlin'?"

Then, playacting, as if he were Shirley Temple making peace between the Yankees and the Confederates, Rusty placed his index fingers in his own honest-to-goodness Shirley Temple dimples and said, "Do you need your cute new boyfriend to come over and protect you from the big, bad God of Physical Perfection?"

"Stop!" Bart squealed with laughter. "You don't know how tough it is to go home and see a naked God coming out from the shower, his body glistening from the oil he uses on his skin, for crying out loud. Stop! Don't! I'm ticklish!"

"And what about catching Narcissus jerking off to his own reflection in the mirrored sliding-closet doors?" Rusty continued as the Littlest Rebel. "What's an all-American queer boy like you s'pose t'do?"

"It's a virtually impossible place for me to live without leaking in my pants," Bart said, picking up the playacting thread and imitating Shirley's pal Bill Robinson. "But I suppose somebody has to make the sacrifice. I'm just a man who wants to make the planet a better and safer place for the rest of the queers of the world."

Rusty sat back. "Then you'll stop complaining?"

"As best I can. I promise *thisssssss* much," Bart said, opening his arms to express the breadth of his devotion to duty.

"That's my brave and courageous man of steel!"

They both laughed and nestled into each other's arms on the sofa. Then, suddenly, they both bolted up straight. Betty was singing "Children Will Listen" in her best Broadway belting show voice. Perfection.

What Bart didn't tell Rusty was that the mere sight of Rod's body was enough to drive him mad, which was one reason he stayed away from his own apartment as much as possible.

The next night was no exception.

Sunday nights had always been sacred to Bart. He never went out, even when he began to date Rusty. It was a time to mentally prepare for the coming workweek. "A school night," he called it. He read the *New York Times,* watched *60 Minutes,* still missed all the years of watching *Murder, She Wrote,* and somehow got through *Touched by an Angel.* The show was sappy, but there was always a good message. And at least the Angel of Death was cute, although the producers obviously couldn't settle on what color his hair should be. Then off to bed.

The very night after he got through telling Rusty about Rod and how difficult it was to be in the apartment with him because he was always horny and seemingly just hanging around, hinting that he was up for any action, Bart turned in for the night. He fell into a deep sleep.

Then, from down in the basement of his unconscious, he vaguely thought he heard the door open to his room. It wasn't long before he was wide-awake. Indeed, the door had opened, and Rod had slipped into bed beside Bart.

"What the fuck?" Bart said, awaking but groggy, feeling Rod's naked body and hot throbbing dagger against his own bare skin.

"Shhh." Rod placed his mouth over Bart's and rolled on top of him. Bart was dumbfounded. But all the images of the nights they had fucked together collided into one huge, passionate, deep kiss.

Thoughts of Rusty and how much they loved each other rushed in, but the painful need for Rod's muscled body deflected all rationalization. Bart hated himself for giving in to animal desire, but Rod was so passionate and demanding, there was no way to escape and to not fall completely in love with him all over again, even if the love was only physical.

The two men indulged their most base desires and engorged themselves in each other's bodies. Rod's body was as hot and as ripped as Bart had remembered and dreamed about ever since their breakup.

A part of Bart tried to convince himself that this was not at all premeditated. He decided that Rusty should never know about this encounter, telling himself that even if Rusty did find out, he was still the most understanding man alive. Surely he would not hold this one incident of bestial sex between him and Rod against their relationship. Anyway, what Rod and Bart did together was not the same kind of passion Rusty and Bart shared. It was something completely different and therefore not an issue in their love for one another.

He could rationalize forever. The truth was he was so engulfed with lust, for the moment he didn't care about the consequences.

"Bart! Oh, Christ, Bart!" Rod groaned. "I am *so* fucking hard for you! I've *got* to fuck you! *Please,* Bart! I've got to fuck your brains out! You want me to, don't you? Yeah, you remember how great it was. You want me up your hot ass, don't you! Say you want it! Say it, Bart! Say it! Please, say you want it!"

"I want it! I want it, *Rusty!* Fuck me, *Rusty! Fuck me!*"

Rusty! Oh, shit, Bart thought to himself as he continued to kiss Rod, pretending the name had not slipped out.

But they both had heard Rusty's name spoken, in the darkness. Instantly, the spell was broken. Although Rod and Bart for a time continued to kiss deeply, and with their respective tongues fighting each other like moray eels in an underwater cave, they slowly drew apart. It wasn't a conscious thing, but both men grew less fervent until they lay merely entwined in each other's arms and legs and their breathing became less heavy, more controlled.

Bart could feel Rod's enormous, erect penis pressing against his stomach, and he longed to reach down and hold it with his hands. Instead, he breathed in the scent of Rod's underarms and felt the sultry heat from his body. Neither man spoke, although they stayed wrapped together for the rest of the night.

In the morning, after Bart had showered and was dressed for work, Rod still lay in Bart's bed. "I'm *not* sorry I came in here last night, if that's what you're hoping for."

"I'm not sorry, either," Bart said, sitting on the edge of the bed. He put his hand out to touch Rod's sculpted chest. "But I'm also not sorry that things didn't go any further—if that's what *you're* hoping for."

"You didn't do anything with me last night that should cause a problem for you and Rusty. Are you going to tell him?"

"What purpose would it serve?"

Rod didn't answer. He guessed it would be stupid to reveal what were essentially two friends enjoying the comfort of being close together. They hadn't even jacked off together, so it was completely benign. The sex, or at least the act of copulation, had been aborted. So, indeed, there was nothing to talk about.

Then, apropos of nothing, Rod said, "I want you to read Jim's manuscript. It's not that I didn't trust you before, but after your display of devotion to Rusty and keeping last night between us, I know you're probably the only man alive who would keep my secret. I'll give you Jim's whole book. I've highlighted with a yellow marker the stuff I intend to use to blackmail the son of a bitch."

Bart was incredulous. "Blackmail? That's a federal offense."

"Your point being?"

"I thought you ripped off his videotapes for that. Is the stuff in the book really worth the trouble of you possibly going to jail?" Bart asked.

"I didn't steal the tapes. I borrowed them and forgot to give them back when I had to leave so quickly. As for the content of the book, I don't know. I need you to be the judge of its potential value. All I know is he deserves whatever happens to him."

"We all do," Bart said. "It's called karma. You know, cause and effect. Be careful."

"It's also a matter of principle. He's ruined my life. I don't want to have happen to some other stud what happened to me."

"Oh, give me a break," Bart said, standing up and looking down on Rod. "You just want revenge. You're not trying to save some other poor street hustler from a fate worse than death. And you're not even going about it the right way. Jim's career is already in ashes. Also, you say he has chronic acne on his butt. I don't know what else you could possibly come up with that would make things worse for him."

"He'll never make a career comeback. I'll see to it. Just read the book." Rod slipped out of bed and padded out to the office-bedroom.

Bart watched Rod and wished to hell he could undress, get into bed, and have the master fuck him until he was so raw he'd be unable to report to work. But Bart knew better than to act on a fantasy that could only land him in trouble.

Rod returned moments later with a ream and a half of paper, held together with rubber bands. He handed it to Bart, who accepted the weighty manuscript and cradled it in his arms.

Rod said, "A lot of the crap in there is really lame and boring. You can skip right to the stuff I've underlined. It'll make you sorry you ever became associated with Hollywood."

"Like I'm not already?" Bart paused. "I'll start as soon as I get to the studio, but this is going to take days."

"Then just read what I've flagged."

"Make up the bed when you're finished sleeping, will you?"

"Sure. I'll change the sheets, too."

"No. Don't do that," Bart said as he left the room. It would have seemed strange to explain, but he wanted another opportunity to lie in bed, even if he was completely alone, knowing that Rod's naked body had left its scent somewhere on the sheets and pillowcases. He grabbed his leather jacket from the hall closet and walked out of the apartment.

In the car, Bart placed the seven-hundred-plus pages of double-spaced text on white bond paper on the passenger seat. He looked at it with the dread of knowing he'd have to at least skim the damn thing.

Once at the studio, Bart first made a pot of coffee. Then he listened to his messages. Shari (angry). Shari (livid). Angelina Jolie (incensed), Shari (furious), Rusty (affectionate), Shari (petulant).

Then he logged on to his computer to retrieve his E-mail. There were twenty-seven postings since the night before. Red flags meant they were urgent. But Bart dismissed them. He'd read his cyber mail when the office officially opened. This was *his* time.

He wasn't in any hurry to begin poring through the voluminous manuscript. He had glanced at the first page while at a stoplight on the way to the studio and immediately noticed long run-on sentences. The book was going to be a chore to wade through; of that he was certain.

Bart hated having to read other people's unpublished work. As the head writer at Sterling and the author of a book about the behind-the-scenes making of *Encino Man* with Brendan Fraser (the only reason to write the book in the first place) as well as some short stories here and there and feature articles, novices were constantly after him to read their stuff. They all wanted the same thing: to be told how wonderful their work was and how, with a little more effort, they would be the next Armistead Maupin or Edmund White. They also wanted access to Bart's agent or publisher with a letter of recommendation.

Finally, with a sigh of resignation, Bart picked up Jim's manuscript. He propped his feet up on his desk and placed the manuscript in his lap. He leaned slightly back in his chair and began to read:

Page 1. Chapter One.

LOVE ME AND LEAVE ME

"I cried for forty-eight hours straight!" Jim began. "When that bitch Meredith on *Totally Hollywood* aired that two-part and completely false and slanderous piece about me, with her doctored videotape, I was so humiliated, I left the studio in the middle of a taping, went to bed, and with my clothes still on, drew myself into a fetal position and cried myself to sleep! I awoke two days later, ready to fight for the truth! This is why I am writing this book, which is meant as an explanation to all my fans and a vindication of my virtue."

The first chapter was wretched. Bart found himself laughing not only at Jim's lack of writing skills but also his whining about the travails of being a star and how his fame got in the way of having an ordinary sex life. While most celebrities complained about lack of privacy, Jim merely griped about sex. He tried to explain how he got caught on a videotape being raped by a gang of mad South Central Los Angeles bangers. He said that he had been followed home from a party by a car filled with six tough guys. They crashed through the estate gate to get to him before he reached the safety of his house and the security alarm system.

"As I pleaded for my life in what was supposed to be the sanctuary of my guarded estate, I was wrestled to the ground and severely beaten!"

he wrote. "When I eventually regained consciousness, I found myself tied up in my own wine cellar! I was a prisoner in my own home, and I was terrified!" Jim ended nearly every sentence with an exclamation point.

"The ugliest of the gang members, the one who seemed to be the leader, decided he wanted to videotape the big, important TV star that he and his cohorts had just bagged! I know some Spanish, from trying to teach my cleaning lady how to properly iron toilet paper, so I understood that they wanted to sell the video to the highest bidder—on eBay!"

Bart groaned. It was highly unlikely that gangstas from South Central would be hawking porn on eBay.

"Then, when I finally thought I had found an opportunity to fight back, I was overpowered by the entire hoard of thugs! They had their way with me. Then they found a cattle prod that had been used as a gimmick prop on my sitcom and they decided it would be funny to use it on me for real! It was the darkest moment of my life! I vowed it was the last time I would ever take home a prop that belonged to the show—especially a potentially dangerous one!"

Bart knew better than to buy any of this. First of all, there had never been a burglary-and-assault situation. The *Star* or the *Enquirer* would have detailed the incident immediately if it had really occurred and been reported to the LAPD. If something as innocuous as George Michael flashing his reknowned genitalia in a Beverly Hills public restroom and could be "News at Eleven" as well as Leno's opening jokes for a week, then surely they couldn't have kept Jim Fallon off the night sergeant's report.

Second, Jim was well known in various communities, not just among gays, for hiring Latin prostitutes to rough him up. Even his neighbors complained about the types of men who didn't belong in the area running in and out of Jim's estate. It was the worst-kept secret that Jim had a penchant for being gagged and hog-tied as a prelude to sex.

Third, the underprivileged from South Central most likely would not know how to use sophisticated video equipment and make such a professional-looking tape.

Fourth, Bart was unaware of an episode of *The Grass Is Always Greener* in which a cattle prod was used. The closest the show came to such a scenario was when Grammy, played by Lily Pudetra, a third-rate road-company version of comic stalwart Doris Roberts, threatened her grandchildren by holding their pet hamster over the open cylinder of a

Cuisinart while turning the machine on and off, making the scalpel-sharp blades rotate like a fan.

With her patented disingenuous smile and sweet-tempered voice, Lily had said, "Alrighty now. Mr. Leonardo DiCaprio here has been awfully depressed lately. Which of you future cocksuckers is going to tell their sweet little ol' Grammy where they hid her brand-new copy of her favorite Freddie Prinze Jr. video before Leo jumps down the chute to commit suicide?"

The slack-jawed kids didn't have to pretend to be mortified. They suspected their TV grandmother was, in real life, quite capable of mixing Leonardo in with the homemade pizza dough she was supposed to be making in that particular scene.

Bart remembered that episode because it was especially hilarious and the fanatics at PETA and Actors and Others for Animals had gone more insane than usual and tried to have the episode banned. Their ads in *TV Guide* and *USA Today* only made the ratings soar. Lily even received an Emmy Award nomination.

And finally, on the tape, why was Jim's cock as hard as the plastic dildos he bought at the Pleasure Chest on Santa Monica Boulevard the whole time he was supposedly being tortured?

"Hell, I'd be as limp as a telephone cord if I wasn't having the slightest bit of fun with sex and if it looked like my final performance might be in a snuff film," Bart said aloud.

Bart recalled that by the time the tape was ready to end, Jim climaxed like a geyser without anyone so much as touching his less-than-average-size dick.

Bart decided that, so far, this book was simply too far-fetched to be anything but fiction. It was as silly as Liberace claiming that three times he'd "come close" to being married (to a woman). It was all horseshit.

A few chapters later, Bart found himself rolling his eyes while reading about the failure of Jim's engagement to a woman that he called "Jenny."

Jim admitted that Jenny wasn't the woman's real name. He wanted to protect her virtue by using a pseudonym. From all that Bart knew of Jim's sexual proclivities—made even more clear by the s/m videotapes, and Rod had absconded with a dozen more from a fully stocked vault—this Jenny was probably a Jeremy. Or, more likely, Rod.

Chances were, like O.J. vowing to find Nicole's "real" killer, Jenny/Jeremy/Rod was probably in the same halfway house occupied by fictional ex-girlfriends and beards of closeted gay stars who were too freaked about their sexuality and thus continued to pass themselves off as breeders in order to keep the public buying their records, flocking to their movies, or watching their dumb-assed television sitcoms.

Jim's reminiscence about hearing the horrifying news of his television show's cancellation was another complete lie. He claimed to be completely mystified about the cancellation of the network's number-one sitcom. He had heard the rumors. The truth was, old enemies were out to defame him. Of course, as soon as his infamous video was leaked to *Totally Hollywood,* he knew the years of rolling sixes or eights had finally hit craps.

Bart's first response to the beginning of the book was to bemoan how poorly the text was written. There didn't seem to be any continuity of thought. Transitions were practically nonexistent. It was like a schizophrenic unable to censor his thoughts or the stream-of-conscious babbling of the venomous Rev. Don Wildmon and his American Family Association, going on about how the Pillsbury Dough Boy commercials and the muscular Mr. Clean solvent ads contained subliminal messages from GLAAD, trying to advance "the homosexual agenda" and corrupting "traditional family values." Bart found himself nearly nodding off from boredom a number of times.

Then, suddenly, like the explosion from a firecracker, the book kicked into some kind of fourth-dimension high gear.

It was as though a voice other than the author's had come along and possessed the pages, like a demon. The prose became startling, as though the combined nefarious spirits of Cindy Adams and Mr. Blackwell had suddenly taken over. It was the Fatty Arbuckle scandal magnified to the power of a billion. Only this time it wasn't an obese comic fucking a starlet to death with a Coke bottle. It was the Gen-X *Father Knows Best* unloading the best of the worst about the nutty, slutty world of Hollywood.

By page 75, Bart was hooked. Until then, the only value of the book was in finding out more than anybody would want to know about the night a drunk Frank Sinatra came to the Comedy Room on Sunset Boulevard and had heckled Jim while one of the cocktail waitresses stooped down and put her head under the dime-size table and in plain sight of the whole room gave "Ol' Blue Eyes" a blow job in the middle of Jim's set. All Jim could say was to parody Estelle Reiner from *When Harry Met Sally:* "I *won't* have what she's having!" The audience tried in vain to suppress their laughter. After Jim's set, bodyguards kicked his ass in the parking lot behind the club.

Then there was the evening that diva Deena Rose brought an entourage that included Bob Mackie and how Rose had talked throughout Jim's entire set. When Jim tried to comically harass the group to quiet down, Mackie became so embarrassed by his friends and sympathetic to the talent onstage that he stood up and, like the gentleman that he is, publicly apologized. This, however, made Jim appear to be a number-one asshole. A tourist from a chartered bus that was idling outside became outraged at Jim for throwing a fit at "that nice costume designer from the old *Carol Burnett Show.*" Then she threw the contents of her glass of watered-down Chablis at Jim's crotch.

Until page 75, Jim had recounted vague incidents of the people he met day in and day out in Hollywood. He talked of the male casting agents who had him take off his shirt under the pretense that the roles most likely to come along were for the daytime dramas and they required guys with decent builds. These so-called agents often took snapshots of Jim with disposable cameras. More than a few times, an agent was obviously jacking off under his desk as Jim bared his chest and showed what at the time was a perfectly acceptable physique. The subsequent years of stardom, with all his drinking, overeating, and indulgence of recreational drugs, had taken their toll. But when he was starting out, he had an above-average-looking upper torso. Although no matter how many exercises he performed, chicken legs would be his lifetime affliction.

Still he couldn't get work. Until the day that the owner of the Comedy Room caught his routine during an open-mike night. Jim retold the oft-quoted story about how she gave him a spot every Monday night for a month. Monday was typically the slowest night of the week, so she felt she had nothing to lose and maybe something to gain. She also made a few phone calls to agents and suggested they come around and take a look at this new guy.

Michael Scott was one of the agents.

Over the years many muffin magazines had printed variations on this theme of "discovery." The only thing new in this book was Jim revealing that Michael, after watching Jim's performance, sensed that a star was about to be born and wound up the evening schmoozing, then fucking the unknown comic to get him to sign an agency contract.

Michael was so stupid, he didn't realize it was supposed to be the other way around: Wanna-bes fucked talent reps. Talent reps made empty promises. Wanna-bes kept fucking talent reps. Talent reps go on to new wanna-bes. That was the typical Hollywood game. In this case, however, Michael was both horny and impressed by this particular wanna-be's stage presence. In short order, there was the series and major stardom for Jim. It shouldn't have worked out so well. But it did.

As 9:00 A.M. loomed, Bart couldn't put down the manuscript. On every page after 75 he read the names of people he recognized, including some of his colleagues: Shari Draper, Cy Lupiano, CEO Rotenberg, as well as star-crossed John Landis, movie-star slut Mare Dickerson, Betty Ford regular Britteny Austin, tempestuous, tantrum-throwing bully Stan Murray, egomaniacal director Michael Mann, Heidi Fleiss, Madonna, Kurt Cobain, Margeaux Hemingway, and Nicole Brown Simpson, among many others.

The pages were peppered with the names of stars, with numerous footnotes about each. They all seemed somehow connected. The "six degrees of separation" link appeared to be dead producer Don Simpson, whose demise was as poetic as justice comes—one of the biggest shits in Hollywood dying on the toilet! While Hollywood pretended to grieve and honor the whacked-out druggie with a memorial service on a friggin' soundstage, practically everybody who ever knew Simpson smiled at the idea that the Wicked Witch of the West was dead—and such an *unforgettable* way to die.

As Bart read along, he decided that truth *is* stranger than fiction, but this was too on-the-nose to be anything but a play-by-play of the people Jim had to deal with at the studio, as well as guest stars on his show.

The door to Bart's door was closed. When Cheets arrived at 9:40, her delight at thinking she had, for the first time, come in before her boss was short-lived when she used the spare key to unlock and open his door. Bart was still reading. "I'm not in yet," he told his assistant. "If anybody asks about me, I had car trouble. Close the door, please."

Cheets was nothing if not happy to be in on something clandestine. She lived to lie. Or, as she called it, "practicing my character study of a sociopath." She closed the door as instructed.

Bart then picked up his cell phone and dialed Rod's private number.

Rod didn't answer. He was probably at the gym. Now that he was out of Jim Fallon's house, he had borrowed enough money from Bart to rejoin his health club and spent at least three hours a day there. His voice mail picked up.

"Rod, it's Bart," he said quietly. "I've read a lot of the book. We have to meet. This is a crazy day for me, but we have to talk. Don't call back at the office. Just meet me at the Griffith Park Observatory at twelve-thirty. If you can't make it, call me at that time—not before—on my cell. Got it? See you then, I hope."

After shutting off the phone, Bart placed the manuscript in his shoulder bag and zipped it closed. He then put the leather bag into the bottom drawer of his filing cabinet and locked the three-drawer unit. Then he opened his office door and acted as though he were ready for a regular day of business.

At noon, Bart reversed the procedure, unlocking the file cabinet and retrieving his bag. He left the office and walked with purpose to the parking structure. All along the way he felt as though he were carrying a load of narcotics and was being trailed by a contingent of DEA officers. He thought he probably looked conspicuous, and if he'd been disembarking from a jet landing in Europe, he'd be stopped at customs.

For the first time, he paid attention to warning signs posted all around the parking structure: "All cars subject to search." He'd never known anyone whose car had been singled out, but he thought, *I'll be the first.* Bart waved to the guard as he drove past the gate and off the studio lot.

Entering the freeway at Riverside Drive, he drove along the 134 to where it split to the 5, taking the off-ramp to Los Feliz, and from there drove up to Griffith Park. On the wide carpets of lawn, Hispanic families were picnicking. Studs from West Hollywood, dressed in Speedo's, getting a head start on the tanning season, also had their blankets spread out. He saw them occasionally reach into their Coleman ice chests for a bottle of Evian water.

Bart took the long, serpentine road and followed the signs that directed motorists to the hilltop observatory, which on a clear day could be seen from all over the city, like the Hollywood sign.

Arriving at the observatory, Bart parked his car, grabbed his shoulder bag, and walked around the grounds outside the massive art deco–style building that always made him think of the climactic scene from *Rebel Without a Cause,* which was shot on this very location. James Dean and Sal Mineo were still both hot guys all these years after their respective bizarre deaths. And with the previously secret details of Dean's gay life now established, Bart could only imagine what must have gone on between him and Mineo.

At 12:30 he saw Rod's Dodge Dart pull up into the parking area. Dressed in blue jeans and a white athletic shirt that showed off his muscles and his tattoos, Rod looked around until he finally spotted Bart standing by one of the many coin-operated telescopes that allowed a viewer to magnify the city below.

"So you must've gotten to the part . . ." Rod began to speak.

"What *is* this?" Bart said without preamble, indicating the manu-script. "Do you believe it's true?"

"Pretty amazing shit, eh? Jim wrote it, I think. But he couldn't have done it just over the past few months," Rod said. "I get the impression that he's been working on it for years."

"Okay. Let me get my bearings straight. Bottom line."

"Bottom line," Rod repeated.

"Shari Draper . . ."

Rod nonverbally coaxed Bart, as if playing a game of twenty ques-tions.

"Someone named Larry Burton . . ."

Rod prodded.

"A jail cell in Alaska with . . . ?" Bart's eyes widened

". . . dead, fucked-up producer . . ."

Bart smiled.

"*Comprenez-vous?*" Rod asked snidely.

"Just about." Bart was still attempting to fathom the scenario he had read and now found reiterated by Rod. "Is this the old 'Mrs. Madrigal' switcheroo routine?"

"Wait'll you read the rest."

When Bart returned to the studio from the observatory, he heard right away that Owen Lucas had been fired.

According to the rumors, Owen was terminated for two reasons: sex-ual harassment and poor job performance. The gossip further claimed that two unnamed guys from the marketing staff had filed a lawsuit stat-ing that Owen had tried to have sex with them. The rumormongers set out like truffles pigs sniffing about to discover who the plaintiffs were. Bart was a prime suspect.

"You told too many people you thought he was cute," Cheets ex-plained when Bart told her he'd overheard a couple of secretaries in the stairwell whispering about him. "What else are they going to think at a time like this?"

"But it's not true," Bart protested. "I'm going to talk to Shari."

He hurried down the hall, passing the judgmental eyes and shaking heads of several colleagues. When he reached Shari's outer office, Mitch looked up at him with an expression that asked, "You didn't, did you?"

Bart responded before Mitch could utter a word. "Of course it's not me," he insisted. "Trust me, Mitch. I'm completely innocent. I would never do anything to hurt Owen."

Mitch nodded to indicate his agreement that it was impossible for Bart to have made any kind of noise about Owen. Even if Owen had come to Bart and had been rejected, Bart was the type who would have said, "I'm flattered, Owen, but you know the old saying 'Don't get your meat where you get your bread.'"

Mitch gave Bart a smile and cocked his head toward Shari's office. "She's in there with Cy. I'll call you when she's free."

But before Mitch could jump up and shield the door with his body, Bart rushed for the handle. As he slammed the tall, solid wooden door behind him, the muted sound of Mitch crying, "No! Wait!" could be heard. But Bart was already inside and locked the door.

A startled Shari looked up from her desk. Cy, who was seated on the Mies van der Rohe chair, turned around and glared at Bart.

"What's this rumor that I'm suing Owen Lucas for sexual harassment," Bart declared.

"You can't fucking just waltz in here, you little cocksucker," Shari cried.

"You guys said you just wanted some ammo in case Owen tried to screw you."

"And, like a good boy, that's exactly what you gave us," Shari sneered.

"How did I . . . ? What did I . . . ? What's he done to deserve this?"

"You don't know the depth of what's going on, so don't jump to conclusions," Cy said calmly. "You're way over your head, son, and I do mean the one on your shoulders."

Shari laughed at Cy's intentionally sexist remark.

Bart said, "All I know is, I'm suddenly a pariah around the office. Everybody thinks I'm one of two guys responsible for Owen being fired. They think I'm filing a sexual-harassment lawsuit. Which I'm not."

"But you've made so many complaints about him. I have proof," Shari said.

"You haven't seemed to care before that the whole studio knows you're a faggot," Cy said. "So why do you give a shit what else they have to say now?"

Bart blanched at the word faggot. He felt as if he were back in grammar school, being taunted by bullies on the playground. "I'm not ashamed of being a fucking queer faggot pansy cocksucker or anything you want to call me, Cy. However, I *am* ashamed of possibly being re-sponsible for a brilliant, creative, and innocent man getting the ax."

Shari groaned. "Oh, cut the bullshit, Bart. We know you wanted to sleep with him. Although 'sleep' is hardly the right word."

Turning to his boss, Bart countered, "All those lies you had me re-hearse about Owen coming on to me. You were setting me up, weren't you? Oh, it's so clear now. Well, you can fire me if you want, but I'm not suing Owen. Instead, I'll have both of you and Sterling up on charges for harassing me into going along with this charade!"

"Oh, aren't you the high-and-mighty one." Shari's voice dripped sar-casm. "We're way ahead of you." She stood up and walked over to him. "You're threatening the wrong people, sweetheart," she said, jabbing her index finger into Bart's chest. "The shit we've got on you stinks like Chris Farley's asshole."

"Leave it to you to denigrate even the dead," Bart retorted. "God knows you probably think yours smells like Chanel No. 5."

Shari snarled at him. "As a matter of fact, I'm calling security now and have you escorted off the lot. You won't even have time to drag that screensaver of your naked Latin lover–friend into the trash-can icon—where you both belong! Oh, yeah. We know all about him. That's merely a fraction of the evidence we've gathered against you. It wasn't very wise to download all that porno, Bart. You know the studio's net-work saves everything. Not only are you a cocksucking pervert; we've got you on so many other charges, from padding your expense account to making personal calls to Paris and London using company time to make sex dates on AOL."

"You'll never eat lunch in this town again," Cy said. "No other stu-dio will ever have you. You're washed up."

"Can't you come up with anything better than an old Julia Philips book title?" Bart mocked, but he was really completely floored. He couldn't be more shocked. Then he paused, pretending to backtrack. "I can't lose my job. What if I did decide to help you? What about that?"

"Too late." Shari smiled evilly.

"What about when this all comes out and I testify and tell the court everything that's happened here?"

"Who the fuck's going to believe some disgruntled employee?" Shari scoffed. "We've got a file on you that's as thick as the girth of your boyfriend's dick, complete with complaints and write-ups and poor evaluations. Even got a few critical letters from celebrities in there! That lovely director Barbet Schroeder offered a good one. So did Mare

Dickerson. She said, and I quote, 'I find Bart Cain to have a lot of anger in him.' It has only been out of the goodness of our hearts that we kept you here as long as we did. You're a disgrace, Bart! You're a sick, perverted, lazy excuse for a staff writer, and nobody's going to argue with that assessment."

Shari picked up the telephone and pushed Mitch's extension number on the keypad. "Get security up here now," she said.

"You're seriously having me thrown off the lot?" Bart said, incredulous in the face of the whole situation.

"You bet your cock-fucked ass, you little creep. I've got a new writer starting tomorrow."

Within moments, there was a knock on the door. A master key opened the lock, and two security guards stepped inside the room.

"Gentlemen, this is Bart Cain," Shari said. "He's just been terminated. One of you please go lock his office. Then collect his studio ID and escort him off the lot."

Mitch stood in the doorway, shocked at what he was witnessing. Then, furtively, he left quickly and ran to Bart's office. He began to drag Bart's personal files—the porno Bart had shared with him—into the computer's trash can.

"Let me at least get my wallet and jacket," Bart demanded. The security men looked up at Shari, who waved them off as if to say, "I suppose that's okay."

As the two security men, one of whom was Rod's fucker Rich, tried to lead Bart away by the arms, Bart shrugged them off. He turned around and spoke one last time to Shari. "Like the lady in the lottery commercial says to her boss after she's won the jackpot, 'I can't tell you what a pleasure it's been working for you. Really. I can't.'"

"So long, fuckup!" Shari said, then blew him a kiss.

As pissed off as Bart was, he made a quick decision not to mention what he now knew—or at least had read in Jim's memoir about Don Simpson, the prison in Alaska, and someone named Larry Burton.

Bart passed Mitch in the hallway and smiled sheepishly. Mitch gave him a wink, in solidarity. Bart led the security team down to his office, where they watched as he picked up his briefcase and grabbed his jacket.

"Don't touch anything else," one of the security men advised. "Your personal stuff will be packed up and sent to you."

Just as the door was being closed and locked, Cheets appeared from wherever she always disappeared when her boss was away. She looked stunned. "What's going on?"

"Looks like you'll have a new boss tomorrow," Bart said. "He or she probably won't be as understanding of you coming in so late each day and leaving early for rehearsals. Better play it safe for a while."

Bart had to wonder how much help Cheets had provided, if indeed there was any evidence of his padding his expense reports and down-loading porn from the Internet. He didn't abuse his expense accounts as badly as most of his colleagues did. Still, Cheets resented having to com-plete the forms and attach receipts for Bart, especially when he left a dozen bills from expensive restaurants on her desk. "You're a cool liar, Bart," she'd said on more than one occasion. "I can't even afford Denny's, and you're taking friends out to the Ivy and Morton's, all on Sterling's dime. Just hope you never get audited by accounting." He now wondered if that had been a threat.

Bart would not have been surprised to find that his assistant had been a spy or even an outright traitor. She was jealous of his salary, his car al-lowance, and of course, the expense account.

"Hey, everybody. Bart's been fired. Come say g'bye," she announced in her most theatrical voice.

The call brought half the staff out of their respective offices and cubi-cles to watch as Bart was led to the elevator.

Once inside the lift, Bart looked out at all the faces of the people he had worked with for so many years. Although he was fond of only a few of them, he felt a huge emptiness knowing that this was the end of the line for his career in the motion-picture industry. At least as a publicist for Sterling Studios.

Chapter Twenty

Months passed since Bart's and Owen's respective terminations. But they had bean holding strategy meetings to retaliate against Shari, Cy, and Sterling. A core group of conspirators had been assembled.

Seated at opposite ends of the dining-room table at Rusty's home were Rusty and Bart. Owen Lucas and Rod Dominguez and Jim Fallon and Mitch Wood occupied the seats on either side. Seated between Owen and Rod was the odd man in the group: Gus Fitterman, Hollywood's most famous litigator since his triumph in *Neal v. Waldman,* the infamous high-stakes lawsuit in which sex and drug-addicted producer Grey Waldman was forced to pay several million dollars to twenty-seven uncredited and unpaid screenwriters who had worked on his hit films.

Two tall gold-plated candelabras, aglow with multiple tapered candles, provided a gentle radiance. John Barry's *Movieola* CD softly filtered through the air. Dinner of chicken paella was over. Gus patted the basketball that passed as his stomach. And the seven men were about to get down to the business that had brought them here in the first place.

Bart was the designated leader. He could feel the ricochet of negative protons and electrons leaping around the room like Lords in a Christmas song. He took another sip of red wine before addressing the guests and looked to Mitch with the eyes of a nervous alien abductee being prepped for his first rectal examination.

"I'm still angry with Rod for stealing my manuscript," Jim fumed for the record, and at the same time draining the room of what little mirth there was.

Now, after the sorbet had been served, the whole place seemed like a summit meeting between Tony Blair and leaders of Sinn Fein.

"I didn't steal it!" Rod snapped back at Jim. "I just printed out a *copy* and took it with me to read. Yours is still in the computer. And anyway, I've apologized about a gazillion times," Rod said, fast melting like the candles. "Jeez, you know how to hold a grudge. If it hadn't been for your fuckin' lousy book that you thought would bring you millions, I'd have only guessed at what a real prick you are. You fucked me over for the rights to my script. Now you can add a new chapter about how Michael fucked *you* over when he formed an alliance with his assistant, Troy, to sell Rod's screenplay and screw you out of the deal. Oh, I forgot—you let him fuck you while you were both fucking me. Anything to be a star again, eh?"

"Again? I'm *still* a star! You ungrateful little thief and prick!" Jim bellowed in his best impersonation of Dixie Carter as an over-the-top Norma Desmond.

"A thief *and* a prick? My, I've moved up a notch." Rod chuckled. "So I made a copy of your stupid book. Mr. TV hasn't had a good zap from a cattle prod in a long time, I can tell. Why don't you go gnaw on a frayed electrical cord or lick a fuse box, for Christ sake!"

"Listen, you cocksucking jerk," Jim retorted. "I'll up and leave right now! The only reason I'm here in the first place is because Mitch and Bart convinced me they had a plan to retaliate against the people responsible for ending my series."

"Okay, guys. That's all blood under the bridge, so to speak," Bart said. "We're soul mates now. We all have a common bond."

Mitch piped in: "Bart and Owen would just be two more victims of Shari's abuse and her lack of conscience if it wasn't for your book, Jim, which I for one am sleepless with desire to read. Hope you included me in one of your more torrid chapters. And you did spell my name right, yes? That's Mitch, with a capital W-O-O-D!"

For a moment, Jim was appeased, thinking of his one-nighter with Mitch and feeling like a real author with a real book and a real fan.

"Are we forgetting I'm about to go to trial for sexual harassment," Owen cut in.

"And *I'm* being countersued by Sterling for my wrongful-termination suit against them," Bart continued. "They're determined to get away with their lunacy and larceny at our expense. Jim's book could help immeasurably with our claims," Bart said.

Owen smiled. "If Bart's tapes and Jim's manuscript can prove my innocence, I'll be taking you all on a cruise. And I don't mean down Santa Monica Boulevard."

"I'm still pissed," Jim pouted. "But I guess if I can help blow the whistle on everybody who's done us all wrong, then my efforts won't have been in vain." He was playing the grand dame suffering for the common man.

"And that's what we're here for," Fitterman finally said.

Throughout dinner the attorney had explained the complicated scenario of fighting Shari and the big Sterling corporation, which was known to be the hardest of legal hitters in town. Fitterman's personality was as dry as Peekabo Street's lips in a Chapstick commercial, and he'd nearly wearied Jim and Mitch with his too-technical dissertation about the law. But he knew precisely what he was talking about. During their appetizers of tamales wrapped in cornhusks, he had recited verbatim the Equal Employment Opportunity Commission's guidelines for sexual harassment.

"Just what is sexual harassment?" he asked the men rhetorically. "Well, it's defined as sex discrimination that is a violation of Title VII of the Civil Rights Act of 1964."

"That was like a million years ago," Mitch quipped. "The last century, as a matter of fact!"

Fitterman looked over the rim of his bifocals, irritated by the interruption. He continued. "And there are two types, quid pro quo and hostile environment," Fitterman said.

"Ally McBeal says, 'Quid pro quo' a lot. What's it really mean?" Rod asked.

"Quid pro quo means 'this for that' or 'something for something,'" Fitterman answered.

"So, when I have sex for money, I'm just doing it quid pro quo?" Rod smiled a sincere question. "They get *this,*" (Rod made a jerk-off motion with his right hand), "and I get ker-ching!" He made the sound of a cash register ringing up a sale.

Bart looked across the table at Rod, who shrugged and added, "A guy's got to make the rent, Mr. Naïveté. You should have known I'd be back at it. No one else is keeping me. No one ever will again." Rod stared at Jim.

"No," Jim said, "that's not quid pro quo. That's simply being a fucking whore!"

"It was good enough for you, Mr. Pimple Butt," Rod countered before Rusty intervened and demanded they both cool it.

"May I continue, gentlemen," Fitterman said. "Thank you. Did you know that sex as a form of prohibitive discrimination was just tagged on at the end of the Civil Rights Act? The famous Civil Rights Act—yes, from the last century." He looked over at Mitch. "It was originally a race-discrimination bill. But at the last minute someone added sex as a category of discrimination."

"That'll come in handy when I'm down to my last lifeline on *Who Wants to be a Fucking Zillionaire,*" Mitch chirped.

Fitterman, not quite getting the reference, eyed him with increasing annoyance. "Hmmm. Yes. Well, in sexual-harassment cases, it means unwelcome sexual advances, requests for sexual favors, and other verbal or physical conduct of a sexual nature where submission to such conduct is made either explicitly or implicitly a term or condition of an individual's employment. Or, submission to or rejection of such conduct by an individual is used as the basis for employment decisions affecting such individual."

"No hablo inglés," Jim said, annoyed by the polysyllabic legalese. *"Speekee de Ing-gee, por favor?"*

"Then what's 'hostile environment' sexual harassment," Owen asked, ignoring Jim's comment to Fitterman.

Fitterman replied, "It has the similar language as quid pro quo but adds; 'Sexual harassment when such conduct has the purpose or effect of unreasonably interfering with an individual's work performance or creating an intimidating, hostile, or offensive working environment.'"

"What determines if the harassment is considered hostile?" Rusty asked, passing the tureen of paella to his guests.

Accepting the bowl and taking an extra-large serving and two more tamales, Fitterman continued: "The court obviously has to look at a number of factors to determine if the environment is hostile. First, whether the conduct was verbal or physical or both. Second, how frequently it occurred. Third, whether the conduct was really hostile and patently offensive. Four, whether the alleged harasser was a coworker or supervisor. Then there's whether others joined in perpetrating the harassment and if the harassment was directed at more than one individual. An assessment is made upon the totality of the circumstances."

"I like the one that asks if others joined in perpetrating the harassment," Owen said. "That in itself should sink Shari and Cy."

"Not so fast," Fitterman commanded. "It's never been possible to find Sterling legally responsible for harassment by a supervisor. Their legal muscle and their brand-name value make unenlightened jurors sympathetic to the company."

Fitterman continued: "The U.S. Equal Opportunities Commission says, and I'm quoting one of their releases, 'An employer is always responsible for harassment by a supervisor that culminated in a tangible employment action. If the harassment did not lead to a tangible employment action, the employer is liable unless it proves that it exercised reasonable care to prevent and promptly correct any harassment and the employee unreasonably failed to complain to management or to avoid harm otherwise.' You know full well that Sterling has a zero-tolerance policy."

"In English, puhl-ese!" Jim begged.

"Sorry," Fitterman said. "Simply, an individual qualifies as a 'supervisor' if he has the authority to make decisions affecting the employee or direct the employee's daily work activities."

"That's me, basically," Owen said, dismayed. "'Tangible employment action' means I had the authority to change an employee's status, like hiring, firing, promotions, demotions, change in benefits compensation, and all that, which I did."

"In our situation it has to do with Owen's—and Shari's and Cy's, too—ability to fire or demote a subordinate because he or she makes sexual demands. We'll get into all the stuff about Owen and Bart's failure to complain about harassment because of legitimate fear of retaliation when we get to trial. But remember, that guy they've got lined up to testify against Owen can use the same excuse—fear—for not going to his supervisor, namely, Shari."

"I'm so bored," Jim said. "Let's get to the good stuff, like how much money we'll make when we win."

"This is by no stretch of the imagination a win-win situation," Fitterman barked. "How can I make it more clear that I will be working extremely hard on behalf of Owen and Bart to bring Shari Draper down, along with Cy Lupiano and all of Sterling, Inc. But this is a steep, uphill battle, gentlemen. Sterling has never lost a sexual-harassment case. They usually settle out of court. What makes this worse is that it is a sexual-harassment case involving males only," he emphasized. "This is going to be a complicated procedure. I need each of you to fully cooperate. If you think Shari has a hair-trigger temper, wait'll you meet the studio's chief counsel. It's going to be messy.

"However, thanks to the recordings Bart made of his so-called rehearsals with Shari, along with the documentation from Jim's notes from when he was in jail, plus corroboration and testimony from dozens of witnesses, we've amassed a substantial amount of evidence proving Shari and Cy are more than the gutter-variety Hollywood crooks and snake-oil salesmen. But you all stand a good chance of losing this trial—and being embarrassed. Your careers and reputations may be destroyed," Fitterman argued.

"Oh, don't spoil this by dashing our dreams for revenge even before the trial begins," Rod pleaded.

"Where's Ling Woo when you need a deviant litigator," Mitch said. "No offense, Fitterman. I was just thinking out loud." He then suggested they all adjourn to the living room for tea or coffee.

"There isn't anyone in the legal business better than Gus," Owen said. "He's never lost a case, and he's not going to lose this one. We've got to be one hundred percent positive that the system will work. Bart and I are completely innocent of all charges and allegations, and Gus is the only man I know who can topple Shari and Cy and Sterling Studios. There's no fooling around here, guys. This is the most terrifying thing that's ever happened to me *and* to Bart. No way are we paying with our careers and reputations—as many before us have done—just because Shari and Cy hate queers—"

"We're fighting evil here," Bart interrupted. "Those two maggots are afraid of Owen's creativity and intelligence."

"And yours, too," Rusty interjected, looking at Bart.

Jim spoke up in a conciliatory tone. "I'm sorry that I've been so self-absorbed. Of course, I'll do whatever needs to be done to help you guys. Since I'll be helping myself, too."

"We're with you all the way," Rod said. "I'm sorry, too, that Jim and I keep bickering like George Costanza's parents. I know how important this trial is. No more animosity." He looked at Jim. "Okay?"

Sheepishly, Jim looked back at Rod. Just feasting his eyes on the sight of this kid in his tank-top shirt with his bronze muscles and gang tattoos on display seemed to give Jim an immediate hard-on. "Absolutely. I'm sorry, too."

Rusty smiled. "Okay, then," Rusty said, relief in his voice. "Who wants coffee or tea? You all go into the entertainment room. Bart and I will be along."

"Don't forget the after-dinner mints," Mitch chirped.

Chapter Twenty-One

———

Rusty and Bart retreated to the kitchen. When they returned to their guests, they each carried a tray. Bart's held China cups and saucers and silver spoons and napkins. Rusty's was burdened with two silver serving pots, one filled with decaf, the other with hot water, and a selection of herbal teas.

"If no one has any objections, let's begin the entertainment with Bart's tapes," Fitterman said, dropping his ample girth into a love seat and taking up much of the space. "Rusty," he said, "would you do the honors?"

Rusty finished pouring hot water over a bag of peppermint tea in Bart's cup. He set the pot back down onto the tray and reached for a cassette tape Fitterman was holding out with his right hand. Rusty went to the stereo unit, hidden behind accordion-like doors of a home-theater unit that occupied one entire wall of the living room. He opened a panel that revealed all the latest electronic home media toys, including a cassette tape player. He inserted the cassette and activated the sound equipment.

"At long last, I'm finally going to get a sample of what's been going on behind Shari's closed doors all these years," Mitch said, as if he weren't a master of eavesdropping, especially on his boss.

Every secretary at any company who has been in his or her position for any period of time knows more than their boss would prefer about the boss's personal life. More than one wife has used her husband's assistant to document his cheating double life and corroborate facts and evidence when it came to getting courts to cough up juicy divorce settlements.

In fact, Mitch had already come to Bart and Owen's aid and given a sworn statement to Fitterman detailing countless criminal acts and atrocities committed by Shari.

It wasn't the little stuff that mattered to Fitterman, such as charging expensive gifts for herself and friends at Tiffany's and expensing the baubles to the overhead accounts for various films. The big stuff that only Mitch could offer had to do with where the proverbial bodies were buried in and around Hollywood. Overnight sensations disappeared into the *Enquirer*'s "Dead or Alive" column. Usually the column had household names that hadn't been seen for a couple of years, like: Bob Newhart. Dead or Alive? Gavin MacLeod. Dead or Alive? Susan Saint James. Dead or Alive? Where did the lesser stars go after one hit sitcom or box-office blockbuster? It seemed only a few insiders, including Shari, knew. Arlene Golonka. Dead or Alive? Mark Goddard. Dead or Alive? Jim Fallon. Dead or Alive?

But Owen's and Bart's bodies weren't about to stay dead, thanks to Mitch. Fitterman was also in a position to exhume more than a few others.

What the group heard on the tape was a less than perfectly clear recording of all the contemptible things Shari had said about Owen. The audio was distorted at times. Bart had turned on his microcassette tape recorder and dropped it into his pants pocket just before entering Shari's office each time he was summoned to meet with her. In the mind's eye of each listener, they could imagine Bart arriving at the dreaded "black corner," which is what Shari's office was affectionately referred to as. At the beginning of the tape they could hear her instruct him to be seated. They imagined his taking one of the chairs facing her desk. The recorder picked up the end of a one-sided phone conversation she was having with Cy Lupiano; at least that's who Bart presumed she was speaking to.

"No one held a gun to Mare Dickerson's head to do this fucking movie," Shari snarled. "Yeah, the director found out. I heard he stormed into Mare's trailer and shouted, 'I just want you to know that I'm proud of everything I've done. Even this!' Mare'd invited the cast and crew to watch a soft-porn tape starring their director. His younger years. Had to earn a living when he first come to Hollywood."

Silence, briefly, while Shari listens to Cy. Then: "Don't ask me! I don't know where Mare dug it up. Just somewhere. *Moi?*" Shari exclaimed in a false stage insult. "You can't imagine I'd want to embarrass that loathsome director, can you? Anyway, isn't Mare a hoot? We should find another film for her. Just wanted you to know. I gotta go. That Bart guy's here. Yeah. We're going to go over the lines. Not to worry."

As the men listened, more than once throughout the playback Bart found himself apologizing to Owen for the attacks on his character that Shari had forced him to recite.

"*Pffft.*" Owen dismissed Bart's attempt to apologize. "This is exactly what will end her reign of terror in Hollywood. Don't apologize. Remember, you did this to help me. We'll put the bitch away for good."

"Perhaps she'll get lucky and have Patsy Ramsey for a cellmate," Rod said.

An hour later, after it was many times positively obvious that Shari and Cy had committed fraud by planning to falsely accuse Owen of sexual indiscretions, the group took a break before agreeing to continue on to hear what Jim's book had to reveal.

Fitterman extricated himself from the love seat, stood up, and waddled to the center of the room. In his best legal-eagle-sounding voice he began to read a prepared synopsis of several chapters from Jim's book. "Mind you, this is abridged material. The full text will be used when Shari takes the stand at Owen's trial. The hoped-for result is that it will so damage her credibility that Owen will be exonerated and Bart's lawsuit will not be contested by Sterling. This is just a sample, but here goes."

Jim was all smiles as the audience of Bart, Rusty, Owen, Rod, and Mitch listened to Fitterman, who exposed one hell of a shocker:

"This is from chapters seven through twelve.

"'Back in the early 1970s, an asshole named Don Simpson was incarcerated in the same jail in Alaska where I was serving six months. His charge: attempted murder. Mine: possession of cocaine for sale. You might have guessed it; this is the same Don Simpson who was the future Hollywood Bad Boy mogul.

"'Then along came a tough little guy named Larry. Larry Burton. He was charged with assaulting his boyfriend. You got it—his *boyfriend*.

"'There aren't any secrets in prison, let me tell you. And it was well known—and proven—that Larry was more than halfway through a transgender operation. His so-called *boyfriend* was a real thug and loser who had been sharing a tiny trailer as a home with Larry. One day he decided life was too dull with a fey Alaska Bell telephone operator, which Larry was at the time. So he found himself a husky—not the breed of dog but a beer-chugging lumberjack—and kicked Larry's sorry ass out of their one-room aluminum-shell hellhole of a traveling house. Larry didn't think that so bad except the creep also reneged on his promise to pay for the final operation that would make Larry the woman he always knew he was inside.

"'Larry was livid. In a premeditated attack, he sneaked up on his beer-bellied ex—who at the time was jacking off at the little sink-urinal in the trailer-home. Larry wanted to start his boyfriend out on the road to the same operation that he was promised. He took a lame swing at him with a wood-handled hatchet. But the boyfriend lunged to the other side of the trailer in the nick of time. The blade sliced the Formica in which their little sink was built. Then the ax-wielding maniac had another go at the scum he had supported on his meager Alaska Bell salary. This time Larry got a good chunk off the fat ass of his b/f. But the genitals were still intact. When the lumberjack arrived, he beat the shit out of Larry and called the sheriff.

"'Long story short, while in prison, Don Simpson, who adopted me the day I arrived, decided he liked the new boy, Larry, better. I ended up being passed around to the other inmates like a blond marine with a twelve-inch dick at a Barry Diller pool party. I've always been very popular.

"'Don didn't have to exercise much force to make Larry his new steady. Although they hated each other at the start, they were cut from the same cloth. They may have been oil and water, but each came to respect the other's devious natures.

"'The fact that Larry was almost a complete woman was a godsend to Don. Although he would poke his pecker into any hole he could find—and I wasn't the only one who suffered the indignity of that pig's oinking and boinking—Don enjoyed Larry's combination of breasts and penis. He actually got off on semiman sex.

"'I think it's ironic that the future lunatic Hollywood mogul who was so infamous in so many ways, among which was his seduction of a revolving carousel of female secretaries and starlets, would get off sucking on cellmate Larry. But as I've said earlier, he was a common barnyard pig. Slop was slop. And those two were both USDA-certified swill.

"'Don actually promised Larry he'd eventually get him all the right anatomical equipment he needed. I'll say this about Don; you couldn't turn your back on him and trust him not to fuck you—literally and figuratively. But when he decided to come through for you, he did. He could be generous. Don and Larry became inseparable.

"'Then, one day, a second-unit Hollywood film crew came to Anchorage to shoot exteriors for a remake of *Alaska Gold Fever*. Don, Larry, and I were loaned out and assigned as "atmosphere." Nothing more than extras on the set. Our job was to hang around, pretending to be walking past the local turn-of-the-century bank or the grocery store or the courthouse, all of which were just flimsy façades.

"'After weeks of excellent behavior and befriending the transportation coordinator and the first assistant director, Don and Larry slipped out of town with the crew as soon as the last frame of film was shot. Those bastards deserted me. Eventually they ended up where most of the world's cons end up: in Hollywood. I promised I'd get even.'"

Jim's text went on to detail that it wasn't long after Don moved to L.A. that he began his meteoric rise in the film biz. He had bullied his way into the studio system. He knew a guy who knew a guy who knew a guy, and in no time he became what all schoolyard thugs become: senior executives at a movie studio. In this case, Simpson landed at Paramount Pictures, where he got an office in the old DeMille Building. He started taking credit for making *American Gigolo, Urban Cowboy, Little Darlings, An Officer and a Gentleman,* and *48HRS.* He conveniently forgot about the directors.

"His real talent was for humiliating underlings and whores, which was practically an oxymoron in his office, and screwing a succession of secretaries and taking credit for everybody's good ideas. The whole town—not just the studio—was petrified of Don. He loved the power. It made him feel that it didn't matter that he only had a fat four-and-a-half-inch dick.

"He then teamed with a beady-eyed, huge-overbite director from the world of commercial advertising named Jerry "the Velvet Scalpel" Bruckheimer. Together they produced *Flashdance*. Despite the film's overall negative reviews, it became a monster hit, raking in millions of dollars in worldwide grosses, as did their subsequent films.

"Simpson was a dichotomy. On the one hand, he was loyal only to the gods of money, power, pussy, Valium, Thorazine, Vicodin, diphenhydramine, lithium, Xanax, promethazine, cocaine, and scotch."

"Say that again ten times fast," Mitch blurted out, interrupting the hanging-on-every-word oration.

Fitterman cleared his throat. "'But he also had a soft spot for the time he spent incarcerated with Larry Burton,'" Fitterman continued. "The drug-induced, self-indulgent, all-black-jeans-wearing fatso tyrant kept his promise and paid for Larry's final operation.'

"So," Fitterman said, taking off his eyeglasses and continuing extemporaneously. "The old *male* Larry Burton debuted as a new but not necessarily improved female." Fitterman paused. "Any guesses who Larry became?"

"Bea Arthur!" Mitch erupted.

"Elaine Stritch?" Rusty toyed with the idea.

"Somebody like Demi Moore?" Owen quipped.

"Oh! Oh!" Mitch exclaimed as though he had solved a mathematical equation in class. "Eleanor Roosevelt. Just like that WACS *in the White House* song!"

Everybody groaned.

Bart and Rod, the only two other than Fitterman who, from reading Jim's book, knew the answer, exchanged smiles.

Fitterman cleared his throat. "First name rhymes with Larry. Second name with Raper."

Mitch, having a ball playing twenty questions, said, "Larry. Barry. Carrie. Shari. Fairy. Scary."

The answer hit everyone simultaneously—except Mitch, who continued with "Wary. Larry. Gary. Shari. Hairy . . ."

"For Christ sake," Jim snapped. "You already said it—twice! *Shari,* for god's sake!"

The room could have exploded and burst into flames and Rusty, Owen, and Mitch would not have been more surprised by the revelation. They were speechless. Bart had wrestled with the idea of keeping this knowledge from his lover but decided to follow Fitterman's request to not tell a soul.

Fitterman continued, this time extemporaneously. "However, the testosterone and estrogen levels in Shari's body apparently couldn't be balanced."

"That explains the hairy mole on her breast and the mustache," Bart said.

"Instead of becoming the soft and radiant Jaclyn Smith, the Breck shampoo girl who turned up as Kelly Garrett on *Charlie's Angels,* became a ball-buster of a woman who could easily take down Mike Tyson and reduce that throwback to *Homo erectus* weeping at a De Beers 'A diamond is forever' commercial."

Jim piped in to take center stage with what he thought was *his* story. "Unlike the original Miss Crossover, Christine Jorgensen, about whom the newspaper headlines had roared: 'G.I. Goes Abroad, And Comes Back A Broad,' Shari was *not* a lovely buttercup of a lady."

"I knew Christine," Fitterman added wistfully. "A real lady."

"But Shari was just a hard-boiled bitch," Jim continued. "It's not that she wasn't aware of how crass she was. In fact, early on she enrolled at the ultraexclusive Miss Peabody's Finishing School for the Socially Inept. She lasted three days of etiquette class and never learned to properly slice a cake to serve with tea.

"Try though her instructors did, they couldn't get Shari to stop saying, 'Fuckin A' when she found something amusing. Finally, Miss Peabody and the school's psychologist-counselor, Miss Allen, called her in for a meeting.

"Miss Draper," Ms. Peabody began, "Dr. Allen has studied your personality examinations and career-placement assessments. According to the standard evaluations prepared by Stanford University, it appears that you could do quite well as an executive in Hollywood."

For the first time since arriving at Miss Peabody's Finishing School for the Socially Inept, Shari's eyes sparkled.

"It is our consensus, and that of the board of directors, that you should be dismissed from this school. Your tuition will be reimbursed if you leave immediately," Ms. Peabody added.

"Fuckin' A!" Shari exploded with pleasure as she jumped up from the burgundy leather chair in which she had been seated and headed for the door. She made a quick stop at her dormitory to pack her belongings and to call Don Simpson, to whom she owed a great debt—but wanted more in exchange for keeping her lips sealed about his being an escaped con. He said she'd have a job the next day. She was to report to the mailroom at Millennium Studios on the West Side of L.A.

From skateboarding mail girl sucking off a succession of producers and creative executives, she moved up the ladder. She began as an assistant to the head of feature-film publicity, wrangled her way into her boss's job, and ended up director of the entire marketing staff.

"Finally, one afternoon she got the call she'd been waiting breathlessly to receive," Jim said. "One of her old cocks, Cy Lupiano, had just signed a contract at Sterling. He missed Shari and wanted her to take over as the new executive vice president of publicity."

"The Gayest Place in the Universe," Mitch sighed.

"And it was," Bart said. "Sort of. At least until Shari came aboard."

Fitterman continued reading Jim's words. "'When I got out of the pen, I went to Hollywood, too. Years passed. Don became a big shot in entertainment. Shari practically ran a studio. I became a household name. Shari eventually deigned to acknowledge me after we reconnected at a party. And, as a Christmas present last year, she sent me a beautiful hustler—already unwrapped and ready to play—batteries and all. The present and I took some videos, and he stole the tape. He was Helen of Troy's pretty brother! Shari got the cassette and had it aired on *Totally Hollywood*. To keep her past a secret, she was making sure I disappeared and never worked again.'"

At last, the evening ended. Bart and Rusty said good-bye to their guests. Rusty thanked Gus Fitterman for his hard work and good nature.

"And then there were none," Rusty said, embracing Bart and telling him not to worry about the outcome of the trial.

Bart began unbuttoning Rusty's shirt and nestled his face into his lover's chest and inhaled the warmth emanating from his skin. "Let's clean this stuff up in the morning," he suggested, looking around the room. "I just want to be in bed with you right now."

Rusty grinned.

"Get yourself ready. I'll lock up and put the kids to bed," Bart said.

Rusty quickly completed his ablutions and took off his clothes. By the time he turned off the bathroom light, Bart was already in bed, covered only to his waist in a sheet.

Rusty, who'd had an erection ever since Bart began unbuttoning his shirt, stood in the doorway looking over at his lover. "I never get tired of seeing you in my bed."

Bart's member did an involuntary jump under the sheet. "And look at you, Mr. Stiffy. Trust me, I never tire of seeing *that!* Bring it over so I can have my dessert."

Rusty moved onto the bed and snuggled next to Bart. After all these months together, neither tired of the same sort of foreplay that had existed from their first time. They began kissing and feeling the contours of each other's chests and reaching over to hold the other's cock.

Rusty straddled Bart, reaching for a bottle of massage oil on the bedstand. He poured oil on Bart's chest, replaced the bottle, and began rubbing the fluid all over Bart's body, which glistened in the dim light that emanated from a halogen desk lamp on the bedstand. Then Rusty lay on top of Bart and rubbed his own body firmly against his lover's, coating his own skin with oil.

Without having to say it, Bart and Rusty both knew they were enough for each other. Neither could conceive of a time when they would want to be physical with anyone else. They felt it almost a miracle that they were together.

After Rusty rubbed more oil on his cock, he slowly humped Bart's ass and then gently slipped into his lover's body.

Chapter Twenty-Two

Sterling's chief counsel, Richard Ward, and his innocuous horde of deputy counsels, Tweedledees and Tweedledums, flanked Shari and Cy as they entered courtroom number 340 on the third floor of the Flower Street Courthouse in Burbank. The trio were the picture of self-confident composure and intimidation. Shari's arrogance wafted around her as palpably as the Samsara she spritzed herself with in the car on the way over from the studio. In a beige suit, accented with a silk Donna Karan scarf and a ladybug lapel pin from Cartier, she looked over at the defendant's table and gave Owen Lucas and Fitterman a slight smirk, as if she were Alex Trebek holding the correct question on *Double Jeopardy*. Owen stared at Shari with dead eyes and did not return the smile. Soon she looked away, unable to maintain eye contact.

Feeling completely at ease in what to anyone else would have been an intimidating environment, Shari looked over at the jury box and summed up the eight men and four women who were the first to be impaneled as possible jurors. They reeked of the lower classes. "Not a jury of *my* peers," she sneered to herself, having forgotten there was a time in the not too distant past when these people would have been socially superior to her. There was not one whom she could remotely conceive of knowing personally. "NOCD," she said to herself, looking down her nose at each of them.

Shari's composure was still unruffled when she examined the others in the room. She wasn't surprised to see Bart Cain seated in the back of the courtroom. When their eyes met, he blew her a kiss—a reminder of the day she fired him. Then he smiled. Shari also spied Mitch—who was supposed to be minding the office—Jim Fallon, and that stud she met once, what's his name, Rod, all of whom were seated together. They gave her a collective glare, which did not achieve the desired effect of eroding her confidence. In fact, their solidarity seemed to backfire, as Shari became as icy as Judge Judy.

Shari glared at them. She never felt for an instant any sense of dislocation or thought that she was being cornered by a pack of ravenous hyenas. She turned to face the bench when the bailiff announced, "All rise. The Honorable Judge Jonathan Carter is presiding, and court is now in session."

The entire room became silent, though not just because of the solemnity of the proceedings and the mandatory respect that was due the judicial system. No, they were more than a little surprised by the man entering the court and taking his place behind the bench. In any other venue there would have been an appreciative gasp of surprise throughout the vast room, because the man who entered, Judge Carter, was not only extremely young—whatever the minimum age was for a judge—but inordinately handsome. He could easily pass as a Richard Gere clone. Even his perfectly combed hair was of an elegant, prematurely grayish black color.

As the judge took his seat behind the bench, Mitch elbowed Bart, who looked at Rusty, who smiled at Rod, who winked at Jim. In the silence of the courtroom their combined gaydar could almost be heard crackling like static, like blips on an air-traffic controller's monitoring screen. But there was interference jamming the signals. Although Judge Carter was a stud, none of the men could say for certain what his sexual orientation was. He was inscrutable.

Judge Carter was also a formidable-looking man who exuded authority. Rod imagined Judge Carter in black leather chaps and vest showing off his endowments; Mitch flashed on his wearing Western drag and doing line dancing at the Rawhide; Bart envisioned himself cuddled in bed on a Saturday morning reciting poetry; Jim got a hard-on thinking of the judge coming to his wine cellar wearing his robe as he sentenced Jim to a lashing by Hispanic prison guards; Rusty's fantasy matched Bart's, right down to the Brownings and e. e. cummings.

Shari was attracted to him, too. Even the court reporter, a cute skinny kid with a diamond stud in his left earlobe and a goatee, could hardly keep his eyes on the keys of his stenographer's machine. Each man and woman in the room imagined what would be revealed if this hunk of judge were to remove his robe. His stature and posture made it a certainty that the guy was an irresistible specimen of perfect masculinity. "I'll wager he's got a gym in his chambers," Rod said to Bart. "Check out those shoulders!"

Aside from the god who sat above the rest of those in the room, the stage setting was just like every episode of *Perry Mason, Law & Order, Matlock,* and *Judging Amy;* indeed, all television courtroom dramas.

Having taken his seat, Judge Carter addressed the plaintiff and defendant and their respective counsel. He looked to each table and glared at Owen and Fitterman, Shari and her Sterling team. Bart and Rusty looked at each other, both registering the judge's look at Owen. They nonverbally agreed there was something ominous in the way the judge observed Owen that was different from the way he looked at everybody else. Perhaps he was homophobic.

"Was it my imagination," Mitch said to Bart, "but did you notice that flesh-and-blood incarnation of David on the bench give Owen a nasty look?"

"No different than the others," Bart said, trying to convince himself that justice was indeed blind. "But I can tell he's a total professional. He won't let the fact that he may think Owen's a total perv interfere with the trial. I think we'll all definitely be witnesses to a well-run courtroom."

"Can you picture him naked?" Mitch asked as an aside, to which Bart laughed just loudly enough for the judge to look up threateningly as he searched the room for the contemptuous transgressor. "Any person who feels this is a court where levity is permitted may leave the room immediately," he barked.

Bart slumped down in his seat.

In what otherwise would have been the most boring part of the trial, the act of the judge reading the case and giving instructions to the potential jurors, all eyes and ears were attentive to His Honor: handsome heartthrob Judge Carter.

"Ladies and gentlemen," Judge Carter began, "this case has been randomly assigned to this court."

"See? No bias," Bart said, this time sotto voce.

"The case that will be tried in this court is exceptional." Carter looked over at Owen. This time he held his gaze. "Would the defendant and plaintiffs please rise and face the jury box."

Owen, the defendant, dressed in an impeccable gray Armani suit, white Perry Ellis shirt, and a necktie bearing the image of Carmen Miranda under her signature tutti-frutti headdress, followed the court's instructions. Owen stood before his accusers at the next table and the men and women in the jury box, who would either side with the immaculate reputation of Sterling or believe his defense and exonerate him of the charges of sexual harassment. His life would soon be in the hands of Fitterman and twelve jurors.

Judge Carter announced, "This is a case of same-sex sexual harassment. In some jurisdictions same-sex sexual harassment is not actionable. However, in California, both on the federal and state levels, it is, most certainly. California is also one of the few states that has sexual-orientation laws. Therefore, this is an extremely important case. I implore those of you who will be selected to serve on this jury to pay close attention to all the evidence presented by both sides.

"You will hear often graphic evidence presented by counsel for Sterling Studios, who have the burden to prove that the defendant was removed from his position as president of motion-picture marketing when it was alleged that he was engaged in sexual misconduct—harassment—of several male employees."

A murmur went through the courtroom, as if the gallery had never seen *Ellen, Will & Grace,* or *The Birdcage.* Judge Carter cracked his gavel and continued.

"On the other hand, the defendant, who is an openly gay man, alleges that he was unlawfully terminated from employment on the basis of false accusations of said illegal conduct.

"It is also alleged that soon after commencing his assignment at Sterling, the defendant began asking Bart Cain, a senior publicist at Sterling, if he would like to have a sexual relationship with him. Mr. Cain allegedly said no, explaining he was not attracted to Mr. Lucas. However, it is alleged that Mr. Lucas persisted in asking for a sexual relationship, including requests to perform oral sex on Mr. Cain.

"You may be seated, Mr. Lucas. Ms. Draper."

Judge Carter folded his hands and peered first at those in the jury box, then out into the gallery and to fifty or so other prospective jurors. He had one more comment to make before the selection of those who would sit in judgment of Owen Lucas and Sterling began.

"Living in the Los Angeles area, as all of you do, perhaps you're familiar with the case of *Shermansky v. Bronze Productions.* I would ask that if any of you are familiar with the case, you advise the court of this knowledge when the voir dire process begins.

"*Shermansky v. Bronze* is a relatively recent case in which one of the employees of management level at Bronze Productions allegedly required as a condition of employment that male assistants stay with him in his hotel room when he traveled and made them watch X-rated films with him. An employee brought a claim of sexual harassment, and the court agreed there was a viable theory of same sex-sexual harassment.

"The court rejected the defendant's argument that upholding this theory would violate the defendant's First Amendment rights, saying that if same sex-sexual harassment was recognized by law, then every employer would have to inquire into the sexual orientation of all its male employees. The court did not agree with that argument, because employers are not supposed to inquire into whether their employees are heterosexual. Please keep in mind that the Civil Rights Act of 1964, the antidiscrimination law, does not include a requirement that the victim and harasser be of opposite genders."

After providing the details of the case, the tiresome process of selecting the jury began. Shari was bored. She would much rather have been getting her pedicure than sitting on the hard wooden chair listening to the long list of prospective jurors go through the voir dire process when all of them seemed for one reason or another to want to be excused from service.

"I'm a Christian woman, I am," announced the first prospective juror, a fat woman wearing a floral print dress that accentuated the rolls of flesh beneath the flimsy fabric. Her Charles Laughton face was garnished with almond-shaped eyeglasses in a blue plastic frame covered in rhinestones. When asked if she could render an unbiased verdict, she replied, "I ain't the type to judge another of God's children, no, sir, Your Honor. But if that there man was fired for being a pervert, then he deserved what he got."

Judge Carter quickly interrupted her and without a moment's hesitation announced, "You may be excused."

"I 'spect he'll be punished more in hell when he gets there, too," the woman continued, speaking more to herself than to anyone in particular as she waddled out of the jury box.

"All prospective jurors are cautioned to disregard all comments that are not testimony," Judge Carter implored, and brought down his gavel with a thundering clap. He was already irritated, and the trial had not yet begun.

The bailiff called another name from the room. That person filled the vacant seat left by the Charles Laughton woman.

This prospective juror looked like a middle-aged redneck wanna-be. He wore a baseball cap backward on his head and a wrinkled T-shirt with a boldly written slogan: I Love My Country. But I Fear My

Government. Irritated, Judge Carter demanded that the man show some respect for the court and remove his hat. The man complied, albeit reluctantly.

Asked if he thought he could render a fair verdict based on the evidence, the man thought for a moment, then delivered a non sequitur. "I think there is a def'nite trend toward sex and violence in Sterling films today," he said. "This makes me biased against that studio, and so I guess also against anyone associated with that studio."

Judge Carter asked if he would not be able to put his displeasure with Sterling aside, give equal weight to all the evidence he would hear, and help deliver a verdict.

"I rather doubt that, Your Eminence," he replied. "You see, my ch'ren watch their animated videos practic'ly ev'ry day of their lives . . ." This response made the entire room erupt with a roar of laughter.

Judge Carter was not amused and pounded his gavel to demand silence. "Sir, you find the product from Sterling to be offensive, yet you allow your children to watch their videos as a matter of daily routine?"

"Oh, kids'll be kids, Yer Holiness, sir. Cain 't keep an eye on 'em fer twenty-four hours a day. They 'specially like the lil' rat in the White House." The man smiled.

Again the room exploded in laughter, which made the man disconcerted, but he continued.

Judge Carter tried to interrupt him again, but he kept talking over Carter's objections.

"I'm afraid these movies today aren't like they were when I was growin' up. Don't you agree?" he asked, as if he were a Christian zealot positioning a debate with "Don't you believe that the Bible was written by God?"

"Sir," Judge Carter said.

"Honestly, where are the old Annette Funicello and Frankie Avalon movies?"

"Sir," Carter tried to intervene.

"And even them Doris Day movies, and Marilyn Mon-row, bless her drug-ravaged, stone-cold soul . . ."

"Sir!" Judge Carter brought down his gavel and startled the man into silence. "As you know, if you were paying any attention to me earlier, this trial is not about the movies created by Sterling. This is a very serious case. A senior executive with a highly visible position was terminated from his employment at Sterling for allegedly perpetrating the act of sexual harassment on another employee or employees.

"This case has nothing whatsoever to do with rats in the White House [another chortle from the gallery] or flying carpets or stories about little orphaned girls who become princesses," Judge Carter admonished. He then reiterated his question about whether or not he could make a determination based on factual evidence and help render a verdict of guilt or innocence of the defendant.

"Oh, if you put it that way, I s'pose I could try to be fair. But deviant sex is immoral and belongs at home, not in the workplace."

Again the gallery thundered with laughter. The brainless man turned bright red, not quite comprehending what it was he said that had brought on such burst of glee.

"What warped parallel universe have we landed in?" Bart whispered to Rusty. "The scary new attraction at the Sterling theme park. Anita Bryant's Wild Ride."

By the time Fitterman and the attorneys for Sterling had asked a few more questions of this man, he, too, was dismissed.

And so it went for the next four hours. Every conceivable reason for not wanting to serve on this jury was heard. Motivations were all over the board. From "Gays have an organized agenda to recruit new members, and red-blooded A-mer-e-cans shouldn't stand fer it no more" to one woman who had filed a sexual-harassment suit years before but had lost the case, which made Bart and Owen's blood run cold with the obvious possibilities of their own case. But finally, twelve jurors and two alternates were deemed reasonably acceptable to all the lawyers. As it was nearly five o'clock, Judge Carter determined they would begin proceedings at nine the next morning. He adjourned his court until the following day.

Bart, Rusty, Rod, Jim, Mitch, and Gus Fitterman left the courthouse and walked toward their respective cars. Their already morose feelings took a further nosedive when a man who appeared to be a vagrant walked up to the group. In a jovial voice the man said, "Which of you handsome gents is the lucky Bart Cain?"

Bart identified himself. "Great!" said the vagrant as he handed him an envelope. "See ya!"

Bart opened the hand-delivered package and found it contained a subpoena. "I'm being charged with defamation of character. Shari's filing a personal lawsuit against me. Jeez! How'd she work that out so fast?" Bart said, stunned at the turn of events.

Fitterman took the document from Bart's hands and quickly perused it. "She suspects what you have up your sleeves and got the wheels rolling. Don't worry. This is going nowhere. She can't know the full extent of our evidence. This is moot, I assure you. I'll take it up with Judge Carter first thing tomorrow."

"You said this was going to be nasty," Bart addressed Fitterman. "I just didn't think of all the other repercussions."

Chapter Twenty-Three

June gloom and the so-called marine layer of clouds and fog seeped from the ocean, all the way into Hollywood and over the hills into Burbank and the Valley. When Bart and Owen arrived in court for the first day of testimony, their early euphoria at the prospect of retaliation against Shari and Sterling for the crimes against them had withered. They were as dismal as Mary Tyler Moore's numerous failed sitcoms and episodics after her classic seventies show.

Bart Cain was the first witness called by the defense. Seated in the spotlight, he looked down from the witness stand and saw Shari's imperious face. Sterling's chief counsel, Richard Ward, asked him to explain the details of Owen Stone's sexual harassment of him.

"The only harassment I've ever received at Sterling is from Shari Draper," Bart declared.

There ensued a lot of coughing and hurumphing from Ward as well as those at the plaintiff's table and the jury box.

"Objection!" after sustained "objection" came from Fitterman, who accused Ward of badgering the witness by asking such questions as "Mr. Cain, do you mean to sit before this court and refute your previous testimony?"

"I have never testified before," Bart reminded Mr. Ward.

"Is that right?" Ward asked in sarcastic mock surprise. At this point, Ward brought out an audiocassette tape. "Your Honor, I'd like to offer this tape as Exhibit A. The evidence will prove beyond any doubt that the witness is perjuring himself."

Judge Carter accepted the plastic cassette box from Ward and examined it for a moment. It was neatly shrink-wrapped. A title had been professionally printed on the inside of the transparent casing:

BART CAIN/SHARI DRAPER
INTERVIEW
FEBRUARY 9

"Very nicely presented," Judge Carter said suspiciously. "Why the 'just-off-the-Virgin Megastore-shelf' look?"

"Er, a proper exhibition for the court," Ward said, sounding somewhat unsure.

Carter returned the tape box to Ward. "Just get on with it. Did you bring a tape player?"

"Indeed, Your Honor." Ward returned to Bart and threatened, "Listen carefully to this tape, sir. You will tell the court, under oath, whether this is or is *not* a conversation you had with Shari Draper in which you accuse Mr. Lucas of sexual harassment."

Ward had a moment of trouble peeling off the tightly wrapped cellophane in which the cassette box was packaged. Finally, he inserted the cassette into the machine and pressed the PLAY button. A few minutes of the tape was played for the judge and jury to hear.

"Well, he was standing there with his shirt unbuttoned, the president of marketing . . . his hairy chest . . . For a moment he just leaned against the doorframe. 'Why don't you blow it off, Bart?' he said. He asked me if I'd eaten anything."

"Dinner?"

"I said I'd grab something at Wienerschnitzel. Then he put his hands in his pockets and started moving them around, like he was feeling for his change or something . . . said he always made it a practice at all the studios where he'd worked before to have a special employee that he found attractive . . . and since I was so cute . . . he said he didn't want to hurt me or create an unpleasant working environment. That's when he asked how much I liked my job and what did I think of him as a man. And what I'd be willing to do to stay on as head writer . . . told me he wanted a blow job every now and again . . . he'd make me happy in return."

Ward stopped the machine in mid-conversation, intending to save the best for later. Smugly, he approached the witness box.

"I ask you, Mr. Cain. Did you or did you not have this conversation with Ms. Draper."

"I had *a* conversation."

"Yes or no, Mr. Cain. It's a simple question."

"This conversation?"

"What other conversation are we discussing?"

"My answer would be no."

"Oh, come on, Mr. Cain. You're an intelligent man. Do you deny that the male voice heard on this recording is yours."

"No."

"Do you deny that the female voice on the recording is Ms. Draper's?"

"No."

"Then how in the name of Pinocchio, if I may use a Hollywood reference, can you sit there and mock this court by lying—under oath—and insist this is not your conversation? Your nose is growing."

"Objection! Harassment!"

"Sustained."

"I'm *not* lying!" Bart said. "With all due respect to the court, I haven't a clue where that tape came from or when it was made. But I assure you, that specific conversation never took place." Bart looked up at Judge Carter.

"I wonder what else you 'don't recall,' Ward asked in his powerful, intimidating tone. "Do you recall what year you graduated college?"

Bart stalled for a moment. "I didn't graduate," he said softly.

"Oh?" Ward pretended to be surprised. "How can that be? I have a copy of your application for employment at Sterling, along with your résumé." He removed the documents from a file, first handing them to Judge Carter to examine before passing them to Bart. "Would you please read for the court your academic achievements?"

Bart again stalled as he silently reviewed the material. Then, in a small voice, "Education. B.S. Journalism, California Polytechnic State University, San Luis Obispo, 1996."

"Please speak up and read that statement again," Ward demanded.

Bart repeated in a louder voice what appeared on his old résumé.

"Quite frankly, Cal Poly has no record of your matriculating in their journalism program. For that matter, they have no record of your attending their fine school, Mr. Cain. Perhaps their dog ate your transcripts?"

Members of the jury laughed.

Bart appeared defeated. He looked over at Rusty and Owen with a look that said, *I blew it. I'm a liar. I blew the case. I'm so sorry.*

"Why did you blatantly lie on your employment application? Didn't you read the fine print at the bottom just below your signature—this is your signature, isn't it, Mr. Cain?—in which it states that you affirm all answers given are true and correct and that you may be subject to legal action if they are found to be inaccurate?"

"I put that on my application because I was embarrassed. I only received my AA degree from Los Angeles Junior College. It's not exactly Ivy League."

"Embarrassed, Mr. Cain? Embarrassed the way you were when Mr. Lucas harassed you in your office? Embarrassed as you must be right now, lying again about not speaking to Ms. Draper about Mr. Lucas's provocations?"

"Objection," Fitterman shouted.

"Establishing character, Your Honor," Ward declared.

Shari sat behind the table, reclining, her arms folded across her chest. She looked straight at Bart with a derisive smile frozen on her face.

"Answer the question, Mr. Cain," Judge Carter said.

"Mr. Lucas never harassed me; that's a fact" Bart stated adamantly. "That tape is a forgery or something."

"Oh, give us all a break, Mr. Cain!" Ward bellowed. "We all have ears. We all heard *your* voice whining to Ms. Draper about harassment. You've lied before, and you're lying now. Am I not correct?"

"You are *not* correct, sir!" Bart turned to Judge Carter. "Your Honor, I, too, recorded meetings between Shari Draper and myself."

Shari suddenly sat up and flashed an angry look first at Bart, then to her attorneys.

"Do you have audio proof?" Judge Carter asked in a compassionate tone.

"My attorney, Mr. Fitterman, has three tapes, Your Honor."

Judge Carter looked at the helium-filled Gus Fitterman. "Do you have evidence to refute opposing counsel's?"

Fitterman nodded. "Indeed I do, Your Honor. May I approach the bench?"

"Objection!" shouted Richard Ward a split second before the entire contingent of Sterling lawyers chimed in, in unison. They all deferred to Ward, who argued that they had not been notified of this evidence and would therefore require time to evaluate the authenticity of the recording.

"I, too, object, Your Honor," Fitterman exploded. "I object to Mr. Ward not providing his piece of evidence for me and my client to study."

"Both of you sit down," Judge Carter said. "Bailiff, allow the court to hear both tapes."

The first cassette played for the jury was the rest of the one presented earlier by Richard Ward.

Bart's voice could be distinctly heard saying, "Shari. This is the most difficult situation I've ever been in. I don't know what to do, so I'm coming to you for advice. Owen Lucas has been hitting on me."

"What do you mean, 'hitting on you'?" Shari asked.

"He came to my office a couple of times when I was working late. His shirt was unbuttoned. He stood next to my desk with his fly unzipped and asked me to give him oral sex."

"Are you sure?"

"Positive. It happens every night."

"And have you gone along with him?"

"I've had no choice. He says he'll fire me if I don't do what he asks."

"Anything else?"

"I've had to spend every weekend for the past two months at his house having sex."

When the tape ran out, it didn't end with any sort of heart-to-heart from Shari, any promise to look into the matter or to file a grievance with human resources. It was clear to Bart that this was simply a "best of the best" compilation tape.

Judge Carter ordered the bailiff to remove that tape and insert the one from Owen and Bart's attorney. It was quite a different conversation that the court heard. All the same words were there, but they were prompted and rearranged.

"How many times do I have to explain this to you, moron? Try it again." It was Shari's voice.

"Okay. Ah. Shari? Ah, this is the most difficult situation I've ever been in. Ah, I don't know what to do, and since you're the only one I can trust, I'm coming to you for help and advice."

"Go on. Owen Lucas . . . hitting on you . . ."

"Right. Owen Lucas has been hitting on me."

"Don't just leave it at that, you simpleton. Tell me, what do you mean by 'hitting on you'?"

"Er, when I'm working, he comes into my office . . ."

"No! When you're working late at night . . ."

"Right. Late at night he comes to my office when I'm working late. His shirt is unbuttoned."

"What else?"

"Oh. Well, he stands next to my desk."

"His pants! His pants! What about his pants, for Christ's sake!"

"Ah, they're unzipped. His fly, I mean."

"Now is where you say he wants you to give him a blow job."

"That's kind of vulgar, isn't it?" Bart was heard questioning Shari. "That's not what I would say. Nobody would believe those words came from me."

"You're such a little pussy! Just say he stands with his fly unzipped and he asks for oral sex. Can you say 'oral sex,' or is that too offensive to you?"

"No. 'Oral sex' is good."

"Are you sure?"

"*Very* good."

"No, stupid. I mean, does it happen every night? You're supposed to say it does."

"It happens every night."

Shari had slumped down in her chair; her arms folded in a display of loathing for the peon publicist who had the audacity to tape their meetings.

The tape continued. "And have you gone along with him?" Shari's voice asked.

"I've had no choice. He says he'll fire me if I don't do what he asks."

"Anything else?"

"I got to spend every weekend for the past two months at his house having sex."

"'Got to spend every weekend . . . ! 'Got to' . . ." Pu-leese! That's stretching it too far. Anybody who heard you say that would think you were enjoying yourself."

"Nobody's going to hear about this," Bart interjected. "You said we were just practicing because Owen was threatening to fire you and you might someday need my help."

"Objection, Your Honor!" Ward screamed.

"Grounds?"

"This is detrimental to my client!"

"It's evidence, you quack! Sit down." Carter hammered his gavel.

The tape continued. "Don't worry your little ass," Shari's voice continued. "You won't ever have to say these things in court. Owen'll be long gone and won't make a peep."

"You can't be serious about being afraid of Owen. He's the first human being to ever occupy that office," Bart said. "As a matter of fact,

I wish he *would* proposition me. But he's such a doll, I'd probably have to take a number and wait in line for about twenty years."

At that Shari exploded. "You fags are all the same! You think he's so great. Let me tell you, he's aiming to can my butt, and he'll can yours, too! In an instant!"

"Are we finished?" Bart asked.

"Get your ass outta here. And don't say a word about this to anyone. Ya hear?"

"Who would I tell? I don't have time for a social life. You keep me too damned busy."

"Then get busy. I want that Mare Dickerson release on my desk before I get in tomorrow."

There came the sound of Bart saying good night to Shari and closing the door to her office behind him. But the audio continued. Bart had stopped for a moment to say good night to Mitch in the outer office.

"Don't worry, you're not the only guy she's got running lines with about sexual harassment from Owen," Mitch said. "Unfortunately, that bleach-blond dweeb, Josh from promotions, is all for going along with whatever Shari and Cy dictate. They've promised him a big promotion if he files a sexual-harassment claim."

"He can't be that much of an idiot," Bart's voice was heard saying. "I guess the fact that he doesn't know if he's gay or straight, just because he fucked April on a dare at the last company retreat, counts for something."

"He's very much like the whiskey-voiced April. She got her vice-president stripes by blowing Cy, didn't she?"

"Ewe! Doesn't Cy have the face of a very old deep-sea turtle?" Bart said as an aside. "That beak of a nose and those wattles under his eyes. And how'd he lose so much hair at such a relatively young age?"

"Sexy stuff!" Mitch said.

"Anyway, Josh sees an opportunity to advance his career, and like so many others in this town, he'll do whatever he thinks he's got to do. What a sorry excuse for a human being. And his hair is turning orange from the peroxide," Bart added before walking away and turning off his recording device.

The bailiff turned off the tape player.

The entire courtroom was stunned. Finally, Judge Carter cleared his throat. In a very civil tone, he instructed counsel for both the plaintiff and defendant to approach the bench. Immediately.

The sounds of wooden chairs scraping wooden floors filled the room as the attorneys and the court stenographer filed up to and behind the judge's bench. He turned off his microphone.

Shari looked over at Bart with an expression of repugnance that in previous times would have made tears come to his eyes. Without words, he knew what she was thinking, that she'd find a way to get even with the little bastard. Judge Carter looked sternly at Richard Ward and his lackeys. "What, gentlemen, and I use the word loosely, are you trying to pull in this courtroom?"

"What, Your Honor?" Ward asked, like an idiot who doesn't know he's wearing a Kick Me sign.

"I'm referring to Exhibit A. Its pretty packaging. Its professional quality. No stumbles or stammers on the tape. It's perfect. Exhibit B on the other hand is something from a Mamet play. What gives? I'm really interested."

"Your Honor," Ward began, "given the sophisticated audio technology available at Sterling, it's not surprising to me that our tape sounds better than the amateur's."

"Considering the technology at Ms. Draper's disposal, it's also not difficult to erase glitches and to fake a conversation from bits and pieces of others," the judge countered.

"I assure you, Your Honor, I have no idea what you're getting at," Ward said.

"Then you're an idiot."

At the judge's bench, Richard Ward announced that they had the authority and were prepared to settle the case immediately. Fitterman argued that the case was just getting started and that he had much more evidence to present. However, they would not meet Fitterman's terms for dropping the case: If they simultaneously settled Bart Cain's wrongful-termination lawsuit, he would consider the motion. That, they said, was an entirely different case, and they refused to consider any such move.

"Your Honor," Fitterman said, "I'm fully prepared to continue with this trial if these gentlemen are ready to proceed.

"We are, Your Honor."

"Very well," Carter said. He made a motion with his hands for the assembly to return to their seats.

"Mr. Fitterman, you may cross-examine," Carter said, resuming control of the courtroom.

"Thank you, Your Honor," Fitterman said as he moved unsteadily toward Bart in the witness box. "Mr. Cain," he began, "you were fired from Sterling Studios. Why?"

"Objection, Your Honor!" Richard Ward bellowed. "No relevance."

"No relevance?" Fitterman bawled. "Indeed, Mr. Cain was fired for *no relevance*. But his termination is relevant to the case against Mr. Lucas."

"Objection, Your Honor!" Ward cried again. "Hearsay and speculative!"

"What's speculative about the fact that Mr. Cain was fired?" Fitterman countered.

"All your objections are overruled, Mr. Ward," Judge Carter said. "Continue, Mr. Fitterman."

"So tell us, Mr. Cain, why were you fired?"

"Because I refused to go along with fraudulent claims that were being concocted by executive vice president Shari Draper and motion-picture chairman Cy Lupiano accusing president of marketing Owen Lucas of sexual harassment."

"Is that the reason that was given for your termination?"

"No. I was told that my work performance was subpar."

"But you have many citations and commendations for your work," Fitterman said, holding up a sheaf of papers with little gold seals affixed to them. There was also letterhead stationery from well-known actors.

"I guess the Lord giveth and the Lord taketh away," Bart said.

The jury sniggered.

"Tell us, Mr. Cain, what is a typical day in the life of a publicist?"

"To be honest, sir, I was only a publicist by title. I didn't pitch stories to newspapers or magazines, and I didn't interact with the press. I just wrote all day; all of the studio's publicity materials. Press kits, cast and filmmaker bios, photo captions, press releases, speeches, responses to complaint letters, film synopses, special assignments, such as feature articles about the stars in our films. I wrote letters on behalf of various stars or producers to the Hollywood Foreign Press Association, or the HFPA, as it's known. Basically everything written about our live-action films."

"Live-action?" Fitterman interrupted.

"As opposed to animated films. Sterling has got a great writer who's also a real publicist to handle animation."

"So you had nothing to do with that cute little rat in the White House?"

"No, sir."

The gallery chuckled at the joke.

"I handled, or used to handle, writing about Bruce Willis, Nightmare Dickerson . . . Sorry, I mean the movie star Mare Dickerson, Angelina Jolie, Jackie Chan, Nicolas Cage . . . and of course the directors, producers, cinematographers, editors, composers, costume designers, etc."

"Sounds like quite a job," Fitterman said. "Did you enjoy your work?"

"Yes, sir."

"Did you like the people you worked with."

"I like most people to one degree or another."

"Did you like your boss?"

"No."

"Why not?"

Bart looked past Fitterman to Shari, sitting at the plaintiff's table, sipping a glass of water, waiting patiently for his response.

"On the whole she is a cruel, devious, vicious human being who takes enormous pleasure in publicly castigating employees for the smallest infraction. And I'm on drugs—antianxiety drugs—because of her daily treatment of me."

"Can you be specific?"

"Objection! Your Honor, Ms. Draper is not on trial here!" Richard Ward complained.

"She's the plaintiff, you knucklehead," Judge Carter said. "She represents Sterling. You may answer the question, Mr. Cain."

"Okay. For instance, when Julia Bob's film *Plain Jane* opened to the largest Memorial Day weekend box office in the studio's history, I was greeted at the following Tuesday-morning marketing meeting by her screaming that my press kit didn't contain enough quotes from the star, although Ms. Draper had previously approved the material. My morale and the entire department's morale was now incredibly low because of her attitude toward us.

"Then there's this one film director she particularly hates. She doesn't think I know why she hates him, but I do. And it's not just because he's fat. She's Miss Perfect, with the life cycle and the trainer and the protein diet and the Mr. Rudolph's hairstyle. She had me research his background and pull newspaper clippings of him being arrested twenty years ago and serving time in an Alaska jail for making soft-porn films. She got hold of some of the videos he did and started a smear campaign. She first invited all of her senior staff to view the tapes. Then she had her friends at the *Los Angeles Times, Daily Variety,* the *Hollywood Reporter,* and *Totally Hollywood* and Roger Ebert see what this guy had been involved in. He was directing a family movie for the studio, and she had him kicked off the picture."

"But don't you think she had a right to do that? To save innocent kids from his perversion?"

"He served his time in jail two decades ago. He hadn't been involved in porn since then. His debt was paid to society. But she brought it back into the news and wrecked his career."

"Why do you think that is?"

"Because she has a secret that she doesn't want anyone to know about."

Shari gave a vigorous nudge to Richard Ward, who immediately stood up. "Objection! Your Honor, where is this leading?"

"I'm sure I don't know," Judge Carter said in his most condescending tone.

At that point, Shari leaned over to Ward and whispered something, frantically gesturing with her hands. "Object or something, you pissers! You promised my personal life would never come up in this trial. You promised, you son of a bitch! Settle this thing!"

Ward stood up and addressed Judge Carter. "Your Honor, may we have a sidebar?"

"For crying out loud! I'll give you a sidebar you'll never forget if this keeps up, Counselor!"

Fitterman looked at Owen. Owen looked at Bart. Bart looked to the back of the room, where Jim and Mitch and Rusty were sitting on the edge of their seats. They simultaneously smiled at one another.

Judge Carter caught the exchange and hammered his gavel. "What's so amusing, Mr. Cain? Would you care to share whatever you think is so funny?"

"Nothing, Your Honor. I apologize to the court, Your Honor."

Judge Carter gave Bart a look of disdain.

Again the attorneys and the court reporter proceeded to the judge's bench. Judge Carter sat behind his desk and poured himself a glass of water from a stainless-steel pitcher. He took several long swallows before allowing Richard Ward to begin speaking.

"Your Honor, I have just been notified by my client that she does not wish to continue with the case. I have the authority to plea-bargain on behalf of my client, Sterling."

"Why the change of heart, Mr. Ward?" Judge Carter asked.

"I'm not sure, Your Honor, but my client is vehement that we resolve the case immediately."

"Mr. Ward," Judge Carter said, "we are in the middle of a trial. Why the hell didn't you all settle this case out of court in the first place? Now you're wasting taxpayers' money and the court's time, which is *my* time! Go back out there and try this case!"

"But Your Honor," Ward whined.

"Go, for Christ sake!"

"Mr. Ward, please call your next witness," Judge Carter intoned.

"I call Ms. Shari Draper."

Shari rose regally from her seat and walked with purpose to the witness box. The bailiff asked her to raise her right hand and to swear to tell the truth, the whole truth, and nothing but the truth.

"Hmmm," Shari responded.

"I know it's a bore," said Judge Carter in mock indulgence, "but would you please answer in the affirmative or negative, Ms. Draper?"

"Yes!" Shari said.

"That's a good girl."

"Woman! I'm a woman, not a girl," Shari protested.

"Just recite your name and address for the record and don't yell in my court," Carter said. Shari complied with clarity and confidence.

Mr. Ward's opening questions revolved around her length of service as executive vice president of Sterling Studios and her association with Owen Lucas and the number of people who had come to her with allegations of the president of marketing's alleged inappropriate sexual behavior.

"Many people came to me to complain that they were being sexually harassed by Mr. Lucas," Shari said. "I taped their conversations as evidence for our human resources department."

"What were the complaints about Mr. Lucas?"

"You heard what was on my tape. He demanded sexual favors in exchange for his employees getting raises, promotions, and in the case of Mr. Cain, keeping his job."

"Mr. Lucas was your superior, the next in the chain of command, so to speak. Correct?"

"Correct."

"Therefore, you were his subordinate, correct?"

"Yes."

"And Sterling has a strictly enforced zero-tolerance sexual-harassment policy, correct?"

"Indeed. That's why I took the matter up with the next-highest level."

"Mr. Cy Lupiano?"

"Yes. He and I both determined it was in the best interest of the company to terminate Mr. Lucas."

"But that wasn't your call, now, was it, Ms. Draper?" Ward asked.

"No. It was at the discretion of Mr. Lupiano, the chairman of the motion-picture division."

"And of course this was done with the full cooperation of human resources?"

"Objection," Fitterman stated. "Counsel is leading the witness."

"Overruled," Judge Owen called.

Shari answered. "Of course. In fact, they had quite a file filled with complaints about Mr. Lucas. Mr. Lupiano didn't require anybody's authorization to do what he felt was in the best interest of his company. He is the final authority. Almost."

Mr. Ward held up a large manila file folder and asked her to read the name printed on a tab.

"LUCAS, OWEN."

"May it please the court, we wish to enter this file and its contents into the record as Exhibit C. It contains numerous complaints from a variety of sources regarding Mr. Lucas's sexual behavior in the workplace. I have nothing further for Ms. Draper."

"Mr. Fitterman, please proceed," Judge Carter said.

Shari remained calm and confident to the point of being almost defiant.

Waddling to the witness stand, Gus Fitterman was all smiles as Shari sat stone-faced, completely disgusted by the man's girth, age, disingenuous demeanor, and halitosis.

"Why was Mr. Lucas terminated, Ms. Draper?"

Mr. Ward stood up. "Objection, Your Honor. The witness has already testified as to cause!"

"Sustained. Please ask another question."

"I'm sorry, Your Honor." Fitterman smiled. "Ms. Draper, you testified that you made audiotapes of those who complained about sexual harassment. May we hear the other tapes as well?"

"I never said I made other tapes."

Fitterman smiled apologetically. "Guess I've got to have my hearing checked," he said, chuckling. "I was sure that you previously testified that you taped conversations with employees who made allegations about Mr. Lucas's supposed indiscretions. My apology."

Shari smiled. Self-satisfied.

Fitterman was about to ask another question when he interrupted himself. Scratching his forehead, he turned to the judge and said, "I'm sorry, Your Honor. Would you indulge this old man and ask the court reporter to read back Ms. Draper's previous testimony. Just at the very beginning, after she was sworn in?"

Judge Carter nodded his agreement, and the cute stenographer worked his way back several feet of rolled paper that had gathered in a Lucite box attached to his stenographer's machine. He found the correct place and read in an antomaton's monotone voice: "Many people came to me to complain that they were being sexually harassed by Mr. Lucas. I taped their conversations as evidence for our human resources department."

"That's the part. That's good," Fitterman said appreciatively. "Thank you. I honestly thought for a moment I might be having a *senior moment* or the imaginings of an old man who should have retired long ago. Whew!" Fitterman pretended to be relieved. "My hearing seems to be fine, after all. But your memory, Ms. Draper . . . You previously testified that you made audiotapes of employees who brought charges of harassment, and now you deny that testimony. Would you please explain?"

"I recorded other conversations. I misunderstood you."

"Where are those tapes, Ms. Draper?"

"Hell if I know. I think human resources lost 'em, or something."

"Or something. Yes. I see. Well, let's move on," Fitterman continued. "Why do you think your audiocassette tape and the audiocassette tape produced by Mr. Cain are so different?"

"I'm sure I don't know."

"Can you speculate, because I'm as confused about this as you appear to be," Fitterman said in his best Matlock slack-jawed wonder.

"Mr. Cain has based his career on lies, as his record proves," Shari said.

"Isn't that a publicist's job?" Fitterman smiled.

"Objection!" Richard Ward shouted.

"I apologize, Your Honor," Fitterman said. "A small Hollywood joke."

"Very small," Judge Carter snarled.

Returning his attention to Shari, he said, "One of my big dilemmas is that the date on the audiotape you provided—and by the way, it's very pretty and was beautifully packaged—is that it says February nineth. That was a Saturday, wasn't it?"

"I don't remember."

"Trust me, it was a Saturday. Here's a calendar," Fitterman said, holding up a daily planner. "You don't remember working on a Saturday?"

"I work seven days a week. One day is the same as another."

"How about Mr. Cain?" Fitterman continued his line of questioning.

"He often works weekends, too."

"But this was also the day of the big bash at Jim Fallon's home. Mr. Cain did not work that Saturday."

"I don't keep his time card," Shari said, sounding bored with the barrage of questions.

"Another thing I keep scratching my head over is I don't understand why it appears you're giving direction on the tape Mr. Cain provided? It sounds like you were setting him up as a pawn in a charade to terminate Mr. Lucas. Am I correct?"

"Objection, Your Honor!" Ward pounced. "Counsel is giving witness's testimony!"

"Overruled. I'm as curious as Mr. Fitterman."

"Of course not!" Shari spat. "Are you now calling *me* a liar?" She gave him a look that would have sent Evander Holyfield looking for his mama.

"I haven't called you anything but Ms. Draper. It is *Ms.* Draper, isn't it?"

Richard Ward leaped from his seat. "What is going on here, Your Honor? The plaintiff has stated her name and address for the record. Mr. Fitterman is just bullying her!"

Judge Carter looked at Ward. "Calm down," he said. Then he addressed Gus Fitterman. "Mr. Fitterman, please make your point. It's getting late."

Shari recognized something in the wheels that were turning behind the eyes of Gus Fitterman. For the first time, she began to lose her composure. She picked up a water glass from the flat railing of the witness box. It was empty.

"Please, allow me to pour you some," Fitterman said as Shari held out her glass. She took her time but swallowed the entire glass of water. "Are you ready to continue?"

Shari simply raised her eyebrows, then looked at Bart and at Owen with the same contempt she offered Fitterman.

"Ms. Draper. And forgive me if I use the feminine pronoun loosely."

Once again Ward erupted from his seat. "Objection! Mr. Fitterman is being downright rude!"

"Your Honor," Fitterman said, "I don't wish to be rude or inconsiderate or to cause the witness undue distress. However, I submit for the record this document from a Dr. Howard Rean, noted transgender therapist."

"Counsel for both sides approach the bench immediately," Judge Owen called, and turned off his microphone. He grabbed the document from Fitterman and examined it thoroughly. Then he looked at Shari before handing the pages to Richard Ward and his army, all of whom looked at each other, then looked over at Shari. She sat motionless, staring at the bailiff who guarded the double doors at the entrance to the courtroom.

Ward and his minions made another plea for a meeting in chambers. Judge Owen turned his microphone back on and asked for the jury's patience while he and counsel stepped away for a few moments. The representatives for Sterling and for Owen and Bart as well as the court reporter disappeared into the room behind the bench. Shari continued to sit stone-faced. For the first time, she had the sinking feeling that something ominous was about to unfold.

Although the walls between the judge's chambers and the courtroom were thick as a fortified castle, the entire jury and those in the gallery could hear shouting. Words could not be distinguished, but the murmur from the volatile conversation seeped into the outer room.

"I have really had enough of you guys *and* Hollywood," Judge Carter roared at Ward and his cohorts. "And you, Mr. Fitterman, you're no better, surprising opposing counsel with this damning evidence. You should have made this material available to them!"

"I'm sorry, Your Honor, I was just provided with these documents this afternoon." Fitterman lied. "The defendant's counsel has the right to a postponement to review this material and to offer a defense," Judge Carter said.

"I still move for a dismissal," Ward stated.

"I'm considering your request," Carter said.

Richard Ward looked at his colleagues, who shrugged their shoulders as if to say, "Let's give up."

"Does counsel for the plaintiff really wish to settle?" the judge queried.

"On the conditions previously set forth?" Fitterman said adamantly.

"Gentlemen?"

"No, Your Honor," said Ward. "Not under those conditions. We may as well see this through."

Chapter Twenty-Four

"All rise," the bailiff demanded as Judge Carter, Sterling's attorneys, Fitterman, and the court reporter returned to the courtroom.

After a moment of settling down, Judge Carter spoke wearily. "Continue, Mr. Fitterman," he said with a sigh.

Shari shot a long look of loathing at Ward, as if to say, "Why didn't you settle? For Christ sake, I told you to settle this mess!"

Gus Fitterman went to his table and picked up several documents. Then he walked slowly over to Shari, who was beginning to look like Allison Janney's character in *American Beauty*—cast down in a gloom of perpetual dejection.

"Ms. Draper," he said. "Would you please look at this document and state for the record what it reveals?"

This time there was no objection from Sterling's attorneys. Neither of them bellowed that the witness had already testified, under oath, that she was Shari Draper of 275 Thorn Hill Drive, Beverly Hills, California.

Shari took a long moment. Bart watched her and for a moment experienced pity for the woman—a pity reserved for one whose world is instantly and without warning wiped away as if it never existed in the first place.

"For the record. Your legal name, please," Fitterman prompted.

Looking up as defiantly as ever and in a voice that filled the room as if to proclaim a victory, Shari said at last, "Shari Draper. My name is Shari Anne Draper!"

"Perhaps I phrased my question incorrectly and you didn't quite understand," Fitterman patronized. "I'd like you to tell the court the name you were born with."

"You heard me the first time." Shari was fast losing her confidence and arrogance.

Fitterman continued. "Well, let's take a different approach. Do you know Jim Fallon? The television star?"

At the reference to his stardom, Jim beamed.

"Yes. I know many stars," Shari said.

"Isn't it true that you knew Mr. Fallon from a time when the two of you were incarcerated in an Alaskan jail?"

There was a loud murmur in the gallery.

Judge Carter brought his gavel down on a wooden block, calling for order. He had to demand silence several times before the crowd settled down.

Shari was flustered and looked with contempt at her team of attorneys. "Certainly not."

"Okay. Did you know a man named Don Simpson? A film producer?"

"Oh, poor Don. What a terrible loss. I was completely floored by his death," Shari pretended to weep.

"How well did you know Mr. Simpson? How far back did you go?"

Shari, working on overdrive to present the image of an ingenue, proceeded cautiously. "Oh, when I was first working in Hollywood as an assistant. I knew Mr. Simpson, and he was so incredibly kind and encouraging and helpful to me—and to all his assistants." With this Shari feigned an emotional breakdown.

"Back to Mr. Jim Fallon for a moment," Fitterman continued. "Where again did you say you met him?"

"I didn't say."

"Do you remember?"

"No." Shari's façade was practically diaphanous.

"Mr. Fallon has written a fascinating book, the manuscript of which is on my table. Did you know you are heavily featured in his story?"

Suddenly, knowing full well where Fitterman was going with his cross-examination, Shari stood up and faced Richard Ward. "Settle, you S.O.B.!" she shouted. "Settle! Settle! You motherfucking bottom-feeder!"

Judge Carter brought down his gavel with a thunderous echo. "The trial will continue," he demanded.

Before the room could settle down completely and before the judge had an opportunity to render any sanctions, Fitterman plowed ahead. Holding a document out close to Shari's face, Fitterman said, "Once again, for the record, your legal name, please."

Finally, with no one to back her up, not even her overpaid lawyers,

Shari stood up in the witness box. With an imperious tone, she proclaimed, "Larry Burton! *Mr.* Larry Charles Burton!"

There was a simultaneous explosive gasp from the jurors and those in the gallery. Fitterman completed his assault by stating, "We also have documentation from the Anchorage County Jail that Larry Charles Burton escaped from jail in 1976, along with the late Don Simpson." He said to Shari/Larry in a compassionate tone, "You are said convict, number 2928272, are you not?"

"So I am," Shari spat, making no apologies. "I suppose this is the point where I'm to get up and start singing a Jerry Herman song. 'I Am What I Am,' or something. Well, that ain't gonna happen, you asswipes!"

In the midst of the turmoil in the courtroom, Judge Carter brought his gavel down one more time and declared the trial over. "I have no alternative but to find in favor of the defendant. Ms. Draper, er Burton, will be held until it's determined if extradition to Alaska is required."

He thanked the jury and apologized to them for not having the opportunity to deliberate the case. Then he looked out at Owen, and while looking into his eyes, he spoke collectively to the attorneys and to Owen. "I want you all back in this courtroom next Thursday at nine A.M. At that time I will determine the monetary damages to be accorded to Mr. Lucas and Mr. Cain." Carter's eyes stayed on Owen a beat longer before he rose from the bench and disappeared into his chambers.

Owen came over and hugged Bart, who by this time was surrounded by Rusty, Rod, Mitch, and Jim. They all thanked Fitterman, who was putting papers into his briefcase.

Sheriffs had surrounded Shari/Larry and placed her in handcuffs. "How could you do this to me, you fucking faggot," she screamed at Bart. With new bravado and knowing that Shari was shackled, Bart left his clique and walked up to his old boss. "I learned a lot from you, Shari. I learned that nothing is ever good enough for you. I learned how not to treat other people. I especially learned what Norman Shearer learned in *The Women*. Does 'Jungle Red' mean anything to you?" Bart held up his hands and bent his fingers as if demonstrating that he'd finally grown claws—like everybody else in Hollywood. "They're the same color as your toenails!"

Chapter Twenty-Five

"Come back to the house and we'll have Wolfgang deliver something to celebrate," Jim said in a moment of unusual graciousness.

Reaching the parking lot, the men split up to find their respective cars. Bart and Rusty walked to Rusty's Jag. Mitch got into his Honda. Owen pushed a button on his key and from ten paces away deactivated the alarm system in his BMW. Rod drove away in his Dodge Dart. Jim made a great show of wiping a spot from the hood of his Rolls-Royce. And Gus Fitterman just barely squeezed into his Volvo. They left Burbank and headed over Barham toward the Cahuenga Pass and up into the hills to Jim's estate.

Knowing all the shortcuts, Jim reached Woodrow Wilson before the others. He parked his car in the circular drive and closed the gate behind him. He raced into the house, where he poured a double gin martini before the first arrival. Soon thereafter, Rod buzzed from the intercom at the gate. Jim pushed the button to activate the system that opened the enormous front gates, and Rod drove up the hill.

When he got inside the house, he immediately inhaled the smell of booze and realized that Jim had already downed a drink. "Ya know, this is the first time I've been back here since the day I found out that you and Michael had screwed me out of my script," Rod said.

"Oh, let's not go into that tonight, shall we?" Jim pleaded. "We have to celebrate Owen's and Bart's victory. Do open a bottle of bubbly. You still know where everything is. Nothing's changed. They'll be here any sec. And would you get Wolfgang on the phone for me?"

"I'm not your fucking houseboy anymore, Jim. You could ask me politely. Anyway, do it yourself."

"Ever the contrary one, aren't you!"

Just then the intercom buzzed. It was Bart and Rusty. "We're here,"

Rusty announced. "And Gus is a moment behind us, so please keep the gate open."

When the men had all assembled in the library and Rusty had time to recover from the shock of seeing the city view for the first time, Rod decided to play host, after all, and poured them all flutes of champagne. "You're a doll," Jim said to him in appreciation.

Jim had even deigned to call Wolfgang to order pizzas. By the time the food arrived, the men were famished. They had been consuming nothing but champagne and melted Brie for an hour and were starting to reminisce about things that should have been kept locked up in the vaults of their respective memories.

"Oh, Rod," Jim lamented. "I was an awful shit to you. I'm truly sorry. You're too handsome to be angry at any longer. I'm even more sorry that they didn't submit my book as evidence. That would have ensured it becoming a best-seller."

"Your manuscript may still be incredibly valuable," Fitterman interjected. "You've documented Shari's attempt at castrating her lover to her being a failed transsexual to skateboarding microskirt-wearing mail-delivery girl at Millennium to queen of marketing at Sterling. With all your footnotes and the stuff about that director she had ruined because she realized they'd been in the slammer together and he knew her big secret, there's no way she'll succeed in harming Bart."

"It'll make a damn good movie," Jim mused aloud. "Yes, and I could play myself."

"When I began, all I wanted was to get my screenplay produced," Rod said defensively to Jim. "None of this would have happened if it weren't for you and that prick Michael! By the way, whatever happened to him?"

"I'm shocked at you," Jim said. "You always used to devour the trades!"

"I haven't been able to afford a shot of tequila, let alone buy *Daily Variety*. What's happened to him?"

"Nothing, dear boy, except he's *persona non grata* in the town he was determined to conquer. He's on an unpaid leave of absence from Actors and Others. It's been a scan-dal—with a capital D-I-S-H."

"What happened?" asked Rusty.

"Seems his assistant, Troy, followed him to the Trap one night. Picture this: Michael sauntering into that scumhole of a dive, laying five hundred bucks on the counter, and the bartender grabbing him by his necktie and dragging him over the top of the bar. With videotape recorder in hand, Troy photographed Michael—in Armani, no less—forced down to his knees, where he became, shall we say, a human urinal not only for the bartender but for half the guys in the place. It was like a gang rape." Jim made the pronouncement as if Michael must have been in heaven.

Jim paused. "Michael's been in the hospital with hepatitis and God only knows what else. He should have stuck with spankings."

Rod wanted to say it served Michael right for all the evil he'd wrought. Instead, self-absorbed to the core, he merely said, "So much for my script."

"As a matter of fact," Rusty said, interrupting, "Troy, his assistant, is one of my clients. Beautiful little shih tzu."

"He's got a cute dog, too," Jim said, smiling at his old joke.

Mitch was just about to throw in another zinger, but Bart gave him a look that immediately stopped him.

"He was always hot for your script, Rod," continued Rusty. "The original script, not the fiftieth draft you subsequently wrote based on Michael's lame suggestions. He told me in the strictest confidence—and I wouldn't ordinarily break a confidence, but since I've had too much to drink and you deserve as much positive news today as Owen and Bart—he's made it his priority to package it for a new discovery he's made. Some Gwyneth Paltrow/Cate Blanchette/Piper Perabo combo. He just negotiated a three-picture deal for her—at of all places, Sterling. He says she's going to be a mega star, and he's calling the shots for her career. So keep your fingers crossed about *Blind as a Bat*. You, too, Jim, because he said the one thing Michael did right was to sign you to the agency and he agrees that the gay building super would be the ideal role for your comeback."

"I never left!" Jim said indignantly before checking his temper and realizing that Rusty was not being insulting.

Owen, meanwhile, quietly sipped champagne and watched the sun go down and the city lights appear below through the floor-to-ceiling windows. Bart and Rusty both noticed how withdrawn Owen seemed. They decided to wander over for a chat. Bart said to him, "A buck fifty for your thoughts?"

"Inflation, eh? I'll never be able to repay you for putting your career on the line for me the way you did," Owen said. "You and Rusty are an amazing couple. I've never been so grateful."

"What'll you do now that the nightmare is over?" Bart asked.

"You don't have to worry about me."

Rusty looked at Owen in a manner that suggested *You want to tell him, or shall I?*

Owen's nonverbal response indicated that he trusted Rusty to do whatever he felt was best.

"Owen's the heir to the Lucas department store chain. He's got more money than God."

"Jeez," Bart said. "Why would you want to work at a hellhole like Sterling if you didn't have to?"

"I love marketing. It's what I got my degree in. Plus it was a big challenge. Also, when you don't have to work, you don't take all the day-to-day politics and bullshit seriously. You tell yourself, So what if they fire me. It'll be their loss. What am I gonna do, starve? Money is merely freedom.

"But it's you I'm now worried about," Owen said, addressing Bart. "Even if Judge Carter makes Sterling reinstate you in your old job, you won't go. What will you do?"

Bart smiled. "What transpired in court today gave me the ending to the novel I've been writing . . ."

Rusty turned to Bart. "I didn't know you were writing a book! That's really great."

"I've been turning in chapters for the past six months to my agent, who's been shopping it around. We made a deal last week with Rocket Books."

"What's it about?" Owen asked.

"About me. About Shari. About Jim. About Rod. About egomaniacal producers like Don Simpson. About Mare Dickerson. About my ex-lovers. About my childhood. It's a *roman à clef*. A real potboiler!"

"What's the title?" Owen asked.

"I'm thinking of calling it *Tricks of the Trade*. But the first thing I plan to do when it's finished is something that Rusty and I have both dreamed about. I'm kidnapping him, and we're going off to live in Scotland!"

Rusty was beaming. Although it had always been a plan to go back to his favorite place on the planet, he didn't foresee a time for a trip anywhere in the near future.

"Wonderful!" Owen said, genuinely happy. "When are you leaving? How long will you be gone."

"We're leaving as soon as both of us can get things together. And we're not coming back—except to visit now and then. I've already got a relocation company checking into cottages and farms for us to rent or buy."

Bart turned to Rusty. "I'm sorry I haven't given you a chance to discuss the details . . . and we don't have to go, really. But we've talked about living abroad so often, I called up an estate agent, and she has some interesting properties. Listen. We don't even have to live there. We'll just take an extended vacation and see how we like it. They're working everything out. But of course I'm not going if you're not, so . . ."

The news couldn't have pleased Rusty more. He put his flute of champagne down on the carpet and placed his hands on Bart's face. He pulled his lover toward his lips, and they embraced in a deep, passionate, long, loving kiss.

"I love you, Bart," Rusty said with tears in his eyes.

"And I love you, Rusty, more than I ever imagined it was possible to love another human being. I just want us to be together in Scotland or Van Nuys or Paris or Tampa."

"In Bellflower, Botswana, Baghdad, Loch Mere—or the moon," Rusty countered. "No matter where we are, as long as I'm with you, I'm alive and in love with you."

"It's true what they say," Owen said. "Money isn't everything. I'd trade the zillions of bucks that keep pouring in, armored truckload after armored truckload, for just a fraction of what you two have."

"What about Judge Carter," Bart said with a mischievous grin.

"What about him?" Owen smiled but remained on guard.

"Were you too nervous today to see the way he looked at you?"

"He looked angry."

"Only in the beginning. It was his macho façade," Bart said. "From where I sat, and the guys will back me up on this . . . Hey, guys!" he called. "Come over here a sec!"

Jim, Rod, Mitch, and Gus ambled over to the window overlooking the city. "Tell Owen how the judge responded today when he got a look at the hot guy sitting in his courtroom," Bart said.

"You mean Scary Shari?" Mitch deadpanned.

"You little twit. No. When he first saw Owen . . . and throughout the proceedings."

"It was obvious to me that there was something sexual going through his brain," Rod said. "And I read men like the menu at IHOP."

"Maybe he just thought Carmen Miranda on a necktie was too outrageous for his courtroom," Owen said.

Fitterman practically gushed, "Hell, I'm straight, but I have eyes. I can see how handsome he is."

"Gee," Mitch teased, "most *straight* men don't admit they recognize it when another guy is attractive," as if to imply Fitterman was concealing an ambivalent sexuality.

The inference went over Fitterman's head. "And I know for a fact he's available. Not married. Not dating."

"Really?" Owen said, becoming more intrigued.

"One of my legal aides is best friends with the court reporter. She was interested in the judge for herself until . . . Well, let's just say she found out that justice may be blind but Judge Carter's scale tips the other way."

Owen beamed at the suggestion that Judge Carter may have found him attractive. "I could tell by his posture. Under his robe was probably the body of a guy who played quarterback for Harvard. Not that I'd know if he went to Harvard, but he was certainly smart and completely understood the letter of the law."

"Isn't that adorable?" Mitch mocked. He pinched Owen's chest, aiming for where he thought his nipple might be. "We point out the obvious to you and suddenly you're smitten."

"Am not!" Owen laughed. "Just curious."

"That he thought you were a stud?" Mitch finished the question. "Duh!"

Mitch rolled his eyes and poured another flute of champagne for himself and refilled Owen's glass as well. "Here, this will muddle your mind further." Then to the group he appealed, "How come there are guys like him who have the looks of Campbell Scott, the brains of . . . of . . . of . . . well anybody who's smart, has more money than God, but they don't think they're worth dating?"

"I know I'm worth dating," Owen countered. "But I don't go around thinking everyone wants me. Especially someone as hunky as the judge. But now that you mention it." Owen had a distant look in his eyes. "I *do* remember sitting at the table and feeling kind of light-headed when the bailiff called, 'All rise.' I mean, am I wrong, but wasn't he just so-o-o-o good-looking?"

"*YES!*" The entire room exploded in unison.

"I'll place odds that after next week's court date, he'll call you," Bart predicted. "Or you'll just have to call him."

"Like I would even dare presume he found me attractive!"

"Don't presume anything," Bart said. "But if we have to get a summons and haul his studdly ass into a restaurant to meet you, we will."

The other men ad-libbed, "Absolutely! Right on! You've got to give him a try. You're a catch. He's a catch."

"Well, this has been some day," Owen finally said. He was basking in both his triumph in the courtroom and the general verdict of his friends that *Love Finds Andy Hardy*. Well, if not Mickey and Judy, maybe Doris and Rock. Or Richard Gere and Julia Roberts.

"Speaking of love," Rusty interrupted, "Bart and I are going to mosey on down the hill. We've got some celebrating to do ourselves."

Bart smiled. He looked first at Fitterman, then to the other men. "This has been one heck of a great day. I can't thank you all enough for everything that each of you did for me and for Owen. You guys are my family. My friends."

At that moment, Rod turned away and went to the bar, clearly ignoring Bart's departure speech. His cold shoulder was so obvious that the other men all looked at each other and shrugged as if to say, "Somebody needs a nap."

"Give me a sec," Bart said to Rusty. He walked to the bar, where Rod was knocking back another champagne. "What's up, man?" he asked, genuinely surprised by Rod's rebuff.

"Nothing. Why do you assume something's up?" Rod poured another glass of champagne.

"Well, for one thing, you've been in great spirits all evening, and now you're behaving as if you're avoiding me."

"If I were avoiding you, I'd hardly be standing here talking to you, would I?"

"Okay. As long as things are cool."

"Cool?" Rod mocked Bart's concern. "Yeah, it's cool that you're going home with Mr. Perfect. I think maybe I'll get back with Jimbo here. He really wasn't all that hideous."

"Not when he's unconscious," Bart quipped.

"Hey, nothing's perfect," Rod said, slurring his words. "Except . . . I'm going to the bathroom. I'll be awhile, so don't wait around."

With that, Rod left the room.

Bart, stunned by Rod's comments, turned and went back to the group. "Jim, it's been a great pleasure. We'll see you soon, I hope? Mr. Fitterman, what can I say?"

"You'll be saying a lot when you get my bill." Fitterman laughed. The others joined in despite knowing he was only half-joking.

Bart continued. "Mitch, we'll keep in touch. And Owen, I guess we'll see you next Thursday, if not before."

Owen opened his arms and embraced Bart. "See you at the wedding?" he joked. "Can a judge marry himself? I'll have to look into that." Owen laughed. "Heck, I haven't so much as had a date with the guy and I'm planning our honeymoon. What a fool!"

"Only fools fall in love," Rusty countered. Then he took Bart by the hand to lead him up the two steps of the sunken living room and into the foyer toward the door.

After Rusty's Jaguar cleared the gates and they moved out onto Woodrow Wilson Drive toward Mulholland, Bart spoke up. "Did you hear what Rod said before we left?"

"We all did. The guy's got some major issues. He's still hung up on you."

"But how do you feel about it?"

Rusty reached Mulholland, checked for traffic approaching, and quickly scooted his vehicle across the street. He stopped at the light at Laurel Canyon and made a right turn before answering the question. "I trust you to do whatever's right."

"Mr. Passive/Aggressive," Bart snorted.

"I trust you completely, Bart. Really. Plus, I'm not giving up this trip to Scotland for anything!"

Both men laughed, agreeing there was nothing for either of them to worry about and that any problem Rod had was his alone. There was nothing Bart or Rusty could do to change the way Rod thought.

Bart leaned over and kissed Rusty on the cheek. "Hurry home, baby," he said. "I need you naked next to me!"

Rusty let the steep, winding road rush them down to Fryman Canyon, where he stepped on the accelerator to avoid a red light. Within minutes they were home, in the garage, kissing passionately to the sound of the dogs barking for their share of attention.

Chapter Twenty-Six

Thursday arrived, one of those perfect Southern California Chamber of Commerce spring mornings. The sky was as blue as it could ever be in smog-choked Los Angeles, and the air was still filled with the scent of night-blooming jasmine. Bart and Rusty met Owen and Gus Fitterman at the courthouse for Judge Carter's final resolution of their respective cases.

Passing through the metal detector at the courthouse entrance, the four walked to their assigned courtroom, which turned out to be the same one in which their lives had been irrevocably altered the week before. The atmosphere was just as formal as when the jury had been present. However, this time, the only people in the room were the court reporter, the bailiff, counsel for the defense and the plaintiffs, Bart, Rusty, Owen, and Judge Carter, who entered from his chambers and settled into the black leather chair behind the bench.

Judge Carter began. "Because of the staggering malice as well as reckless and reprehensible indifference to Title VII of the Civil Rights Act perpetrated by Ms. Shari Draper, acting for Sterling Studios, who openly and admittedly engaged in discrimination against president of marketing Owen Lucas, I hereby order Sterling Studios to pay compensatory and punitive damages totaling $4.5 million to Mr. Lucas.

"With regard to Bart Cain, who served as senior publicist at Sterling Studios, I decree the studio shall pay compensatory and punitive damages in the amount of $2 million. Also, if Mr. Cain or Mr. Lucas desire, they are to be reinstated in their respective positions, with compensation doubling the salary they have missed since their wrongful terminations."

With this command, he slammed down his gavel.

Nonverbal sounds of disagreement and disgust issued from Richard Ward. Ward broke a pencil in half to display his anger.

Bart was stunned by the settlement. Simultaneously, smiles and sighs of relief came from Bart and Owen, with Rusty calmly nodding his head, acknowledging that justice had indeed been served.

"And one more item on my agenda," Judge Carter announced. "I am issuing a formal statement warning the plaintiffs from attempting to practice any type of retaliation against either of these men. The following note has come to my attention. It was addressed to both Messrs. Lucas and Cain, which leads me to believe someone from Sterling is responsible. The note says, 'I am warning you to hand over all materials said to be evidence in any case or complaint about Shari Draper. You are despicable sneaks and cheats. If you do not comply with this request, you will suffer dire consequences for your abominable, cowardly transgressions. With deepest contempt, Your Worst Nightmare.'

"This type of behavior will not be tolerated by the law. As an aside, I trust you know that statistical surveys indicate that 50 percent of working women in the workplace and 10 percent of working men have been sexually harassed on the job. I will personally see to it that these two innocent men are also awarded a staggering sum of Sterling Studios's money if this case is appealed and you lose. Am I completely clear, gentlemen?"

Richard Ward grudgingly responded. "Yes, Your Honor."

"Then court is adjourned," Judge Carter announced, and brought down his gavel one final time.

Bart and Rusty and Owen rose. Fitterman came back over and shook each of their hands, offering his congratulations. Rusty and Owen exchanged words of appreciation for all that Fitterman had done for them. The other attorney and the judge left the room. For a long moment, the three simply looked at each another. They were relieved to be rid of Shari and to have the trial completely over.

Finally, Owen said to Bart and Rusty, "Once you guys are settled in Scotland, I'm coming to stay with you for six months. Maybe I'll buy myself a castle. Or maybe the entire country. But I'm definitely getting away from Hollywood for a while. Who needs it?"

"Of course. You're always welcome," Bart said, and Rusty readily agreed. Just as they were about to leave the room, the court reporter came up to the trio. "Excuse me, gentlemen," he said, pushing his eyeglass frames up the bridge of his nose. "Judge Carter asked if you wouldn't mind meeting with him for just a moment in his chambers."

The men looked at each other, not completely surprised. "Sure," Bart said. "Lead the way."

The court reporter escorted them back into the vast room, past the jury box and witness stand and the judge's enormous bench. He knocked on the wooden door that was off to the side behind the bench. *"Entréz-vous,"* an affable voice responded.

The court reporter opened the door for the men, who entered the private chamber feeling a little like Dorothy and her friends entering the Great Hall ruled by the Wizard of Oz.

Inside the room, just as Mitch had predicted when he first saw Judge Carter, there was indeed a bench press, Stairmaster, and treadmill. The office was also decorated with floor-to-ceiling shelves of law books. And there, removing his robe to reveal a hairy, pec-pumped Adonis in faded blue jeans, stood Judge Carter, every inch the hard-bodied specimen the defendants and their cohorts had lustfully imagined.

Judge Carter explained why he wasn't wearing a shirt. "The robe gets too hot." He pulled a tank top from his gym bag, lying next to the treadmill, and pulled it over his head.

"Quite a case, wasn't it, guys?" the judge declared, making conversation. "I just love it when I get to make all that noise with my gavel. It's my favorite part of the whole job," he said, metamorphosing into a regular guy, the persona of the tough authority figure completely dissolved. "That and prying out all sorts of mucky dish from witnesses on the stand. What you guys came up with about that Shari/Larry person was just too much. What a caution he/she is! How on earth did you stand to work for the bitch?"

Bart uttered, "Well, Your Honor . . ."

"Oh, don't 'Your Honor' me when I'm off duty. I'm Jonathan, and I'm happy to finally meet you guys under more positive circumstances." He held out his hand for Bart, Rusty, and Owen to shake, a formal greeting that was perfunctory until he shook Owen's hand. The two men's hands were locked together more than a moment longer than necessary. When the motion stopped, they didn't immediately disconnect from each other's grasp. "Especially nice to meet you, Owen," Jonathan said.

"Same here," Owen responded. "By the way, we're going over to Morton's for a celebratory dinner tonight. Care to come and join us."

"Really?" Judge Carter looked as if he were a child being invited to another child's birthday party.

"Absolutely," Rusty chimed in.

"I'm there!" the judge accepted. "What time's the reservation?"

"Sevenish," Owen said. "Andre, the maître d', will hold a table if you're busy and want to make it later."

"Terrif. I'll be there at sevenish."

"It's a plan," Owen nodded. "We'll see you there."

Bart, Rusty, and Owen left the room, appearing to be very dignified. However, once outside the court building, they broke into smiles and nonverbal squeals of laughter. "Now do you believe that 'Jonathan' is interested in you?" Bart chided Owen.

"And did you get a look at those arms and his chest." Owen smiled. "He should never wear robes!"

"Something tells me we'll have to put a king-size bed in the guest room at the farm," Rusty said. "Something big—to play in."

Owen pretended to protest. "Oh, stop! We don't even know each other." Owen smiled again. Owen sang an old Dusty Springfield gem "Wishing and Hoping" as they got into Rusty's Jaguar.

"You can have the nuptials in that castle you threatened to buy," Bart said as they drove off toward Owen's Beverly Hills house. Owen was already asking Rusty and Bart what he should wear to dinner.

The banner headline in *Daily Variety* announced: "Draper Hangs at Galaxy." The story that followed revealed that after being released from her contract at Sterling, Shari Draper had landed safely at Galaxy Studios. The press release from which the story was taken sounded a lot like something Bart Cain would have written.

FOR IMMEDIATE RELEASE

Shari Draper has been appointed to the position of president, worldwide marketing and promotions, for Galaxy Pictures, it was announced today by Bert Heinz, chairman of Galaxy Studios. Draper will report directly to Heinz.

Commenting on the announcement, Heinz said, "Shari Draper is an outstanding motion-picture executive. She has done extraordinary work throughout her career, and we are delighted that she has chosen to accept this position at Galaxy. We know she will play a vital role in helping us meet our expanded production schedule and maintain the high standards of quality that have been

*a hallmark of her career. She is tops in her field and will be a tre-
mendous asset to our team."*

The articles that appeared in *Daily Variety* and the *Hollywood
Reporter* only briefly touched upon her recent dismissal from Sterling.
There was no reference to the sexual-harassment trial or reports from
the media about her transgender identity. Her clout in Hollywood was
still so strong that there was hardly any negative publicity. She simply
and blissfully continued her upward spiral as a power-hungry studio executive.

"She's got an itchy clit today." Mitch Wood whispered the warning to
Galaxy Studios' staff writer Tim Waters, who had just been summoned
to Shari's office to rewrite a press release he'd been rewriting all day.

Tim, in his mid-thirties, was a rising star in the Galaxy Studios publicity department, where he'd been the staff writer for five years. His
awards for excellence from the Publicists Guild made him an easy
choice when other studios needed a qualified writer for their marketing
divisions. But he turned down every offer, fully expecting to one day re-
tire from Galaxy, which he considered the preeminent studio in
Hollywood. He loved his job. He loved Galaxy. He loved his colleagues.

Until Shari Draper came aboard.

It took Tim only one private meeting with Shari for him to know his
days were numbered. Shari had practically said as much. "You've got a
great reputation in town, Tim. I've only heard good reports." Tim had
smiled self-consciously. "So how come all the good writers are queer?"

Tim blanched from the sucker punch.

"You know, Tim, Sterling Studios is desperate to find a new writer.
Perhaps you'd fit in better over there."

Tim teetered out of that introductory meeting in a daze. He knew
right away that nothing he ever did from that moment on would please
his new boss. He was right. POOR SYNTAX. POOR SENTENCE
STRUCTURE. POOR EDITING. I COULDN'T FINISH READING
THIS CRAP! was scrawled across his press-kit notes and press releases.
Now he wished he'd accepted that last offer from Disney. At least their
marketing department was known to be run by intelligent human be-
ings—the operative word being "human."

Now Tim looked at Mitch and swallowed hard as he prepared to
enter Shari's office for her to review the press release she'd made him
rewrite five times.

"Is it finally finished?" she sneered.

"I guess you'll tell me."

"Don't get sarcastic with me."

"I was only—"

"Whoever said you could write, for Christ's sake?"

Mitch, listening to the repartee, was experiencing déjà vu.

Although Mitch himself had betrayed Shari, she was incapable of doing her job without him. *She* had the balls and hairy scrotum, but *he* had the brains and ability to anticipate potential publicity land mines before they detonated. (He had tried to warn her about WACS *in the White House,* but she wouldn't listen.) As is the case with most Hollywood executives, they're not too bright when it comes to the details of running an office, and they need their underpaid assistants, who, if they had to, could easily perform most, if not all, of their boss's duties.

A mere few hours after Mitch had read in the trades about Shari's new job, the telephone rang in his apartment. Blessed with a kinky version of ESP that was an equal to his discerning gaydar and never one to play the sycophant (regardless of how well hung a studio messenger or water-delivery guy may be), Mitch didn't even say hello when he picked up his cordless phone.

"Look, missy," he hissed, knowing it was Shari. "I want half your yearly bonus and a car allowance. I come in at ten and leave at six. I don't play sentinel while you're screwing on studio property, and I don't massage your feet or trim your nose hairs."

"You little-dick shit," Shari bellowed her introduction, "I wouldn't have you back if—"

"I want all the terms *in writing,* honey. Notarized. And maybe I'll remember not to ever *accidentally* call you . . . *Larry.*"

"Have your skinny ass at the desk tomorrow!"

"Monday. This is only Wednesday, and I'm expecting a UPS delivery at any moment. Oh, and a platinum parking sticker so I can park in the reserved spaces," Mitch added.

"Gold. It's still subterranean."

"Platinum."

"Gold, I said! You little fucker!"

"Platinum."

Shari paused. Then: "Platinum."

"Oh, and—"

"Fuck you, Judas," Shari screamed. She hung up the telephone.

Mitch was actually thrilled to be getting back to work, and at a new studio. While still holding his cordless telephone, he thought, "New office. Fresh meat. And the guys at Galaxy are reputed to be just as cute as the ones at Sterling or Disney."

Epilogue

"Quiet on the set!" screamed the first assistant director. *"Blind as a Bat!* Scene twenty-seven! Take ten!"

"Action," roared the director, Rodrigo Dominguez, as he watched the monitor on which was projected each frame of film that his cinematographer was shooting. It was the movie's most dramatic moment. The two main characters, David Morgan and Martin Stone, a wealthy gay tenant and his nefarious slumlord, respectively, argue about the costly renovations to David's apartment in a dilapidated brownstone in Chelsea. As the actors began their repeated altercation, the tension on the soundstage kept the entire crew silently transfixed on the scene.

Just a few moments into their dialogue, director Dominguez called, "Cut!" He left his chair beside the monitor and walked slowly to the set, which was a precise replication of an apartment near Greenwich Village in New York.

"Jimbo, Jimbo," Rod said in a deprecating tone, placing a hand on Jim Fallon's shoulder. "Subtext, man. Subtext! We've had two weeks of rehearsal. How many times do I have to tell you, this is where you pour out all your bitterness and anger at the inequity of not getting what you want from this scummy slumlord. No offense, Ben. How's this for a reference? Just think of the animosity you had when your freakin' *The Grass Is Always Greener* sitcom was so unceremoniously canceled. Remember that, Jimbo? Or maybe just dig down and find that hostility you felt for your old agent, Michael, rest his soul. I don't care what you have to do, just *do it!* We're behind schedule!"

Rod turned to Ben Affleck. "By the way, Ben, you're doing a great job." Rod's voice became honeyed, which he hoped would irritate Jim to no end. "Okay, guys, back to work!"

It took another five takes before Rod was satisfied with the scene and called, "Cut!" for the last time that day. It was Friday, and the first assistant director yelled for everyone to check their call sheets for the time they were expected on set Monday and also to bone up on what scenes were scheduled to be shot. Jim walked off to the makeup trailer to get the gunk off his face and have his hair washed.

Rod separated himself from a conversation with the script supervisor when Troy, who was producing the film, came up to him. "Hey, Rod, I've been watching the dailies. I knew you were the ideal guy for the job."

Rod nodded his head in agreement, indicating he never had a doubt that he could direct his own screenplay; nothing to it. "At last I finally have that fucking Jim Fallon under *my* domination." Rod chuckled. "What goes around comes around, eh? I'm making a public asshole of him in front of the entire crew. I humiliate him, and he hates me. He should have heeded that famous warning Be nice to the people you meet on the way up. Of course he loves *you*, 'cause you convinced the studio to take a chance with him."

"You're getting a damned good performance out of him," Troy countered. "So far he's walking away with the picture."

"It's not Jim, it's the role," Rod said as they began to walk off the set. "It could be played by Tom Arnold. Even he couldn't screw it up."

"Well, the suits are starting to smell a winner. I think Bruckheimer wants you to direct one of his pictures next. At least I've heard talk."

"Ha! That prick couldn't pay me enough!"

Troy hesitated before revealing another piece of news. "There's also talk of another series for Jim."

Rod stopped in his tracks. "Good. He'll sink or swim. God knows he's no Bob Newhart. But maybe this film will give him another shot."

"You're not still angry with him?"

"Too much waste of time. I'm not into getting even. The way I've been treating Jim on the set, it's really just so he gives value to the words I wrote. This is *my* picture, all the way, and I won't let him fuck it up with a mediocre performance."

Troy smiled. "And that's precisely why I hired you. 'Cause you're one of the most manipulative sons of bitches I've ever known."

By the end of the summer, Bart and Rusty had ensconced themselves on a small farm in Loch Mere, Scotland. Two horses, as well as twenty-four head of sheep and a border collie, came with the property.

The cozy thatched-roof house was filled with music and books. One of the first items on their agenda was to hire a woman from the village to cook and clean for them. Mrs. MacBurney served a two fold purpose. First, she was a terrific housekeeper. But more importantly to Bart and Rusty, she was a gossip. The men deliberately wanted a woman who would take positive impressions of them back to the village.

It had been suggested by their real-estate agent that this was the best way to become accepted by the people in the village. Soon they weren't just a pair of rich interlopers from America, but rather the two nice gentlemen who were sharing the old MacEwen place, Glenlough Cottage. Everyone who met Bart and Rusty agreed they would be hard-pressed to find two more interesting and delightful men. Mrs. MacBurney had only glowing things to say about them, and her chatter at home and in the village shops and church soon made the men less of a curiosity and more of an accepted part of the community.

The area where Bart and Rusty had decided to settle would have seemed miserable to many people. It rained almost daily. The cold was as bitter as either had ever experienced. And the wind at night would often shake the sturdy old house in a way that reminded them of the earthquakes of Los Angeles. But those were the best nights, the nights when, snuggled together in bed beneath a thick down comforter, they found the most peace. While the wind and rain lashed the outside world, inside they felt completely protected, as if they were in a cocoon.

On such nights, as chill air permeated the house—they did not have central heating, and the warmth from the fireplace on the first floor failed miserably to reach the bedrooms upstairs—Bart and Rusty raced into bed. The first biting coldness from the sheets (even the flannel was cold) was soon replaced by the warmth of their two bare bodies, entwined. Their nightly lovemaking soon had the bed and room engulfed in warmth. They were the happiest men on the planet.